LETHAL PASSAGE
Grave Diggers Series
- Book 6 -

by
Chris Fritschi

DISCLAIMER

This is a work of fiction. Names, characters, businesses, places, events and incidents are either the products of the author's imagination or used in a fictitious manner. Any resemblance to actual persons, living or dead, or actual events is purely coincidental.

Lethal Passage
by
Chris Fritschi

Vi

ISBN:
ISBN-13:

Click or visit
chrisfritschi.com

To my wife. Thank you for your endless patience and support.

ACKNOWLEDGMENTS

This book is the product of countless hours of lost sleep, divine inspiration and madness. Enough can't be said for the tremendous encouragement and support of my readers.
Thank you for your great reviews, emails and social media posts.

1

OUTSIDER

The train bumped to a stop, jolting Ichika out of her fog. She looked out the window to the station sign and squeezed her eyes closed in a silent scream.

I missed my stop.

Ichika Asami cursed herself under her breath. *Bakka, stupid!*

The most meaningful day of her life, and like everything she touched, she was messing it up.

The sign outside the window said Osaka, Takaida Station. Her hand closed around the crisp paper in her pocket, but she didn't need to read it to know she was in the wrong place.

"Sumimasen," she muttered, just above a whisper, through her mask. She pushed through the crowded metro car towards the open doors. "Excuse me. Excuse me."

She didn't need to look at the people she brushed past. She could feel their impassive disdain as they shifted out of her way.

The metro doors hissed closed behind her as she stepped onto the station platform. In front of her was a wall of faces; commuters crowding together, waiting for the next train. Only their eyes were visible over their bite-masks. Nobody looked at her. No one ever did.

She shunned. A Soto; what the Japanese called an 'outsider.'

It was a word that symbolized her life.

In a society deeply in tune with the nuance of each person's place in life, it only took a brief glance to recognize Ichika was soto. Even though she occupied space and time, she was invisible to everyone around her.

Behind her, the metro train pulled away, quickly speeding up. Its gentle wash of turbulence tugged at her hair and clothing.

She turned, watching as the train and people inside blurred together until the last car disappeared into the darkened tunnel. In its wake, bits of trash fluttered and skipped over the tracks.

That's me; a piece of scrap chasing after something I can never catch. Maybe that's where I belong, down there.

Looking the other way, she leaned out a little, peering into the mouth of the tunnel, wistfully hoping to see the distant lights of an oncoming train.

Nothing. Just darkness.

I could wait until the next train approaches; step off the platform and become another piece of scrap.

A sharp cough brought her eyes up. A nearby metro policeman was frowning at her, reading her intentions. Crime was uncommon in Osaka, but suicides weren't.

Ichika flushed, embarrassed that the policeman had guessed what she was thinking. Eyes down, she quickly crossed the platform and climbed the stairs to street level.

Fresh air.

She breathed deeply, smelling the earthy air as it filled her lungs. The rush of cars, busses, and people couldn't sour this rare moment of pleasure. Then she felt the press of the short sword in her waistband and the moment was gone.

She didn't know how others felt about carrying a sword. She'd never asked, but Ichika had never gotten used to carrying it. She was always aware of its awkward bulk on her hip. But today it felt especially heavy, as if it were waking up, filling itself with anticipation.

She glanced around at the bustle of people hurrying by, each of them carrying a kodachi short sword at their sides. Some were modest yet stylish with a simple lacquered wooden scabbard, while others, befitting the person's status, were ornate with gold or pearl inlay. Ichika's was a drab, uninspired government-issued sword.

It was the law that each citizen of Japan carried one.

The outbreak of Vix had been the death knell for entire populations across the world. In a country as densely populated as Japan, the undead should have turned the island into a slaughterhouse within days. But the Japanese have a long memory.

As far back as the Mongol invasion of 1274 to the fire bombings of World War Two, those experiences were folded into the cultural mindset; a reflex memory added to the lexicon of self-preservation and passed down from one generation to the next.

The Vix took their toll on the country. Surprise and panic allowed them to feed and swell in number. A refusal to accept the horror of what was happening almost doubled the death count, but news of the raging undead spread ahead of the Vix and the Japanese people cleared the streets and locked themselves away.

The spread of Vix halted. Then the military moved in and the real battle for Japan began. It was a short but furious and bloody war.

Six months later, the last Vix on Japanese soil was killed.

Scientists argued each other's findings, but the majority of them eventually agreed that the bite of a Vix would infect a living person.

Soon after, the parliament passed a set of laws making it mandatory that every man, woman, and child must wear a bite mask. Much like a surgical mask in form, the bite mask was made of a hard material, wire mesh, acrylic, that covered the mouth yet allowed for unobstructed breathing with a simple but sturdy strap that clasped behind the head.

Many in the government complained that the mask wasn't enough, but they were labeled as fear mongers and sidelined by the media.

Three months later, those 'fear mongers' were proven right.

Of the few details collected from survivor accounts, a homeless woman had inexplicably become a Vix one night.

An autopsy couldn't find any bite marks on her body. The

evidence was clear; she hadn't been bitten by a Vix, yet she became one.

Barely over five feet tall and only ninety-three pounds, she was as far from intimidating as you could get, but as a Vix she was a nightmare.

Before the police arrived and killed her, she had ripped, maimed and disemboweled twenty-seven people.

Pictures of the carnage spread like wildfire. Public panic and fear boiled into outrage. Headlines blanketed the news with accusations that the Prime Minister didn't care about the public. This was a particularly painful claim because the truth was the PM honestly felt responsible for the people of his country.

That same day, the Prime Minister called an emergency session with parliament. Hammering the podium with his fist, he demanded a solution must and would be decided.

The situation was fertile ground for pushing party agendas and soon each side was playing politics. Furious, the Prime Minister ordered his Security Police into the chamber and threatened to have members of the parliament arrested, dissolving the cabinet entirely.

The room fell silent in shock. The Prime Minister glared at the gawking faces, daring them to test him. None of them did.

The question of how to protect the people was both complex and simple.

The military wasn't large enough and increasing the size of the police force was financially impossible.

The answer was as pragmatic as it was Japanese.

Arm every citizen. Not with a gun, but with a sword.

Parliament members who were descendants from noble houses of samurai loudly protested. The katana, the symbol of the samurai, was not a menial object like a broom to be carried by the lower classes.

The PM negated their grandstanding by pointing out the drawbacks of requiring everyone to carry three and a half feet of steel everywhere they go.

They needed something more compact, less intrusive and intimidating.

The answer was the kodachi.

Smaller, lighter than a katana, they could be quickly mass-produced. The choice satisfied the government and was approved.

It wasn't the solution the Japanese people expected, but it was the one they got and reluctantly accepted.

Ichika watched as a mother and young daughter walked by, hand in hand. The child-sized pink and white handle of the little girl's dagger poked out from under her jacket. A brightly-colored cartoon kitten charm swung from the handguard by a colorful piece of cord.

An unguarded smile softened Ichika's face, but the little girl only vacantly stared back without returning the expression.

Outsider. Even the child knew it.

Ichika shifted her sword out of sight under her shapeless sweater, and looked away; self-consciously through the limp curtains of hair that hung down the sides of her face.

She was sure she'd let go of the note in her pocket, yet it seemed to keep finding its way back into the palm of her hand. It wanted her attention.

She took it out and unfolded it. The message was simple, written in a clear, gentle hand. *An enlightened death saves all. Go to the Mori no Kuki kindergarten.*

Missing her train stop had put her miles away from the kindergarten. She didn't have any money for another train ticket. She'd left everything at home; those things weren't important anymore.

The sun was taking on a purple-orange cast while deepening blue shadows crept up the walls of the concrete buildings around her. The rich display was a mocking reminder the day was slipping away from her.

She thought of the kindergarten filled with children. So many souls she could have saved. They would have accepted her sacrifice. But, that wouldn't happen now. By missing her stop she would never get there before it closed. She had failed them.

A roar and sudden whip of wind snapped her back to the present by a car racing by, an inch from hitting her.

She froze mid-step. Lost in thought, Ichika had wandered into the middle of the road. Heavy traffic rushed past her and she dared not move, sure at any moment there would be the horrible sound of crunching bone and twisting metal.

This is my chosen day. I shouldn't be afraid, but I am.

Before her death was given purpose, she had already decided to kill herself. She cared more about where to die than how. She could imagine her death being the subject of gossip; her neighbors would sneer over her lifeless body with pity and contempt.

She chose to die the same way she had spent her life; alone, unseen in the Sea of Trees.

Nestling against Mount Fuji, the Aokigahara forest had earned the sad reputation as the suicide forest, the Sea of Trees, long ago.

As a child, Ichika had heard the stories of many who had gone there to end their lives. Now, their spirits roamed those dark woods. The thought of those mournful ghosts had given her chills.

The police used to travel into the depths of the forest, hoping to rescue the unfortunate people who had given up on life. Then rescue workers began to disappear.

Nobody had seen what happened to them, but people stopped showing up for the monthly sweep of the forest. Now nobody went in unless they intended to never come out. The Vix were in there.

The thought of never coming out had become like a narcotic to Ichika.

Whenever she felt herself sinking into the dark waters of loneliness and depression, she would picture herself passing into the forest where the woods would strip away the demons dragging her down.

Two weeks earlier, she'd decided to travel to the forest to die. The decision had made her feel so strange. At first she felt as light as a feather, but over the hours of the journey to the forest, she began to see that her life really wasn't as bad as she thought.

Not everyone ignored her. The elderly landlady always checked on her and would bring her steamed buns on cold days. The bus driver, on her morning commute, would tell her the funny thing his dog had done. And Yoshi always seemed to be at the office door at the same time she came to work and left.

A new thought hit her so hard she stopped breathing for a moment.

Does he... like me?

Her mind turned to the rumors of the kami; ghosts, that roamed the forest. She didn't believe in them and yet the thought frightened her. Were they real? Did they know she was coming? Were they waiting for her?

Perhaps she wouldn't die, not abruptly. Maybe the longer she wandered in the forest, her body would fade away and become a spirit.

At last, she had arrived. Grey mist shrouded the tops of the forest in every direction. She stood, feeling doubt for the first time.

The woods crowded the edge of the wide, empty parking lot. They loomed above Ichika, eerily silent, like the forest was holding its breath in expectation of her venturing in.

She turned around, looking at the world she was leaving behind. She felt nothing. Her head tilted to the side in mild surprise at the lack of any emotion. It was curious, but not troubling.

She turned back to the woods. Softly biting her lower lip, she stepped inside.

As she continued deeper into the woods, a tangible quiet closed around her, like she had entered a shrine. Her sense of connection to the outside world faded away.

The mossy, damp carpet of the forest floor deadened her footsteps. The forest wanted silence.

Ichika continued to wander until early evening, not sure what she was looking for. Maybe the forest would give her a sign; to do what she didn't know, but she had felt drawn to come here. Surely the forest had called her here, but the endless woods offered her no answers.

Tired, she sat against a gnarled tree and looked at her surroundings. She picked up a twig, tapping it on her knee impatiently. What if this whole thing had been another of her foolish mistakes?

She snapped the twig and tossed it away. There was nothing spiritual or otherworldly about this place.

An angry tear stung her eye as she stood up.

I'm so stupid! I talked myself into believing fairy tales and where did it get me? Lost.

The reality of her situation began to fill her mind with unfeeling clarity. This wasn't going to end with her softly fading into an ethereal transformation of stardust. She was going to suffer a long, slow death from starvation or exposure from the cold.

I have to go home.

She glanced around, hoping to recognize the direction she'd come from. Anything that offered the smallest promise of a way out. Fear and despair squeezed her heart.

"Someone, please help me," she said, as panic clutched her chest. "I don't want to die like this."

"No one wants their death to be meaningless."

Ichika yelped; her heart jumped into her throat as she fumbled for the handle of her sword. She tried to pierce the gloom for the source of the disembodied voice; half believing a ghost would appear.

"Don't be afraid," said the voice. "You are welcome here. You are safe."

"Who are you?" Ichika said, whimpering.

"You came here hoping for death, for meaning," said the voice. "I am here to help you find both."

"Then do it," she stammered. "But don't hurt me."

"Dying here is not the answer you're searching for, but don't be sad. I will tell you where and how to die. My guidance will bring you an endless bliss and the gratitude of the souls you will save. Is that what you want?"

"I'll save? How can someone like me... you're teasing me."

"I am the Keeper of the Sacred Gate. Listen carefully and follow my instructions."

Now, two weeks later, she stood on a narrow strip of pavement with cars whipping past her on both sides. She tried to follow his instructions and failed.

The sidewalks were filled with people. Why hadn't anyone called out a warning or tried to stop her? Why wasn't anyone trying to help her?

The car that almost killed her never honked; hadn't even tried to avoid her. Why?

Outsider.

The truth of that word pierced her heart with pain like never before. There was always a small part of her that believed she was overly dramatic. She had come up with the label of outsider to justify her self-pity. She could blame everyone else for her social exile when the truth was her exile was self-imposed.

But now she stood in a blur of crushing steel and nobody said a word. Nobody lifted a finger to help. That wasn't her imagination.

She really was an outsider.

A delivery van blew past her, its side-view mirror inches from shattering her face. No one cared.

A bitter tear pooled in the corner of her eye and spilled down her cheek.

Her body began to tremble. Was it fear, self-pity, or rage?

She closed her eyes, feeling the gusts of passing cars trying to tug her into their path as a new truth revealed itself.

The Keeper had said she'd find peace by saving the souls of children. He was wrong. She would find revenge.

She opened her eyes. Her warm, walnut brown eyes had become hard and dark.

Across the street flashed the multistoried sign of the huge Yama Soyokaze shopping mall. Thousands of people came every day to shop, socialize and enjoy the upscale yet classic architecture of the tall building.

Ichika stepped into the street, heedless of the traffic. The air exploded with screeching tires and blaring horns as she crossed the busy street towards the mall. Angry drivers swore at her, but she didn't hear them.

Ichika would find death today and when she did, nobody would dare ignore her.

The Yama Soyokaze shopping mall was a monolithic testament to Japanese technology and ingenuity.

Every person that walked in was scanned and recorded by an advanced facial recognition system. Their image was referenced against a massive database of the shopper's history, what stores they went to, who they came with, time spent, and countless other data points.

An artificial intelligence 'shopping friend', customized to each person's tastes and personality, was instantly created and uploaded to the shopper's phone.

The shopping friend was built around behavioral analytics, intuitive and dispositional personality factoring and a mind-numbing array of other human sciences. It was wildly expensive but gambling and porn couldn't hold a candle to the profit margin of consumerism.

Each person's shopping friend would cheerfully greet them. Drawing from the shopper's conversations the system had eavesdropped on, it would chat about topics they would likely enjoy. It would suggest exciting products and provide directions to the stores. Shoppers were tracked as they moved through the mall, and algorithms monitored their body temperature, respiration, and activity level. If it determined they were tired, the system would suggest something to eat or drink, based on their eating history.

Even their facial and physical cues were analyzed to determine the shopper's mood. The system would modify its suggested products to match.

No opportunity to sell something was left to chance.

When Ichika entered the mall, the facial recognition system did an algorithmic equivalent to a double take. She wasn't anywhere in the database. In a blinding flurry of calculations, a generic shopping friend was created for her, but it couldn't upload the AI. She didn't have a phone.

The system puzzled over this for a moment, then switched to a light-form augmented reality presence.

Ichika shuffled to a stop as a projected image of a young woman appeared in her path.

"Welcome," said the LARP, bowing. "I'm so glad you're here. Would you like..."

"Go away," said Ichika, her voice flat and cold.

The shopping friend winked into nothingness. The AI decided to monitor the stranger, collecting data points until it could compile a working profile.

She walked among the throngs of shoppers spread out along the store-lined avenues. While everyone else was looking at the eye-catching window displays, Ichika was looking at the people. An idea was taking form as she noticed the easy ebb and flow of the shoppers. She wanted somewhere congested.

The moving walkway brought her up to the food court. A ring of quick order restaurants encompassed the entire floor, creating a stadium effect.

A skylight spanning the entire ceiling poured light down on the dining area, where hundreds of shoppers were gathered.

Ichika walked into the food court, surrounded by the loud buzz of voices trying to be heard over each other and a cacophony food smells.

This felt right.

She wandered into the center of the arena, looking for a place to sit. No sooner had she thought it than an elderly man, at the table next to her, wobbled to his feet.

"Please," he smiled, gesturing to the chair. "You look tired. Take my table."

He wheezed as he bent over to clear his meal, but she stopped him.

"It's fine," she said.

The old man kindly bobbed his head and shuffled away.

Ichika stared down at the green, synthetic tray, scattered with the debris of the old man's meal.

A robotic hand appeared as a courtesy-bot cleared the table and wiped it clean. Its face was a display screen with human-like features, but not so human to be unnerving.

"Good afternoon," said the bot, bowing. "It's my pleasure to serve you today. Would you like to see a menu?"

The robot produced a data pad with a selection from the different restaurants in the food court.

Ichika took the note out of her pocket and gazed at it, ignoring the bot. She dug out a tattered book of matches from her small bag. The paper cover was frayed from age. She'd forgotten how long ago she'd stopped going to her grandfather's shrine and wondered if anyone was lighting a candle for him now.

She opened the book of matches and plucked one-off. The match head sputtered into flame as she struck it across the friction strip.

"Please excuse me," said the bot. "This is not a smoking area."

Ichika put the match to the corner of the note and watched the flame take hold and consume it until it was nothing but ash.

The robot's eyes tried to mimic polite confusion but failed. "Perhaps you'd be more comfortable somewhere else?"

"Go away," said Ichika.

"I'll return after you've had time to consider your selection." The bot bowed and left.

Ichika glanced around, but nobody was watching her, not that it mattered. Her path was clear and she wouldn't be stopped.

She reached behind her head and unfastened the bite mask. She felt a surge adrenaline as it fell off her face, anticipating shouts of protest and criticism from the people around her.

Nothing happened. Nobody had noticed her naked face. There was only the drone of endless chatter.

She looked down, feeling something hard and round in her hand. It was the pill the Keeper had given her to deaden the pain of what was to come. She hadn't been aware of taking it out of her pocket.

She rolled it between her fingers, wondering how such a small, inert thing could defeat human pain.

She put it back in her pocket. She wanted to pass into the next existence with complete clarity.

It was time.

Ichika took a cleansing breath, feeling a calm settle over her as she gripped her sword under the table. The action curled her lips with an ironic grin.

For once in her life, she didn't want people to notice her.

She hadn't drawn the sword since mandatory training several years ago, and it took a sharp tug to work it free of the scabbard.

She turned the blade around, pointing the chisel point at her abdomen. She grasped the handle hard with both hands, trying to squeeze the shaking away. The sword felt heavier than she remembered.

Ichika swallowed hard. The unknown yawed open in front of her. Would there be a welcoming light promised by the Keeper? Or would it be silent blackness? Would there be anything at all?

She glanced down, seeing the tip of the sword tremble and the weight of the moment struck her; if she pointed the tip a few inches to the left, the sword would glide back into its sheath.

A few small inches to the side means I can go back home.

The point of the sword wavered, then slowly drifted away from her stomach.

Back home to what? More of this?

A tear squeezed from her eye and ran down her cheek. The polished, razor sharp tip shifted back to her middle.

Her arms bumped the table as she stretched them out, thinking she'd need the momentum to cut through her clothing. She greatly underestimated the honed edge of the blade.

Squinting her eyes closed against the coming pain, Ichika plunged the sword into her gut. The blade was so sharp, she only felt a burning sting. It wasn't nearly as bad as she'd feared.

That only lasted a moment; then the real pain came.

It boiled up like an angry storm, twisting and tearing, igniting every nerve in her belly with unimaginable agony.

She doubled over with a groan, unable to draw a breath, and laid face down on her table.

A few people glanced over, but Ichika's hair hid the writhing torment on her massless face.

She clutched the sword, hoping if she kept it still the pain would stop. She remembered back to the forest. The Keeper of the Sacred Gate had told her the pain would be brief. Just as she damned him for lying to her the pain began to fade. He had told her the truth! In place of the pain came a spreading cold.

A later autopsy would find that her sword had severed the descending aorta, the largest artery in the body. The internal bleeding was sudden and massive.

Ichika's thoughts drifted without form, fading quickly into blackness. A thick rivulet of blood pumped down her belly in her few remaining seconds as her heart desperately tried to push life through her body. The last electrical spark in her brain winked out and her heart shut down.

The courtesy-bot returned to see if she was ready to order and noticed something had spilled on the floor, under the table.

The bot rolled away, leaving a track of bloody tire prints on the polished marble floor and reported the need for a maintenance bot to clean up the mess.

Riko and her friends were wrapping up their meal and making plans about which store they'd go to next.

Reaching down for her shopping bags, Riko frowned at the dirty path the bot had left behind. Her eyes followed wet streaks until they stopped at the spreading pool of blood.

She knew what she was looking at, but denial and confusion clashed with reality, leaving Riko blinking in shock. She looked at the girl in the drab sweater, slumped over the table.

"Excuse me," she said, worry spreading through her. "Are you okay?"

Her friends stopped chatting to see who she was talking to; fear's cold fingers began to squeeze their hearts.

Relief washed over Riko as the girl at the table began to move.

"She's fine, Riko," said her friends, not believing that for a second. "We should go."

Ichika's pale hands landed on the tabletop as she turned her face towards the girls.

Riko's face twisted in a silent scream Ichika's milky, dead eye peered at her through the drape of lank, black hair.

The Vix came to its feet with a hiss, the kodachi still in its belly.

The chatter of the food court was cut by a soul-rending scream.

Every head turned; some stood up, looking for what was going on. Somewhere in the middle, people were running, crushing against each other to get away. Panic rippled through the food court and in the middle of it all, a Vix was ripping its way through them, leaving a trail of bodies in its wake.

Soon those bodies rose up from the carnage. The Vix swelled in numbers, spreading out and running down the horror-stricken trying to escape.

2

THE DIVE

"I had a dog once," said Rosse wistfully.

The rest of the group around the table looked at him in anticipation of a story, but the stocky sergeant only gazed at the ceiling with a smile on his face.

"Oh, come on," said Monkhouse. "Don't leave us hanging. I bet he was all fangs and scared the neighbors."

"Who, Doris?" said Rosse.

"You named your dog Doris?" asked Wesson, her pale green eyes sparkling with amusement over the lip of her cup.

"Better than some stupid name like..." Rosse searched the air for a suitably bad dog name.

"Spot?" offered Fulton.

"Yeah," said Rosse, jabbing a finger in agreement. "Who names their dog Spot, fer cry'n out loud?"

"What kind of dog was she?" asked Fulton. "Like a Bull Mastiff or something?"

"Naw. She was little. Could sit in my hand," said Rosse, holding out his palm.

"If that's where my tip's supposed to be, you're not funny," said the waitress, coming by with a fresh round of beers. She cleared the table of empty foam cups and set out new ones of cold, amber goodness.

Fulton gave her a big smile as she leaned over his shoulder and put a glass in front of him. Before he touched it, Monkhouse reached across and took it.

"Hey," protested Fulton.

"You've had enough, young man," said Monkhouse, taking a sip of the stolen beer.

"Anyways," grumbled Rosse. "My Doris was always happy to see me when I got home from work. Jumped around and barked every time. Made it nice after a long day."

"She sounds sweet," said Wesson.

"Yeah, she was," he nodded. "Crapped in my slippers a lot. Don't know what that was about."

"Maybe because you named her Doris?" smirked Monkhouse.

Ota nearly sprayed his mouthful of beer and swallowed quickly before laughing.

The rest of the table broke up in laughter. Ota nearly sprayed his mouthful of beer and swallowed quickly before laughing.

Rosse shrugged, cocking his head for lack of a good comeback.

The Dive was buzzing with good-natured conversation tonight. It was the favorite club on Fort Hickok because it was the only club. The tricky part was knowing where to find it.

Compared to the previous base commander, who abruptly left without notice, the new commander was a big improvement. Colonel Stockland understood the culture of her posting and didn't come in full of piss and vinegar, thinking she'd snap the place into shape overnight.

She was content to institute small changes, one at a time, and give people time to acclimate to the new way of things.

Unfortunately, she also believed in the system of rewards and consequences. You didn't get things for free; you had to earn them. Generally, most could accept her methods until she closed the club in the fort.

Before she'd approve its reopening, the fort had to meet a number of her standards.

In true military fashion, the soldiers took the decision with a stoic, 'Yes, Ma'am', and a crisp salute, then immediately began planning their own speakeasy.

Hence The Dive was born. All that was needed was four walls and a roof. Sometimes even that didn't matter. Everything else was portable and easily set up in a matter of minutes. Folding tables and chairs, chem lights, and collapsible water bladders filled with beer.

The entire bar could be taken down and disappear without a trace in three minutes. They had this down to an art. If they needed to bug out, the patrons had to fend for themselves. The management made it explicitly clear they were not responsible for your sorry butt if you were passed out.

When the MPs showed up, on the rare occasions someone blabbed, they found nothing but an empty room and one or two drunks sleeping on the floor.

Fort Hickok had grown a lot over the past few years, but it wasn't so big that there was a limitless choice of secluded locations The Dive could appear. The management of The Dive had to be creative. If that meant getting your drinks in a garage bay with a partially stripped-down transport truck or smelling cordite in the back room of the practice kill house, nobody complained, just as long as the beer kept coming.

Many welcomed the change of scenery.

Tonight's setting was an empty barracks recently vacated by a platoon of noobs who were out for three days of wilderness training. The furniture had been moved to the back of the long, rectangular room, and Dive supporters had promised to move everything back before leaving for the night.

Good humor and camaraderie flowed easily around the table, except for the team's leader. Jack Tate wasn't in the mood.

From the time he'd sat down, he'd been lost in his own thoughts. Judging by the way he frowned at his half-empty beer, the rest of the team decided to let him be.

"Hey," said Rosse, brightening up. "D'ya think the new colonel would let us have a dog?"

"What? And have to check my boots every morning for dog crap?" grinned Monkhouse. "No thanks."

"It's just like you to put a price on unintentional love," said Rosse.

"Unconditional," said Wesson.

"That's what I said," mumbled Rosse.

"It could be like our mascot," said Fulton. "Every cool team has a mascot. I bet the colonel would make an exception for us."

Rosse nodded in approval, pointing at Fulton as he took a pull of his beer.

"That's what happens when you think you're better than everyone else," called a voice from another table.

The team, except Tate, craned their head to see who was talking. Two tables away, they saw five soldiers smirking back at them. Four of them were hunched over their drinks, but the fifth one, a staff sergeant, was stretched out in his chair, looking pleased with himself.

All of them were large and rough around the edges. Their Army Combat Uniforms were smeared with dirt and hung limply on them from humidity and sweat. Their muddy boots completed the picture of a squad recently returned from a hard patrol through the jungle, hunting Vix.

"They think they're better than the rest of us," said the grungy sergeant. "They don't have to follow rules."

The expressions around the Grave Diggers' table darkened as their good mood deflated.

"Someone ought to shut that loudmouth up," grumbled Rosse under his breath, his big hands ominously curling into fists.

"Sorry you feel that way," said Wesson to the far table, hoping to deescalate the situation. "You guys have the next round of beers on me."

"Do we look like we need your charity?" said the staff sergeant, sitting up.

"Terrific," mumbled Monkhouse as a couple of The Dive's bouncers perked up from across the room and stared at them. "Guys, I really don't want to get banned from here, you know?"

"We take the same risks as everyone else around here," said the staff sergeant, undeterred. "We got jumped by fifteen, maybe twenty

Vix today. Sam's lucky to be sitting here." One of the men patted another, presumably Sam, on the shoulder as the other soldiers nodded in agreement. "When was the last time you put your butts on the line?"

"I ain't kid'n," growled Rosse. "I'm about to tear this guy a new hole to talk outta."

"You don't know what you're talking about," stood Fulton, surprising everyone at the table.

"Sit down, private," said Wesson, firmly. But it was too late; the barn door had opened and the horses were running out.

"We do way more dangerous stuff," said Fulton. "Important stuff you guys don't even know about."

"You saying what we do isn't important?" said the staff sergeant, getting to his feet.

Ota took a handful of Fulton's shirt and pulled the drunk private down onto his chair.

Confused about how he ended up back in his seat, Fulton looked around until he met Ota's Nordic, deep-blue eyes. He put his finger to his lips, cutting off Fulton's protest.

"What's the matter, bub?" said Rosse, rising from his chair. "Your feelings hurt cause nobody gave ya a gold sticker and a cookie for do'n your job?"

The staff sergeant's chair scraped loudly over the floor as he stood up and the room fell silent. Everyone watched as he walked over to Rosse's table, anticipating the coming storm.

The bouncers closed in, but the staff sergeant's big friends headed them off, creating a barrier between them and the inevitable fight.

The staff sergeant glared down at Rosse, but the difference in height was meaningless to the ex-prison guard. Rosse planted all of his two hundred and twenty pounds solidly in front of the staff sergeant and stared up into his eyes. Muscles bunched in his arms like thick cords of steel cables as he balled his hands into fists.

If the staff sergeant was hoping to intimidate the barrel-chested Rosse, he would have to seriously up his game.

"We're out in the muck and wet and heat every day," growled the staff sergeant. "And every day we're taking on those stench-filled killing machines, hoping all of us come back alive. Every day. But, every time I see you people, you're looking fresh as a daisy. When was the last time you made a difference?"

Every expression at the table was different. Fulton's eyes shimmered with excitement, knowing Rosse was about to wipe the floor with this loudmouth. Monkhouse winced, knowing they'd never get another beer until the official club reopened. Wesson shook her head, resigned that nothing she could say would stop the explosive chaos of the next three seconds. Ota sipped his beer, completely okay with what ever happened.

Rosse's knuckles cracked as he tightened his fist an instant before he launched it into the staff sergeants face, but before he swung, Tate put his hand on Rosse's arm.

Both men watched as Tate stood up next to the staff sergeant. There was nothing in Tate's expression except a weary indifference, confusing the staff sergeant.

"Just sit down, Rosse," said Tate, exasperated.

Rosse looked at him, his dark expression melting from his face; why Tate wasn't backing him up?

"What did you say?" asked Tate, turning to the staff sergeant. "We aren't making a difference?"

The staff sergeant glowered down at him, ready to take on this newcomer, but there was no hostility in Tate's grey-blue eyes.

The staff sergeant mentally stumbled, feeling like the situation had made a quick turn and he'd missed it.

He glanced at Tate's fatigues just to make sure the next person he took a swing at wasn't an officer. Tate wasn't wearing his rank, which only perplexed the staff sergeant more.

Whatever was happening, the staff sergeant was in the mood to process. All he knew was that no officer would walk around without his rank. That made Tate fair game, and that was good enough. He fell back into his comfort zone of being pissed off and ready to fight.

"Yeah," he said. "That's exactly what I'm saying. You guys don't do spit."

The bouncers knew the verbal sound of a trigger being pulled but couldn't push past the barrier of friends.

The staff sergeant's fists bunched up, anticipating Tate's swing and ready to hammer him.

"You're right," said Tate. "We're not making a difference." He looked at the rest of his team, who gaped in stunned silence. "He's right."

Tate walked away, leaving the big sergeant looking back and forth between Tate's receding back and the table of speechless Grave Diggers.

Even though the other guy backed down, it didn't feel like a victory to the staff sergeant. In fact, it felt like he'd lost.

"Yeah. Well..." he said in a last attempt to save face. "Okay then."

He went back to his table with his friends in tow, leaving Wesson and the rest of the team awkwardly avoiding each other's gaze.

Monkhouse flicked at crumbs while Rosse picked up his cup but changed his mind and put it back down without taking a drink.

"I don't get it," he said.

"Yes, you do," said Wesson. "We all know what he was talking about."

The others fidgeted in silence.

"I don't," said Fulton, looking at the others for an answer.

"Just what he said, kid," said Rosse. "The stuff we're doing ain't making much of a dent."

Fulton glanced around the table in disbelief.

"What do you mean, no dent?" said Fulton. "We killed a bunch of Vix. That's something. We stopped that general guy from poisoning, like, millions of people or something. We got that secret satellite thing before...," Fulton's voice dropped to a whisper, "...The Ring got their hands on it."

Heads nodded in agreement, but Fulton felt like he was pulling teeth. "What about that Russian dude? The one Wesson sho..."

Wesson quickly looked up at him and he realized he had hit a painful nerve.

"Who was going to launch a nuke," continued Fulton, quickly changing direction. "And what about that drug lord creep?"

"San Roman?" said Monkhouse. "He got away."

"Yeah, but we blew up his house, right?" said Fulton. "Wrecked his operation."

"An we stole his helicopter," smiled Rosse.

"See?" said Fulton. "We do stuff."

"What Top means," said Wesson, "is it doesn't feel like we're doing enough."

"Guys," said Fulton, throwing up his arms, not believing what he was seeing. "We stopped a war. That's got to count for something."

"He's got a point," said Monkhouse. "Not too many people here could say that."

"Thank you," said Fulton, feeling vindicated.

Wesson finished off her beer and masked a burp behind her fist.

"Look at it this way," she said. "When you kill a Vix, there's less Vix in the world."

"Until someone dies and then you have more Vix," said Monkhouse.

Wesson dropped her chin and looked at him from under her eyebrows.

"Shut up," she said.

A lopsided grin spread across Monkhouse's face.

"What I'm trying to say," she continued, "is that every time we get rid of something bad, some other bad thing takes its place. Top's feeling like we're not making any headway."

"Good and bad are a balance," said Ota.

Everyone at the table stopped and looked at him in surprise. They could almost count the number of times Ota had spoken on two hands.

He ran his hand over his head, pushing his blond hair out of his eyes, glancing at his friends.

"Good and evil can't conquer each other," he said. "There can be more good than evil, or the other way around, but the balance always returns."

"I don't mean ta step on your toes," said Rosse, "but I don't buy that Zen stuff. I know good can win."

"Because you were a prison guard?" said Ota.

"Yeah. What I did kept a lot of scum off the streets."

"You didn't reduce the evil in the world," said Ota. "You just moved it from one place to another."

"Zen is depressing," said Monkhouse. "You're saying that no matter what we do, how hard we try, we can never make the world a better place?"

"The only place we can conquer evil," said Ota, "is inside ourselves. Every time a person chooses to do good, they make the world a better place."

"But that still leaves the bad guys," said Fulton. "How do we make them decide to do good?"

"Ya kick their butts till they're too scared to be bad," said Rosse, cutting off Ota's answer.

Wesson groaned, rolling her eyes.

"What'd I say?" asked Rosse.

Ota smiled good-naturedly and sat back in his chair, content to let Rosse be Rosse.

3

OUTSIDE WORK

Two targets rushed Tate the moment he rounded the corner. His Heckler & Koch 93 was instantly at his shoulder. He snapped off two shots, dropping both targets. He kept his eye glued to the gunsight, the barrel leaving a trail of smoke as he swept his sight picture to the right for more surprises.

Nothing moved.

He followed a snaking trail that led him into a wide alley between a storage building on his left and stacks of crates on his right.

Ahead, the building and crates ended and Tate would have to choose to turn left, around the corner of the building, or right, around the corner of the crates. Either way meant that for a critical second he had his back to the unknown.

His finger rested lightly outside the trigger guard and he took a controlled breath, forcing his shoulders to relax.

Make a choice. The clock's ticking.

Just as he decided to go left, a bead of sweat caught the corner of his eye. The salty drop stung and blurred his vision. He switched the rifle to his other shoulder and clear eye.

That would have been the perfect time for the range master to spring a pop-up target on him, but he was either being kind, not paying attention, or playing a psychological game with him.

Moving quickly, Tate stepped into the open, turning left.

Clear.

He spun, checking his six.

Clear.

He'd anticipated a target popping up in front of him. It always happened before. He swore under his breath at the range master who was clearly messing with him, trying to amp up the tension.

His dominant eye wasn't stinging anymore and he tested it. He could see clearly and switched his rifle back to his right shoulder.

In mid-motion, targets sprang up. One ahead, static.

CRACK.

Two on his right, speeding at him. His gun bucked twice, dropping them. He spun, anticipating another threat.

Nothing.

A shadow filtered over him.

Son of a ...

A target came over the top of the building, falling at him fast. He ducked away, shooting three times; two more than he should have. Tate grimaced at his lack of self-control.

That target was new. What else had changed on the course?

Five more hostile targets sprang up around him and charged.

Easy money.

Around them, seven innocent targets sprang up, moving in every direction.

What the...?

Fighting back the reflex to spray in every direction, Tate put his sights on each hostile, shooting around the innocents. The timing of each shot felt like a lifetime, but in reality each shot was a tenth of a second.

CRACK, CRACK, CRACK... click.

The rifle's bolt locked open on the empty magazine.

Reload.

In a blur, Tate hit the magazine release. As the empty mag fell, his free hand snatched a fresh one from his combat vest.

The targets were closing fast. Really fast.

The new mag snapped into the gun. The bolt closed.

Got ya.

He pulled the trigger.

Click. Misfire.

Endless hours of training and combat experience took over. Tate dropped the rifle, immediately drawing his Colt 1911.

The hostiles were on top of him. The big .45 flashed twice; a split second before the targets bumped into Tate, a smoking hole in each one's head.

He glowered down the barrel, looking for another threat.

He heard a buzzer through his earplugs, signaling the end of the exercise and the loudspeaker crackled to life.

"Clear," chuckled the range master.

"You put duds in my spare mags?" shouted Tate.

"You said you wanted a challenge," said the range master, breaking into a laugh.

"You're a dick, you know that?" growled Tate, but he couldn't hide the smile curling the corner of his mouth.

"You should have seen the look on your face," said the range master. "I thought you'd pull your axe-thing and start swinging for the fences."

"Only if someone screwed around with my Colt," said Tate with a subtle warning.

"Give me some credit. I know better than to mess with your baby."

Tate nodded in approval as he thumbed the safety on his pistol. He slid it back into its weathered holster and closed the flap.

It was an original 1912 holster, carried by his great grandfather in World War Two. Tate meticulously cared for it, ensuring its longevity. The brass hardware was scuffed, but clean. The embossed 'US' was still clearly legible on the flap. It was a working holster, not a display piece. The leather showed the scuffs and wear of use over the course of three generations, but the hide was still strong.

Tate crunched over the pebbled dirt, the fine red dust kicking up and coating his boots. He made his way back to the beginning of the course and the welcomed shade of the covered patio.

His eyebrows arched in mild surprise as he saw Kaiden lounging on one of the benches, waiting for him.

"Look what the cat dragged in," he grinned.

Kaiden gave him a sad smile, shaking her head.

"Is that any way to talk to a friend," she said, taking a sip from her thermal bottle of cold water.

"It's exactly the kind of thing you'd say to me," said Tate.

"True," she said, "but it's charming when I say it."

Tate eyed her cold drink then his scratched and dented water bottle. He knew the water inside would be hot and as appealing as a mouthful of sand.

"Don't look so glum," said Kaiden, producing another cold bottle. She tossed it to him and the fresh condensation sprinkled his face as he caught it. "See how I look out for you?"

He flipped open the cap and relished the cold water as it washed the dust out of his mouth.

"Speaking of looking out for you," she said.

A warning flag went up in Tate's mind. The puzzle piece of why she was here fell into place.

"I've heard you've been moping around, generally being a buzz kill."

"Who told you that?" he asked.

Kaiden smirked, tilting her head in disappointment.

"I thought I'd ask," he said. "Okay, sure. I've been feeling off. No big deal."

"It's been going on for a few months," she said. "Kinda sounds like a big deal."

"It happens," he said, and began cleaning his rifle. "You get depressed."

"But then I shoot someone and I feel better."

Tate smirked, wondering in the back of his mind if she wasn't joking. Kaiden wasn't burdened with by the lengthy moral dilemmas most people faced when it came to pulling a trigger. She didn't take killing lightly; Tate knew that for a fact. She killed when there was a reason to kill. It was just that the grey area between black and white was much smaller for her.

Seasoned professionals played out the situational ambiguities of combat before going on a mission; trying to anticipate the 'ifs' and 'whens' of pulling the trigger.

There was no way to cover all the scenarios, but the mental preparation could mean shaving a tenth of a second off your hesitation, and that saved lives.

"You should try it," said Kaiden. "Somebody in the world always needs shooting."

"We've shot a lot of bad guys," said Tate as he wiped down his assault rifle. "It hasn't changed anything."

"That's it," she said.

"I'm right?" he asked, not sure if he was surprised or troubled.

"I mean, that's it," said Kaiden. "That's officially the stupidest thing I've heard you say. Look around. Okay, not here." She waved her hand dismissively. "This place is a dump. Look at the bigger picture. Because of us, the world has changed for the better."

"It doesn't feel that way," he said.

"What are you expecting? That everyone you ever helped should send you a card and a box of chocolates?" Tate opened his mouth to answer. "Quiet," she said, "that was a rhetorical question."

He closed his mouth and Kaiden continue. "I know what you're thinking. Every time you kill a bad guy there's more to take their place. Sometimes that's true. But each time you plant a bad guy in the ground, good people get stronger. We show them that bad guys can bleed and die. Because of what we do, there's more good people than bad."

Tate finished with his rifle and started on his Colt. He wasn't convinced and she could see it in his face.

"You're forty something..."

"Thirty-six," he grumbled.

"Thirty-six?" she said, studying his face. "Huh."

Tate gave her an annoyed look.

"Okay, thirty-six. Sorry. Anyway, we've been doing this for a while. Tell me, when was the last time you saw an old bad guy?"

Tate holstered the Colt, his gaze drifting up as he searched his memory.

"I don't know. It's been a long time," he said.

"There's a reason the bad guys are getting younger," said Kaiden.

"They don't live long enough to grow old," he smiled.

"Or at least, you know, thirty-six," she said, taking a drink after her glancing swipe at Tate's ego.

Tate took the good-natured jab with a smile and sat on the bench across from her.

"You make a good point," he said, feeling better.

She only nodded, content to listen to the chorus of birds in the surrounding trees.

"Thanks," he said.

She looked at him, slightly puzzled.

"For coming all the way out here to cheer me up," said Tate.

"That's not why I'm here," said Kaiden. "Well, not entirely, but you're welcome."

"Then why?"

"I heard about someone looking to hire a security team and thought you'd like a change of scenery."

"I'm not a private contractor," he said, tapping the flag patch on his fatigues. "You might have noticed I'm in the Army."

"That so? When was the last time you ran a sanctioned military op?" asked Kaiden. "And Colonel Hewett doesn't count. He's Army, but he's got you running his personal black ops against The Ring."

Tate had no answer. No good answer. He looked at Kaiden, waiting for her to get the point that he'd already reached.

"You're a contractor," she said, "but there's nothing wrong with that. I'm a contractor, and you like me."

Tate grinned, making a 'so-so' gesture with his hand.

"Ouch," she said.

"A security team for what?" he asked.

"I don't have all the details. Someone's looking for a team to babysit a client."

"I haven't trained my team for security work," said Tate. "Is there a high risk of attack?"

"I don't know," said Kaiden, scooting off the benchtop and dusting off her pants. "If you're curious, you can ask him yourself."

She fished out a note and handed it to Tate, who read it with surprise.

"This is for tonight," he said.

"I'm sorry. Is this your date night?" she said.

Frowning, he looked at her out of the corner of his eyes.

"You wouldn't just throw this at me sight unseen," said Tate. "What do you know?"

"I can't tell you," she said.

"Don't do that," he said, getting frustrated. "You know that 'need to know' crap pisses me off."

"I know," said Kaiden, "and I really am sorry, but it's up to the client to tell you what he's comfortable with. If it helps, you know I wouldn't let you walk into a meat grinder."

Tate let his stare speak for him.

"That's not fair," she said. "You can't hang Singapore on me. You know that had nothing to do with me, and I'd appreciate it if you stopped rubbing my nose in it."

"Okay," he said, sighing. He took a long drink from his water. "At least give me a reason why I should consider this job."

"You get an all-expense paid trip to Japan," said Kaiden.

"Japan?" he said, his eyebrows arching in surprise. "It's still there? I mean, it wasn't wiped out?"

"It's still there," she said.

Tate looked at the note in his hand. Learning there was another country that had survived the outbreak had a profound impact. Since the outbreak, he'd had a mental image that the world had been turned into a graveyard, overrun by the Vix. He hadn't seen or heard any news to justify that image; it was just a feeling, but one that had shaped his belief and it had weighed heavily on him.

The sudden revelation that Japan belonged to the living created a ray of hope in his bleak perception.

He put the note in his pocket and nodded.

"I'll be there."

Tate struggled with the pros and cons of taking a contract job during his drive to the Blue Orchid. At least the meeting was on familiar ground. But was that really a good thing? Maybe it was too familiar. He considered that he had conducted a lot of business from there.

He pushed the thought out of the way. That was a topic for another time. He returned to the question about this potential job. If he took it, what did that make him? A mercenary?

He hadn't seen himself like that until Kaiden pointed it out.

The operations he'd taken against The Ring had been orchestrated by Colonel Hewett, so by extension, that made them military, except... and that's where his logic fell apart.

He had to face it. Colonel Hewett was Army, but the missions he gave Tate and his team had nothing to do with the Army, or any military objective.

There was no other way around it. Tate was a contractor, but his sudo-boss wore a uniform.

Tate pursed his lips, refusing to give into the idea. Maybe he was a contractor; didn't mean he'd work for anyone.

On the heels of that thought, he remembered a joke about a lawyer and a witness to a crime.

The lawyer was defending a man who was accused of robbing a bank. The witness had told police that he was in the bank at the time and could confirm the lawyer's client and the robber were the same man.

The lawyer, knowing this witness was big trouble, had learned that the witness had lunch in the same place, every day, and waited for him there.

The witness was surprised and upset when the lawyer sat down at his table.

"You're not supposed to be here," said the witness. "I'm not talking to you."

"You don't have to talk," said the lawyer. "Look, my clients' had a hard life. He's robbed a lot of people and yeah, maybe hurt a couple, but he really wants to turn his life around. If you send him to prison, he'll never have that chance."

"That's not my problem," said the witness. "He made his choices and now he's paying the price."

"Well, that's where you come in," said the lawyer. "See, you're the only eyewitness. If you don't testify, they don't have a case."

"What are you getting at?" said the witness, looking worried. "Is that a threat?"

"No, nothing like that," said the lawyer. "Listen, if I paid you a million dollars, right now, would you change your testimony and say my client is innocent?"

The witness perked up. This was more money than he'd ever seen in his life. He glanced around nervously and hunched over the table, lowering his voice.

"Yeah," said the witness. "I could say it was someone else."

"Great," said the lawyer. "What if I paid you a hundred instead?"

"A hundred?" said the witness, flushing red. "What kind of man do you think I am?"

"We already established that," said the lawyer. "Now we're just haggling over the price."

Tate wondered, did he have a price?

As a Delta Force operator, he had been proud to wear the uniform of the United States military. He was proud to wear it now, even though it was secondhand surplus. But did he need to wear a uniform to take pride in defending his country?

There was a tap at his window, snapping him out of his introspection.

Outside stood a giant of a man in a tight-fitting doorman's coat.

"Evening, Mr. Jack," said Rocko. "Everything okay?"

"Uh, yeah," said Tate, answering a little too brightly. "Yes, just thinking about something."

In fact, he was so wrapped up in his thoughts that he wasn't aware he had arrived at the club. He had driven on autopilot for miles.

"I'll have the valet take your car when you're ready," said Rocko.

"I'm good to go," said Tate, and Rocko opened the car door for him.

"Thanks," said Tate, giving the doorman a generous tip. He always did with Rocko, but sometimes worried if it looked like he was showing off. He genuinely liked Rocko, who had gone the extra step for Tate a few times. "How have you been?"

"Had the flu, but better now, thanks," said Rocko.

They walked up the short steps to the club's double doors and Rocko opened one for Tate.

"Have a good evening," he said.

"Thanks," said Tate, and stepped inside the Blue Orchid.

4

JACK OF ALL TRADES

Entering the club, Tate let out a long breath and felt the tension drop from his shoulders. The comfortable settings of the Blue Orchid was a welcomed change and a place he could be alone to relax; except for those rare times when the outside world intruded, like tonight.

The club looked like it had stepped out of a Bogart movie. The wood, brass and leather decor was accented by the live band on stage at the back of the room. He didn't know the name of the music, but knew it had to be from way back in the 1940s. It was Teddy Moon's style and the man wouldn't have anything else.

"Jack," called Teddy from several tables away. He always made his greeting sound like a mix between a welcome and an announcement. He crossed the room with a bright smile and outstretched hand.

Teddy's love of the 40s extended to his style of clothing. He was always well dressed with hair slicked and parted on the side. His attire was accented with cufflinks and tie pin. His black Oxford shoes were polished to a shine that could be seen even in the subdued lighting of the club.

"How are you, Jack?" he said, warmly shaking Tate's hand. Teddy's white, double-breasted jacket accentuated his tanned face. "You're looking aces."

"Thank you, Commodore," said Tate, making Teddy beam with pleasure. Teddy insisted that his good friends use his nickname, Commodore. Tate didn't know the origins of the nickname and felt a little silly saying it, but it was a small price to pay to make his friend happy. "I'm doing okay."

"Word is you had a scrape with San Roman," said Teddy, lowering his voice. "That cat's bad news." His eyes became solemn as he studied Tate's face, then just as quickly, his smile and good cheer returned. "But here you are, all in one piece. All's well that ends well."

It troubled Tate that Teddy always knew about things that were supposed to be secret. He didn't suspect Teddy was the kind of person to use that information against him, but the man was connected, and someone who knew Tate was talking.

"You have nine lives, Jack," said Teddy with a grin. "I understand tonight's more business than pleasure. Your associates are waiting for you in the Marlowe room."

Tate took a moment to catch up to the change in subject.

"I'll have a whiskey waiting for you at the bar when you're done."

Teddy had a knack for anticipating what Tate wanted before he knew himself. It made him feel like he was easy to read, but like it or not, he had to admire the club owner's talent for keeping his customers happy.

Teddy walked Tate towards the back of the club and the door leading to the private rooms. Standing next to it was another doorman; not as big as Rocko, but big enough. Nobody was getting past that door without Teddy's approval.

The doorman took a key out of his jacket, unlocked and opened the door.

"See you later," said Teddy, and left to mingle with his other guests.

Tate stepped into the hall, feeling his shoes sink into the plush carpet. The door clicked behind him as he headed down the hallway.

Brass wall sconces lit his way past rich, wood doors that led to other rooms.

The Blue Orchid's private rooms were intended for just that. Privacy. There weren't any windows, only one door and soundproof-

36

ing. Two comfortable but small couches sat against opposite walls with a short coffee table in between.

Tate stopped, reading the polished brass plaque on the door. The Marlowe Room.

It was unlocked, and he walked in and swore.

Sitting on the couch were the two ex-FBI agents that had nearly gotten Tate and his team killed in Cuba.

"Good to see you, too," said Jones, blowing out a cloud of cigarette smoke.

"I thought someone dumped you guys in a lake along with all the evidence of your bungled operation," said Tate.

"Thought, or hoped?" smirked Jones.

"Same thing," said Tate.

"Please come in," said Smith, gesturing to the other couch.

"Or leave," said Jones, "but then..."

He stopped there, smiling and sat forward, tapping the ash off the end of his cigarette.

The smile told Tate they knew something he didn't, but whatever it was, they knew it would be important to him.

They were slimy idiots, but they had connections to information that Tate didn't. If they were feeling this smug, it had to be something significant.

He closed the door but remained standing.

"You're looking for a security team," he said, making it both a statement and question.

Jones tapped his cigarette on the ashtray again, even though there wasn't any ash. Tate sensed they needed him more badly than they were letting on, but for what?

"Yes. A person of interest is conducting some business in Tokyo. You're not on their radar, are you?"

"Japan? No," said Tate. He'd operated in Japan before, but it was off the books; nobody there would know his name or face.

"We want you to babysit this person," said Smith.

"Does that sound like something you can do?" asked Jones.

"What's the threat assessment?" asked Tate. "I'm not walking my people into another of your shoot-outs."

Jones took a long pull on his cigarette, making the ember glow bright. "No need," he said, blowing out smoke. The ventilation system quietly but quickly it drew away, clearing the air.

"We're not expecting anyone to attack him. He's involved in a dull contract negotiation. It's not worthy of a criminal organization's interests."

"If it's so simple," said Tate, "why are you coming to me?"

Jones looked at him with a smile that Tate wanted to slap across the room. The agent absently tapped his cigarette; this time dropping ashes on the carpet. Tate imagined how annoyed Teddy would be when he found out.

"We like to cover our bases," said Smith, "You and your people are travel insurance."

"Stuck in that armpit of an army base," said Jones, "you don't get out much, but we know how chaotic the world can be. Innocent people get mixed up in all sorts of trouble they had no part in creating. I bet a gung-ho type like you has been on both sides of situations like that."

They were holding something back; Tate could feel it. The two ex-agents were so textbook spook it almost made him laugh. He studied them, hoping to see behind their poker faces and nondescript black suits, white shirts, and red ties.

Whatever it was, he couldn't get a read on them.

All right. I'll play along.

"How long will he need a team?" asked Tate.

"A week. Two at the most," said Smith. "All the expenses will be covered."

"That doesn't include any medical or burial costs," said Jones. "That's on you."

"When is your man making the trip?" asked Tate.

"Details are still being worked out," said Smith. "In two months, give or take a week."

Jones snubbed out his cigarette, then rested his elbows on his knees, peering at Tate.

"What kind of personal security training does your team have?" he asked.

"I thought you guys had files on everyone," scoffed Tate.

"We've been... involved with other matters," said Smith.

"Matters that don't include you," said Jones.

"We know you Delta types are a Jack of all trades," said Smith. "Did any of your ops include personal security?"

Tate paused as an uninvited memory flashed in front of him. The scene was chaotic and desperate and one he hadn't thought of in many years.

"I'll take that as a yes," said Jones, seeing the look on Tate's face.

"A few times," said Tate. "My team doesn't have the same length experience as I do, but they're good."

He swallowed back the half-truth, but he wanted to know what the agents were up to. Or maybe it was the prospect of going somewhere new after being cooped up in the same place for so long.

His team didn't have any personal security experience, but Tate told himself he wouldn't agree to anything that would put them at risk.

They'd been in enough tight situations; he knew they could be counted on to work under pressure and follow his instructions if things went sideways, but this job sounded like something they could easily manage.

He'd put the next two months to good use, training them for the unique needs of protection duty.

"Well, it's not a demanding job," said Smith. "I think you're a good fit for our needs."

"At least if you live up to your reputation," said Jones.

"What reputation?" asked Tate.

"Things happen. People talk. Word spreads," said Smith, letting the subject drop. "I'll send you what you need to know about our guy. There is one thing I need to be specific about. He'll be carrying a gate-drive. That is your top priority."

"In fact, to clear up any misunderstandings," said Jones, "that gate-drive is your only priority."

"What about your guy?" asked Tate.

"Secondary," said Jones, waving his hand.

"But a very high secondary," said Smith, frowning at Jones. "Neither are disposable."

And now a new detail was finally revealed. Why didn't they mention their priorities from the beginning? Protecting someone's life was entirely different from safeguarding an object.

Tate wondered what else they were holding back.

"It sounds like that gate-drive is important," he said.

"It is," said Jones, reaching inside his jacket for a cigarette. He took out a leather case and opened it, revealing a neat row of bleach-white cigarettes. This was the first time Tate had seen him smoke. The leather case looked new and the way Jones took his time, it felt like he was making a show of a status symbol.

Tate wondered if the 'other matter' Smith had mentioned had something to do with it. The last time he'd dealt with them, they were running their own covert ops out of an unused room in the basement of the Pentagon. Was it possible they were moving up in the intelligence community?

"Custom made," said Jones, seeing Tate looking at the cigarettes. He reached the leather case across the table. "Go ahead. Take one."

"No thanks," said Tate. He enjoyed a good cigar from time to time but had never developed a taste for cigarettes.

Jones held the case out for a half a beat longer before snapping it closed and tucking it in his jacket pocket.

"Why us?" asked Tate, voicing a question that had been on his mind since Kaiden told him about the job.

"Why not?" answered Smith.

Tate didn't respond, not accepting the deflection.

"Why us?" said Jones, striking the tip of the cigarette. A small flame sparked to life, lighting the end of the cigarette. "You mean why would I want to hire a backwater team of inexperienced people to protect my valuable property?"

"Those weren't the words I was thinking," said Tate. "But since you put it that way, yes."

"You tell me," said Jones. He smiled at the subtle flash of annoyance on Tate's face. "I'm not trying to be a jerk."

"Too late," said Tate.

"Funny," said Jones. "But seriously, why do you think we're reaching out to you?"

"Maybe you're looking for a team that's disposable," said Tate. "There won't be anyone to complain if the entire team gets smoked."

"Wow," chuckled Jones. "You go right for the drama."

"It's why you picked us for the last operation," said Tate. "Tell me I'm wrong."

Jones pinched the cigarette between his lips and straightened his jacket before sitting back.

"You're not on anyone's radar," said Smith. "Especially with security contractors. That's a tight community, lots of chatter with those people. If I'd hired any of them, the gossip would spread and everyone would have their nose in our business, asking questions and drawing unwanted attention."

"It's a low threat operation," said Smith.

"A walk in the park," said Jones. "That's why you're a good fit."

That sounded right. It even made sense to Tate, but there was something about the whole thing that got the little voice in the back of his head worried.

These two spooks were opportunists, looking to make a name for themselves. If they scored a big enough win, maybe it would wash away the stain of being in the FBI.

Tate had a feeling this job was their shot at that big win. It was a good bet they wouldn't lose sleep over burning him and his team to get it. He didn't need to know anything more.

"We're not the team you're looking for," said Tate, standing up.

"What?" asked Jones, getting to his feet. For just an instant, Tate caught a glimpse of desperation. "We haven't talked about money."

"I'd appreciate it if you stay out of my club in the future," said Tate.

He left the room, wondering what kind of trouble he'd just dodged.

Entering back into the club, he relaxed. He wasn't playing psychological chess anymore.

He headed to the bar; true to Teddy's word, the bartender was pouring a fresh whiskey just for him.

A large mirror covered the back wall of the bar and Tate kept one eye on it, watching for the two agents to exit.

They never appeared during his whiskey, and he assumed Teddy had let them use the back door so they could leave unseen.

Always playing cloak and dagger.

During the drive back, Tate tried to forget the meeting with zero success. It was like a bad song stuck in his head. It wasn't just that the agents knew something; they knew the information would be important to him.

Maybe they don't know anything. They're trying to bait me into another of their dumpster fire operations.

But the question of what they did know kept circling back to his mind.

He gripped the steering wheel in frustration, not knowing what to think.

Why do I let those idiots mess with my head?

Through the mental static, one thought began to stand out from the rest. His gut was telling him it wasn't over.

Paranoia wasn't part of Tate's vocabulary, but he did believe in instinct. He paused, having caught himself being sucked back into thinking about the meeting again and chuckled to himself.

"You're getting twitchy in your old age," he said.

The front gates of Fort Hickok came into view and he pushed himself to think about something else.

He liked the new base commander. She was tough and didn't feel like she had anything to prove. She expected respect for her rank but made the effort to earn the personal respect of others.

After the new commander had settled in, Tate decided to have a frank conversation with her about the irregular comings and goings of the Grave Diggers team.

This was the first time he'd met with the new colonel and Tate had a well-earned reluctance when it came to officers. Some were good, some were inept, and others were career climbing evil bastards who didn't feel like their day was complete until they'd exercised their power to make someone's life miserable.

He'd started the conversation with a boatload of diplomacy. He hadn't gotten far when she waved him off with a tired smile.

"Relax, Sergeant Major," she said. "I've already filled my quota of human sacrifices for the day. I don't have the patience or desire to play counterintelligence with people. Just say what you want to say."

That didn't make it any easier for Tate. If anything, it made it worse because now he either had to jump into the subject with both feet or retreat. His choice wouldn't have surprised anyone who knew him. He was definitely a 'both feet' kind of guy.

"I'm in charge of a special team," he started.

He skillfully avoided giving away too much information about their history, formation and unique operations, but the colonel could connect enough of the dots to draw her own conclusions.

Having heard enough, she'd held up her hand, stopping Tate in mid-sentence.

"I got it," she said. "You keep odd hours."

"Yes, ma'am," said Tate. "That about sums it up."

"I'm going to ask you some questions," said the colonel. "I want truthful answers."

A dark expression clouded her face and she looked at Tate with cold death in her eyes.

"If I find out you've lied to me," she said, "there's no version of your worst nightmare that'll compare to what I'll do to you. How copy, Sergeant Major?"

"Loud and clear, ma'am," he said, knowing she meant it.

Her expression cleared, returning to the casual interest she'd shown before.

"Are the actions of you and your team supporting anything illegal?" she asked.

"No."

"Are you doing anything that threatens this base?"

"No."

The colonel's questions continued. It was a short list and he answered them honestly.

"One last thing," she said. "If any of you screw the pooch during one of your side activities, I won't allow it to blowback on me, this base or the United States army. Don't look to me to save you. If I have to choose between you and the Army, I'll hang you out to dry every time."

"Understood," said Tate.

"Great," said the colonel. "Are we done?"

Her tone said it wasn't a question. The meeting was over and it was time the he got out of her office.

"No, ma'am," said Tate, getting to his feet. "Thank you for your time."

They exchanged salutes and Tate left her office feeling good about their understanding. But he also felt the weight of responsibility to abide by her rules.

Rules were like plans. They were easy to stick to until you got punched in the face. Anyone who'd been in combat knew how true that was. Committing to the colonel's rules promised to be difficult. Tate knew there would be unforeseen situations that could put him right up to the edge of crossing the line. But it was useless to play 'what if'. He'd cross that bridge when it came.

The big upside was that the Grave Diggers could come and go as they needed.

All right, he admitted to himself, that was an exaggeration. But they did have more latitude when it came to leaving the base.

Tate flicked on the light as he walked into his quarters, smiling as cool air wafted over him. The finicky air conditioner had chugged away like a champ for the past few days. The last time it broke down he'd sworn to use it for target practice, and he toyed with the belief the threat had worked.

He paused, unlacing his boot, thinking he'd heard something.

He heard it again. It came from his backpack.

Tate fished out his sat phone, the blinking light on top confirming a missed call.

Paging to call history, he saw an incoming call logged only a few minutes ago. The caller's number was masked.

The agents.

He didn't know why he thought that, but it hit him with undeniable certainty.

That they discovered his sat phone number and broke the encryption irritated him beyond description.

More angry than curious, Tate mashed the call-back button.

The call was answered before the first ring had finished.

"Thanks for calling back," said Smith.

Tate swore under his breath as he remembered, too late, the trace device Nathan had given him months before. If he'd taken a moment to think about his next move instead of acting on impulse, he could have used the device to expose the agent's number and location.

Now he could add frustration to his anger.

"How'd you get my number?" he growled. "Forget that. Tell me what's really going on. No more screwing around. Don't piss in my ear and tell me it's raining."

"Okay," said Smith. "I know you're mad but hear me out."

"You have five seconds." Tate was squeezing the sat phone so tightly he thought it might shatter.

Let it break.

He was going to take his frustration out on something and he wasn't picky about what it was.

"I'm breaking a lot of protocols by calling you," said Smith. It might have been an act, but the man sounded genuinely nervous. "I shouldn't be telling you any of this."

"Time's up," said Tate.

"The man we want you to protect is defecting from The Ring," blurted Smith. "We want you to bring him in."

5

KILL TEAM

Tate's thumb hovered over the disconnect button, his mind stumbling to process what he'd just heard.

"Say that again," he said.

There was a long pause. Tate waited, listening to the static.

"I'm really putting my neck on the line, here," said Smith. "But I know you're the right team for this."

"You don't know anything about me," growled Tate.

"I know you joined them before you learned what they were doing. I know you're using connections inside The Ring to take them down. And I know you feel like they're winning."

Tate bit back the questions whirling through his head. He remained silent, waiting to see how Smith filled the empty air.

"Like I said at the club, people talk," said Smith. "Word gets around."

Tate pinched the bridge of his nose against the throbbing of a growing headache. He was tired of the word games. A wave of old, familiar anger began to well up in him. That anger had the same nervous energy he felt every time he dealt with spooks. He'd never met one he could trust.

He hated the way they played people against each other. He really believed they played with truth like a game; one they were addicted to, trying to see who could outwit and misdirect the other. This was exactly the same feeling he was getting from Smith.

He shook off his personal dislike for the two rogue FBI agents and focused on the bigger picture.

"A defector," said Tate. "Did you confirm your sources?"

"I talked to him," said Smith. "And he's bringing crucial data about the entire organization and their operations."

That kind of information could be enough to destroy the organization if he was safely delivered into the hands of the good guys.

With sudden realization, Tate understood the huge significance of protecting the defector. He would never know another moment of peace if he turned down the job and another team botched it.

It had to be him and his team. Nothing else was acceptable.

"Are you still there?" asked Smith.

"You know I am," said Tate. "Tell me about your defector. How's this supposed to play out?"

"Mullen is traveling to Japan on Ring business," said Smith. "He believes putting distance between him and his handlers will create a window of opportunity to escape before they can react."

"What's the meeting about?"

"He wouldn't tell us," said Smith. "We don't care. We just want him and the gate drive."

"They won't let him out of sight that easy," said Tate. "The Ring'll have a security detail escorting him everywhere he goes, twenty-four, seven."

"Yes and no," said Smith. "They don't want to risk drawing unwanted attention by sending Mullen and his entourage of heavies through customs at the same time. The security team will arrive covertly using a chartered flight a few days later."

"And that's where me and my team come in?" said Tate.

"You will intercept and neutralize the security detail before they connect with Mullen."

"What happened to this being a 'walk in the park'?" said Tate. "You said we were escorting. Now we're taking on a trained security detail."

"You did walk out before we got to the details," said Smith.

"You have resources specially trained to counteract a team like that," said Tate. "Why aren't you using them?"

"We're executing an operation in a foreign country," said Smith. "We have to maintain a small footprint. That means a multifunctional team. Yours."

"We don't do wet work. We're not assassins," said Tate. "We're not killing anyone just because they're in the way."

"We're not asking you to," said Smith. "Especially on foreign soil. More importantly, you can't afford to kill them."

"Another wrinkle?" said Tate.

"A safeguard," said Smith. "After landing, the security detail must check in with a confirmation code. Only after they've been verified will they'll be given the secured sat phone number to reach Mullen. It's the only time they'll be off the clock and have their guard down."

"What do we do with them once they're out of action?" asked Tate.

"Leave them wrapped up," said Smith. "We'll send someone to sit on them until the op is finished."

"Anything else?" prompted Tate.

"I've already said too much," said Smith. "Considering your history with The Ring, I can't think of a more highly motivated team for this operation than yours."

"I need to pass this by them before I give you an answer," said Tate.

"I advise you make that a fast conversation," said Smith. "There's a lot of time sensitive complexities to this op, and we can't afford to wait long for your answer."

"I'll be in touch," said Tate.

"Great. When will you..."

Tate hung up.

———————

"We're going to Japan?" said Rosse excitedly.

"Really?" scoffed Monkhouse. "That's your takeaway?"

"What's your problem?" asked Rosse.

"We're going to a place where we don't speak the language," said Monkhouse, counting on his fingers. "We don't read Japanese. We don't know the currency. We don't blend in, especially you, unless you're in a sumo parade."

Rosse glanced at his stomach, frowning.

"We don't know the laws. And if you don't like seafood, you're screwed."

"Yeah but, you know," mumbled Rosse, "we're going to Japan."

"I think Monkhouse touched on some of the difficulties we'll be facing," said Tate, "but I need to address the most important hurdle you face. None of you have any experience in personal security."

He let that hang in the air for a moment. Everyone of his team had a past and all of them had shared small windows into those lives. But just fragments; he suspected none of those pasts included working security.

Another factor was everyone in the room was a product of the All Volunteer Expeditionary Force; an impressive name for the military equivalent scraping the bottom of the barrel.

The primary role, in fact the only role of the AVEF soldier, was to kill Vix. Boot camp took only long enough to train a recruit from accidentally shooting themselves or each other.

The life expectancy of the average AVEF soldier was ten Vix patrols. Twelve tops. The army made no attempt to hide this fact from the public and yet there was no shortage of people wanting to sign up.

The reason people ignored the risks was that the payoff for completing your time in service was you could literally come out a new person. All crimes, debts, everything, wiped clean. You got a new name and identity.

Just to make sure their past didn't catch up to them before their tour of duty was over, some people signed up using a false name. The army didn't care. There were millions of Vix roaming freely and the faster they were wiped out, the happier the president would be.

Tate didn't know if the names of his team members were real or fake. Frankly, he didn't care. They had proved themselves to be loyal and courageous in a fight. He trusted each of them with his life. What more did he need to know?

"I was a guard," said Rosse. "That's kinda like personal security."

"We have combat experience," said Fulton, raising his hand. Tate had told him over and over he didn't need to do that, but it was just his way.

"There's some overlap," said Tate, "but there's a lot of differences between combat and engaging an active shooter in a civilian environment. I have two months to train you. That's not much. The training will be concentrated and intense. It's going to be physically and mentally exhausting."

Their expressions ranged from unhappy to outright discouraged and Tate realized he had laid it on too thick.

"I'll put it this way," he said. "The training will be challenging, but I know all of you can do it."

The encouragement raised their spirits and they looked ready to take it on.

"But first things first," said Tate. "Whether we move forward on this or not is up to all of you. So, let's make this simple. Who's out?"

He didn't feel the need to remind them there was no shame or pressure to decide either way. Everyone knew they wouldn't be judged by him or their fellow teammates. This wasn't a mission sanctioned by the army. The same rules didn't apply and Tate wasn't going to push anyone into a potentially dangerous operation.

"Anyone?"

Nobody spoke.

"We're going to hit the ground running," said Tate.

He glanced at his watch, showing them he wasn't exaggerating.

"Okay," he smiled. "Grab your gear and meet up at the kill house in one hour."

"It's the middle of the night," said Rosse. "I'm beat."

Tate stared at him without expression or comment.

Rosse got the message.

"Yeah, yeah," he said. "I'm going."

Chairs scraped as everyone got up and hurried out the door.

"Gun, gun, gun," yelled Wesson, as she moved in front of the client and herded him towards the car.

"I don't see them," said Fulton, aiming down his gun site and panning the crowd.

Gunfire crackled as Rosse and Ota crouched, searching for the shooter, but seeing only civilians.

Wesson stumbled and fell against the client, knocking them against the closed car door. The client scrabbled to get inside but couldn't open the door with Wesson's weight pushing on them.

The chaos was pierced by a shrill whistle as Tate stepped through the rows of dummies to the collective groan of the entire team.

"Wesson's dead," he said flatly. "The client's dead and the shooter got away. Where are the points of failure?"

"Somebody didn't open the door," said Monkhouse, looking accusingly at Fulton.

"I thought I was supposed to cover Wesson," said Fulton.

Tate could feel his frustration wanting to take over. Chewing them out would help him blow off the monumental amount of steam built up, but that would only erode their confidence.

"Remember why you're divided into teams," he said. "Wesson is the Principal Protection Officer, directly responsible for protecting the client. That also includes getting them into cover. Fulton, you're Personal Escort Section One. You're responsible for clearing the path, opening doors and getting people out of the way. Rosse..."

"I know," he said. "Me an Ota are the PES Two. We engage and suppress the shooter."

"Who was the shooter?" asked Tate. He was met by a wall of blank faces. "Who called 'gun'?"

"I did," said Wesson, looking dejected. "I screwed up. I didn't identify the shooter to the rest of the team."

"Everyone meet for debrief and theory in thirty minutes," said Tate as he walked away.

They had improved faster than he'd expected and he had sped up their training, but maybe he'd moved too fast. They were screwing up on basics.

They were two weeks away from Japan and there were a lot of rough edges he needed to fix.

He was concerned they wouldn't be ready in time and his worries were mounting. On paper there was no reason to suspect anyone would attack the defector, but Tate knew from first-hand experience how quickly things could go to hell.

The memory of that operation had never left him.

———————

Davorin Volansky was an out of work cold fusion engineer in a country that was slowly, but inexorably circling the drain of bankruptcy. The specialty of his skill set made finding a job that much harder than the average laborer.

The last of his money went toward keeping food on the table.

He was behind on his rent, utilities had been shut off, and the reality was they'd be living on the street within a few short weeks.

In a master stroke of luck, he was approached by a small investment group and offered a job with a handsome paycheck.

Davorin couldn't accept fast enough.

He would be part of a larger project involved with research and development to enhance the energy interaction between tiny amounts of hydrogen and palladium.

Davorin saw the potential to change the face of energy around the world. It was very exciting.

The process required a containment device capable of withstanding an extreme amount of pressure and demanded it be engineered to precise standards.

The materials for the device included rare earth elements that were very expensive. Under the wrong conditions, they were also violently unstable.

Davorin raised his concerns to his employers who were quick to agree. He was told there was another team working on the necessary countermeasures to ensure the safety of the device and he shouldn't concern himself about it any further.

He should have been satisfied with their response. They were attentive to his concerns. Their explanation was sound and by all appearances, they had the matter in hand. But... a ripple of doubt began to nag at him. He tried to ignore it, but it wouldn't go away.

Quietly, carefully, he began to dig into what was going on outside of his small engineering team.

What he discovered shook him to his core. The investment group turned out to be nonexistent. A front. A nameless organization was pulling the strings from the cover of shadows.

They didn't hire him to design a new source of energy. He was unknowingly helping to create a cold fusion bomb with a potentially destructive force that would make a nuclear explosion look like a firecracker.

Panic and horror twisted his gut. He had to get out, but that was impossible. The instant they suspected he knew something, they'd kill him, and probably his family. If he said nothing and finished his work, they'd kill him to cover their tracks. No matter what he did, he was a dead man.

Rumors about the development of a new type of super bomb had caught the attention of the CIA and in the process had connected with Mr. Volansky.

Now it was up to Tate and his Delta team of Night Devils to extract Davorin and his family.

After two months of surveillance, the Night Devils were ready. They had cautioned Davorin to stop his criticism of the company, but by then it was too late.

The company knew Davorin had become suspicious. That made him a threat, but the people behind the company had dealt with threats before and had set up a team of watchdogs in a house across the street from his home. His family's every move was being watched around the clock.

They were instructed that if Davorin or his family showed any sign they were attempting to flee, the watchdogs would execute all of them.

The Night Devil's extraction plan was based on divide and conquer.

Staying within the confines of the family's routine, they would wait until the family members were spread out, the daughter at the mall, the son at home and the wife grocery shopping. This would dilute the watchdogs into smaller teams, reducing their effectiveness.

The timing of the extraction had to be down to the second, taking possession of every family member at the same time.

The Night Devils had broken up into teams of two. Tate and Sergeant Charlie 'Mojo' Woodmen were assigned to extract Davorin's fourteen-year-old daughter, Celeste. One of the many challenges they faced was that Celeste was deaf, but Davorin said she was very good at reading lips. As an extra aid, Tate was bringing a small whiteboard and grease pencil.

In a risky, but necessary meeting in a library, Tate explained the details of the extraction with Davorin. It was paramount that his family understood they must act normally; not talk about it to anyone. On the day of the extract, they shouldn't change their behavior, dress differently, take any mementos or anything else from the house they normally don't carry.

Davorin promised his family would do as they were told.

Over the following weeks, Tate and Mojo had gradually inserted themselves into Celeste's environment as stock clerks at one of the stores that Celeste and her friends loved to shop in.

Each family member knew where they were supposed to be at the exact minute of the following day.

The Night Devil teams were in place and ready. Now they waited as the minutes ticked down to the critical minute when everything went into action.

. . .

54

No plan was perfect. Variables were impossible to anticipate. Adapting to the unexpected while under pressure was part of the Night Devil's training.

But none of the Night Devils were fathers to a teenager, or knew how disastrously one could unravel a life and death operation.

Celeste's mom dropped her off at the mall, just as she'd done many times before.

"I'll pick you up in the afternoon," said Mara.

It's what she always said, but they both knew today was going to be different. The next time they'd see each other would be at the Night Devils' safe house.

Mara tried to keep her smile from cracking under the weight of fear. The lives of her family were in the hands of strangers. Her heart ached to hold her daughter and never let go.

Celeste rolled her eyes and reluctantly hugged her mom, feeling the eyes of her friends watching.

"You're embarrassing me," she signed. "I'm not a little girl anymore."

Her mother clicked her tongue, hoping to mask the sting of tears threatening to well up in her eyes. She gripped the steering wheel to keep her hands from shaking.

"See you later," she said.

But Celeste had already got out of the car and didn't see her mother's lips.

Mara drove off as Celeste waded into the clique of friends and together, they headed into the mall. All of her friends knew sign language and saw it as their secret code. They'd gossip about boys they liked and girls they didn't. Celeste was as chatty as any of them except for today. She was reluctant to take her hand out of her pocket to sign. She was carrying something special from home and was afraid of losing it.

. . .

Davorin's son, Able, was the last to leave the house. Like clockwork, the last two watchdogs left their house and followed at a discrete distance. Unknown to them, two Night Devils were behind them.

"This is Toaster," radioed one of the Devils. "We have the last two watchdogs in sight. Everyone's accounted for."

"Copy," replied Tate.

Except that wasn't true.

Hamit, the ninth member of the watchdog team had been missed during their initial reconnaissance.

Minutes later, he walked out the door of the surveillance house and crossed the street to Davorin's home. He opened the door with a master key and went inside as he had every time the house was empty. It was his job to sweep the home and see what Davorin was up to.

Starting in the living room, Hamit compared the room to the photographs he'd taken on the first day of this assignment.

Mementos, family photos and items of sentimental or monetary value were cataloged. Basically, anything someone might take with them if they were never coming back.

It was tedious work and Hamit resented having to do it. But he was the low man on the totem pole. Regardless if it was a corporate office, or a death squad; it was all about seniority.

Satisfied everything was in place, Hamit moved on to the next room with a disgruntled sigh.

Tate and Mojo started their day stocking shelves at the Supra designer store, each of them keenly aware the minutes were counting down to their meet with Celeste.

Across the mall, Celeste glanced at the clock on the wall as she took a sip of her custom ordered coffee. It was time.

"There's a new top at Supra I want to try on," she said.

Her friends were all on board and left the coffee stand, ready to do more shopping.

The watchdogs watched the girls leave in the reflection of a store window, following after them.

Celeste hadn't met Tate and Mojo and didn't know what they looked like. Her father had told her they would identify themselves with the keyword stagecoach.

It had annoyed her how he had made such a big deal about it.

"Follow their instructions," he'd said.

"I know, Dad," she had signed, exasperated. "You don't have to keep telling me. I'm not a child."

The girls poured into Supra and Celeste glanced around, but didn't see anyone making eye contact and assumed her escorts weren't there.

The watchdogs split up at the store's entrance. Raul went inside and Viktor loitered outside. Neither of them stood out from the crowd of milling shoppers, except for their concealed automatic pistols and the willingness to use them.

Celeste glanced over the rack of clothes, confident she'd be able to pick out the two old guys that were supposed to meet her.

She shrugged her shoulders, not seeing anyone that stood out, browsed the blouses until she found the one she liked.

Taking it off the rack, she headed into the changing rooms at the rear of the store.

Raul walked over to a table of sweaters next to the entrance of the changing area. It was as far as he could go and that's what Tate and Mojo had counted on.

Celeste passed open dressing rooms until she came to the one with a unicorn on it. The door was closed but unlocked. She paused in surprise at the two big men waiting for her inside.

They waved her in and she closed the door behind her.

"Stagecoach," said Tate, mouthing the words.

Celeste nodded and stepped inside.

He checked his watch and held up two fingers.

"I'm Tate and this is Mojo," he mouthed. "I know you might be a little scared, but..."

Celeste frowned, gesturing something.

Tate took out the small whiteboard and pencil and handed it to her.

She took it with an air of disappointment.

"I'm not scared," she wrote.

In spite of the strict rules, Hamit had taken a beer out of the family's refrigerator. He saw it as compensation for doing menial work.

He went into Celeste's room and pulled up the photographs on his data pad. His gaze flicked back and forth between the photos and the left side of her room. The place was a cluttered mess of clothing, posters, stuffed toys and makeup.

He moved on to the next wall, quickly becoming impatient to finish and move on.

He shook his head, looking at her TV and stereo.

Spoiled.

Taking another drink, he moved on to the next wall, but stopped in mid swallow.

Hamit held the data pad at arm's length and compared it against Celeste's bookshelf. Both were a menagerie of colors, shapes and textures, but one was not like the other.

Something's missing.

He magnified the image and saw a small, antique broach. They knew it was a prized memento from Celeste's grandmother. Nobody was allowed to touch it.

The kid's taken it!

Hamit dropped the beer as he scrabbled for the radio on his belt and keyed the mic.

"The kid's got the broach," he blurted. He shook his head, knowing the team wouldn't understand what he meant.

"The family's escaping!"

Celeste's watchdogs were now a kill team.

6

SAY ROOKIE ONE MORE TIME

People shouted in angry protests as Viktor barreled through them to reach Raul at the sweater table.

The indignant shoppers suddenly fled as fully automatic pistols appeared in the men's hands.

They charged into the changing area and headed for the first dressing room.

Raul pushed open the door, shattering the mirror inside. The room was empty.

They moved to the next room. Empty.

Raul pushed on the door with the unicorn. His pulse quickened when he discovered it was locked.

Both men opened fire, stitching the door with bullet holes. Capturing the girl was not their priority now.

They kicked in the door to confirm their kill, but the dressing room was empty.

A quick glance around revealed a door marked employees only. It opened into a stock room with another door at the other end. The two men split up; Viktor searching the stock room while Raul headed for the opposite door.

Stepping through, Raul entered a long hallway just in time to hear a distant door slam closed.

"This way," he said, taking off with Viktor right behind.

Tate's plan had been to exit the mall through the utility door, which opened onto a second level parking lot. From there, they would use the public to screen them from view until they got to their car. It was a simple plan until everything went to pieces.

Panic had spilled out of the designer store and had spread throughout the mall.

The chaos rose to a fear-fueled pitch when the fire alarm went off. Thousands of people, pushing and yelling, trying to be heard over the blaring. The mall's speaker system came alive with a nervous voice, snapping instructions for everyone to hide and wait for the police.

Everyone in the parking lot flew back to their cars to get out of there and instantly jammed the driveways.

"We go on foot," said Mojo, tossing the keys over his shoulder.

Tate nodded; with Celeste in-between them, they fast walked to the stairwell.

Viktor and Raul rushed out of the door and into the parking lot. They briefly paused, scanning the situation. Cars were stacked up, bumper to bumper with frightened people blaring their horns.

They knew the girl didn't drive and if anyone was helping her, they wouldn't be sitting in that traffic jam.

They were running on foot.

Raul and Viktor ran to the nearest stairwell.

Tate, Mojo and Celeste came out of the stairwell on the street level. Just like upstairs, this lot was a snarl of congestion.

A driver had rear-ended another car at the exit of the parking lot, and now the two drivers were out of their cars, yelling at each other.

"We'll use the fight as a distraction," said Tate, leading them towards the accident.

He flinched as a bullet ripped past his ear. They ducked into a crouch, leaving Celeste looking at them in confusion.

Mojo yanked her down. Her angry protests were ignored as they dragged her off her feet, racing towards the fighting drivers.

"Get her in," said Tate as they reached the front car.

He circled around to the open driver's door and got in, unnoticed by the arguing drivers.

Mojo pulled open the rear passenger door and pushed Celeste inside. Scared and angry, she had enough sense to pull her leg in before the door slammed closed.

Mojo reached for his door. Two bullets punched him in the back, knocking him against the car.

"Get in," shouted Tate.

"Can't," wheezed Mojo, slumping out of sight.

Tate saw the kill team racing for him.

The passenger window spiderwebbed as bullets smacked the glass.

Tate gunned the engine and Mojo rolled away as Tate barreled into oncoming traffic. Cars twisted and screeched, trying to avoid him.

The arguing drivers gaped at the chaos as Viktor shoved past them to the remaining car.

"I'm driving," he snapped, rushing to the driver's side.

The owner caught sight of Viktor's gun and didn't say a word.

Raul stopped at the passenger door and aimed at Mojo who could only watch his approaching death.

"He's not our target," barked Viktor, starting the car.

Pausing a beat longer, Raul lowered his gun and got inside. The tires screeched as they took off after Tate and Celeste.

Tate grabbed his radio out of his jacket. "This is Razorback. Mojo is down and needs medical care."

"This is Red Man," answered the radio. "I copy. We'll get to Mojo as soon as we can. Everyone's got their hands full. Something tipped the watchdogs off that the family's bailing. We're scattered all over the place trying to escape and evade."

"Same here," said Tate, glancing at his rearview mirror.

A car violently spun out of control as his pursuers plowed into it, shoving it out of the way.

"They're on my six," said Tate. "I'll report when I can."

"Good luck," said Red Man.

Tate dropped the radio on the seat as Celeste popped up from the rear seat, waving her hands in angry gestures, demanding answers.

"Sit down" barked Tate, shoving her away.

He pushed the accelerator to the floor. They were going too fast. The car was skittish, overreacting to the smallest movement of the steering wheel. He hoped the fates were on his side and didn't throw an idiot driver on their phone in front of him.

The kill team was gaining.

The light was green at the intersection ahead, but it wouldn't stay that way much longer. Tate crushed the gas pedal, trying to squeeze more speed out of the car.

Almost there.

The traffic light turned red.

Tate's jaw clenched, gripping the wheel with white knuckles as cross-traffic rolled into the intersection.

Horns blared, rubber screamed as Tate shot into the closing window of escape. The side of his car scraped across the front of a truck, ripping a gash down the length of the car.

He fought the car under control and was through to the other side.

Glancing in the mirror, he saw the pursuing kill team blocked by the havoc he'd left behind.

A grin curled the corner of Tate's mouth, unaware his victory was short lived.

Outside, a razor point of jagged metal from the ripped front fender lingered inches away from the tire.

At the next corner, Tate turned, driving the sidewall of the tire into the metal, instantly shredding it.

The car nosed into the asphalt in a spray of sparks as the tire blew and they slid into oncoming traffic.

Tate threw the wheel hard, trying to counter-steer, but the car wouldn't respond.

A violent jolt threw him against the door as a truck clipped him, spinning his car and crashing into the curb.

A crowd started to gather around as Tate fought through his swimming head and got out of the car. He pushed away the helping hands and grabbed his radio, then retrieved Celeste. She wobbled on her feet, but nothing looked broken and she wasn't bleeding.

Good enough.

He had to get them out of the open and Tate led her through the crowd and into the nearby block of apartments.

The kill team smoked the tires, screeching to a stop and jumped out of their car.

"Which way?" snapped Raul.

Startled by the show of guns, the crowd were quick to point where Tate and Celeste had disappeared.

Tate felt a stabbing pain in his side. He gingerly explored the area and winced as he felt the break in his rib. Running was still an option but running fast wasn't. He had no choice but to change his tactics.

They paused in the narrow courtyard of the multistoried apartment complex as Tate weighed his options. Rows upon rows of doors and windows made it a perfect place to hide, and chances were high that the kill team would run through and out the other side of the complex, assuming Tate and the girl had gone that way.

"We're going up," he said.

Celeste hotly stared at him.

"Now."

He grabbed her hand and started up the stairs. His rib was punishing him, but he pushed himself to climb.

They reached the fourth floor and he stopped in a small recess on the landing to fish out his radio.

"This is Razorback," he said. "We're on foot, still heading to the safe house. ETA..."

Celeste pulled free from his hand and gestured angrily at him.

"I don't know what you're saying," said Tate.

He handed her the mini whiteboard and she snatched it from him, scribbling on it then shoving the note at him.

"This is stupid. We can hide at my friend's house."

"Listen to me...," began Tate, and she rolled her eyes at him. Pain fanned his frustration, but he fought to keep a level head. "Just do what I tell you and we'll get through this."

She signed something and he held out the note board. Celeste grunted, taking the board and flung it over the railing, defiantly crossing her arms across her chest and glaring at him.

Viktor and Raul entered the complex, moving quietly but fast. They could see where the complex opened to another street in the distance.

They tucked their guns out of sight and picked up the pace to reach the other side.

Raul saw a small, white panel on the ground, dismissing it until he saw writing on it.

This is stupid. We can hide at my friend's house.

He put his hand on Viktor's arm and gestured up. The two men left the courtyard and headed up the stairs.

Tate grimaced every time Celeste shuffled her feet or sighed impatiently. Glancing at his watch, he determined the kill team should have passed by now.

He stepped out onto the landing to see if it was clear below.

Gunfire cracked and bullets seared the air around Tate's head.

He ducked back, pushing Celeste against the wall.

The kill team was at the other end of the walkway. Tate pulled out his Colt, glancing at the stairway behind them. They could take it down to ground level, but the kill team would only follow them, and with Tate's injury, it would be a short chase.

He aimed down the length of the walkway, waiting for his pursuers to stick their heads out.

· · ·

Viktor peeked around the corner. A .45 slug shattered the plaster in front of his face and he pulled back, swearing. Angry, he stuck his gun around the corner and blind-fired down the walkway, hitting nothing.

Beads of blood seeped from his cheek and he tried to blink the dust and debris from his eye.

"Hold him here," said Raul, heading back to the stairs. "I'll go underneath and come up from behind them."

Viktor nodded, wiping his eye on his sleeve.

Tate peeked around the corner, ready to fire.

Keeping his gaze on the other end of the landing, he motioned for Celeste to stay put, then slipped around the corner towards the kill team.

Angry and scared, Celeste backed away until she reached the stairs.

She took out her phone and went down the stairs until she reached the courtyard. She spotted the busy street to her left and ran out of the complex.

Raul stopped looking up as gunfire cracked above him but couldn't see what was happening. He reached the courtyard just in time to see Celeste disappear as she exited the buildings.

He briefly thought about getting his partner, but the girl was alone now. This would be easy.

Tate knew he'd rattled the men at the other end of the walkway because they'd were shooting wild and staying hidden behind the distant corner. He was blind to them, but only for a moment. As quietly as speed would allow, he rushed their position.

Viktor wondered why he hadn't heard Raul shoot yet. It had only been a few seconds of quiet, but in combat a few seconds was an eternity and anything could happen. Where was Raul? More alarming; where was the girl's protector?

Alarms were going off in his head that he was in danger. Still blind in his eye, he stuck his gun around the corner to shoot.

Tate reached the corner as a gun appeared, inches from his chest. Reflexes took over and he grabbed the gunmen's hand and twisted. Bone snapped and he heard a scream around the corner as the gun clattered to the floor.

Gasping in pain and surprise, Viktor reached for his back-up knife. Tate came around the corner and pistol-whipped Viktor in the temple with the heavy Colt, instantly dropping him.

Where's the other guy?

Tate scanned for the second gunman.

He went downstairs to circle behind us. Celeste!

Tate charged back the way he'd come, filled with dread.

Crack!

A single shot. Ice filled his veins, but as he ran it dawned on him the sound was oddly distant.

He peered over the railing and saw the other gunman tucking away his pistol and drawing a knife.

He disappeared from view, heading out of the complex.

Celeste stopped at the street and opened her phone. A bus was approaching and she glanced at it, deciding if she'd get on or text her friend for a ride.

"Can you pick me up? Everything's crazy and my bodyguard's a jerk."

Raul paused inside the complex to line up his shot. He squeezed the trigger at the same instant the girl dropped her head to text on her phone. The bullet missed. The girl never heard the shot.

Before he fired again, a bus stopped and people got out, milling around his target. He put his gun away and took out a small dagger.

Up close it is.

He walked over to the people at the bus and slowly sifted his way through them, moving closer to the girl.

She was texting, but turned, looking up the street; maybe expecting someone.

Raul didn't know if she'd recognize him and angled to get behind her. He flexed his grip on the dagger. He'd have to be fast and get it right the first time. His target was the popliteal artery at the back of the knee. She would hardly feel the sting, but she'd bleed out in seconds.

Raul would disappear in the confusion of the crowd.

"I'm almost there," messaged her friend.

Celeste smiled, texting a heart emoji as a man moved close behind her and knelt down, pretending to tie his shoe.

She yelped as something bumped the back of her leg. She looked down as a strange man collapsed at her feet and she jumped back.

As the startled crowd backed away, a rough hand grabbed her by the arm. She looked up into the glowering grey-blue eyes of Jack Tate.

Before it disappeared inside his coat, she glimpsed a blood-stained knife.

They left the milling crowd staring at the body on the sidewalk. Celeste didn't resist.

―――――――

"That one looked perfect to me," said Wesson. "What about you, Top?"

Tate stammered as his mind jumped into the present. He had no idea what he'd just missed.

"Uh..." he began.

"You guys have really improved," said Kaiden.

Tate was surprised to see her standing next to him.

"You're getting a good sense of positioning and overlapping sight-lines."

Wesson smiled at the uncommon complement and turned to Tate for the final say.

"Good work," he said, trying to sound like he knew what he was talking about. "Run it again."

"Okay," she said. "You heard him. Let's go."

The rest of the team groaned, shuffling without enthusiasm. They'd repeated the exercise several times already.

"Cry me a river," said Wesson. "Get in your positions."

She walked off, organizing the team into their places.

"When did you get here?" asked Tate.

"Somewhere in the middle of your daydream," said Kaiden.

"You saw that, huh?" he said.

"Everyone saw it."

"I figured," said Tate.

"You were thinking about the deaf girl?" she asked.

He looked at her with a mix of wonder and suspicion. "How did you know?"

"I've had clingy boyfriends who have less trouble letting go than you do," she smiled.

They watched the team as they practiced escorting Monkhouse. They swept the crowds of dummies, looking for signs of threats.

"Do you really think they're good?" asked Tate.

"Considering the threat level?" said Kaiden. "Yes. They're... okay."

"Maybe you could impart some of your glowing knowledge about close protection tactics."

"Maybe that's why I'm here," she said.

"I didn't thank you for setting up the meet with your agent buddies," he said.

Kaiden glanced at him, the corner of her eye crinkled with a grin.

"If I told you it was them, you wouldn't have gone," she said.

"You knew what the operation was."

"I guessed," she said. "They dropped a couple of hints."

Tate's eyebrows came together in a frown.

"You're kidding. Who else are they talking to?" he asked. "If this leaks back to The Ring..."

"The agents are a little desperate for validation," said Kaiden. "But they're not complete idiots."

"That's your opinion," he grumbled. "I'm not walking my team into a trap. If those..."

"I get it," she said, "but I promise you, they haven't compromised the operation."

He stared at her a moment longer.

"All right," he said.

"I thought you'd be more excited," said Kaiden. "Your principal isn't some self-important Senator on a photo op. He's defecting from The Ring. He's a once in a lifetime match that just might burn the entire organization to the ground. It's a lot to put on a rookie team."

"Hey!" said Wesson sharply.

Engrossed in their discussion, Tate and Kaiden hadn't seen her approaching.

"First off," she said, glaring at Kaiden, 'if that rookie team hadn't carried your shot-up carcass through a jungle and gotten you to a hospital, you wouldn't be standing here. Second, maybe they're not at the same god-like level of special forces you're used to, but they're committed, loyal and willing to risk their lives. If they don't stack up to your standards..."

"Thank you, Sergeant," said Tate, cutting in. "I think you've made your point. Kaiden?"

Fire was in Wesson's eyes and Tate felt himself tense in case he had to intercept a punch.

Nobody could accuse Kaiden of talking behind people's backs, and she didn't feel like she'd been caught secretly maligning the team, so there was no sense of shame or embarrassment, but Wesson had made a good point. Sometimes tenacity was better than skill.

"You're right, Sergeant," said Kaiden. "I should have picked my words better."

"You still meant what you said," accused Wesson.

"Calling them rookies?" asked Kaiden. "Have you ever been a close protection operator? Have they?"

"No," said Wesson in a voice like she was chewing nails.

"I didn't say you're not a solid team," said Kaiden. "None of you have done this before. No more, no less."

Wesson was still angry, but the fire had gone out of her eyes.

"Kaiden's here to help train the team," said Tate. "I'll leave the decision to you, Sergeant. Can you use her?"

Wesson shifted from one foot to the other, studying Kaiden. In spite of her irritating nature, Wesson knew they would all benefit from her guidance.

"Fine," she said, putting aside her personal feelings and turning back to join the team.

"I think I'm growing on her," said Kaiden.

"Like a fungus," muttered Wesson under her breath.

7

CUSTOMS

As Tate and the team rolled onto the tarmac, he was pleased to see the Gulfstream Lux was fueled and waiting. The ex-agents hadn't missed a beat. Everything was where they said it would be, and when it would be there. It was an encouraging sign they weren't trusting the running of this operation to one of their minions.

It was hard not to appreciate the beautiful lines of the jet, as the dusky sun painted the fuselage with purples and oranges.

Wesson and Tate supervised the crew as they loaded their bags while the rest of the team climbed the stairs to the cabin.

The interior was compact but decorated like a five-star hotel room. Each of the plush, leather seats laid flat for sleeping, and had its own entertainment center and a privacy curtain.

Compared to the spartan living conditions of Fort Hickok, this was the kind of luxury of billionaires and sultans.

Tate smiled as they marveled over each new discovery but wondered how they'd feel after thirteen hours confined in the small tube.

"Buckle up," said the pilot over the intercom. "We're starting our taxi for takeoff."

Everyone picked a seat and put on their seatbelts with anticipation. Their sense of adventure was infectious and even Tate was feeling excited about the trip.

"Prepare for takeoff," said the pilot, as the jet bumped to a stop at the end of the runway.

The twin Pratt & Whitney electric engines spun up but were nearly silent inside the cabin. They could feel the Gulfstream vibrate under their feet as the landing gear brakes fought back the mounting thrust of the engines.

The pilot released the breaks and the team sunk into their seats as the jet sprinted down the runway. A moment later, their stomachs dropped as the pilot pulled back on the wheel and the Gulfstream soared into the air.

As Tate had expected, the honeymoon had worn off after eleven hours.

Monkhouse, the team's engineer, was pacing the aisle, restlessly tapping his thighs with boredom and impatience.

Wesson's curtain was closed, but every few minutes Tate could hear the rustle of her blanket and an annoyed sigh as she tossed and turned in the narrow seat.

Tate thought Rosse would be the one climbing the walls but hadn't considered the ex-prison guard's career was spent in confined spaces for hours on end.

The big medic was somewhere in the back, contently reading a book. Behind him, Tate could hear the heated clacking of buttons while Fulton continued his video game marathon.

The biggest surprise was Ota, who Tate would have bet a year's salary would have quietly disappeared behind his privacy curtain until they touched down.

Instead, he spent the flight behind the cockpit, talking with the pilots. Tate could count the number of conversations he'd had with the sniper on two hands, and none of them were more than a few minutes long.

To lessen the effects of jet lag, Tate had given everyone a sleeping pill with instructions to take it eight hours before they landed. It wasn't working for him. He had only gotten a few hours' sleep and it didn't look like anyone else had slept at all. The jet lag was going to a real...

"Rise and shine," said the pilot. "We're making our approach to Tokyo. It's 6:10 am, November twentieth. The current temperature is a brisk forty-two degrees."

Tate glanced out the window to the ocean below. Fishing boats dotted the grey, morning sea. Wisps of clouds shot past until his view cleared again and they were over land. Japan.

He could feel the Gulfstream gently nose down and heard the hum of the landing gear extending.

The tires touched asphalt with a single bump as they landed on a private airstrip. The engines built up to a roar when the pilot reversed thrust and the plane quickly slowed.

The jet taxied in front of an open hanger before shutting down the engines.

Tate watched as the pilot left the cockpit and unlatched the cabin door. With an easy push, the door opened and cold air flooded. Everyone was on their feet, more than ready to stretch their legs.

Walking down the stairs, they headed for the hanger, where they saw a man and woman standing near two large SUV and a table. The woman broke from her conversation and walked towards the gathered team.

"Ohayo gozaimus," she said, bowing with a smile. Her dark hair, tied in a ponytail, fell over her shoulder and she brushed it back as she straightened up.

"Good morning," said Tate, returning the bow. Following the example, the rest of the team bowed.

"I am Kiku Ogawa. Please follow me inside." She motioned towards the hanger.

As she turned to lead them inside, they noticed the Katana sword in her belt. At five foot four, her small frame made the sword look much larger than it was.

Inside the hanger, they were protected from the chilling breeze and the team glanced at the pilots unloading the jet, anxious to dig their heavy coats out of the baggage.

"I have been hired to be your guide while you are in Japan," said Kiku, her walnut brown eyes appraising each of them. "Some of you may be here for the first time. You will find that the Japanese culture is very different from yours and there are many opportunities for inconvenience."

"Huh?" asked Rosse.

"She means it's easy to get in trouble," said Tate.

Rosse nodded in understanding.

"We will appreciate your help in avoiding unneeded attention," said Tate.

"I have worked for your CIA in the past. I understand the need for discretion."

CIA?

Tate knew they weren't here with the CIA's authorization, or knowledge. They hadn't been in the country for five minutes and already the ex-FBI agents had put Tate and his team in jeopardy.

If the guide reached out to her CIA contact, she'd quickly discover she'd been lied to. Whatever the fallout from that, Tate couldn't guess, but knew it included prison.

Kiku opened a box and took out several small devices.

"What are these?" asked Fulton.

"They are your phones."

"Hey," he said with a grin. "We got phones."

"Yes," said Kiku. "Each one has been preprogrammed with the numbers for your other teammates."

Monkhouse examined the small, glossy rectangle, curiously turning it over in his hand. "Where's the buttons?"

"I'm sorry," said Kiku, with a small frown of confusion.

"How do we dial?"

"Ah," she said. "There is no dialing. You speak to the phone what you want. If you want to call, you say call; to take a photo, say photo, like that."

"What's this?" said Wesson, taking a bite mask out of her bag.

"That is a courtesy mask," said Kiku.

Wesson looked between her and the mask in confusion.

"It is for safety," elaborated Kiku. "In case you turned into a ghost."

"You mean Vix?" said Tate. "You mean in case somebody dies. Then they can't bite anyone."

"Yes," she said. "That is what it is for. But happily, you don't have to wear them. That is also part of my duty."

"What duty?" asked Fulton.

Kiku paused, trying to think of the English translation until her eyebrows raised in success.

"I am your lifeguard," she said. "In case you become a Vix then I will save everyone's life."

"What good's a lifeguard if I'm already a Vix?" asked Rosse.

"No, Rosse-san. Not *your* life."

"I think she means a type of Kaishakunin," said Ota.

"Oh," said Rosse. "That cleared everything up."

"Hai," nodded Kiku.

"Her job is to cut your head off before you kill anyone," grinned Ota as Rosse looked at Kiku's sword with new understanding.

"I'm ready to go home now," he said.

The rattle of wheels signaled the pilot bringing in the cart with their baggage stacked on it.

The team gratefully grabbed their bags and rummaged out their coats.

Kiku saw the hard cases containing the team's weapons and hissed with alarm.

"Are those guns?" she asked.

"Yes," said Tate, unsure why she was asking.

The FBI agents had set up this operation, including Kiku. They wouldn't have divulged the details of Tate's operation to her, but at the very least they would have told her they would be operating outside the law.

"You cannot have guns here," said Kiku.

"We'll make sure they're secured out of sight," said Tate.

"Excuse me," she said. "Guns are forbidden in Japan. If the police discover you with a gun, they will execute you."

Everyone traded looks of surprise.

"We're not going to hurt anyone," said Wesson. "We need them to protect our client."

"I ain't walking around naked," said Rosse, reaching across the table for his gun case.

Kiku's hand flashed to the handle of her sword as her face turned hard and cold. "Tomare," she growled.

He didn't know what she said, but there was no mistaking her meaning.

Scowling, her eyes were locked on Rosse's every move.

He froze in place, sensing that with the slightest twitch she'd take his arm off at the shoulder.

"Okay," he said. "I'm cool. You can have it. Okay?" He carefully drew is hand away from the case as everyone held their breath.

Satisfied, Kiku let go of her sword and her expression switched back to a pleasant smile. The transformation was unsettling.

If there was any confusion about their guide, the last few seconds brought them into crystal clarity. Under her ready smile and respectful manner was a Onna Bugeisha; woman warrior. Tate rightly surmised that if you got on her bad side, she was as hard as nails and deadly with a sword. There was a very narrow grey area before crossing the line with her. He made a mental note to talk to the team later, just in case anyone needed reminding about not pushing their guide's buttons.

"Thank you for understanding," she said. "I will arrange for your weapons to be stored in a safe place. They will be returned when you leave."

"I apologize for the misunderstanding," said Tate, cursing the idiot agents under his breath. "This is a problem. How can we protect our client without our guns?"

"Ah, one moment," said Kiku, and she disappeared around the back of the SUV. She returned with a duffle bag and placed it on the table.

Opening it, she took out a kodashi.

"Please accept," she said. Holding it with two hands, she bowed, offering it to Tate.

"Thank you," he said, bowing in return.

He looked at the glossy, black-lacquered sheath and his mind reeled, trying to grasp the impact this would have on their mission. All of the team's training for personal protection had just gone out the window. Ranged combat, covering fire, even body armor. Useless. They were now facing the purest meaning of close quarter combat with a weapon they'd never trained with. It was a disaster.

One by one, Kiku handed each of the team their own short sword.

Fulton was grinning, a twinkle in his eyes, as she handed him a sword and Tate felt a tremor of alarm.

"Fulton," he said, making him jump. "Don't draw that sword without my express orders. Do you copy?"

"Uh, sure, Top," said Fulton, looking a little hurt. "I wasn't going to play with it."

Tate held the young private in his stare until he wilted.

"I copy," said Fulton.

"That goes for the rest of you," said Tate. He could imagine the blood bath of one of them screwing around and opening an artery.

"There are belts in the bag to carry your kodashi," said Kiku. "If everyone is ready, we can go to your hotel. I have arranged for your breakfast."

The mention of breakfast brightened everyone's mood and she gestured for them to get into the SUV.

They carried their baggage to the back of the SUV, careful to leave the gun cases alone.

Tate picked out his backpack and slung it over his shoulder, giving the gun cases one more look.

"Your weapons will be safe here," said Kiku, picking up on his hint. "My people will collect them very soon."

He wasn't happy about it, but there wasn't anything he could do at the moment. Tate sat in the front passenger seat, tucking his backpack between his feet.

Inside of it was the key to the success of the operation; the M63 Data Relay Trap. The DART was a piece of tech Tate had used years ago. It was a finicky piece of junk back then and he suspected it hadn't improved with age.

Its purpose was to intercept and listen in on encrypted sat phone signals. He didn't know what museum the agents had dug into to find it, but they made it clear it was the best they could do "under the circumstances".

Tate had worked with intel spooks and understood the ambiguity of their explanation was code for 'underfunded operation'. The agents were probably running their own op, off the books, and the DART was the best they could do. They assured Tate they had tested it and it worked.

Don't complain. Make it work.

What else could he do?

Tate sat up as the car's seat moved under him, conforming to his shape.

"Whoa," said Fulton. "Are you guys feeling this?"

Tate eased back in his seat as Kiku got in the driver's side and put her sword in the door bracket.

She spoke something in Japanese and the dashboard, which was one large screen, came to life. It was impressive, but everything was written in Kanji and incomprehensible to Tate.

A voice answered from the dashboard.

"English," said Kiku, and the symbols change to English.

"Good morning," said the car. "What is your destination?"

"Satsudo hotel," she said.

There was a brief pause and a map appeared, displaying their current location, route and destination.

The SUV rolled smoothly out of the hanger without a sound.

"Each seat has personal ear pods if you'd like entertainment or news," said Kiku.

Always up for new experiences, Tate put in the ear pods.

"Good morning, Tate-san," said a voice in his ear. He recognized it as the same voice of the car. "Would you like to read the news?"

A newspaper was superimposed on the windshield in front of him.

"No," he said. "Maybe later."

The newspaper disappeared.

He looked at the Gulfstream, wondering if he should have taken this job after all.

"That is a Gulfstream, Lux," said the car. "Would you like to know more about it?"

Tate blinked, glancing around for an explanation. "How did you know that?"

"I have extensive information about...,"

"No," he said. "How did you know what I was looking at?"

"There are several cameras that allow me to track your eyes," said the car, as the windshield in front of him changed to a virtual diagram of the interior of the car. Multiple circles blinked, indicating the locations of micro-sized cameras.

He looked over at Kiku, who was absently looking out her window.

"That is Kiku Ogawa," said the car. "She is a translator and guide. She is educated in several languages, Japanese, European and American history. She is a 6th Dan of Kenjutsu live-blade martial arts. Her cat's name is Goku. You need her permission for personal information. Shall I ask her for you?"

"No," flushed Tate. "Stop narrating for me."

A large part of his career in Delta Force included reconnaissance and gathering intel on people and places, but this was the first time it made him feel creepy. Just as bad was knowing the car was watching his every move, bordering on mind reading.

"Travel time to the hotel will be forty-five minutes," said the car. "Would you like me to recline the seat so you can sleep? I'll wake you before our arrival."

"Turn off," said Tate

"What would you like me to turn off?" asked the car.

"Just... shut up."

Tate paused, tensing for another reply from the car, but it was silent. He let himself settle back and relax.

"Excuse me, Tate-san," said Kiku.

Tate's eyelids felt like lead as he struggled to open his eyes.

"We are nearing the hotel," she said.

"Yeah, okay," he said, sitting up.

The scene outside the windows had dramatically changed from rolling hills of lush green pastures to the crowded streets and densely packed buildings towering overhead.

Shop signs competed for attention, hanging from buildings like leaves on a tree, all clashing with different colors and images. People filled the sidewalks, all of them wearing masks and swords.

"Who are they?" asked Tate, spotting two men in identical dark blue overalls carrying the longer katana sword.

"Those are policemen," said Kiku. "You should know, it is very important that all of you show great respect to the police. You must do as they instruct."

Tate didn't have a problem with cops. They had a tough job and he appreciated they spent their careers dealing with the ugly side of life so the rest of society didn't have to. But Kiku's advice sounded more like a warning.

"What do you mean?" he asked.

Looking over his shoulder, he could see the rest of the team had detected the tone of warning and were listening to the conversation with interest.

"The Japanese people are respectful of the law and tradition, but everyone carries a sword," said Kiku. "There have been incidents."

Tate waited for her to continue, but she was reluctant to elaborate.

"What kind of incidents?" asked Wesson, leaning into the conversation.

"Before the public carried swords, the police weren't armed," said Kiku. "Then it became mandatory everyone carry one. The government required everyone to train with them for self-defense against Vix. It's a short course. Most never practice after that. But some criminals practice often and become very skilled. Gangs formed and became a great danger to people and police. In ancient times, there was great peace in Japan. The samurai were the police then."

"Weren't they also judge, jury and sometimes executioner?" asked Tate.

"They what?" said Monkhouse.

80

"In order to keep the peace, samurai had free license to kill anyone causing trouble," said Tate.

"Are you saying the cops can kills us?" said Fulton, snapping his fingers. "Just like that?"

"Um, they are authorized to keep the peace, yes," said Kiku, and she looked out the window, satisfied to leave it at that.

"Hang on," said Rosse. "I could be turned into sushi for sneezing wrong? Top, you can turn the car around and take me back to the plane."

"Everyone dial it back a little," said Tate. "Kiku-san, you make it sound like the police kill people every day."

She put her hand over her mouth and chuckled. "Oh no," she said. "No, it hardly ever happens. I apologize if I alarmed you."

"You all feel better now?" said Tate to everyone in back, inwardly feeling his own anxiety coming down.

The car effortlessly navigated the traffic up to the lobby entrance of the hotel and stopped in front of the doorman.

"Everyone must stay with me," said Kiku. "Once you put your swords in your belts, do not touch them in public. It's very rude."

"This place has a lotta rules," grumbled Rosse as he climbed out of the car.

"Is there anywhere you don't complain about something?" teased Monkhouse.

Rosse didn't take the bait.

Everyone collected around Kiku under the curious stares of the people around.

The bellhop unloaded the car and offered to take Tate's backpack.

"I'm good. Thanks," he said, looping his arm through the sling.

"Force of habit," he said to Kiku's curious look.

It wasn't the only old habit he'd developed over the years. Another was not putting all of his eggs in one basket. In this case, he had packed his Colt .45 in his backpack before they'd left Fort Hickok. Considering they were cut off from all of their weapons, this was one habit that paid off.

Kiku's earlier readiness to carve up Rosse made Tate very aware of the trouble he'd be in if he was caught with a gun. Weighing the risks between breaking the law and being defenseless in a fight, he deferred to the old saying; better to be judged by twelve than carried by six.

The Colt 1911 wasn't designed for concealment and the more he carried it around, the greater the risk of it being discovered. He didn't like his options, but Tate decided he would only carry it when absolutely necessary.

"This way, please," said the bellhop.

Tall glass doors slid open as the bellhop wheeled their bags into the hotel lobby.

"Would ya look at this place," said Rosse as they crossed the polished, black marble floor towards the front desk.

They passed by a long mirror pond with two bronze dragons rising fifteen feet high.

"I'm officially impressed," said Monkhouse

They drew looks of alarm and curiosity; foreigners without bite masks, but as soon as people saw Kiku, everyone went back to their own business.

There was something indiscernible about Kiku that made other people move out of her way. Tate suspected it was her katana and her air of confidence. They distinguished her from everyone else. In any case, people accepted that the foreigners trailing behind her were under her responsibility.

Nobody raised any objections to them not wearing masks.

Kiku spoke to the clerk before turning to the team.

"Your room is ready," she said, gesturing to follow the bellhop.

The bellhop opened the door and ushered them inside with a smile and bow.

Entering the suit, they were treated to an impressive view of Tokyo. The living room wall was floor to ceiling windows that opened onto a generous balcony. The cold, grey weather did not invite anyone to step outside and appreciate the view.

"Your rooms," the bellhop said, gesturing to three doors on either side of the living room.

"We're sharing rooms?" said Monkhouse.

"They are very spacious," said the bellhop.

"Thanks," said Tate, bowing to the bellhop. "This will be fine."

"I am in the room across the hall," said Kiku. "Call me if you must leave the hotel."

"I don't have a room key," said Fulton.

"Yeah, me neither," said Rosse.

The bellhop looked at Kiku in confusion. She spoke to him in Japanese and he nodded with a faint smile as he glanced at the team with amusement before leaving.

"There are no room keys, Rosse-san," said Kiku. "Your faces were scanned in the car. When we arrived, your images were transferred to the hotel. Your hotel door now knows your face and will open for you."

First the car and now this. With growing unease, Tate was beginning to see how deeply integrated technology had become in everyone's lives. Every move and word he spoke was being documented. It made him wonder if there were cameras inside their hotel room.

He scoffed, thinking it was a stupid question. Of course there were.

"Where else do our images go?" asked Tate.

"I don't understand," said Kiku.

"You can track us by our phones," he said. "Our images are recorded. Who else has access to all of the information that's being accumulated on us?"

"Shades of big brother," scoffed Monkhouse.

"Do not be concerned," said Kiku. "Your information is safe from criminals. Only the local government has access to your information."

"Where we come from," said Rosse, "that's a lot to be concerned about."

Kiku frowned as she processed Rosse's comment.

"It must be unpleasant to live in a country where the government is untrustworthy," she said.

"I ain't say'n... America's not like..." sputtered Rosse.

"Let's just say we have a healthy distrust of people in power," said Wesson.

"I would enjoy talking to you about this at greater length," said Kiku. "But I imagine you must be tired after your long flight."

"I could use some rack time," said Fulton, yawning.

"I will see you later," said Kiku.

Everyone bowed in response to hers and she left the room.

"All right," said Tate, looking at his watch. "Things are going to get busy, quick. Our first task will be disabling the Ring security detail. Before you ask, I don't know when that happens. Our contacts will advise us twenty-four to forty-eight hours before the bad guys are in-country."

"And don't forget these," said Monkhouse, pulling the sheathed sword out of his belt.

"We don't know anything about sword fighting, Top," said Wesson. "What if the other team knows how to use them?"

"We'd get hacked to bits," said Rosse. "What if they're foreigners like us? What if their lifeguard ain't as picky about the rules and lets them keep their guns? Ya don't bring a knife..."

"To a gunfight," finished Tate. "I know. Everyone take a step back. We don't know the details and until I hear from our contact, all of you stop playing worst case scenario. But I agree with you," he said, stopping Rosse's objection before he could speak. "We need training with these."

"I can help," said Ota.

Everyone looked with surprise.

"You know sword stuff?" asked Rosse. "Forget I asked. Of course the Zen guy's gonna know it."

Tate had his own questions. Ota was a complete unknown. All Tate knew was the man was one of the best snipers he'd ever met, meditated and subscribed to Zen philosophy. He hardly ever spoke, making him nearly invisible, but he was part of the team and had never let anyone down. Tate couldn't ask any more of him, but he wanted to. He imagined, of all of the team, Ota had the most interesting life story of any of them. He'd tried a few times to get Ota to open up, but the man was content to remain silent.

84

"Good to hear, Ota," said Tate. "Get something going as soon as you can. We don't have a lot of time, so just a few sword basics that'll give us a fighting chance."

"I'll be in the lobby," said Ota to Kiku.

"I'm beat," said Tate. "We have three rooms and six of us. Wesson, you get first choice of a roommate."

"Why she get first pick?" grumbled Rosse. "Because she's a ..."

His mouth plopped closed as he realized he'd just walked into the middle of a minefield.

"I'm a what?" asked Wesson.

"A, you know," he fumbled. "Second in charge."

"Oh, nice save," laughed Monkhouse. "Way to pull out of that nosedive."

"She gets first pick because I don't want her to get stuck sharing a room with you," smirked Tate.

"Fulton," said Wesson.

"Uh, sure," he said, blushing.

"Ota," said Tate. "That means Monkhouse and Rosse."

"What did I do?" protested Monkhouse.

"Hey," said Rosse.

"I'm sacking out," said Tate. "Either of you wakes me up with your fighting so help me, I'll hang you off that balcony by your thumbs."

His head hit the pillow and he quickly fell into a deep sleep.

8

HE'S AN ENGINEER

When Tate opened his eyes, it was night outside. The glow of the city lights filled the room enough to see his way around.

Ota was sitting in his bed, legs crossed and eyes closed. Whatever he was doing, Tate chose not to disturb him.

He quietly made his way into the living room and found the rest of the team sitting there.

"Did anyone get some sleep?" he asked.

The general answer was slim to none.

"My internal clock is way off," said Wesson.

"The jet lag," groaned Monkhouse.

"We been cooped up on the plane, in the car, and now here," said Rosse. "That's Japan out there," he said pointing out the window. "I don't know about you guys, but I never been here before."

"Me neither," chimed in Fulton.

Monkhouse and Wesson nodded in agreement.

"Wadda ya say, Top?" said Rosse. "How's about we get out a little? See some of the night life."

They saw Tate glance at the front door and read his thoughts.

"We don't need a babysitter," said Monkhouse. "We'll wear our masks. And besides, I've been checking out my phone. It's got a translator on it."

Tate couldn't deny he was desperate to stretch his legs and get some fresh air. He had to give his team the credit they were due. They were adults and understood the reason why they were in Japan. He trusted them to protect each other's lives in a firefight; why shouldn't he trust them to stay out of trouble?

"Okay," he grinned. "Let's get out of here."

The group broke into a cheer and everyone jumped to their feet to head out.

"I expect all of you to follow my rules," said Tate, looking at each of them. "Keep your phone with you at all times. Be nice to everyone. Keep your masks on, no exceptions. And be back here in five hours."

"Sounds good to me," said Fulton.

"And keep your hands off your swords," growled Tate. "I don't care if it looks like you're going to take a beating. Suck it up. Better than someone taking your head off."

"You got it, Top," said Rosse, stuffing his sword in his belt. "I do better with these babies anyway."

He kissed his fists in a ridiculous show and everyone busted up laughing.

The cold night air energized the team as soon as they stepped out of the hotel lobby.

They selected a cluster of clubs, suggested by the phone, and made their way to the underground metro rail.

It was 1 AM, but Tokyo didn't sleep. People started moving as soon as the train doors began to open. It was a little hit and miss, but all of the team made it into the same train car. It wasn't claustrophobic inside, but there was little room to move. Wesson looked around until she found the rest of the team.

"Let's see how Tokyo parties," said Monkhouse.

The train doors closed, accompanied by a polite voice over the PA system, announcing the next station. With a subtle lurch, the train left the station and picked up speed.

It was awkward being shoulder to shoulder with so many people, and nobody spoke or made eye contact.

Wesson grinned, thinking how it would be the same in a crowded elevator. Nobody has personal space but pretends there's nobody else in the steel box with them.

"Excuse me," she said out of reflex as something brushed against her thigh.

She shifted what little she could to avoid bumping into whoever it was, but only had inches of room.

A moment later she felt it again and realized it wasn't by accident. She looked at the people around her, but they were so closely packed it was impossible to tell.

Setting her jaw, she flexed her hands and waited. It wasn't long before the molesting hand returned. The moment it touched her she gripped it like a vise. The person tried to pull away, but Wesson only squeezed harder.

Now that she had them, what was she going to do about it?

She tried to find the culprit in the sea of impassive faces.

How can nobody know what's going on?

She nodded to herself, accepting the rules of the game. If everyone was going to pretend this creep wasn't trying to molest her, then they could pretend she wasn't going to teach him a lesson.

With a quick twist, she bent the molester's fingers back until she heard a snap.

There was a satisfying yelp of pain and the hand disappeared the instant she let go.

"Anyone else?" she said.

Tate looked at her quizzically from across the crowd.

She smiled, shrugging her shoulders.

The expressions of the people around never changed, but Wesson suddenly found that everyone was giving her more space than she'd had before.

"That's right," she muttered.

The train came to a stop at their station and the sea of people flooded out as soon as the doors opened.

Wesson craned her head, looking for anyone nursing an injured hand, but it was too crowded.

The team gathered around Monkhouse, who had become their default party guide, and with the aid of the phone's directions, he led them up the stairs to street level.

Streets ran in every direction with narrow, single lanes branching off. The night was filled with lights that spilled out of shops, small mom and pop restaurants, clubs, and sake bars.

Clicks of people passed by, all having a good time. Monkhouse led them off a main street, onto a lane hardly wide enough to be an alley, but it was busy with foot traffic.

Tiny eateries and bars sat shoulder to shoulder as far as they could see; all of them buzzing with conversations.

Tate noticed two police quietly standing on a corner, looking at him and his people. He smiled and nodded and they did the same.

Monkhouse led them further down the alley, but the cops didn't follow.

Tate felt he could breathe a little easier. The last thing he needed was unwanted attention.

"Lady and gentlemen," said Monkhouse with a flourish. "Welcome to club Goku Up."

The outside of the club was a strange blend of traditional and modern Japanese architecture.

Next to the door stood a woman in traditional kimono, smiling at them.

"Good evening," she said, bowing.

There was a stiffness to her movement and they realized she was a robot.

"Hi," said Monkhouse. "Table for five."

"Of course," said the bot. "Someone is coming to take you to your table."

"Great," said Fulton. "I'm starving."

"We have the best selection of fresh fish in Tokyo."

"I'm not a fan of fish," said Wesson, wrinkling her nose.

A woman dressed in black with a stunning red and gold comb in her hair stepped out, holding open the door for them.

A heavy smell of cigarette smoke followed her.

"I'm not going in there," said Wesson.

"I don't blame you," said Tate. "We're going to find someplace else. You guys have a good time."

"No prob," said Monkhouse cheerfully.

Tate suspected he didn't mind being out from under the sergeant major's watchful stare.

"Behave," he said, pointing his finger at the three of them.

Rosse, Monkhouse and Fulton disappeared inside with the hostess leading the way.

"What are you in the mood for?" asked Tate.

"You know, I've always wanted to try one of those hot baths," said Wesson. "Maybe get one of those famous massages."

"A shiatsu?" he said. He'd gotten one... once. He didn't care how much people raved about them; getting a massage shouldn't make a grown man cry. The last time he'd been that badly worked over was by a couple of thugs he owed money to.

"Yeah, that," she said brightly.

"Okay, but just a warning," said Tate. "When they say deep tissue, they don't stop until they reach the floor."

Wesson grinned with a spark of adventure as she took out her phone. "Bring it on."

The noise and lights thinned out as they followed the phone's directions until they turned down a deserted street with a single light casting a lonely puddle of light.

"Are we in the right place?" asked Tate.

"There," said Wesson, spotting a small wooden tub next to blue painted, double doors.

A preserved pufferfish hung from a sign and Wesson held up the phone which translated the sign into English.

Steam rose from the small tub and a statue of a smiling raccoon reclined in the simulated hot water.

"This is it," she said.

They stepped inside a small alcove. Across the room, an old woman frowned disapprovingly from behind a desk.

Arrayed around the edge of the floor were several pairs of shoes.

The old woman's gaze flicked meaningfully to the basket of slippers in the corner, then returned to Wesson and Tate.

"We'd like..." began Wesson as she walked up to the desk, but the woman interrupted, hissing and chastising her.

"I'm sorry," said Wesson. "I don't..."

The woman pointed at Wesson's feet and shooed her back to the alcove.

"I'm sorry," she said into her phone. "Should I take off my shoes?"

The phone translated and the woman listened with sour disapproval.

"Of course you do," said the woman. "This isn't a barn."

Grumbling, the woman went back behind the desk and perched on her stool.

"Ignorant foreigners," translated the phone. "No respect for anything."

Wesson and Tate looked at each other in surprise, knowing the woman didn't know the phone could hear her.

They sputtered, trying to hold back their laughter which only earned them another scowl from the woman.

Both of them sat down and took off their shoes.

"Use the slippers," scoffed the woman. "I have to tell them everything."

Tate couldn't find a pair that fit. It didn't matter to the woman that half his feet were hanging over the back of the sandals as long as he was wearing them.

"We'd like the hot bath and a massage," said Wesson.

"No men and women together," said the woman. "I run a respectable shop."

"Of course," she said, bowing.

The gesture wasn't lost on the woman. Still stern, she smiled and gestured for Wesson to follow.

"This way," she said. "Nothing artificial. We have authentic onsen. You," said the woman, leveling a finger at Tate. "Stay here until I come for you."

"Yes," he said, bowing.

Apparently, the woman was only good for one bow a night because she didn't warm up to him the way she'd done with Wesson.

The woman showed Wesson the locker room, bathing area and entrance to the onsen.

Beyond the double glass doors was a steaming pool of water. It was surrounded by flagstones with rich, green palms and bamboo behind it.

It looked amazing and Wesson could hardly wait to get in.

"Thank you," she said.

"Call if you need anything else," said the woman.

Curiously, she gave Wesson's arm a little pinch.

"You'll be fine," said the woman. "Many foreigners aren't used to the heat and wilt like soggy noodles."

She bowed and left.

Wesson eyed the soothing onsen with anticipation.

"Come with me," grumbled the woman to Tate.

She turned without waiting and he quick marched to catch up.

"No smoking," said the woman.

"I don't smoke," he said.

The woman only huffed. She opened the door to the men's locker room and pointed out the facilities.

"I don't know if I have a kimono to fit you," she said. "Give me your shirt and I'll see if I have a match."

Tate expected her to step outside but she stood her ground, looking at him with annoyance.

He wasn't bashful and stripped off his shirt.

"What's that?" said the woman, pointing at Tate's arm.

She was looking at the tattoo on his right arm. It was from his days as a Delta Force operator. Inside a shield, a snake wound around a double-headed axe. Bordering the shield were the words, luxe indices carnificem; Latin for Judge, Jury, Executioner.

"I'm in the military," he said. "It's from my unit..."

"No tattoos," said the woman, shaking his shirt at him. "No Yakuza allowed here. Go now."

"I'm not a criminal," explained Tate. "I'm a soldier."

"Ha," scoffed the woman. "So are they. Go on before someone sees you and my reputation is soiled."

Before he could put his shirt on, she was shooing him down the hallway and into the lobby.

"If you had any honor," she said, "you would leave that nice girl alone. Let her find a good man."

Tate could only stand there, gawking in disbelief at the tough old woman.

With his shoes and shirt in hand, he walked out into the chilly night and instantly started shivering. His breath came in short, foggy gasps as he quickly got dressed.

"I need a drink," he said.

"I'm from America," said Fulton, knocking back another bowl of sake.

The shapely girl smiled at him with deep brown eyes.

"It sounds very exciting," she said. The small hint of an accent only made her more exotic to the men around the table.

"I'm American, too," grinned Rosse.

She was sitting between him and Monkhouse but had inched over to be closer to Monkhouse.

They were lucky to find a girl who spoke english because the phone was working overtime trying to accurately translate Monkhouse's slurred words

"And you're an engineer," she said, turning her sparkling gaze back to him.

In spite of Rosse piling on every ounce of charm, she wasn't interested.

"Yes," said Monkhouse, lost in her eyes. "I do that."

"I'd love you to tell me more," she said. "You could take me somewhere else to talk. Someplace more... intimate."

A grin unevenly spread across Monkhouse's face as she put her arm around his shoulder.

"Hey," said Fulton, nudging Rosse. "She's talking about..."

"Shadup," snapped Rosse. "I know what she's talk'n about."

"I'll see you two losers later," said Monkhouse, smirking as he got up from the table.

Fulton watched them leave with a mixture of admiration and longing, while Rosse's glare could have burned holes in his back.

"Why him?" ask Fulton.

"Because he's an engineer," mocked Rosse.

Monkhouse smiled happily, looking at the attractive girl on his arm.

"I just remembered that I don't know your name."

"Amai-chan," she said.

"Amaah... Ami," stumbled Monkhouse. "Hang on. I'll get it."

Amai-chan pronounced her name slowly so Monkhouse could follow along.

"That's a great name," he said. Have you been to the US?"

"No," she said. "But I've always wanted to."

"I'll give you my number," said Monkhouse. "I'll show you around."

Amai-chan giggled as she guided him around a corner and onto a quiet street. His head was swimming with sake and Amai-chan's enchanting eyes.

"We can go in here," said Amai-chan.

Monkhouse came out of his spell and looked around in surprise. He couldn't remember how they'd gotten there, but when he saw she'd brought him to a hotel he stopped caring.

He wobbled his phone up to the sign for the translation, 'Leave Happy'.

"I like a place that believes in truth in advertising," he said, as she tugged him inside.

It took a moment for his eyes to adjust to the brightly lit lobby. It was decorated with pink and purple hearts on the walls. Green vinyl couches bordered a large screen TV with a loop of waves rolling in on a sandy beach.

Amai-chan walked them up to the front desk where a thick, transparent window separated them and the clerk.

As Amai-chan spoke to the clerk, Monkhouse's gaze wandered around the clashing-colored surroundings.

The phone buzzed in his hand and he glanced at it as it translated Ami-chan's conversation with the clerk.

"... Ready in ten minutes..."

Not this guy, grinned Monkhouse to himself.

Posted on the wall was a sign with three cartoon panels. The first showed two cartoon fish kissing, outside their room with a red circle-slash no symbol. The next image was of them inside the room with oversized locks on the door. Several cameras are looking at the couple and a big thumbs up. The final image showed the happy fish taking off their masks and kissing.

Monkhouse frowned at the cartoonish locks and cameras.

"Are we like the fish?"

Amai-chan tilted her head and winked her nose as she looked at the phone.

"Your phone doesn't make sense," she said. "Are you ready?"

"Um..." he said, as doubts began eating at him.

She looped her arm in his and escorted him to the elevator which smelled like disinfectant.

They stepped into the hallway of the third floor and Amai-chan walked him to their door.

"Whoa," said Monkhouse.

The inside of the room was something from a science fiction movie. The walls looked like windows on a spaceship and outside was deep space with twinkling stars and gas nebulas. Shooting stars randomly zipped by. The bed had a futuristic shape as did the small nightstands on either side.

Winking lights from a starship control panel covered the liquor bar.

The moment was broken as Amai-chan closed the door behind them and Monkhouse heard locks slide into place. The sound was a disquieting blend of vault door and jail cell.

He was reminded of the cartoon with the cameras and looked at the corners of the ceiling, but if there were cameras, they were hidden in dark shadows.

"Let's start here," said Amai-chan, and took off her mask.

She was gorgeous. She smiled at him with pearl-white teeth and planted a slow, soft kiss on his cheek. She reached around his head and took off his mask.

"I could tell by your eyes that you were handsome," she said.

"If I had a nickel for every time I heard that," grinned Monkhouse.

Amai-chan looked curiously at the phone translating into Japanese, then at Monkhouse.

"What's a nickel?" she asked.

"Never mind," he said. "It's just an expression." He looked at the bed with a wide smile. "Shall we?"

"Not yet," said Amai-chan, taking him by the hand.

The warmth of her soft hand pulled his attention away from the thoughts of cameras and she led him through the bathroom door.

"Oh my..." said Monkhouse in amazement. "Are you kidding me?"

A huge, bubbling hot tub sat in the middle of the room. Blue lights glowed from inside and steam rolled over the edges. Threads of neon purple lined the outside of the tub as a field of stars shined on the ceiling above.

"Get in," purred Amai-chan. "I'll make some drinks and join you in a minute."

"You bet," said Monkhouse, trying to pull off his shirt and pants at the same time.

She disappeared into the bedroom as he tested the water with his toe. The steam wasn't just for show. The water was hot.

"When in Japan," he said and gingerly eased himself into the tub.

The hot water had a soothing effect he hadn't felt before, as beads of sweat began to dot his face.

To his right was a console of dials and buttons. He experimented with a couple and the lights in the room dimmed and the starfield above took on a 3D effect.

"Hey, Amai-chan," he called. "This place is amazing."

He lost himself in the artificial stars as the hot water gently bubbled around him.

Sweat trickled down his face and a drink was sounding better and better, but Amai-chan hadn't returned.

"Hey, you okay?" he called, glancing at the bathroom door.

He heard her say something, but it was muffled by the door. There was something hurried in her voice that didn't sound right.

Monkhouse got out of the tub on rubbery legs and grabbed a towel.

When he opened the door, Amai-chan was ransacking his clothes.

"Hey, what are you doing?" he said.

The girl looked at him like a deer in headlights, with her hand stuffed in his boot.

"You're robbing me?" he said, sounding hurt. "But... I liked you."

Amai-chan dropped the boot, her alluring expression changing to a snarl.

She said something in a string of angry words as Monkhouse grabbed his boot.

He caught a glint of steel and Amai-chan had her sword out. The sharp point wavered inches from his nose.

"Take it easy," he said.

Monkhouse backed away, hoping that putting distance between them would calm her down.

He was wrong.

Monkhouse winced as she started screaming; before he could do anything, she smacked a large red button next to the door. The room lights instantly changed to bright white and an alarm went off.

Everything was happening so fast, he didn't know what to do as she kept her back against the wall, inching towards the door.

He couldn't understand what she was screaming. Without risking getting too close to the sword she was waving around, he fumbled around until he found his phone on the floor.

He held it out, hoping he could make sense of her when the door slammed open and two police charged in with swords drawn.

"Oh crap," said Monkhouse.

Amai-chan rattled off something to the police, pointing at Monkhouse, tears streaming down her panicked face.

The police turned to Monkhouse with dark expressions.

"No, no, no. She had my boot," he said. "She's trying to rob me."

The police split up and approached him from both sides, their long blades ready to strike.

The color drained from Monkhouse's face, images of being hacked to death racing through his mind.

He threw himself to the ground with his arms outstretched, praying to whoever was listening to see him through this alive and in one piece.

"Thank you," said Tate, holding up the small bowl of warm sake.

The bartender nodded with a smile and turned back to a pot of frying oil.

Tate had picked out the small hole in the wall pub for its quiet, out-of-the-way feel. The other customers, who he assumed were regulars, looked at him with open curiosity, but the novelty eventually wore off and they went back to their conversation.

For the first time since he'd gotten off the jet, he was enjoying himself. There was a difference between lonely and alone. The latter never bothered him.

Losing their guns was a problem that he still hadn't figured out how to solve. He smiled, thinking that normally it took twenty-four hours for something to go wrong on a mission. This was a new record. That deserved another drink.

The sake went down his throat in a warm stream. The alcohol bloomed in his belly and a wave of warm relaxation spread through him.

The small sake bowl was halfway to his mouth when his phone started chirping. Tate eyed the bowl, wishing he could pretend he hadn't heard the phone, but put it back on the bar.

"Tate," he said, picking up the phone.

"There's been a change of plan," said agent Jones.

Tate frowned, trying to place the voice.

"Smith?" he asked.

"Jones," he said, annoyed. "The Ring's security team is arriving tomorrow."

"You told me they weren't due for two more days," said Tate, feeling the relaxing effects of the sake fade away.

"That was then. This is now," said Jones. "The timeline's been moved up. They're touching down tomorrow. You need to intercept their check-in call with the keyword."

"Are they armed?" said Tate.

"Of course," scoffed Jones. "Why?"

"The guide you set us up with took our guns," said Tate. "She said they're illegal in Japan. Did you know about that?"

"Didn't you? You were supposed to keep them out of sight."

"You were the one making the arrangements," said Tate. "If I'd known we'd have to smuggle our weapons..."

"Calm down," said Jones.

Few things made Tate angrier than someone telling him to calm down. It never failed that the person talking was safely out of harm's way while he was the one up to his neck in trouble.

"I'll work something out," said Jones.

"You have six hours," said Tate, looking at his watch. "You better deliver. I'm not walking my team into a gunfight with these weed-wackers."

"If you don't intercept that security team," snarked Jones, "this entire operation will be a failure. That's on you."

"You slimy son of a..."

"I'll be in touch," said Jones.

Tate gritted his teeth as the line went dead. Anger boiled over and all he could think of was beating the smug smile off agent Jones's face.

That's not helping.

He breathed deeply, pushing his temper back until he began to think clearly.

Starting with the worst case, he had to come up with a plan to grab the security team without guns.

His gaze landed on the sake and he tapped his fingers on the bar, fantasizing about bowls of sake and letting the mission fail just to spite the agents.

Reality quickly stepped in and he slid the bowl away.

Right now, he needed to figure out a way to grab the other team and not get his own people slaughtered in the process.

"Excuse me, Tate-san," said Kiku.

Tate turned, surprised to see Kiku standing next to him. He instantly knew something was wrong. Her customary smile had been replaced by worry.

Something was very wrong.

"Kiku-san?" he said, confused. "How did you...?"

"There has been an incident with one of your people," she said gravely. "We must go to the police station."

9

INTERCEPT

The sun was cresting the horizon but did nothing to dull the sharp chill of the winter's morning.

Tate and Kiku arrived at the police station, finding Wesson, Rosse, and Fulton looking cold and guilty.

"Sorry, Top," said Rosse. "We didn't know this was gonna happen."

"It's my responsibility," said Wesson.

"We have bigger problems than playing the blame game," said Tate, waving them off.

He gazed up at the ugly, concrete building.

"Bring me up to speed."

"I saw him as they hustled him inside," said Rosse. "All's I know is the girl he left with tried to rob him. When the cops showed up, she said he attacked her."

"Was he hurt?" asked Tate.

"I didn't get a long look," said Rosse. "But if yer ask'n if he had all his fingers and toes, yeah, it looked like it."

"Kiku-san," said Tate. "Can you fix this?"

"Fix?" she asked.

"Can you get Monkhouse out?" he said.

"I am familiar with what's happened to Monkhouse-san," said

Kiku. "It's a common trick prostitutes use to rob men. They will accuse the man of attacking them if the police get involved. They are more inclined to believe the girl instead of foreigners."

"Great," said Tate.

"She was a prostitute?" said Fulton.

"Really?" said Wesson. "That's what you got from this?"

"Well," he said. "I never seen one before."

"What's Japan got against foreigners?" asked Rosse. "We didn't do anything."

"It's not personal, Rosse-san," said Kiku. "We are a complex culture with an ancient history. We can be both accepting and reluctant of new things from outside our country."

"What happens now?" asked Tate.

"They will want to interview you, Tate-san," said Kiku. "Your teammate has created a curiosity in you."

Tate noticed a man in a wrinkled suit standing across the street. He lit up a cigarette and leaned against the wall, squinting through the smoke at them.

"We're getting too much attention," he said, guessing the man was a cop. "You three get back to the hotel and stay there. I'm going to see what I can do about Monkhouse."

"I will go with you," said Kiku.

She spoke to the desk sergeant who told them to wait until they were called.

The interior was as dull and bleak as any governmental waiting room that Tate had seen the world over.

The furniture was worn, and he guessed the tattered magazines that littered the side table were as old as the hard chair he was sitting in.

Had the waiting room been crowded with people, he could understand why they were cooling their heels, but there was nobody else except for him and Kiku.

It was an old but effective tactic to wear someone down before interrogating them.

An hour and a half later, the office door opened and a tired-looking detective called their names.

They checked in their swords at the front desk before following them through the door.

They walked past three rows of cluttered desks before the detective gestured for them to sit down.

"I am detective Makado," he said as they sat down. "May I see your identification?"

"In all the confusion, I left it in my hotel room," said Tate.

Makado looked at him for a long moment, then picked up a pen.

"As a foreigner, you are required to carry your identification," he said.

"I'll remember to do that," said Tate. "I'd like to see my friend."

"Are you in Japan for business or pleasure?" said Makado.

"My friend got rolled by a hooker," said Tate.

"She says he attacked her," said Makado.

"Detective," said Kiku, "Wouldn't a review of the security cameras inside the hotel room produce the facts?"

"The manager said the cameras have been broken for some time," said Makado.

"Can I see the woman's statement?" asked Tate.

Makado looked up from his paperwork and stared at him with a stony expression.

"There is no statement," he said. "She left the scene as the officers were arresting your friend."

"If she's not pressing charges, it sounds like you can let my friend go," said Tate, thinking he could see the light at the end of the tunnel.

"How long will you be in Tokyo?" asked Makado.

"A few days," said Tate. "About my friend."

"We'll be holding..." Makado looked at his papers, "Monkhouse-san for seventy-two hours."

Tate began to protest when his phone began chirping. He took it out of his pocket and hit decline.

"Seventy-two...?" he started.

"Excuse me, Makado-san," interrupted Kiku. "Would you please consider releasing him to my responsibility?"

"You are their kaishakunin?" he asked.

"Hai."

"I appreciate..." Makado stopped as Tate's phone started chirping again.

"Sorry," he said, silencing the phone.

"Even though the girl is unavailable," said Makado, "the hotel clerk was able to corroborate the account. The charges are serious and require us to hold this man."

He stared at Tate, who was fuming behind a mask of calm.

"You never answered my question," said Makado, folding his hands. "Why are you in Japan?"

Tate's phone began chirping.

"I have to take this," he said.

He got up and moved away until he was satisfied he wouldn't be overheard.

"What?"

"I have the information for the security team," said Agent Jones.

"Go ahead," said Tate.

"They've landed and are in transit to an abandoned library. They'll make contact with The Ring from there. I've sent the address to your phone."

"Got it," he said. "Anything about our assets?"

"I have someone who can supply you," said Jones, "but they're outside of town."

"How far outside?"

Tate knew it was a bad sign the moment Jones started getting vague.

"As in too far to get there and back in time to intercept the call?" he asked.

"That's what I said."

"There's not enough time," said Tate, feeling the muscles in his back tighten.

"You're the man with the special operations background," said Jones. "This is why we chose you. Make it work."

"What about the sentry team?"

"They're in position," said Jones. "Once you have the security team under control, the sentries will take over responsibility of the prisoners."

Tate hung up and headed back to the detective's desk.

"Thank you for your time, detective," he said. "I'll be back when my friend's released."

"Tate-san," said Kiku, standing up. "You're leaving?

"I would appreciate it if you could help to get Monkhouse released as soon as possible," he said. "I have an appointment I can't miss."

He knew his sudden exit would only stoke Makado's curiosity, but there was nothing he could do about it now.

He glanced at his watch. He didn't know how much time he had, but each minute weighed on him with urgency.

He needed the DART.

The SUV got him back to the hotel with no delays, but everything felt like it was taking too long except the clock, which was ticking faster.

Everyone's head snapped around as Tate ran into the hotel room and grabbed his backpack.

"What's happening?" asked Wesson, getting to her feet. She looked ready to follow him into whatever he was racing towards.

Questions and answers raced through his head. Should he take the team? Without guns? How would he feel if any of them were hurt, or killed? That would be on his head.

If he told them what was happening, they'd demand to go with him, and do what?

Get mowed down, that's what.

Tick, tick, tick...

"Everyone stay put," said Tate. "I'll call if I need you."

"If there's trouble," said Rosse, "we're going."

"You don't bring a knife to a gunfight," said Tate, before the door closed behind him.

Everyone looked at each other, all sharing the same troubling question.

"Does anyone else feel like things are getting worse?" asked Fulton.

. . .

Tate pushed through the elevator doors and people looked up, startled, as he ran through the lobby.

He'd left the SUV in front and climbed in, tossing his backpack on the seat next to him.

"Satsumurda library," he said, and the SUV pulled away from the hotel and into traffic.

"Hurry up," said Tate.

"I cannot exceed the posted speed for this road," said the car.

He grabbed the recessed steering wheel and pulled it out until it locked in place. "I'm driving. Show me the route."

Pale arrows appeared on the windshield, superimposed over the street in front of him.

"Driver's controls are now manual," said the car.

Tate floored the accelerator and the SUV leapt forward with surprising speed.

"You are exceeding the speed limit," said the car.

"Sue me," he growled. "Show me time and distance to the library."

Numbers appeared on the dashboard.

"You are approaching the intersection too quickly to stop for the red light," said the car.

The majority of cars were ultra-compact and the big SUV tore through their midst like a whale through a school of fish.

The intersection came at him fast. Hitting a tiny car broadside wouldn't slow him down much, but everyone in the car would die; of that he was sure.

"Route me through the intersection," he yelled.

Tate watched the cross traffic, looking for an opening and hoping he wouldn't have to make one with his front bumper.

Arrows flashed up on the windshield and disappeared just as quickly as the car's computer frantically tried to plot an impossible path.

Tate grimaced as the window through the cross-traffic rapidly closed.

A freight truck rolled out and he leaned on the horn. It lurched to a stop, but not soon enough.

The SUV jolted violently sideways in a spray of sparks. Tate flinched, anticipating the horrible crunch of ricocheting into the cars on his left. But it never happened.

He was through. The SUV was shuddering and the steering was sloppy, but he was still moving. He risked a quick look over his shoulder and saw the intersection shrinking in the distance.

The dashboard glitched then cleared up and showed four kilometers to the library as he skidded around a corner into an abandoned neighborhood. Empty homes and shops lined the street; many of them husks hollowed out by fire. Dead grass and weeds filled the cracks that crisscrossed the road.

The windshield HUD warned him that this area was deemed safe from Vix, but to exercise caution.

The SUV couldn't go any faster, but Tate's foot crushed the accelerator, hoping to squeeze more speed out of the car.

Hardly looking away from the road he grabbed his backpack and pulled out the DART, flipped open the cover and turned it on.

The antiquated LCD screen faded to life and it began looking for the Ring's security team's sat phone.

Searching.

He was getting closer to the library and the DART was in range, but nothing was happening.

Tate glowered at the device, willing it to pick up the signal.

Searching.

The DART wasn't going to work. He just knew it.

The most critical part of the operation relied on the weakest link.

Unable to detect signal. Reset and try again.

The library driveway came into view. Tate's head rapid fired through his options. The chance to cripple, maybe destroy The Ring was just inside that building and it was slipping through his fingers.

He couldn't let it happen.

Tate pulled out the Colt 1911. It had never looked so small.

Rays of dusty light flowed in from the dirty windows, splashing on the scuffed, weathered floor.

The few tables and chairs had been pushed out of the way to make room for the men to lay down and play catch up from their jet lag.

Cowboy stopped pacing and checked his watch again, his lips moving as he counted down the seconds. "It's time," he said, getting no reaction from the others.

"Where's the phone?" he asked.

Nobody answered.

"Hey, dipsticks," he said, raising his voice. "Who's got the phone?"

"By the door," said someone.

Cowboy sighed, looking at the two stacks of black duffle bags sitting on either side of the open door.

"I don't have time for this," he said. "It's check-in time. Which bag, Levi?"

"Check the ones on the left," said Levi, as he pushed himself off the floor with a groan.

"Keep it down," said one of the men on the floor and rolled over, closing his eyes. The other two were already breathing deeply.

"All these guns and we're not killing anyone," said Cowboy.

"Don't start," said Levi.

"My country was the home of art, education and purity for centuries," said Cowboy. "Then the white people came and look what happened."

"I'm white people," said Levi, wondering if it was a good idea to have his back to Cowboy.

"Yeah, but you're the most Japanese white guy I know. Foreigners brought the outbreak here. They should pay for the death they brought here."

Levi rifled through the bags to the right of the door until he found the phone.

"Here," he said, tossing it to Cowboy. "Save the ethnic cleansing for later."

Cowboy sat on the stacked bags and opened the cover on the satellite phone. The display lit up and beeped that it had acquired a signal.

· · ·

The SUV hardly stopped before Tate raced up the stairs to the library's front doors. He thumbed the Colt's safety off and stepped inside.

This was the stupidest thing he'd ever done. He didn't know how many hostiles he was facing, how they were armed, or what he'd do when he faced them. The only plan he had was to go for the head of the snake. He chuckled as he followed the footprints in the dusty floor.

Great plan, Jack. What's it mean?

Cowboy thumbed the speed dial and held the phone to his ear as Levi leaned against the other bags, looking haggard and uninterested.

"Tell our client to stop interfering with our schedule," said Levi. "We have enough experience to do this with our eyes closed."

Cowboy waived him off then scrunched up his face as he looked at the phone's display.

"It's not working," he said.

"Press the activate button," sighed Levi.

Cowboy pressed the button and gave a thumbs-up as he heard the other end ring.

"This is the security team," he said. "We're checking in."

He nodded, listening to the person on the other end.

"Yes, sir," he said. "Stand by for keyword confirmation."

Levi went rigid as a hand holding a gun came around the doorway and bumped against the back of Cowboy's head.

Tate eased into the room, revealing who was holding the Colt and put his finger to his lips, urging both men to be quiet.

Cowboy moved the sat phone from his ear, looking for help from the three men on the floor, but they were asleep.

A voice on the other end of the line was angrily demanding to know what was happening.

"Is this the team leader?" demanded the voice. "I demand to talk to the team leader!"

Cowboy slowly reached the phone across to Levi.

"It's for you," he whispered.

"Oops," smiled Levi, guessing from Tate's expression he just realized he was holding the gun on the wrong guy.

"Hey," said Cowboy, as Tate yanked him to his feet, using him as a meat shield.

In a blur of motion, Levi's pistol appeared in his free hand as he cautiously got to his feet.

The commotion woke the sleeping men, who quickly understood what was happening. They jumped to their feet with guns drawn, aiming at Tate.

Levi put the phone to his ear, never taking his eyes from Tate. "I'll call you back," he said, and thumbed off the phone.

It was a standoff and Tate had grabbed the wrong guy. The seconds were ticking and he knew it wouldn't be long before somebody decided that losing Cowboy was no great loss if they could get a shot at Tate.

"If someone doesn't kill this gaijin," growled Cowboy, "give me a gun and I'll do it."

"Shut up," said Levi flatly.

Tate kept Levi in his sights, who was satisfied to stay put for the moment, but the other three men were fanning out, working their way to Tate's flanks, looking for a better shot.

The doorway was to Tate's back, but backing out of the room meant taking the gun off the leader. Having a clear shot at Levi was the only leverage he had, but he needed to do something right now.

He backed into the corner of the room, only a few feet from the door, effectively reducing the angle the other men had on him.

"Do what I say and you get to die an old man," said Tate to Levi. "Move in front of the door."

"I like it here," smiled Levi.

His smile lost its humor when Tate thumbed the hammer back on the Colt.

"You're going to like it a lot less with a shattered kneecap," he said, lowering his aim to Levi's leg.

Keeping his gun steady on Tate, Levi stepped in front of the door.

"The next part is simple," said Tate. "You're going to back out of the room. Then I'll follow you. The rest of you stay here."

"What about me?" asked Cowboy, who was looking at his other teammates with the growing realization that his value to the team was rapidly shrinking.

"You're coming, too," said Tate, "and closing the door behind us. Then you two get on the floor and we'll have a little chat."

"A chat?" said Levi, confused.

"I need information," said Tate. "I'm not interested in killing you."

"I wish I could say the same," smiled Levi.

Getting the leader out the door was the only card Tate had to play, and it looked like Levi was calling his bluff.

Tate eased his head behind Cowboy's, exposing only the eye he was aiming with. He tried to judge where the other three men were without looking away from his target.

Air in the room became charged with tense static. The leader had drawn a line in the sand. Taking the hint, the other three men began slowly moving to find a clear shot at him; stalking their prey with predatory caution.

Tate's mind was racing as a trickle of sweat betrayed his mask of calm.

If the shooting starts. No, when the shooting starts, corrected Tate, I have to drop the leader first; a round to the leg. Please let it not hit a femoral artery. He's the only one with the keyword.

The next fatal threat will be the man with the cleanest line of sight. That was the man to his right.

Tate knew before he could shift his aim, that man would shoot. He had no choice but hope he'd miss. He knew the guy wouldn't.

A split second later, the other two would open fire, pumping a hail of rounds into Cowboy until he dropped and turning Tate's body into hamburger.

Fractions of a second; that's all Tate needed to take out the three shooters. If only he wasn't dead before his third pull of the trigger.

He slowed his breathing, gently putting pressure on the trigger.

The laser focus on Tate was broken by a glint of light flashing next to the leader's head.

Levi's smile of confidence changed to confusion, then horror as his ear slid down his cheek and tumbled to the floor.

"The next thing you lose will be your head," said Kiku as the full length of her sword appeared alongside Levi's neck.

All of these men were seasoned professionals, accustomed to the sight of gunshot wounds, but the horrific, mental image of what two feet of razor-sharp steel could do to a body stopped them cold.

"Guns down," said Kiku.

There was no argument. The men couldn't drop their guns fast enough.

A few minutes later, all of the men were tied up and Cowboy glared at Kiku.

"You're a traitor to your own people," he said.

"I've seen men like you before," she said. "You don't care about our people. They're just an excuse to justify your hate."

Cowboy started to speak, but Kiku's hand dropped to her sword.

"Speak again and I'll do what Tate-san was too civilized to do," she said.

After finding a med kit in one of the bags, Tate crossed the room where Levi was being kept apart from the rest of his team and bandaged his head.

When he finished, Tate crouched down in front of Levi and locked eyes with him. There was no gloating in Tate's expression.

People like them shared a mutual understanding that came with the profession. In every encounter, one of you would win and the other lose.

"What's the keyword for your principal?" he asked.

He knew the principal's name was Mullen, but operational security meant keeping the other side in the dark about your objective.

Levi looked at the others in his team for a beat before looking back at Tate.

"They're getting out of this with both ears," said Tate. "They're not going to throw you under the bus for giving me information."

Kiku stood next to Tate, looking down on Levi. From where he sat, her sword was as big as her, and he knew she wasn't shy about a little butchery.

"Causeway," he said.

"Is there anything else I need to know?" asked Tate.

"No," said Levi.

"Coming in," called a voice from the other room.

Tate stood up and arched his eyebrows as the sentry team came in.

"Only two?" he said.

"Did you do a good job securing them?" asked one of them.

The question sounded rhetorical and insulting.

Tate didn't answer.

"Then the two of us is enough."

"Hi," said the other sentry, putting his hand out to Tate. "I'm Alan. That's Nelson."

"Jack," he said, shaking Alan's hand. "No offense about there just being two of you."

"Nah," said Alan. "I'm not happy about it either, but a job's a job. Have you worked for these guys before? They sounded like..."

"Dicks?" grinned Tate. "Yes. Once before, but I'm trying not to make a habit out of it. Don't trust them too much and you'll be okay."

"Good to know," said Alan.

"Okay, then," said Tate, crouching eye level with Levi. "I'm taking your weapons, phones, ID and money. These two are going to drop you on a cargo ship out of the country."

"I'll be back for you," said Cowboy. "I'll wash away this dishonor with your blood."

Tate turned back to Levi with a smirk.

"Where'd you pick up the drama queen?"

"He was part of a package deal," said Levi. "It's not like the old days when you could bring your best people with you. You're wasting your time, you know. As soon as the principal knows you're not with The Ring he'll destroy all of his intel and disappear."

"How do you know about them?" began Tate, before Nelson chimed in.

"Yeah, right," he said, strapping on his tactical vest. "He's the one who invited us here."

"Hey," snapped Tate. "Shut up."

Nelson frowned, realizing he'd said too much, and felt his partner's reproachful stare.

"Come on," said Nelson. "They probably already figured it out."

The flash of shocked realization on Levi's face said otherwise, but now the cat was out of the bag.

"He's defecting," said Levi.

"See? I told you," said Nelson.

"If he says one more word," growled Tate to Alan.

"I got him," said Alan.

Unlike the rest of his team who had accepted their defeat, Levi looked at Tate with grim confidence. He was telling Tate he hadn't given up.

"Don't take your eyes off of him," said Tate, jabbing Nelson in the chest with each word.

Nelson's bluster melted under Tate's withering glare and he nodded in agreement.

Without another word, Tate and Kiku walked out to the SUV. Long gouges of bare metal ran along the sides of the car from grill to tailgate.

Kiku mumbled something in Japanese, heavy with disapproval.

"The car is destroyed, Tate-san," she said. "You were involved in many hit and runs. You are making my job very difficult."

"You aren't the first person who's said that," he grinned. His joke bounced off Kiku's stony expression.

"Japan has suffered from much chaos because of the Vix," she said. "Obedience to rules is how we maintain harmony."

"I'm sorry for the trouble." He bowed low, hoping his apology would be accepted.

Whatever Kiku felt was hidden behind a stoic mask in true Japanese custom. The matter was dropped.

Glancing down, Tate saw the sat phone in his hand and suddenly remembered The Ring was still waiting.

He hit the autodial and waited for the line to pick up.

"Where have you been?" demanded the voice. "I've been waiting twenty minutes. Do you have any idea how important this trip is?"

Tate didn't speak but gave the man on the other end of the line room to vent until he had nothing left to say.

"Are you there?"

"Yes," said Tate.

"Well, uh, give me a minute," said the voice.

Tate could hear paper rustling in the background.

"Okay, uh, what's the keyword?"

"Causeway," said Tate. He couldn't help feel his gut twist with doubt that Levi might have given him the wrong keyword as a final 'screw you'.

"Confirmed," said the principal. "Now listen. Mullen's meeting with Mr. Tanaka is critical. You'll give his security team your full cooperation."

All of this was new information to Tate. Smith and Jones' intel was thin regarding Mullen's meeting. He was going to have to wing this next part.

"Understood," he said. "I haven't received the details of that meeting."

"Of course not. Mullen will provide you with that."

"That's what I meant," said Tate. "Sorry. We just got in and the jet lag is catching up to us."

"That's everything on my end. I just notified Mullen of your confirmation and contact details. Sit tight until he's ready to call you."

"Understood."

"Hang on," said the voice. "The boss wants to talk to you."

The boss?

Tate glanced back at the library as it was beginning to dawn on him that the security team he'd tied up in there weren't outside contractors.

The line clicked and a new voice came on the sat phone.

"Hi, Levi. How are you liking Japan?"

Tate froze. The boss knew Levi. The second Tate spoke, he'd know it wasn't him.

Thinking quickly, he slid his thumb over the mouthpiece creating the sound of static and gave a noncommittal grunt.

"I know you think this job is beneath you," said the boss, raising his voice over the static. "But Mullen's been acting more paranoid than normal. I reviewed your report again and I'm going with your recommendation. He's becoming too much of a security risk. After the meeting with the Japanese, bring him to the penthouse."

"Okay," mumbled Tate.

The call went dead and Tate put down the sat phone.

"Tate-san?" said Kiku. "Are you ill?"

"I was just talking to the head of The Ring," he said, hardly believing what had just happened. "He's here in Tokyo."

10

EVIDENCE

After wiping the car's computer, they abandoned Tate's SUV for the sentry team to dispose of.

Kiku hadn't said it out loud but had made it clear she was taking the driver's seat for the trip back to the hotel.

The mood in the car was tense and Tate looked for a way to smooth things over.

"Thank you for helping me back there," he said.

Kiku nodded curtly and continued to look out the window.

That didn't go the way he was expecting.

"What am I missing?" he asked.

"You hid your gun from me," she said. "You used my trust against me."

Of the consequences he had considered, insulting Kiku had not been one of them.

"It was a necessary evil," said Tate. "I'm sorry I had to hide it from you."

"Yet you would do it again."

"Yes," he said without hesitation. "I'll lie, cheat and steal if it means I can destroy The Ring."

She glanced at him, her eyes hard as flint.

"Why would you say things like that?" she asked.

"The Ring is trying to destroy my country," said Tate. "What would you sacrifice to save yours?"

He watched the play of emotions on her face as she thought about it. She didn't speak, but he saw her expression soften.

"I'll make you a promise," he said.

She looked at him with a mix of irony and skepticism.

"I'll keep my gun but will only use it if someone is using a gun against my people or me."

Kiku crossed her arms and frowned in through for a moment.

"I accept," she said. "But Tate-san, if you break that promise..."

Her hand rested lightly on the handle of her sword. The implication wasn't lost on Tate. He hoped he didn't die keeping this promise.

He was glad that was cleared up but getting that out of the way only made room for the next problem to come forward.

"At the police station, you said you thought you could help get Monkhouse out of jail?"

"Hai," said Kiku. "Monkhouse-san is not the first client of mine that has encountered this situation. Getting the evidence to prove he's innocent may involve... complications."

"The story of my life," he said.

The headache was getting worse and Tate rubbed his temples, hoping for relief.

They'd been in the Yaki club, waiting for Amai-chan, the girl who'd robbed Monkhouse.

Tate had been in firefights and artillery barrages that paled in comparison to enduring four hours of karaoke.

Three businessmen were drunkenly belting out Staying Alive and Tate was losing the will to live.

"Doesn't this bother you?" he asked, his eyes stinging from the cigarette smoke.

Kiku turned from valiantly scanning the club and smiled.

"Yes," she said, even though she looked completely unphased. "Look behind you, at the bar."

Looking over his shoulder, he saw a slim, blond-haired man sitting halfway off his barstool. He was dwarfed by four big Japanese guys that were laughing with him. The blond stood up, looking like he was about to leave and one of the big guys put a hand on his shoulder as the other three talked him into sitting down.

"The drunk guy," said Tate. "What about him?"

"The other men are not his friends," said Kiku. "They are keeping him there until a girl comes."

He looked back again, just in time to see a girl saunter up to the blond. She matched Rosse's and Fulton's description.

"That's our girl," he said.

The man perked up as she began talking to him. She tugged playfully at his shirt and the other men chuckled encouragingly.

The blond got off the barstool and Amai-chan led him out of the club.

Tate and Kiku left their table and followed them outside.

The crisp, winter air was the refreshing slap in the face Tate had been longing for.

Amai-chan and the blond man were nowhere in sight.

"This way," said Kiku, heading for a side alley.

They reached the mouth of the alley and saw two people silhouetted in the neon glow of a sign.

As Tate and Kiku got closer, they recognized Amai-chan and her prey. The blond guy was pretty drunk and while he was focused on kissing her, she was picking his wallet clean.

She saw them out of the corner of her eye and sensed they were coming for her. As they got closer, she pressed a red gem on her bracelet.

"She's made us," said Tate.

"Made us?" asked Kiku.

Suddenly, the back door of the club flew open and the same four big men from the bar came charging out, glowering at Tate and Kiku.

"Ah," she said, nodding in understanding. "Made us, hai."

One of Amai-chan's guards barked at them and Tate reached for his phone to translate but stopped. In the dark alley, the motion could be misunderstood as reaching for his sword.

Kiku snapped back at the bodyguard in Japanese.

"Let me guess," said Tate. "They want us to leave."

"Yes," she said.

The guard waved for them to go away as he growled a command.

Without knowing what they were saying, Tate felt awkwardly out of this fight.

Kiku's voice dropped to a low snarl, yelling something back.

Shock flashed across the four men as if they'd been slapped.

"What's happening?" asked Tate.

All four men lowered their shoulders, grumbling in anger and started coming toward them.

"Never mind," he said. "I'm up to speed."

Kiku's katana flashed out of its scabbard as she crouched, ready to fight. Tate's hand went for his hidden pistol, but hesitated and he reached for his short sword instead.

"Stay back," snapped Kiku. "You will only be in the way, Tate-san."

Tate took a step back as the big men all drew their blades. They carried the same sword as Tate, but it looked very small in their big hands. They stopped out of range of her blade, barking insults, but none of them looked eager to go against Kiku. She stood her ground, silent and poised to spring.

The air was brittle with tension and Tate could see the men working themselves up to attack.

As formidable as Kiku appeared, she was outmatched by sheer weight of numbers.

Tate felt the weight of the Colt tucked in his belt. There was no way he would stand by and let them kill her. He'd given his word not to use his gun. If he broke his promise, even to save her life...

"Stop," shouted Amai-chan from behind her wall of guards. She said something else and the guards glanced at her but relaxed. One by one, they put away their swords.

Cautiously watching their actions, Kiku sheathed her sword too.

"What do you want?" asked Amai-chan.

"Did you rob a gaijin at the Leave Happy love hotel?" asked Kiku.

"Who are you?" asked Amai-chan suspiciously.

"The man is our friend," said Tate.

"Your friend caused me a lot of trouble," said Amai-chan.

"He caused you trouble?" he scoffed.

"I can't go to that hotel anymore," she said. "The manager says I brought him problems with the police."

"We can go to a hotel?" asked the blond drunk.

"We can help you with the manager," said Tate.

"But you help us get the gaijin out of jail first," said Kiku.

"How?" said Amai-chan, looking suspicious again. "Talk to the police?"

"Yes," said Kiku.

"This was your plan?" asked Tate. "Ask a thief to confess and get arrested so Monkhouse can get out?"

"Even thieves have honor," said Kiku. "The gaijin is innocent," she said to Amai-chan.

Amai-chan's giggle bounced off the alley walls.

"Not this one," said Tate.

"If you can help me with the manager," said Amai-chan, "I'll help you."

Kiku looked at Tate with a knowing smile.

"But I'm not talking to the police," added Amai-chan. "Talk to the manager. He's got video of everything that happened."

"He told the police the cameras are broken," said Kiku.

"He lied," said Amai-chan. "He showed me the recording and said if I don't give him money, he'll give them to the police."

"There you go," said Tate. "We buy the recording, Monkkhouse gets out. Problem solved."

"No, Tate-san," said Kiku. "The police are already suspicious of you and your people. If you appear with the recording, they will detain you too. There are ways of doing things here you do not understand."

"That's an understatement," he said.

"We will talk to the manager," she said.

Amai-chan nodded in agreement and said something to her guards. Their leader grunted something and the four brutes went back inside the club.

Amai-chan gave the drunk a long kiss before walking out of the alley. He watched her shapely form disappear from view before staring at Tate and Kiku.

"You guys know how to wreck a good time," he said.

———

Tate and Kiku stood under the Leave Happy hotel sign as it blazed away in flashing colors.

Tate looked at the twenty-foot-high video screens of couples kissing fading into a shower of bright pink hearts.

"Real subtle," he grinned.

He took his phone out of his pocket as the glass doors slid open and they walked into the lobby. Warm, perfumed air and cutesy music surrounded them as they stepped up to the counter.

The clerk pulled himself away from his TV show and shuffled to the counter.

"Nine thousand yen for all night," said the clerk. "Seven thousand to stay and rest."

"Isn't that the same thing?" asked Tate.

"Rest is polite way of saying sex," said Kiku.

Tate briefly toyed with the joke of telling the clerk 'stay and rest' to see Kiku's expression. As quickly as the thought came, he knew it was a disastrously bad idea. He was running on little sleep and it was showing.

"Are you the manager?" he asked.

The question caused the clerk to look at the two of them with guarded interest.

"Yes," he said.

"You might remember a friend of mine. He came here the other day with a good-looking young woman."

"I don't think so," said the clerk. "I see a lot of you people."

"Sure you'll remember him," said Tate. "Short brown hair. Blue eyes. Skinny guy about five nine. Oh yeah, and under arrest."

The clerk tried to look bored, but they could see the worry in his eyes.

"Oh yeah," he said. "I remember now. He attacked that girl."

Cold air rolled in as the glass doors opened and a couple walked in. They were whispering and laughing as they got in line behind Tate and Kiku.

"I have customers," said the clerk. "Next!"

The couple started to walk around them, but Kiku politely motioned them back. Frowning, they backed up, but soon were distracted in verbal foreplay.

"You have a video that proves he didn't attack her," said Tate.

The clerk shifted on his feet as Tate frowned down on him. New confidence filled the clerk as he glanced at the sturdy, clear shield between them.

"I want you to give it to the police and get my friend out of jail," said Tate.

"Why?" said the clerk. "What's in it for me?"

"I'll pay you," said Tate.

The clerk's interest dialed up and he looked Tate over, assessing him.

"Ten thousand," said the clerk.

Tate could feel himself relax. Ten thousand yen worked out to about a hundred dollars.

"Not yen," said the clerk, as if knowing Tate's thoughts. "Dollars."

"You're watching too many episodes of Bay Watch," said Tate. "Real people don't have that kind of money."

"You have money to travel here," said the clerk. "Your friend has money for an expensive girl. Come back when you're ready to pay. Next!"

The couple started to walk around, but Tate stopped them. "We're not done," he said, holding up a finger.

The couple stopped short, holding each other tighter and took a few steps back.

"He was drunk," said Tate, turning back to the clerk, heating up. "He didn't know she was a hooker."

"Not a hooker, Tate-san," said Kiku.

"Pretending to be a hooker," he said.

"Leave," said the clerk, "or I'll call the police, then you can join your friend in jail."

Tate inhaled, ready to level a dark threat at the clerk when Kiku interrupted.

"I apologize for the gaijin," she said, bowing to the clerk. "He does not understand our ways."

Tate tried and failed to hide his surprise. *Who's side is she on?*

"Please wait outside, Tate-san," said Kiku briskly.

He hesitated, unable to read anything in her expression other than disapproval.

"Please do not embarrass me further," she said.

There was no arguing with her and he walked out, swearing under his breath. "The guy runs a sleaze hotel and *I'm* embarrassing one?"

Steam puffed out between Tate's fingers as he blew warmth into his cupped hands, pacing outside the hotel. The cold was getting to him and his curiosity was making him impatient. He glanced from the door to his watch, growing aware of the curious looks he was getting from passersby.

"Sure," he mumbled to himself. "A strange guy loitering outside a love hotel."

He heard a click as someone took a selfie with him in the background.

"Hey," he said. "Knock it off."

His head whipped around to the hotel as a scream pierced the air. The glass doors rattled as the romance couple banged through the doors in panic and ran down the street.

Tate charged for the lobby but pulled up short as Kiku met him at the entrance with a satisfied smile.

"Thank you for your patience," she said, holding out a small green rectangle.

"You're welcome?" said Tate, taking it. "Is this the recording?"

"A copy," she said. "The clerk offers it with his apology for inconveniencing your friend."

Tate looked past her and saw the clerk, pale as a sheet, the clear shield on the floor, cleaved neatly in two.

"He will take his copy to the police," she said. "In the morning. Monkhouse-san will be released afterward."

Tate enjoyed a thick wedge of toast and small link sausages as he waited for a phone call from the police.

The rest of the team were in good spirits and chatting over their food as Kiku sipped her tea.

"These sausages are really good," said Wesson.

"Yeah," said Fulton, spearing another with his fork. "I can't tell if they're beef or pork."

"Neither," said Kiku simply.

"Chicken?" asked Wesson.

"No," said Kiku. "Our country is very crowded. We don't have space for farming animals."

Rosse's fork stopped halfway to his mouth and his eyebrows knitted together as he frowned at her. "What kind of farming do you have space for?"

"People," said Kiku, sipping her tea.

Shocked silence jolted everyone at the table. Fulton opened his mouth, dropping his food onto his plate. Wesson's shoulders hunched as she fought against gagging. Ota popped another sausage in his mouth and kept reading the news.

Kiku's face split into a smile before she covered her mouth with her hand, giggling. Her whole frame shook with laughter and she tried to talk between gasping for breath.

"I'm joking," she said. "You should see your faces."

Some of them laughed with her, while others looked relieved. Rosse left his sausage on the plate.

Tate cocked an eyebrow as his phone chirped.

"Hello," he said.

The others watched expectantly as Tate listened, nodding briefly.

"Thank you," he said and hung up. "Monkhouse is out."

The team cheered and thanked Kiku for her help as Tate got up from the table.

"Great news," said Wesson.

"I've got to sign him out," said Tate. "Save some breakfast for him."

He grabbed his jacket and slid his sword into his belt. He wasn't surprised when Kiku appeared next to him.

"I'm just going to pick him up," he smiled. "I promise I won't get into trouble."

"I don't believe trouble offers a man like you a choice."

11

POWER STRUGGLE

When they got back to the hotel room, Monkhouse walked in like a returning conqueror to the cheers of his teammates.

"Thank you all," he said, arms raised. "I can honestly say I missed you guys."

Wesson broke off from the others as Monkhouse sat down to regale them with his story of adventure.

"Your bag's been beeping," she said, gesturing to Tate's backpack.

"Thanks," said Tate. "I think we're about to take the next step in this fun-filled operation."

He took out the sat phone and saw there was an unread message.

Your meeting with Mr. Tanaka's security team is tomorrow.

Tate read the message and put the phone away.

"Sorry to interrupt your tales of daring," he said. Monkhouse smiled, appreciating the attention. "I just got word. Our meeting with Tanaka's security team is set for tomorrow. I want everyone to be rested and up early. We'll leave at zero six-thirty," said Tate. "Okay hero, you can finish telling how you got rolled by a hooker."

Everyone laughed and Monkhouse blushed, shrugging it off good-naturedly.

Tate didn't rejoin the group, instead looking out the large windows to the broad cityscape; how unique it was to see someplace different and foreign. There was a time in his life when he was traveling so much he stopped paying attention to where he was.

He went out onto the balcony, wanting to capture this rare moment. A moment later he heard the sound of the big glass door slide open.

"Aren't you cold?" asked Wesson.

"I spent enough time sweating in the jungle," he said. "I'm basking in the cold to have something to remember before we go back."

"I hope I'm not intruding," she said.

"No. I'm just... thinking."

Tate leaned on the railing, feeling the cold metal through the sleeves of his shirt. He'd been in the jungle for so long now that it was hard not to see things through those eyes. The city stretched out in rolling hills and valleys, but instead of a canopy of endless green trees and the chorus of animals and insects, it was tight packed buildings, some reaching high into the low, murky grey tatters of clouds while others were smaller, more humble structures with clay tiled sloped roofs. The sound of people rose up to their ears from below.

"It's still a jungle," he said. "Just made of cement and electricity."

Wesson looked at him for a beat.

"That sounded like there was a deeper meaning," she said.

Tate stood, rubbing his arms to warm up, but kept his gaze out towards the city.

"Yes," he said. "Maybe. I don't know."

"You haven't been the same for a long time," she said. "They notice it. So do I."

"Notice what?"

"The thousand-yard stare," she said.

Tate looked at her, curious.

"You're feeling restless," said Wesson.

He shrugged. "Unsatisfied."

"I think I get it," she said. "Before you were Jack Tate, you were living a very different life. You don't talk about it, I respect that, but I've heard enough to know why you left it behind. Frankly, Top, you're smart enough to know that never works. We never get away from who we were. We just bury it, hoping it never comes back. Maybe, if we're lucky, we forget about it, at least for a while."

"Speaking from experience?" he asked.

"Does it show?"

They both chuckled and Wesson rubbed her arms but relished the feel of the fresh breeze.

"I'm worried you're thinking of making a change," she said.

That prompted Tate to look at her. The concern in her eyes was clear and he wondered how he hadn't seen it before.

"This team," she said, "it's my family. I think you want more than what we're doing, but maybe you're afraid that what you want is too dangerous for the rest of us. But if you go, the rest of us will drift apart, be assigned to other units, something like that. What you're after... I think the rest of us want that too."

Wesson's words revealed a side of things he hadn't considered.

"I feel like we're stuck," he said.

"That *we* are stuck?" she asked. "Or that *you* are stuck because we're holding you back?"

Tate shifted his weight, feeling like he was under a microscope. Clearly, he wasn't the closed book he imagined himself to be.

"Getting this defector could be a death blow for The Ring," he said. "Maybe not all at once, but the ripple effect will be devastating."

"But you're not satisfied," she said.

"Before the Vix, I'd been deployed all over the world," he said. "You saw the news about what was going on out there. It was some bad... evil stuff. Me and my team, we weren't staying at home reading about it. We were taking the fight to them."

Tate didn't say anything more. He was gazing at the city, but in his mind, he was miles away.

"I can guess what you're thinking," said Wesson. "But I'm not a mind reader."

Tate came out of his fog and smiled ironically.

"You'll laugh," he said.

"Maybe," she said, "but that's never stopped you before."

"Did it ever bother you, knowing what was happening out there?" he said. "You know you could do something about it, but you didn't."

"We've lived two different lives," scoffed Wesson. "If you had asked me six years ago, I would have been happy where I was. All the bad stuff... it's always been there. You can turn to any page in a history book and they'll be someone doing terrible things."

"But," he said, "when you keep reading, you get to the part where someone took a stand and beat them."

"That's why we were different," she said. "I read about evil in a newspaper. You read about it in a mission plan."

"I've wondered about what you did before... this," he said.

Wesson appraised him for a moment, thinking about telling him or not.

"Sure," she said. "Why not."

"You have my full attention," smiled Tate.

"I was a wilderness outfitter and hunting guide."

She cocked an eyebrow when Tate chuckled.

"No," he said. "I'm not laughing at you, but that explains why you're good at tracking. I thought, I don't know, maybe you were a bounty hunter."

Wesson's pale green eyes brightened and she laughed.

"A what?"

"It's a fair guess," he said. "You track. You can handle yourself in a fight. Where'd that come from?"

"My dad," she said. "He was a street cop. He got injured on the job. Long story. They wanted to retire him, but he fought to stay on and ended up as an instructor at the police academy. I wanted to learn and he was happy to train his little girl."

"It's hard to imagine you as someone's little girl," said Tate.

"I'll always be to my dad," said Wesson. "The training was tough but came in handy when hunters would drink too much and I had to break up a fight."

"You miss it?"

"I miss being in the middle of nowhere. When you're miles away from people, the world feels..."

"Uncomplicated."

Wesson nodded, appreciating that they shared the same experience.

"I miss that too," he said.

"You miss a lot more than that," she said.

Tate gave her a brief, knowing glance.

"I'm feeling restless," he said.

"Even before you started talking about it, it showed," she said. "We're feeling the same way."

Surprised, Tate looked over his shoulder at his team, lounging inside.

"Really?" he asked. "I didn't know."

"Nobody's saying it out loud, but you can feel it."

"Maybe you can," he said.

"You could too if you weren't..."

"Feeling sorry for myself?"

"Preoccupied," grinned Wesson.

Tate laughed, standing up from the railing.

"Thanks. That's the nicest chewing out I've ever gotten," he said.

"One of the perks of my job," she grinned. "I can't feel my fingers anymore. I'm going inside."

"Right behind you, Sergeant," said Tate.

Following the instructions, the SUV eventually took them away from the busy pace of the city, through suburbia, and into a small rural village nestling in a blue-green valley forest. Tate took the opportunity to sleep, a habit of his years in the military. The others found distractions from the car's entertainment screens.

Wesson watched the passing landscape, occasionally talking to Kiku.

"We're almost there," announced the car as it turned down a private gravel road.

Tate blinked the sleep out of his eyes as they drove past rich, green fields of crops. Patches of wild shrubs crowded the sides of the road as it turned towards the foothills of the valley.

The house sat in a pocket of tall pines, enclosed by a low stone wall. The car stopped at the gate, waiting until a man, bundled up against the cold, got up from his stool and pushed them open. He nodded a greeting as they drove into the courtyard.

"All of you will need to leave your phones in the car," said Kiku. "It's a security measure against anyone listening. I will translate for you."

Cold mist was coming off the mountain and wrapped around them as they got out of the car. The left half of the courtyard was taken up by a garden of tall, narrow boulders surrounded by carefully arranged grass and plants.

"It looks prehistoric," said Fulton.

"They look like oversized headstones," said Monkhouse.

"They're gorgeous," said Wesson. "Like they're reminding us that nature is strong. Timeless."

"Check out who's getting philosophical," grinned Monkhouse.

The two-story house sat opposite the garden, its simple, cream plaster walls contrasted against the grey slate roof tiles.

The bundled-up man led them up the stone steps to the main entrance and into an alcove to leave their shoes.

Their guide got out of his heavy coat as Rosse grunted, bending over his gut to reach his boot laces.

"I never had to take my shoes off so many times before," he said.

"It would be easier if you lost..." began Monkhouse.

"Shut it," said Rosse, cutting him off.

They finished swapping out their shoes for slippers and the man led them into a large, open room where Tanaka's security team waited.

The security team sat opposite a sunken fire pit and low table in the middle of the floor. Grey, winter light filled the room through the lattice wall of wood and glass behind them.

They quietly watched, with deadpan faces, while Tate and his team entered the sparsely furnished room.

One of the men stood and bowed. He spoke in low tones to Kiku while looking at Tate.

"This is Satori-san," said Kiku. "He is the team leader for Tanaka-san."

132

Kiku introduced Tate, then Wesson as his second in charge, followed by the rest of the team, each of them bowing in turn.

Satori bowed and gestured for them to sit at the table. They sat on the tatami-covered floor, which gave off a subtle scent of grass, and Satori returned to his seat, next to his men.

Satori's men were dressed in identical black suits and ties in contrast to the more casual dress of Tate's team. He made a mental note of it, wondering which of the two teams would blend into a public setting better. Then he remembered their western features, which made the question pointless.

Across from Rosse sat a huge man who made a point of looking at Rosse's clothing, smirking at him with his dark beady eyes.

There was instant bad blood between the two men. Rosse pretended to ignore him, but already knew he didn't like the guy.

Satori said something as he set a small device on the floor. A white light emerged, like a beam from a laser, then broadened to a flat plane.

Tate watched with interest as a three-dimensional city map grew from the plane until it was sharply defined.

A green line followed Satori's finger as he drew a circle around a building.

"This is the site of the meeting," said Kiku.

Gesturing over the map, it zoomed onto the circled building, becoming semi-transparent.

Satori spoke as he pointed to a room on the ground floor that opened directly to the street.

"The first floor has been reserved for the meeting," said Kiku. "Satori's men will be stationed at..." She paused as he pointed to different areas of the building. "The front door and rear exit."

As he continued to gesture, the building rose, revealing stairs and elevators leading to the underground parking structure.

"You and your people will stay at the garage entrance," said Kiku, "and secure the cars."

"Looks like he's decided our assignments," said Wesson to Tate.

"I hope he didn't spend a lot of time on it," he said, "because that's not going to happen."

Satori looked up from the map and glanced at Kiku for the translation.

She looked at Tate for direction.

"I appreciate the planning you've put into this," said Tate, "but you have all of us outside."

Satori nodded, hearing the translation.

"Satori-san says he selected your locations which are best suited to your skills," said Kiku.

"Here we go," said Wesson under her breath.

"What's he mean, best suited?" said Rosse.

"He means we suck," said Fulton.

"Both of you quiet down," said Wesson.

Tate smiled at Satori, but it didn't reach his eyes.

"Our principal is my responsibility," he said. "Me and Wesson will be with our man the entire time. The rest of my team will be here, here and here." He pointed at map locations, leaving a blue dot with every jab of his finger.

Satori shook his head and his men grumbled objections under their breath. Waving his hand, Satori erased the blue dots and repeated the positions he'd selected for Tate's team.

"Satori-san appreciates your suggestions but reluctantly insists that you follow his instructions to act as the support team," said Kiku, framing Satori's reply more tactfully.

"Support?" began Tate, waving Kiku from translating.

He took a breath, holding Satori in his stare while he sized him up. Tate's skin was tough enough to let things like this roll off his back.

Satori wasn't the first person, not even the hundredth, who tried to muscle him into the back of the bus with a show of superiority.

Tate had haggled with sheiks, tribal chiefs, revolutionaries, rogue paramilitary generals, senators, terrorists, and three New York cab drivers. Satori didn't know it yet, but he was punching way above his weight.

There was no way Tate would leave Mullen without protection in that meeting room. At the first sign of trouble, Sataori's team would hustle Tanaka out of danger, leaving Mullen a sitting duck. Satori wanted Tate out of the way so he'd have clean exits. It was that simple.

He wasn't going to win this by arguing with Satori. They'd be going back and forth all night. It was time to switch up the game.

"We're leaving," he said, collecting his sword as he stood up.

Satori gasped as Kiku translated and his team clamored in shock as the rest of the Grave Diggers got up.

Satori protested in rapid-fire, but Tate cut him off.

"Your arrogance disrespects me, my team and my principal," he said. "You wouldn't insult us without Tanaka-san's approval. We're going back to our boss and I will explain Tanaka-san's contempt for him."

The lag of Kiku's translation was only a few seconds. Tate didn't have to wait long for the expected reaction.

Satori's team looked like they'd been slapped and shouted angrily, jumping to their feet.

The man opposite Rosse scowled at him, gesturing at him with curses.

"Come at me, big boy," said Rosse. "See what happens."

"What's happening?" asked Fulton, looking worried. He didn't know if he should be ready to fight or run.

Wesson stood next to Tate, quiet but menacing as she sized up the man across from her.

"Say the word, Top," she said, "and I'll drop him like a bad habit."

"Sit tight, Sergeant," said Tate cooly.

He stood unphased and let the other side bluster until they ran out of steam.

Satori saw Tate wasn't arguing with him and he realized he'd been outmaneuvered. He couldn't storm off because Tate had already shown he was about to leave. He couldn't attack without looking cowardly because Tate wouldn't fight back.

Tate had baited him by hurting his pride and Satori had foolishly walked into the trap. The only way to save face and not dishonor Tanaka was to return to the planning map and accept Tate's revisions.

Hushing his men, Satori straightened his suit and composed himself.

"I apologize for the misunderstanding," related Kiku. "The meaning of my words were obviously lost in the translation."

Tate glanced at Kiku, who remained stone-faced at the insult.

"Kiku-san," he began.

"It's all right, Tate-san," said Kiku. "Do not be concerned. He is only trying to lure you into another fight so he can save face."

"I suggest we take a break," said Satori. "Please have some tea and enjoy the fresh air. We will return here in half an hour, if that's acceptable."

"It is," said Tate, bowing. "Thank you."

Satori and his men bowed, but the big man only nodded towards Rosse. The gravity of the insult was lost on Rosse, but he didn't need another incentive to dislike the guy.

"Yeah, walk away," said Rosse.

"That's enough, Sergeant," growled Tate.

The big guy glared at Rosse but didn't speak.

"Chicken sh...," mouthed Rosse.

"Sergeant," snapped Wesson. "One more word and you'll be marching up and down this mountain until I sweat the stupid out of you."

"You heard her," said Tate, when Rosse looked at him to intervene.

"What's Satori's problem?" asked Wesson.

"Where do you want to start?" said Tate. "We're foreigners. In his eyes we're not as good as them. He's used to getting his way. And he's kind of a dick."

"Copy that," she chuckled.

Tate thought through his security plan for anything he'd missed, but it was solid.

"Where do you want to be stationed?" he asked.

"Here," said Wesson, pointing to the fourth floor of the building across from the meeting. "I'll have a bird's eye view of the street and foot traffic from both directions. I can coordinate my team from there."

"Good choice," he said. "When we pull out of the garage, I'll be in the lead car with Rosse, Fulton and Mullen. You, Monkhouse and Ota will follow."

"If we weren't so thinned out we could use a lead car."

"It's overkill for this op," said Tate, looking at her closely. "You're starting to make me anxious. What do you know that I don't?"

Wesson looked at him and smiled, the concentration melting from her face.

"You're the one that trained me," she said. "I see bad guys in every corner."

"Is that paranoia or preparation?" said Tate.

"A little of both, I think."

"Yeah," he said. "You're going to do just fine."

"Kind of surprising this country," she said. "If you ignore the swords and masks, it's like nothing happened here."

"I wasn't expecting this," said Tate. "Scratch that. I didn't know what to expect. It makes me wonder what's going on in the rest of the world."

"Maybe a lot more than we're told."

News of the outside world had dwindled until there was only silence.

Speculation about the radio silence ranged from the reasonable to the preposterous; collapse of power grids, state sponsored black outs, and even the near annihilation of the population. That last one would have seemed impossible, but Tate only had to look at South America to know it was entirely plausible.

But even in the face of that, he still couldn't accept that no one from the outside world hadn't tried to contact the US.

In the beginning, there were scattered reports from around the world. Countries like his were in chaos. As the remnants of his own government came out of their bunkers and began to rebuild itself, information outside the country slowly tapered off.

Was there a correlation? He didn't like to dwell on the implications of that question. It left a bad taste in his mouth.

Until he came here, he'd had no idea what had happened to Japan. The same was true for Africa, but he had been there too and seen it for himself.

Why hadn't there been any news about these countries?

He thought about Kaiden and wondered what she knew. She was tied up with some shady elements in the intelligence community and often knew more than she'd say.

He decided to ask her about it when he got back home, then changed his mind. Maybe it was better not knowing. If she confirmed his suspicions, it would only spark the more troubling question of why his own government was keeping the information from the public.

Digging for the answer to that was a bitter pill he didn't want to swallow and a fight he wasn't ready to take on.

At least not today.

Tate looked at Wesson, who was studying the map with thoughtful concentration.

"What is it?" he asked.

"Nothing," she said. "Just getting the lay of the land."

"The meet should go smoothly," he said. "There's nothing in the intel that suggests either Tanaka or Mullen are under threat."

"Maybe," she said.

"I'm listening," said Tate.

"If The Ring knew what Mullen was up to..." she said, trailing off.

"There's no way for them to know," he said. "We have the sat phone. After he meets with Tanaka, we'll deliver him to the agents and he'll be in the wind before The Ring can do anything about it."

Wesson shifted on her feet and gave him an ambiguous smile.

"You don't look convinced," he said.

"I'm wondering how many missions I need under my belt before I have your kind of confidence in a plan."

"Me?" chuckled Tate. "Plans never work out. The only thing I'm confident about is that we can handle what happens when it all goes wrong."

12

SWITCH SIDES

By the time the small boat bumped against the side of the Hiryu Maru, Levi and his men were soaked and shivering from the spray of waves.

"Here we are," said Nelson, cutting the engine. "Home sweet home."

Alan tied a rope around a cleat on the Hiryu's hull while Nelson kept an eye on their prisoners.

A stairway ran from the deck above them, down to the water, ending in a landing.

"I'll go first," said Alan. "You got them?"

"Sure I do," said Nelson. "It's not rocket science."

"Take it easy. I'm just making sure."

Timing the gentle ocean swells, Alan stepped onto the landing and climbed the stairs. Nelson waited until his partner was at the top, then got the prisoners on their feet.

"Okay, everybody up the stairs," he said. "One at a time."

The prisoners had to work at keeping their footing as the small boat rocked. Their hands flex-cuffed behind them added an extra challenge to keep their balance.

Alan stepped back and directed the captives to line up along the railing.

"Stand facing the water," he said, his assault rifle at low ready.

He didn't expect anyone to put up a fight, but it was foolish to ignore that he was outnumbered.

Levi was the last up the stairs and took his time to take in his surroundings.

The Hiryu was a coastal freighter and only forty meters long, not made for the open ocean.

"I thought we were getting a long cruise out of this," he said.

"Your cruise was from the dock to here," said Nelson.

His boots clomped on the steel deck as he walked over to the bridge superstructure and opened a hatch.

"Let's go," he said. "Through the door and down the stairs. When you get to the storage area..."

"The cargo bay?" said Levi.

"Move all the way to the other end," grumbled Nelson.

"This is how foreigners have always treated us," said Cowboy.

"Not another word," warned Levi.

The prisoners went single file through the hatch and down the steep stairs into the cargo bay below.

The space smelled of old oil and saltwater. The white walls and ceiling were damp with condensation and streaked with rust.

Mattresses and blanket were stacked against the bulkhead.

The shivering men moved to the other end of the sixty-foot bay and waited for their next instruction.

"We're holding you here for the next few days," said Alan.

"And then?" asked Levi.

"Then we let you go," said Nelson. "Unless anyone causes us trouble. Then it's a whole new ball game."

He patted his gun

Alan rolled his eyes.

"These guys are cold," he said. "I'm going to get coffee going."

"What about these?" asked Levi, turning his back to display the thick flex cuffs binding his wrists.

"We'll cut those off later," said Nelson. "For now, everyone plant your butts."

Alan's boots rang off the stairs as he climbed back up and headed for the galley.

Nelson watched the men sit down and leaned against the hull with a sigh.

"Long day?" said Levi

"Where do I start?" said Nelson. "It's going to feel longer having to sit in this tub until we cut you loose."

"I remember those days," said Levi. "Everyone else was getting the sweet contracts. All I got were the scraps."

Nelson studied Levi's clothing and gear.

"You can afford some nice gear," said Nelson, "but it didn't keep you from sitting, tied up, in this bucket."

"Eh," said Levi, crossing his legs and leaning back. "You know the job. Sometimes you catch a bad break."

"Sometimes?" scoffed Nelson. "I've been doing this since I got out of the service. It's always the same. I'm living on dried soup noodles until someone scrapes the bottom of the barrel and calls me."

"Too bad you weren't on my crew," said Levi.

"And then I'd be tied up with you. No thanks."

"Win or lose," said Levi, "my contract pays the same. There's a big bonus attached if we complete it. If you got part of that, you'd never have to eat soup again."

"Is that a bribe?" frowned Nelson.

"It's a job offer. I've worked for my client a long time. He trusts me to pick my own crew. You'd get full benefits, but I could only pay you for half the contract."

"What's that come to?"

"Pull up your account on your phone," said Levi.

Nelson looked at him then glanced at the stairs behind him.

"It's up to you," said Levi.

Nelson slung his assault rifle behind his back and fished out his phone. He tapped in the passcode and showed it to Levi, who smiled and gestured to his bound hands.

Nelson drew his combat knife and paused.

"If you try to jump me," he growled, "I'll kill you."

"Do you want the job?" said Levi.

Nelson hesitated, then reached behind Levi and cut him loose.

Nelson stepped back and brought up his gun as Levi rolled his shoulders and flexed the feeling back into his hands. Then he held his hand out to Nelson.

Keeping his gun on Levi, Nelson gave him his phone with his free hand.

Levi tapped information into the phone for a few seconds and offered it back to him.

Nelson took his phone and stepped back, then glanced at his phone. His eyebrows shot up as he did a second take.

"It's already in your account," said Levi. "You're on the team. What do you say?"

"Uh..." stammered Nelson. "Yeah. Um, yes boss. What do we do now?"

"Put your gun on the floor."

Nelson balked, but Levi stepped back with his hands up.

"I won't touch it," he said. "I don't want any accidents. Put it down and cut the other guys free. When your ex-partner comes back, we'll tie him up and head back to shore."

Nelson looked doubtful, then nodded and unstrapped the gun and put it down.

Levi didn't give the gun a second look as Nelson freed the other men.

"Guys," said Levi. "We have a new..."

The cargo bay flashed with a loud crack and hammered off the steel walls of the hull; Nelson tumbled back with a hole in his head.

Levi flinched but quickly recovered and looked at Cowboy in surprise.

A wisp of smoke trailed out of the gun-barrel as Cowboy offered him Nelson's gun.

"You have a serious hate for foreigners," said Levi, taking the gun.

He bent down and picked up Nelson's phone and dialed a number.

"Buy me a beer sometime," said Cowboy. "I'll tell you where I dump the bodies."

"Hello," he said. "I just made a transaction... yes, that one. Cancel it. Thank you. I hope you have a good day too."

Levi hung up.

13

ENEMY OF MY ENEMY

After Satori had collected himself, he returned to the map to work out the security assignments with Tate for the upcoming meeting.

Now they had an understanding, Tate assumed working out the details would go smoothly, but Satori continued to lock horns with him.

Tate could feel himself winding up to an argument, but before things got heated, Satori would agree to his condition as if it was his idea.

Tate suspected it was Satori's way of saving face in front of his team, and Tate helped him by showing gratitude for the man's patience.

Negotiations could be a tricky thing. For every win you had to lose something to the other side. The trick was losing something you didn't care about. Win too much and the tedious allegiance would fall apart, or worse. The other side would sell you out when you were most vulnerable.

It was a lesson he learned in East Kilbride, outside Glasgow.

The Maggy Dirks were making a name for themselves as a human trafficking enterprise. Although the CIA had a file on them, they had decided there were more immediate threats that got a higher priority.

That changed when a busload of American exchange students went missing. The CIA had picked up reliable intel that the Dirks were behind it. The problem was, the Dirks had gone dark. CIA assets hadn't seen or heard from them and, in spite of mounting pressure, the CIA was coming up empty on what happened to the kids.

There is truth to the saying "The enemy of my enemy is my friend"; the CIA didn't think twice when the Bulgarian arms smuggler called Cherna Reka (Black River), reached out with information about the Dirks.

The Maggy Dirks had ambitions outside of human trafficking and once they had accumulated enough financial backing, they decided it was time to branch out into other profitable areas; specifically, arms smuggling. The Black River ran a small operation and was the perfect small-time organization for the Dirks to practice their hand at taking over.

Ironically, the Black River didn't have the firepower to stop the Dirks. They needed an ally. When they heard that the CIA was looking for the exchange students, the Bulgarians were only too happy to help.

The Black River were undermanned, but what they lacked in numbers they made up for in eagerness to see the Dirks wiped out. The problem was the Maggy Dirks were based somewhere in Scotland; a place as foreign to them as the moon. Yet, where there's a will...

Sending two of their best enforcers, the Black River kidnapped and tortured their way to someone high enough in the Maggy Dirks to put a finger on the map where they could find the American students and head of the organization.

Working with criminals was the CIA's stock in trade. When it came time to hashing out the details of their deal, the Bulgarians came to the negotiating table with their intel and an unrealistic expectation of what they could get for it. The CIA came to the table with a small checkbook and a big ego.

Under pressure to get the American kids back, the CIA was impatient to execute the operation and gave the Bulgarians some generous concessions. But the Black River wanted more. They knew America had deep pockets and heavy influence, even in Bulgaria. They raised the price of their finder's fee and dug in their heels. After all, what's a couple more million dollars to one of the richest countries in the world?

The CIA didn't like being extorted and they pushed back. Hard.

To the shock of the Bulgarians, the CIA slashed their offered concessions in half, then told them, in no uncertain terms, that if they didn't take the deal and help them get the Dirks, the CIA would focus their considerable resources, including the skilled men and women of their special forces, on the brief task of wiping the Black River from existence.

With their back to the wall, the Bulgarians had no choice and agreed. But the strong-arm tactics of the CIA would plant seeds of resentment and revenge, and that took root quickly.

A week later, the Night Devils touched down on a small airstrip on the east coast of Scotland. They stepped off the jet into the tail end of a rainstorm and tossed their gear in a rented SUV.

Standing under the wing, they stretched their legs before embarking on the long drive of cramped comfort.

They were scheduled to meet with six members of the Black River the following day. It was unusual for the 'other side' to volunteer their own people for a strike, but the Night Devils didn't mind as long as the rookies didn't get in the way.

They came off the M8 motorway into Calton, looking for a hot meal and a drink. The low, grey sky cast a murky light as they drove by terraced concrete apartment buildings and brick rowhouses.

They were operating in the country with limited and unofficial permission from the Scottish government. Other than a select few, nobody else knew who they were or their operation.

There was no intel to suggest the local police were on the Maggy

Dirks' payroll, but the Night Devils decided against the risk of letting the cops know they were in town.

Like other cities they'd been to in the world, there was always a rough area where the police avoided. As they drove into the dark pocket of Calton, they recognized it was one of those places. That suited the Night Devils just fine.

The SUV splashed over the cracked stone as they pulled into the narrow parking lot next to the Piper Fox Pub.

The regulars, who considered the pub their second home, watched the strangers with resentment and distrust.

Jack Tate and his team ignored them and found a table away from the television that was blaring a rugby game.

Sergeant First Class Robby Fin shifted on the cracked, vinyl seat, feeling every lump.

"It's only fair to tell you," he said to Tiller, "if you want to win my affections, you better start taking me to classier places."

Sergeant Donnan Keith chuckled, tucking his gloves into his jacket.

"I told you he was only interested in your money," he said, winking a green eye.

"Then he's in for a lot of disappointment," said Tiller.

The team's sniper, Sergeant Charlie Woodman, had his nose buried in the menu and wasn't listening.

"Anyone else hungry?" he asked.

"Yeah," said Sergeant Willie Carson. "What do they have?"

"The real question is," said Fin, "what do they have that won't kill you?"

A pretty girl behind the bar saw Woodman glance at her and took the cue to come over to their table.

"Hi," he said, giving her his best smile. "Who are you?"

"Allie," she said, unimpressed. She rattled off something that sounded like a question, and they looked at each other, baffled.

"What did you say?" asked Carson.

"Ah, Americans," she said. "Ya not been in here much, have ya?"

"Does it show?" asked Fin.

"A wee bit," she said. "What do you want to order?"

"What's good?" asked Tiller.

"If ya want good, ya shouldn't a come here," she smirked. "I'll get ya some pies and a pint."

"Like cherry?" said Carson.

"Meat," said Allie slowly, like she was explaining something to an idiot.

"Sounds great," said Woodman, eager to hurry up the order.

"I'll have a coffee," said Tiller.

Allie nodded and headed off, leaving the team to talk over tomorrow's operation.

"Who's volunteering to babysit the Bulgarians?" asked Tiller.

Everyone sighed, looking anywhere but at him.

"Okay," he said, "Woodman and Keith. Thanks for volunteering."

"Aw, come on, man," said Woodman. "Why not Fin?"

"Hey," objected Fin. "Don't drag me into this. Clearly, the boss has bigger plans for me."

"The objective is in a tunnel, under a church," said Tiller. "Not exactly the optimum environment for a sniper."

"It could be if you gave me a chance," said Woodman.

"I don't like them tagging along," said Carson. "We're in a tunnel with a bunch of nervous gangsters on our six. If we start taking fire, those goons will start shooting without worrying who's in the crossfire."

"And that's why Woodman and Keith are watching them," said Tiller.

"I'm with him on this one," said Keith. "Why are the Bulgarians even here?"

"They lost people to the Dirks," said Tate. "They're looking for their pound of flesh."

"Even worse," said Carson. "The Bulgarians are hungry for revenge. They'll pump rounds into every Dirk they see. There won't be anyone left alive to interrogate."

"All right, everyone take it down a notch," said Tiller. He looked at Woodman and Keith. "What's your operational role tomorrow?"

"Don't let the Bulgarians shoot us in the back," said Woodman.

"And?" prompted Tiller.

"Don't let them shoot the prisoners," said Keith.

"There you go," said Tiller, looking satisfied. "Everyone's happy."

Keith raised his hand, but Tiller cut him off.

"I said everyone is happy," he said, stressing that his decision was made.

Allie appeared a few minutes later with their meat pies and drinks. Woodman wasted no time digging in, but the others picked at their food with healthy skepticism.

"I distinctly remember my recruiter telling me this job would take me to exotic places," said Fin, frowning at his plate. "Full of adventure."

"You have a plate full of adventure right there," grinned Tiller.

Woodman looked at his teammates in confusion.

"Generations of Scottish people have lived on this," he said. "This is what real, unprocessed food looks like, man. All those big meat companies back home use a whole bank of chemicals you don't even know you're eating."

"Here it comes," said Fin.

"They're messing with our DNA," said Woodman, undaunted.

"Which 'they' is it this time?" asked Carson.

"That's just it," said Woodman, growing excited. "They all got a finger in the pie."

They sipped their drinks, letting Woodman run out of steam before paying their bill and leaving.

Stepping outside, they breathed in the damp, fresh air, happy to leave the noise and dark stares of the pub behind.

They turned the corner into the parking lot and saw a guy in a dark hoodie trying to jimmy open the door of their SUV.

"Hey, dipstick," called Fin. "You're going to cost me the rental deposit."

The man spun around, a switchblade instantly appearing in his hand.

"Back off, or I'll stick ya," said the thief. His pale face was drawn and his eyes nervously flicked from one man to the next.

"What's happened to the world?" said Keith.

"I blame the educational system," said Fin.

"Ya call'n me an eejit?" said the thief, pointing the knife.

"I don't know what that is," said Fin, "but I'm going out on a limb and saying yes."

The thief flushed red and took a step at them but abruptly stopped in his tracks when the team drew their pistols.

Looking into the barrel of five guns took the wind out of the thief's sails.

"Get out of here," said Woodman.

"And leave the knife, dirtbag," said Carson.

The thief bent down and put the knife on the ground.

"Hang on," said Fin. "How do you expect the guy to make a living without the tools of the trade? It's okay. You can keep the knife."

Bewildered, the thief cautiously picked up the knife.

"Leave it," commanded Tiller.

The thief hesitated a moment, wondering if anyone else would tell him what to do, then dropped the knife.

They put their guns away as they brushed past the thief without giving him a second look. Woodman picked up the knife and put it in his pocket as the others climbed in.

Once they were inside, the thief's courage returned and he started swearing at them.

"Try'n fight me one on one," he yelled. "See if I don't kick ya head in."

They pulled out of the parking lot with the thief still waving his hands and shouting.

The following night, the team's SUV idled on a darkened street, while four of the five men enjoyed the last moments of warmth from the heater.

They were about to meet with the Bulgarians, who would take them to the old Setton Gate and the tunnel entrance.

"Toaster, this is Razorback. You copy?" asked Tiller. The use of their call signs removed any doubt they were now in mission mode.

Woodman watched six human-shaped thermal images through

his sniper scope and keyed his radio. "This is Toaster. Good copy, Razorback. I bet that heater's feeling pretty good."

"I'd be lying if I said it wasn't," smiled Tiller.

He knew Toaster must be pretty cold after being perched on his vantage point for the last half hour. The Night Devils had left their hotel early and stopped a short way from their meeting location to observe the members of Black River before meeting up with them.

They didn't expect the Bulgarians were up to trouble, but it was good practice to check out strangers.

"Anything to report?" asked Razorback.

"Six adult males," said Toaster. He panned his scope for any other heat signatures but saw nothing. "Everyone's in the open. They're just waiting on us."

"Copy that," said Razorback. "We're on our way to pick you up. Razorback, out."

A few minutes later, Toaster was in the car, gratefully warming his hands as they drove to the meeting.

Streetlights ended where the road changed from asphalt to dirt as they passed through the open chain-link gate and into the housing development site.

Darkness surrounded them as they drove by unfinished houses, their windowless frames like hollow eye sockets watching them drive by before they turned down a side street.

At the end of the road were the headlights of a single car with figures milling nearby.

"Remember," said Razorback, "we're all friends here."

"Because I always pal around with arms dealers," scoffed Fin.

"Then this won't be any different, Huck," grinned Razorback. "

Red Man and Mojo," he said, nodding to Keith and Carson. "You two act as our wide ends. I don't want any of these guys wandering around our flanks."

They gestured their understanding as the SUV came to a stop and the team casually got out.

The Bulgarians' gaze fell to the holstered pistols on the Night Devil's hips, but they seemed unconcerned by the Americans.

Razorback walked forward to indicate he was the leader. One of the Black River men squinted at him as he took a last drag on his cigarette, then flicked it away and walked up.

"Vaska," he said, putting out his hand.

"I'm Razorback," he said, shaking Vaska's hand.

"Strange name," said Vaska, cocking an eyebrow.

"I get that a lot. Are we still on for tonight?"

"Dancho," called Vaska over his shoulder. He asked something in Bulgarian and Dancho replied. "Yes. Dancho's been watching the church. He says they're still there."

He eyed Razorback and his team with a grin.

"Only five of you? Doesn't seem like much."

"Eleven," said Razorback.

"Eleven?"

"Your men and mine," said Razorback. "Unless you're not going in."

Vaska chuckled. "Yes. Eleven."

"We're ready when you are," said Razorback, aware the night wouldn't last forever.

"Yes," said Vaska. "Follow us. The church isn't far."

Everyone got into their cars and the Night Devils followed the Bulgarians out of the construction site.

"That wasn't weird at all," said Huck.

"Maybe he skipped math in school," said Mojo.

They drove the rest of the way in silence until the lights of East Kilbride fell into the distance behind them.

Vaska's car turned off its lights and pulled to the side of the road next to a stone and wrought iron fence.

Mojo stopped the SUV behind them.

Vaska walked over to Razorback as the Night Devils geared up.

"We walk from here," said Vaska, looking at the team with interest as they put on their body armor.

"The road goes to the top of the hill," he said, pointing towards the broken iron gate. "The tunnel entrance is in the graveyard, behind the church."

Red Man joined them, handing Razorback his ballistic helmet.

"We're set," said Red Man.

"Cowboys," chuckled Vaska, eyeing their helmets.

"It protects my good looks," said Red Man.

"I'd like your men to keep behind us," said Razorback. "But you be up front with me and guide us to the tunnel."

"Sure," said Vaska. "I was going to say the same thing."

The rest of the team had gathered round and Razorback quickly recapped their movement formation.

After staging outside the gate, Razorback gave a short, 'Go,' and they threaded through the broken gate and up the road.

The team kept their suppressed M4's at low-ready in contrast to the Bulgarians, who casually walked, unconcerned about encountering any of the Dirk's lookouts.

As they neared the top of the hill, Mojo kept an eye on the church through his night-vision goggles.

The gothic steeple silently loomed over them as they moved around the weathered sandstone building.

The night sky was masked in clouds and Vaska could only make out the dark silhouettes of headstones in the graveyard but soon identified the crypt that marked the tunnel entrance.

"Here it is," he said, drawing a SIG Sauer pistol.

"We'll take the front from here," said Razorback, half expecting Vaska to object out of pride.

"No problem," said Vaska, and left to join his men.

The entrance was barred by an iron gate secured with a lock and chain.

"Cutters," said Razorback into his mic.

Mojo came up and pulled a small pair of bolt cutters from his pack and made quick work of the chain.

Razorback eased the gate open to reduce noise from the rusted hinges. It wasn't soundless, but it was better than nothing.

Past the gate, a set of worn stone stairs descended down a claustrophobic, narrow hall, heading deep below.

Using his night vision, Razorback crept with his assault rifle up and ready.

He reached the bottom of the stairs and the tunnel thankfully widened to allow them to move two abreast.

Huck moved up next to Razorback, who motioned to move forward.

They passed side tunnels, but they were either closed off by iron gates or collapsed rubble from a cave in.

Razorback hadn't considered that possibility as he glanced at the stone ceiling inches above his head. If the ceiling gave in, they'd never get out.

Not helpful.

He shook the thought from his mind and refocused on the here and now.

Ahead, he could see the wall of the tunnel was lit where it turned a blind corner.

He eased up and stopped at the corner, listening as he flipped up his goggles.

He heard voices, but they were faint. He couldn't make out what they were saying and considered they may not be speaking English.

Huck nodded, confirming he heard them too.

Quickly, he peeked around the corner.

"The tunnel runs twenty feet past the corner," he said over the radio. "It opens into a large chamber. I don't see anyone."

Red Man's voice crackled over Razorback's radio.

"Hey, Top. The natives are getting restless."

Red Man and Toaster were at the rear of the team, with the Bulgarians behind them.

"What's up?" said Razorback.

"There's a lot of whispering going on," said Red Man in a low voice. "I don't know what they're saying, but it's making my spider-sense tingle."

"Toaster?" said Razorback.

"Yeah. Same here. I don't know if they're getting excited for a fight, but I'm not digging the way they keep looking at us."

"Copy," said Razorback. He added this new complication to their situation.

They were underground, in a narrow tunnel, with an enemy somewhere ahead and a possible threat behind, blocking their only exit to the surface.

Perfect.

Mojo was crouched at the corner, waiting for the signal to go. Razorback put his hand on his shoulder and gave a quick squeeze.

Looking down the sights of his M4, Mojo went around the corner with Razorback and the rest of the team following.

The Bulgarians hung back in the tunnel as the team pushed past the unlocked gate and filed into the chamber, alternately moving to the left and right.

Aiming down their gun sites, they swept for hostiles.

The chamber was empty.

Stone pillars reached up, supporting a domed ceiling where two naked bulbs hung, casting long shadows.

Aside from a small vent hole in the ceiling, the only opening was a gated passageway on the opposite side of the chamber. A quick glance showed the other gate was locked.

"This doesn't feel right," said Mojo.

Razorback agreed.

"Everyone out of the cha— ," he started.

"They're locking us in," shouted Red Man.

The Bulgarians, still in the tunnel, yanked the chamber gate closed.

His back against the wall, Toaster grabbed for the gate, but instantly pulled back his hand as gunfire erupted and bullets sparked off the ancient iron.

A moment later, they heard the snick of the lock, sealing the team inside the chamber.

"Huck. Mojo," snapped Razorback. "Cover the other gate."

The two men trained their M4's on the opposite gate, ready to shoot.

"What's going on, Vaska?" called Razorback.

"Ask your CIA," he shouted, his voice echoing from the dark tunnel. "We offered them a chance to rescue the American students for a fair price and they threatened to beat us, like mongrels!"

"It's nothing personal," said Razorback. "They're jerks to everyone. I have money. I can pay you if you open the gate."

"Sure," chuckled Vaska. "Put your guns down and step out where we can see you."

"What are we doing, Top?" asked Huck anxiously.

"Toaster," whispered Razorback into his mic. "On my go, toss a flash-bang through the gate. Red Man and I will smoke these morons."

The two men confirmed and Toaster took a stun grenade out of his vest.

"You guys smell gas?" asked Mojo.

The moment he said it, the others detected the unmistakable scent of gasoline.

Something flickered as it fell from the vent hole in the ceiling. Glass shattered, followed by a blazing roar as a Molotov cocktail exploded from the center of the chamber.

Fingers of flaming gas splashed in all directions and the team backed themselves against the wall, out of reach of the fire.

"Have a warm welcome from the Maggy Dirks, mate," yelled someone from the hole in the ceiling.

"Crap," said Mojo, feeing the flash of heat wash over him.

"Looks like the Bulgarians made a new deal with the Dirks," said Huck.

"What was your first clue?" said Red Man.

"Still a wee bit cold down there?" yelled the voice from above.

Another flaming bottle fell down the hole and burst into a firestorm on the chamber floor.

Razorback risked a peek around the corner of the wall to see if Vaska and his men were still there.

He pulled back, swearing, as bullets ripped past his head.

The pool of burning gas was growing but still short of reaching the team. That changed when another bottle dropped, sending up a tower of flame. Tendrils of flaming liquid snaked out in all directions and the team could feel the intense heat pressing through their clothes.

"The next one's gonna cook us," said Mojo, fear rising in his voice.

Their breaths came in shallow gasps as the hot air scorched their mouths and nostrils.

"Toaster," snapped Razorback. "On my word, suppressive fire on the Bulgarians."

"Copy," said Toaster.

Less than a second later, they saw a glint of light fall from the ceiling.

"Now," barked Razorback and sprang from the wall.

Toaster angled his rifle around the corner and blindly snapped off shots into the tunnel.

The others gaped in disbelief as Razorback charged into the fire and jumped, grasping for the falling Molotov.

His fingers bumped the bottle and it tumbled past him. With a wild grab, he reached out and caught the bottle before it hit the ground.

Razorback hit the ground, the melted sole of his boots nearly slipping out from under him. Without breaking stride, he flung the bottle at the Bulgarians as Toaster jumped out of the way.

The firebomb smashed against the iron gate, splashing into the tunnel with liquid hell.

"Cut that lock," shouted Razorback, as screams of pain and panic echoed out of the tunnel.

Mojo whipped the bolt cutters out of his pack and bit through the lock. The team instantly moved into the tunnel, shooting anything that moved. Advancing quickly over flaming bodies, they were soon past the fire and into the tunnel.

Refreshing cold air washed over their sweat-streaked faces as they retraced their steps. A new sensation took hold as Razorback felt the sting of his burned legs building in pain. Anger seethed in his gut, driving him to finish the job before the agony overwhelmed him.

He only got a few more steps before his knees buckled and he slumped against the wall with a moan.

"Hold him up," said Huck, as he knelt next to their leader.

Firm hands braced him and Huck deftly cut away the scorched pant legs.

"Don't let them get away," said Razorback through gritted teeth.

"Shut up," said Mojo. "They're not going to leave until they know we're dead."

Huck opened his med kit and took out a small can of burn spray and deftly coated his legs.

"You smell like a cookout," said Red Man, getting a chuckle from Razorback.

The fog of pain cleared from his head as the burn spray did its work.

"You'll live," said Huck, putting away his kit. "But you don't have to worry about shaving your legs for a while."

They let go of him and Razorback tested his legs.

Good enough.

They moved on until they came to the stone steps leading to the surface. They saw a shadowy head disappear from the opening above.

"I told you they'd be waiting," said Mojo.

The narrow stairway was the textbook example of a fatal funnel; a deadly choke point with no cover.

"There's no pretty way to do this," said Razorback. "We go up those stairs one at a time and they'll pick us off."

"We go together," said Huck, "and they toss a Molotov..."

They all got the picture.

The team had been through more combat than anyone wanted to think about. It had forged the individuals into a whole. It only took a moment before they all came to the same decision.

"Together," said Mojo, the others nodding in agreement.

"Give me your flash-bangs," said Razorback. "It's open terrain up there," he said, shoving the grenades into his vest. "The crypt is the only cover they have. That's where they'll be clustered."

"Why not frag'em?" asked Toaster angrily.

"We need someone to tell us where the exchange students are," said Razorback. Toaster nodded, clearly disappointed. "Then we'll frag them."

Everyone chuckled, breaking the tension.

"Everyone got their heads on straight?" said Razorback. "Let's go."

They moved up the stairs, confined to single file, Toaster trying to cover the opening over Razorback's shoulder, who was leading the way.

They stopped short of the exit, Razorback setting the flash-bangs on the stair in front of him.

"Throwing flash-bang," he said, and pulled the pin on the first one.

"Party time," said Red Man.

The first grenade had barely left his hand when he was pulling the pin on the second, quickly followed by the third.

The night flashed with a deafening crack of blinding light and the Night Devils flowed out of the exit and fanned out.

Several people were hunched around the crypt, disorientated and holding their ears.

The Night Devils moved in, roughly shoving them to the ground. In seconds they had the Dirks and Black River flex cuffed.

Vaska and one of his men were the only two who made it out of the tunnel. He swore at the team until Red Man stuffed a rag in his mouth.

The Maggy Dirk prisoners sat against the crypt, some with cocky smiles and others with open hate; they stared at the Delta Force standing over them.

Mojo and Huck collected their ID and took photos of each of them.

"Where's the American students?" asked Razorback.

"Nice legs," smirked one of the Dirks.

The other prisoners chuckled, but Razorback was unphased.

Ignoring the pain, he crouched in front of the joker.

"Right now," he said, gesturing to Huck, "that man is running your faces through our system. In a few minutes I'll know more about you than your mother."

Razorback looked at his watch and glanced at the horizon. "Before the sun comes up, I'm going to make everyone you know disappear into a black hole. Your wives, girlfriends, kids, gone. Like they ever existed. I'll even take your dog."

"He's blow'n smoke up yer arses, lads," said another Dirk, trying to calm the fear rippling through the prisoners. "He's got no authority in Scotland."

Razorback leaned in, locking eyes with the man.

"Why do I need authority?" he said. "I was never here, and in a few minutes, you won't be either."

He stood up and watched their faces as his words sunk in. The Dirks were shifting nervously and Razorback could see this coming to a head.

"They're in the church basement," blurted one of them.

"Shut ya gob, Danny," snapped the cocky Dirk.

"Toaster and Huck," said Razorback. "Check it out."

The two men nodded and left at a jog.

A few minutes later, Razorback's radio crackled in his ear.

"We got them," said Toaster. "They're all here and can walk."

"Copy. Bring them here and we'll exfil."

"What about these guys?" asked Mojo, nodding to the prisoners.

"We'll call the local newspaper on the way out," said Razorback. "By the time the cops get here, these guys'll be all over the morning edition. If the cops are dirty, they won't be able to cover this up."

14

DEATH TRAIN

The team's energy lifted as their SUV rolled smoothly up to the entrance of their hotel.

"I'm starving," said Rosse. "I'm gonna get me one of those big bowls of noodle soup for dinner."

"Udon?" said Wesson, please to be picking up on the local language.

"Yeah, that," he said.

It was dusk and everyone was tired and hungry. The planning session had taken twice as long as it should have because of Satori's grandstanding, but Tate was determined not to leave the table until he had gotten everything he wanted.

Part of his stubbornness was for the safety of Mullen. The other was because his team was watching.

Before the meeting, Tate didn't think ahead about his team's dynamics as spectators and what it would do to their opinions of him if he got pushed around by Satori.

Tate believed a leader should show his team he wasn't perfect. But it was important to be selective about which imperfections were revealed. The right one created a stronger bond between a leader and their team. The wrong one could create distrust and loss of respect.

Neither of those things happened today.

"I'm dying for a pizza," said Fulton.

"I'll second that," said Wesson. "They don't put seafood on pizza."

"We do, Wesson-san," smiled Kiku.

Tate took out his sat phone and dialed Mullen.

The phone didn't finish the first ring before Mullen picked up.

"Yes?"

"This is.."

"I know who it is," said Mullen. "Is the meeting set up or not?"

Tate rolled his eyes and took a breath before speaking.

"Everything's been arranged," he said. "We'll pick you up tomorrow."

"That's good news," said Mullen, sounding calmer. "Nice work."

"I'm sending the details now..."

Mullen hung up.

Levi smiled, hearing Mullen hang up on Tate.

It's a thankless job.

He switched the sat phone back to 'monitor'.

Levi credited unlocking the sat phone's secure frequency to luck and fast thinking when Tate had crashed his team at the library.

Now anytime Tate made or received a call, Levi was listening in.

He punched a number into his phone and waited for the answer.

"Haruki," he said, "Get the team together. We're on for tomorrow."

Levi walked down the narrow street alive with sounds, smells and light.

He passed a long line of trendy kids, laughing and smoking under three-foot-tall letters pulsing with light in sync to the music pumping from the doors of the dance club.

He turned the corner where the lights were more practical than spectacular. Two glowing vending machines bordered a narrow alley, hardly more than a gap that led behind the club.

Levi picked his way around puddles of oily water and empty cans into the darkness of the alley where the light didn't reach. He stopped at a grey-streaked metal door and swiped a card over the security sensor, hearing the lock click.

The door cracked open and he went inside, into a hallway splattered with ugly colors and ripped posters. He smirked over how hard people tried to appear edgy. He stopped at the third door in the hallway and went in.

Five strongly built men watched as Levi entered and walked over to the table covered with assault rifles and pistols.

"Do you have what we need?" asked one of the men, joining him at the table.

"That's why I called you, Haruki," said Levi. "Give me the table."

Haruki turned to the other men and snapped something in Japanese. They quickly cleared away the weapons and watched Levi as he took out his sat phone and a small black cube. He set them on the table, connecting the phone to the cube.

The table's surface flickered with light until forms took shape into an identical copy of the holographic map used by Tate and Satori.

The men gathered around the table, dwarfing Levi, as they examined the map. Cowboy was the last to join them at the table.

"Our target is meeting here," said Levi, pointing to the same room identified earlier that day.

"Who's team is this?" asked Haruki, pointing to the blue icons.

"That's Satori's team," he said. "The green markers are security for our high value target."

"You told us the security would be light," scoffed one of the men.

"It will be," said Levi. "Satori's men don't care about our HVT. They'll clear out with Tanaka the first sign of trouble. That just leaves Tate's team. He's got his people split between the principal security unit," he said, pointing to their assigned locations, "and exterior overwatch."

Cowboy said something in Japanese, his black leather coat creaking as he angrily pointed to the green icons.

"Be quiet, Cowboy," snapped Haruki. "This is not your operation."

Levi looked at the Cowboy who stared down his nose at him.

"Come on," said Levi. "You're a big boy. If you have something to say, say it to me."

Cowboy's eyes flicked to Haruki.

"Don't hide behind him," said Levi.

Cowboy flushed and he swore under his breath.

"It's a foolish plan," he said. "You tie our hands by forbidding us to use our guns."

"I can't believe I'm having to spell this out for you," said Levi with a weary sigh. "We're using suppressive fire because I don't want our HVT hit by friendly fire. Tate believes the meeting is low threat and won't be armed. Do you get it now, or should I use hand puppets?"

"And when they see that we are afraid to harm them, they will tell others we are weak," said Cowboy. "More gaijin will come. Maybe stay and bring more Vix. They'll pollute our cities with their stupid white faces. No! We kill the entire team. Leave their bloody bodies as a message to..."

"Enough," barked Levi, his brown eyes burning with cold fire. Cowboy's mouth hung slack before he snapped it shut. "I'm paying you to do a job. It's my operation. My rules. I thought I hired a professional, but all I see is a whiny old woman, beating her chest about Japanese superiority."

Cowboy shook with rage, clenching his jaw. He glanced at the other men around the table for support, but nobody would look at him.

"If you lack self-discipline and courage, get out," said Levi. "Otherwise shut up and follow orders."

The air was brittle with tension as the two men faced off. Levi felt the weight of his pistol, tucked under his shirt. He didn't want the situation to go that way, but he wouldn't hesitate to blow the back of Cowboy's head all over the wall.

Cowboy's gaze moved over Levi's small frame, judging his opening strike, but then he returned to the man's eyes. They were calm, even amused. Cowboy's anger was quenched with a shiver. Levi was looking at him like he was already dead and he believed it.

"I apologize, Levi-san," said Cowboy, bowing low. "I was wrong to let my personal opinions cloud my judgment. I will serve according to your expectations."

"I accept," said Levi formally. "Our team will be better with you on it."

Levi knew the value of letting a man save face and hoped it would buy him a little more of Cowboy's respect.

Judging the customary amount of time had passed, Haruki broke the silence.

"Levi-san," he said. "Where will you be positioned?"

Levi turned back to the table and pointed to his assigned location.

"We'll strike after the meeting is over," he said. "Do you have the override device?"

"Yes," said Haruki, reaching into his coat pocket. He handed him what appeared to be a cell phone and pointed to a button. "Yamutsu will put this in the follow car. It will override the car's onboard systems and send them miles in the wrong direction."

"Our timing becomes critical when their meeting ends," said Levi. "Tate's team will escort our HVT to the lead car in the underground garage, here." He pointed to the map. "They'll follow standard security protocols and load the HVT then wait until the follow car is on the way. When the lead car leaves the garage, Kenji, you jam their comms."

Kenji gave him a curt nod.

"As soon as that happens," said Levi, "Yamutsu activates the override for the follow car and we split the team's effectiveness in half. From there, we disable the lead car... use suppressive fire to keep the security team pinned down. Grab the HVT and exfil. We'll split into two different directions to add to their confusion."

Levi glanced at Cowboy, searching for any hint of resistance, but everything about him reflected a calm, dispassionate professional. Satisfied, Levi wrapped up the final details with Haruki.

Behind Cowboy's mask of indifference was a mind rapidly developing his own plan.

After Levi left in the car with the HVT, there wouldn't be anyone to stop him from killing every one of the foreign security team. He knew Mitsuo and Ryoichi shared his hate of gaijin. They wouldn't interfere. And if they tried, he'd kill them too.

Tate and the team were up before the sun and burning off pre-mission adrenaline in the hotel gym.

They were scheduled to pick up Mullen in four hours and it would be the first time he'd come out of his safe house.

Tate had only spoken to him once, but he pegged him as the high-strung type. He couldn't blame him. After today's meeting, they were going to deliver him into the warm embrace of the CIA, effectively knifing The Ring in the back and making himself a dangerous enemy.

Mullen had been sitting on his secret plan for weeks and the closer he got to the finish line, the more his fear ratcheted up.

Hanging over his head was the dread that The Ring would find out. If they did, he knew they'd make a horrifying example out of him; a warning to anyone with wavering loyalty that this was the price you paid for betrayal.

Tate decided he needed a break before getting on the stair-master. He hated that thing almost as much as it hated him. Wesson was on the treadmill, running at a pace that he was sure would make his heart explode.

He grinned, remembering the punch line from a joke; I don't have to outrun the Vix, I just have to outrun you.

He got up with a sigh and headed to the stair-master.

You're not going to get any faster sitting on your butt.

Yaki waited on the Tokyo train station platform, reading and rereading the message on the small square of paper.

An enlightened death saves all.

He smiled, taking a deep breath, feeling the weight of the world slip off his shoulders.

Yaki looked at the people around, not caring if they saw him staring; all of them dressed in business suits, each of them tiny cogs in a soulless machine. They couldn't feel what he felt. He was more alive than any of them and the thought made him giggle.

He caught himself and looked down, embarrassed. His gaze met a small girl peering up at him behind a scarf wrapped around her face. Her shiny eyes smiled at him and he smiled back. He felt warm inside. He was going to save her from the fate that had already imprisoned everyone around them.

The young girl grunted, shifting the weight of her bright yellow school bag to a more comfortable place on her small shoulders.

"They make you carry a lot, don't they?" asked Yaki.

"Yes," she said. "It hurts, but momma says it's good practice. I will need strong shoulders when I grow up."

"What if I told you," said Yaki, "you'll never have to carry those heavy books again?"

The little girl happily nodded.

The girl's mother gave her arm a tug of disapproval.

"Don't talk to strangers," she said.

The little girl obediently looked away, but Yaki didn't mind.

The child had been sent to him as a symbol, a beacon to prove he had chosen the right path.

The SUV pulled out of traffic and rolled up to the designated spot where they'd pick up Mullen.

Tate easily picked out the short, heavy man from the busy foot traffic as he fidgeted with his tie, looking at every passerby, expecting one of them to scream 'traitor' and butcher him with their sword.

"Mr. Mullen," said Tate evenly. "I'm Tate. Please follow me."

Mullen took a pull from his coffee cup, flexed his grip on his briefcase and brushed past Tate to the waiting SUV.

He opened the front passenger door to the surprise of Monkhouse, who was riding shotgun.

"Sir," said Tate, catching up. "You'll be in the back seat."

"I get car sick," said Mullen.

Monkhouse looked at Tate for direction.

"Come on," said Mullen. "Out."

Tate shrugged and gestured for Monkhouse to relinquish his seat.

Monkhouse waited for Mullen to get inside before closing the door behind him.

"A real people person," said Monkhouse, before opening the back door.

Tate kept his poker face but nodded, then went around the front of the car and got in the driver's seat.

"These people," he said, motioning to the rest of the team, "are your security team. To ensure your safety, please follow any instructions they may have for you."

"Take it down a notch, Rambo," said Mullen. "It's just a business meeting. Nobody's interested in what I'm doing. Even I'm bored with the whole thing." He took a drink of his coffee and Tate doubted the man's hands were shaking because of the caffeine.

"All right," he said. He gave the car the address for the meeting with Tanaka and the SUV pulled out into traffic.

"We are approaching Kasuga station," announced the polite female voice over the train's speakers.

Yaki glanced up with anticipation at the map display of the rail line. This was the last stop before his destination.

He held on to the overhead support as the train slowed to a stop. Chimes rang and the doors opened with a hum. People met in a jostled knot as those getting off the train worked past others trying to get on.

Yaki felt sad for the commuters who were leaving, missing the opportunity to end their misery.

A flash of yellow caught his eye and he saw the little girl was still in the same car as him.

He waved at her and she smiled back before the fresh throng of people filled the car between them.

Happiness swelled in his chest. He accepted that he couldn't help everyone know the peace he was about to find, but at least he would help the little girl.

His hand drifted towards his sword, but he stopped himself before anyone noticed. He didn't need to worry about it jamming in the scabbard. After practicing last night, he knew it would draw like silk.

He put his hand in his coat pocket and felt the cool metal of the gas grenade. He flicked the ring-pull, enjoying the sound of it tinkling.

"Next stop, Suidōbashi station," chimed the automated voice.

Almost there.

"Hey, car," said Mullen. "Take me to someplace that has good coffee."

"Motosashi's Coffee House has good coffee and it's on your way," said the car. "It's a favorite of commuters using the Suidōbashi station. Would you like to go there?"

"Mr. Mullen," said Tate, keeping the irritation out of his voice. "You should avoid any unnecessary exposure. It's a risk to your safety."

"This," said Mullen, tapping his coffee cup, "is empty. Me not having coffee is a risk to my safety."

"Sir," began Tate.

"Let's get something straight," said Mullen, flushing pink. "The whole reason you have a job is because of me. You and this entire clown car would be swapping stories about your glory days in a sweaty merc bar if it weren't for me. So, chill out while the grown-ups do their thing. Anything else?"

Tate folded his hands just in case one of them decided to slap Mullen around and looked out the windshield.

"No, sir," he said.

"Take us to Motosashi's," said Mullen, staring at the side of Tate's head.

. . .

The clock over Yaki's head showed they would arrive at the station in a few minutes.

It was time.

He closed his eyes and muttered a short prayer as he gripped the gas grenade.

He breathed deeply, feeling peaceful as he finished his prayer and took the grenade out of his pocket, then pulled the safety ring. He dropped it on the floor and dense white smoke began jetting out. It was louder than he had imagined.

For a moment it seemed like nobody but Yaki could see the smoke quickly building up around everyone's feet. Doubt and worry gripped him as he wondered if this entire train ride was another of his hallucinations. He feared that at any moment his eyes would clear and he'd be back in his living room.

A cry of panic echoed through the train car and Yaki smiled.

It's all real.

Chaos broke out, people crashing into each other, blindly pushing to get away from the gas.

He took a deep breath, feeling thankful that the Keeper of the Sacred Gate had chosen him.

The rising gas stung Yaki's eyes, but he kept them open. He didn't want to miss any of it.

At first the commuters only coughed, but as the smoke-filled the car, they gagged.

Desperate for air, they ripped off their masks, just like the Keeper told Yaki they would.

He grabbed his sword, but several panic-stricken people fell against him, pinning him in place. He struggled against them but couldn't move. For a horrible moment he feared his plan was going to fall apart, but then they were gone, lost somewhere in the billowing gas. He was free.

In one fluid motion, he drew his short sword and plunged it into his abdomen. The sword was so sharp there was only a hint of pain, but he knew it was coming. He had to keep going before the pain kept him from his final reward.

With a terrific yank, he pulled the sword across his belly. Something warm and wet fell on his shoes, but all he felt was searing pain exploding through his body.

He stopped feeling the pain as shock and massive blood loss washed over him. He crumpled to the floor, shrouded in the gas among the thrashing panic of the commuters.

Arms outstretched, a businessman groped for the emergency switch and tripped over Yaki's body.

The man fell hard, gagging on the gas and blinked through his tearing eyes, seeing Yaki's pale face.

"Get up," croaked the businessman. "You'll be trampled down here."

When Yaki didn't answer, he moved closer to examine his face.

"Hey, wake up!"

Yaki's eyes flicked open. They roamed for only a second before fixing on the man in front of him.

His lips curled back as he snarled and grabbed the man with inhuman strength.

The choking gas did nothing to stop the man's guttural scream of raw terror before Yaki ripped out his throat.

Now there were two.

By the time they reached Suidōbashi station, the train would be a writhing chamber of undead.

The commuters waited on the station platform with bored impatience as the train pulled in. Confusion swept through them as they puzzled over the swirling opaque cloud behind the train car's windows.

The chime rang and the doors slid open.

Billows of gas spilled out, spreading over the feet of the people closest to the train. They backed away in alarm, trying to get away from it, bumping into the people behind them.

A mangled face appeared out of the train car and someone screamed. Another face appeared, hissing and sputtering, then another and another.

Suddenly, Vix surged out of the train car, crashing on the commuters like a tidal wave.

Primal fear gripped the crowd and they ran in blind panic. People charged off the other side of the platform into the path of an oncoming train.

The platform turned into a seething pile of savage carnage that boiled up the stairs to the city above.

It was cold in the Suidōbashi station's security office. Mitsuru had complained about the broken heater to his boss, who cared more about the annual budget than the guard's comfort.

Mitsuru came back to his desk and sat down with a hot cup of tea and a steamed bun. He breathed in the aroma of the tea and blew to cool it off as he glanced at the platform monitors.

He didn't feel the scalding tea splash on his legs when he dropped the cup as his chest squeezed the air out of his lungs.

Transfixed, he watched a little girl with a yellow school bag viciously rip off a woman's arm. Blood sprayed, coating the little girl's face as she sunk her teeth into the meat.

The guard snapped out of the trance and jumped to his feet. He yanked open the protective switch cover and slammed his hand on the red containment button.

The station filled with blaring alarms and flashing hazard lights.

Steel shutters rolled down, sealing off the exits to the streets above, but it was too little, too late.

15

THE BELL TOLLS

"No foam. Understand?" said Mullen. "I'm not paying for half a cup of air."

The barista smiled, nodding several times politely.

"She doesn't know a word I'm saying," said Mullen.

"If she spits in his coffee more than three times," smirked Rosse to Fulton, "she understood him just fine."

Wesson was outside the coffee shop, watching the passersby and marveling how the city had thrived after the outbreak.

She'd imagined a near total destruction of the planet, but if Japan could bounce back then maybe...

Commotion across the street caught her attention. A crowd of people around the subway entrance started shouting, confused then anxious.

Wesson heard an alarm.

"Top, something's happening out here," she said into her mic. "I think we should leave right now."

"Copy," said Tate. "Bring the car."

Wesson took off to the parking lot, next to the coffee shop, at a fast walk, trying not to draw attention. She didn't have anything to worry about; everyone was looking at the station entrance.

Hearing the exchange between Wesson and Tate, the rest of the team went into action as Tate moved next to Mullen.

"We have to leave," said Tate, taking Mullen by the arm.

"Hey," he protested. "Let go of me."

Rosse appeared and took Mullen by the other arm; the two men practically dragged him out of the coffee shop.

The color drained from their faces as a flood of Vix vomited out of the station across the street from them.

No nightmare could ever capture the horror growing in front of them.

"There's so many," muttered Rosse, feeling his stomach drop.

Panic shot through the crowds like lightning, scattering them in a mad run. Mullen shuddered in panic and fought to break free from Tate and Rosse. The two men clamped down on his arms like vices.

"Everyone in the car right now," yelled Tate into his mic. "Wesson!"

"There's too many people in the way," she said.

"We go to her," ordered Tate.

A wave of people smashed into them, tearing Mullen from their grasp.

"Help me," he cried.

Tate reached out, catching the man by his coat and pulled him back as Rosse moved in front.

"Stick with me," he said, dropping his shoulders and bulldozing his way through the streams of people.

The SUV instantly appeared as the panicked crowds suddenly disappeared. They knew the terrible meaning of that alarm.

They sprinted for the SUV. The passenger door opened. Monkhouse jumped inside, shouted for them to hurry.

Tate pushed Mullen to the car when a bloody hand clamped down on him with startling force. Before he could react, the Vix yanked him off his feet, pulling him to its jaws.

In a fleeting second, Tate saw the decorative bite mask covering the Vix's mouth and hoped it worked.

Its head reared back for the bite and in a moment of surrealism, he saw a wink of light as the head rolled off the shoulders.

"Get to the car," said Ota, holding his bloody sword and yanking the dead hand from Tate's arm.

Vix were sprinting at them from across the street and any hope Tate felt in escaping was snuffed out like a match.

"Move," snapped Ota.

He reached across and grabbed Tate's sword; to Tate's utter disbelief, Ota walked towards the Vix.

"Come on," shouted someone over the radio, snapping Tate out of his haze; he ran for the car.

Ota began whipping his two swords, arcing in front of his body as the Vix ran at him. He dodged, scything into them. Arms, legs and heads tumbled in a grotesque rain of blood as he moved like smoke around and between the mass of undead.

He grimaced as his arms began to tire and a Vix slipped through his defenses. The thing went for his leg and Ota swept his sword down, taking off both its arms.

Everything that got near the glittering blur of his swords was cut down, leaving a trail of limbs and torsos.

The SUV pulled alongside and with a final stroke, Ota jumped in.

"Thank you," said Tate, as everyone else stared at Ota with awe.

"Here," said Ota, offering Tate his sword.

"You keep it," said Tate, smiling. "That's wasted on me."

"What are we going to do?" asked Wesson, her face drawn with dread.

"Are you kidding?" stuttered Mullen. "We get the hell out of here."

An apocalypse raged outside the windows of the SUV. Vix charged mindlessly in every direction. Bodies carpeted the street, some never moving again and others jerking to their feet in a nightmarish dance as the dead came to life.

Down the street, survivors stood on top of a bus, waving their swords at the growing horde of Vix encircling them. The Vix couldn't climb up, but the people were stranded.

"I'm going to save as many as I can," said Tate. "The rest of you have to decide for yourselves."

The car fell silent as each of the team considered their odds of life and death.

"There's no shame in…" began Tate.

"Where you go, I go, Top," growled Rosse.

"Me, too," said Fulton.

Wesson nodded in agreement, followed by Ota.

Monkhouse looked at the others and pointed at Ota.

"I'm staying next to him," he said.

Tate nodded gravely, silently thanking them. Unbidden images of their deaths flashed through his mind and he breathed deeply, wrestling back control of his thoughts.

"We start by helping those people on the bus," he said.

"What's the plan?" asked Wesson.

Tate smiled at her.

"Car," he said. "Switch to manual control. Everyone, put on your seatbelts."

Wesson gripped the wheel with grim determination.

"You have full control," said the car.

Wesson pushed the accelerator to the floor and the car leaped forward.

A sea of Vix heaved around the bus, snarling and grasping for the survivors on the roof. For the people, they already knew they were going to die. The only choice was between their own sword or the Vix.

A blaring horn pulled their eyes away from the sea of twisted faces below as a black SUV rammed into the Vix like a wrecking ball, flinging bodies into the air and crushing them under its tires.

The SUV shot out of the other side of the horde and hit the brakes. The back end swung around as the screeching tires left a cloud of burning rubber.

"What was that?" gasped Tate, staring out of the shattered windshield.

"I thought that's what you wanted me to do," said Wesson.

"No. Drive around them and use the horn to lead them away from the survivors."

"Oh," she said.

"Never mind," said Tate. "Your idea works too."

"Hang on," said Wesson, stomping the accelerator.

The mangled front end of the SUV did nothing to slow it down as it mowed through the Vix.

Tate reached under his seat and took out his tomahawk.

"Let's clean up the stragglers," he said, getting out of the car.

They made fast work of the remaining Vix and helped the survivors down from the roof.

"Use the bus," said Tate to the least hysterical survivor. "Get away from here."

Several of them hurried inside the bus, but others didn't move.

"We stay," said one in halting English. "Fight."

The others gripped their swords, all voicing their agreement.

Everyone watched as a distant Vix raced down the street and disappeared from view.

"Good luck," said Tate, bowing.

The survivors bowed in return and began finishing off the mangled Vix that were still moving. The team got back in the SUV.

"Where do we go now?" asked Wesson.

"Search and destroy," said Tate.

They'd only gone a couple of blocks when they heard wailing sirens growing louder.

A line of armored personal carriers raced around the corner and flew by them. Some of the vehicles split off and went down other streets.

"See?" said Mullen. "They got this under control. We're only going to be in the way."

"We've kept you alive this long," said Tate. "Do you really want to take your chances without us?"

Mullen slumped into a disgruntled quiet and said nothing more.

"Hey, there's someone waving from that building," said Fulton.

They looked up and saw a woman leaning out of the window of her apartment building, waving a green towel.

Wesson put the car in gear and drove down the street, stopping in front of the building.

"Front is clear," said Tate.

Everyone scanned the area around the car for Vix close enough to be a threat.

They all reported clear and the team got out of the SUV, leaving their worried client inside.

They craned their necks to see the woman, five stories above, who screamed for help.

"How many?" yelled Monkhouse, holding up his phone to translate.

Ota, Tate and Wesson stood watch against incoming Vix, but they were too far to notice the exposed team.

She kept crying for help and Monkhouse couldn't get anything useful from her.

"All right," said Tate. "We go in blind. Ota, watch our six. I'll take point."

The glass doors to the building's lobby were scattered shards on the floor.

An automatic security door had been triggered to protect the building's inhabitants, but the bodies of people who died trying to escape had wedged the door open enough for Vix to get through.

Swords in hand, the team threaded past the door and started up the stairs.

They moved, stressing stealth over speed, straining to hear the slightest noise of Vix.

Rosse looked over the railing, seeing the stairs switch-backed into the gloom below.

"Anyone think about what happens if them Vix come at us from front and back?" asked Rosse.

"Jump," hissed Tate. "Shut up and listen."

They reached the fifth floor and cracked the door open, ears aching to detect the slightest sound.

The door opened up in the middle of a long hallway. Tate could see one end of the hall was clear but would have to stick his head around the door to see the other way.

He wiped the sweat from his face, blaming it on the climb of stairs, but knew it was fear. His arm still ached where the Vix had grabbed him; a reminder of how close he'd come to dying.

He eased around the edge of the door and quietly blew out a sigh of relief at the sight of an empty hallway.

They crept out, taking a moment to figure out which door belonged to the stranded woman.

Hers wasn't the only open door and the idea that Vix could swarm out of any of them at any time cranked up the team's tension several notches.

As they approached the woman's door, they could hear growling under the sound of the television.

They lined up against the wall and Tate motioned that he was going to look inside.

He took a breath and flexed his grip on the tomahawk, then slowly leaned around the door jam.

The Vix was right there and saw him. Tate pulled his head back as the Vix jumped at him with incredible speed. It charged into the hallway, smashing into the opposite wall, black ooze flying from its lips as it jabbered.

It bounded off the wall as Tate swung his axe and caught it in the face with a bone splintering crunch.

The grisly corpse fell to the floor alarmingly loud and Tate ordered everyone into the apartment. They hurried inside and he closed the door behind him.

They heard the woman moaning on the other side of the bedroom door and knocked, telling her she was safe.

"What if she's changed?" said Fulton

They stood back, tensing as the doorknob rattled and opened.

A tear-streaked face peered out, glancing past them for the Vix.

"It's okay," said Wesson, her phone translating for her. "You're safe now. You can come out."

The woman nodded, muttering under her breath and followed them into the living room.

They told her to stay in her apartment, something she readily agreed with.

With a cautious scan of the hallway, the team left and made their way down to the car.

. . .

Just as they were climbing in, an armored car pulled up and several police piled out and drew swords. All of them were dressed in full riot gear and paired off in teams of two.

Behind them, huge trucks carrying portable walls lumbered past them.

"This area is being walled off," shouted a cop. "Leave while you can."

"What's that mean?" said Mullen. "We're going to be trapped with these Vix?"

"How long do we have?" asked Tate.

"Minutes," said the cop. "Once the barrier trucks deploy the walls, you won't be allowed to leave."

Tate looked at his team. They knew he was giving them a chance to get to safety.

A scream echoed in the distance and the team got in the car to investigate.

"I feel like we're fighting a forest fire with spit," said Rosse.

"It's not a lost cause," said Tate. "I think all of these buildings have automatic security doors in case of Vix."

"We saw how well they worked here," said Monkhouse.

"Between the bite masks and steel doors, it'll slow down the Vix from spreading," said Wesson.

As they raced towards the source of the screaming, Vix appeared from buildings and side streets, madly chasing the SUV.

Wesson stopped and put the car in reverse.

"Everyone brace," she said and hit the gas.

The SUV charged into the knot of Vix, scattering their broken bodies into the street.

"I'm getting the hang..." began Wesson, when the rear window shattered.

Glass flew in as a Vix rammed its head through the window, shearing the flesh from its face.

It peeled back the glass to reach inside and everyone ducked as it slashed the air above their heads. Wildly clutching for its prey, its hand came down on Fulton's coat and yanked.

"It's got me!"

He struggled as the Vix pulled him backwards over the rear seat.

Rosse fumbled to draw his sword in the confines of the car.

"Screw this," he yelled and shoved the door open.

"Sergeant," barked Tate, but Rosse wasn't listening.

Rosse charged around to the back of the SUV and grabbed the Vix by the legs.

With a grunt, he heaved on the Vix, yanking it out of the window and flung it in the air.

The Vix flailed as it cartwheeled and landed hard on the asphalt but sprung to its feet and bolted for Rosse like a missile.

Instinctively, he reached for his gun. He hesitated only a moment and shifted his grab for his sword. The Vix was almost on him.

He gripped the kodachi like a baseball bat.

"This stupid thing better work," he said, grinding his teeth, and swinging with all his might.

His powerful arms drove the sword in a sweeping arc, chopping through the Vix from hip to shoulder; its body tumbled past him, splashing him in a sheet of gore.

Rosse blinked in surprise and looked at the sword in his trembling hands.

"Rosse, get in the car," ordered Tate.

"Thank you," said Fulton, almost hugging the ex-prison guard.

"I got'cha kid," said Rosse.

They took off, hoping to find where the screams had come from.

Making a best guess, Wesson pulled over as another armored car ground to a halt across the street.

Police in protective gear jumped out and split off into teams, forming a defensive line. A female officer got out of the passenger side and eyed Tate and his people with a critical stare.

No Vix appeared and she ordered the two-man teams to clear the area of Vix.

"What are you doing here?" she demanded.

"Same as you," said Tate.

She keyed the mic attached to her riot vest and snapped an order before turning her attention back to Tate.

They were all watching for movement, on guard against attacking Vix, but she kept her gaze locked on Tate as if no Vix would dare to interrupt her.

"We have harsh laws against looting," she said. "You better get in my truck. We'll escort you out of the area."

"Officer," began Tate.

"Captain," she snapped.

"Captain," he said. "We're saving lives."

"That's our job," said the captain.

"It's a big city," said Tate. "We can help."

The captain looked at the gore-splattered, mangled SUV and the grim determination of the team.

"You're help is welcomed," she said, changing her mind. "But I demand that you wear masks," she said. "I won't have you being a threat to my officers if you foolishly get yourselves killed. Yakamuta! Get these people masks."

"Hai" said Yakamuta with a sharp bow and disappeared into the back of the truck.

He trotted back and handed out bite masks to the team.

"Thank you," said the captain. "Good hunting."

Before Tate could answer, she marched back to the truck and they drove off.

"I'm hating this," said Wesson, trying to adjust the mask.

Rosse put his on and frowned. "Is this what my breath smells like?" he asked.

"Welcome to my world," said Monkhouse.

The deep toll of a bell resonated down the street and the team looked around, wondering who could be ringing a giant bell.

"It's a temple," said Ota. "That way."

He pointed up the street to a set of tall, peaked roofs.

Tate was suddenly aware that the sun was getting low on the horizon. He couldn't believe time had passed so quickly, but then felt the fatigue in his limbs and realized what seemed like only minutes had been hours.

"I feel it too," said Wesson, reading his expression. "What about Mullen's big meeting."

Tate looked around the eerily deserted streets and shrugged. "Called on account of Vix."

They climbed back into the SUV, which thankfully started up with little complaint and headed for the temple.

"If it matters to anyone," said Mullen, "I'm starving."

"Let us know when you spot an open sushi bar an' we'll get ya fixed up," grumbled Rosse.

Tate was about to tell off Rosse for being rude but decided against it. Everyone was operating under intense pressure and a little venting wouldn't hurt.

Wesson stopped in front of the temple grounds, seeing a long walkway that stretched through open gardens and ended at large temple doors.

The bell rang again as they got out of the car with swords in hand.

"That bell's like a Vix magnet," swore Tate.

Heads on swivels, the team headed up the wide path and stopped at the imposing temple doors. Strong bands of black iron held the thick, ancient doors closed against all intruders.

Tate hammered on the door and shouted for someone to answer.

Something heavy rumbled on the other side of the door as voices grunted to unlock the door.

The team stood back as the door opened and an old man in orange robes stepped out and bowed.

"Are you in trouble?" asked Tate.

"Yes," said the monk. "Several of our brothers are missing. They ran into the old storage house, chased by those unfortunate creatures."

Through the shadows of dense foliage and old pine trees, they could see the thick wooden timbers of a single-story building further back in the temple grounds.

"It's going to be dark soon," said Tate. "Does that building have lights?"

"It hasn't been used in generations," said the monk.

"The ghosts live there," said a young monk, peering over the older man's shoulder.

"Ignore him," said the old monk.

Ghosts?

Tate sighed, rubbing his face. His fingers rasped over the rough stubble of his beard and he suddenly felt old and tired.

"Do you have flashlights?" he asked.

"Yes," said the monk and spoke over his shoulder. The young monk nodded and disappeared.

Cold crept through their clothing as the pink and orange hue of sunset faded, casting the temple grounds in a darkening blue.

Some of the team were rubbing their arms, trying to stay warm. If Tate's suspicions were right, as soon as they went into that old building, things would get hot, fast.

Three monks appeared, two with trays or steaming tea and the last with flashlights.

"You will need your strength," said the old monk. "We appreciate your help."

They took the small bowls and knocked back their drinks.

"Yikes," said Fulton, as powerful warmth bloomed in his belly.

"Sake?" said Tate, surprised by the effects.

"We do not drink," said the monk, "but understand its fortifying nature for others."

"Mother Mary," said Monkhouse, feeling warmth filling his limbs.

"I can't feel my lips," said Rosse.

Kicking himself, Tate blamed himself for assuming they were given tea. He didn't believe it was enough to make Fulton drunk, but he might be a hair slower.

His irritation faded as he realized he was feeling pretty good. His fatigue was gone and he felt remarkably refreshed.

Tate saw the old monk studying him with a smile in his eyes.

"It is our special blend," said the monk. "I hope it aids you in your task."

"Thank you," bowed Tate and turned to his team. "Let's go."

Leaving behind the welcoming glow of the temple lights, they moved into the deepening shadows of the woods, towards the old building.

184

16

NOT AS I DO

The beams of their flashlights swept across the shrubs and gnarled tree trunks with growing tension.

Rosse gasped, startled when glowing eyes appeared in his light. Everyone crouched, ready to fight, adrenaline charging through them.

The eyes hesitated, then turned and disappeared and they caught a glimpse of brown fur.

"Just a deer," said Rosse, feeling his heart in his throat.

Tate didn't have to tell anyone to stay alert. Their nerves were stretched taunt. He prayed nobody panicked and started wildly swinging their sword.

They stopped at the door of the old storage building. Green moss clung to the base of the stout structure, adding to the feeling of long disuse, but the door was ajar.

Wesson bent down and examined the footprints in the dirt, leading inside.

"There's blood," she said simply.

Tate flexed his grip on his tomahawk, cursing, not for the first time today, their lack of guns.

There was no question that their swords were lethal, but a gun had the huge advantage of not having to wait until the Vix could touch you before you could protect yourself.

"We're going to be bunched up," said Tate. "Don't slash the people around you."

They nodded and Tate pushed against the heavy door.

Any hope of a quiet entry was crushed when the iron hinges broke the silence with a rusted groan.

"That's just perfect," mumbled Rosse.

There was no chance of stealth now and Tate shoved against the door, throwing it open.

They stood outside, waiting, anticipating the sounds of pounding feet running at them, but nothing happened.

The dark interior swallowed their beams of light, giving nothing away of what might be waiting for them.

"Wedge formation," said Tate quietly, reminding them they were a fighting force, trained and skilled.

The floor creaked under their feet as they moved inside. As their eyes adjusted to the dark, they could make out a long, wide interior. Sagging crates and weathered barrels huddled in the far corner.

Specks of dust danced in the beams of their light, but nothing moved. No sounds. The building looked deserted.

"Maybe they went out another door?" asked Monkhouse.

"Wesson?" said Tate, calling her tracking skills into play.

She crouched down and examined the wooden floor, seeing things the rest of them never could.

"There's a mix of sandal and shoe prints," she said. "They lead to the right."

They trained their lights in the direction but didn't see any door.

"They had to go somewhere," whispered Tate.

The team spread out and crept deeper into the building, the rasp and creak of the floor marking every step they took.

Tate heard Monkhouse murmur quietly over the radio. "I see a trapdoor in the corner."

Tate was about to tell him to wait for the team when a horrible screech and cracking of wood shook the room.

Monkhouse's scream was cut short as everyone turned their flashlights to the sudden noise.

All they saw was a spreading cloud of dust and a ragged hole in the floor where Monkhouse had been standing.

"Monkhouse," yelled Tate. "Do you copy?"

Their blood turned to ice as horrible snarls and chattering rose out of the hole.

Tate didn't think, didn't pause. He vaulted into the gaping hole, knowing what was waiting for him.

He landed on something firm, but it shifted under his weight and he fought to keep his balance. Out of the dark, a clawed hand blurred through the beam of his flashlight. He tried to dodge it, but the Vix raked his shin, sending Tate toppling back.

Monkhouse gasped as Tate landed on him, coughing in the thick dust.

Jumping to his feet, Tate cocked his hand, ready to bury his tomahawk in the first thing he saw, but there was no one but him and Monkhouse.

Quickly looking around, he saw they were partially surrounded by musty sacks of rice.

"Top," cried Wesson.

"I'm okay," he said, crouched and ready to fight. "I have Monkhouse."

"Are you alone?" asked Wesson.

A burst of guttural rage broke out as rays of flighlights strobed from the floor above, whipping the Vix into a frenzy. The wall of stacked rick sacks shuddered as the mob of Vix banged into it.

"Next question," called Tate. "How bad is it?"

Tate heard Rosse swear as they realized his predicament.

"You are one lucky nut job," he said. "If you'd fell the other way you'd already be a hamburger."

Tate looked behind him but didn't see a way out. If they could climb on top of the sacks, someone could reach down and pull them out.

He felt the sting of pain from his shin and realized the Vix would be able to reach them too. They didn't have another option and they'd have to move fast or get pulled into the maw of the growling Vix.

"Test the floor around the hole," said Tate after explaining his plan. "We don't want anyone else falling through."

Groaning, Monkhouse got up, sucking air between his teeth as he put weight on his left foot.

"I think it's broken," he said.

"You can stand," said Tate. It wasn't a question; if Monkhouse was going to survive, he had to push through the pain.

Tate stared into Monkhouse's eyes with brutal seriousness.

"Okay," said Monkhouse. "I got this."

"I'll help you up," said Tate, forming a saddle with his hands.

Monkhouse grabbed the highest sack and pulled himself up, but the sack fell back on him, spewing crumbling rice.

Tate realized what was happening before Wesson confirmed it.

"They're clawing through the sacks," she said.

The weight of growing anxiety in her voice told him it wouldn't be long before they would rip through the sacks.

"I can buy you some time," said Ota. "Fulton, I need your help."

The pile of sacks were beginning to wobble as their sturdiness spilled onto the floor.

There wasn't time for an explanation and Tate didn't ask.

Ota led Fulton to the open trap door and looked down. Rough-hewn wooden steps lead to the basement below.

"Stand behind the trapdoor and wave your light down there," said Ota. "Whatever you do, don't stick your arm out."

Fulton nodded with tentative understanding as Ota drew both his swords.

He slapped the flat of his blades together, filling the room with the sound of ringing metal as Fulton waved his flashlight down the stairs. The reaction was immediate.

The Vix charged the stairs, clawing and climbing over each other to reach the opening above.

A grisly face appeared; ribbons of torn flesh and scalp flapped as it gnashed its teeth.

Ota's swords hummed as he sliced the top off its head. Before the

Vix tumbled back down the stairs, two more scrambled into view. One of them lashed out for Ota's leg and its arm fell off its shoulder by the invisible whirr of a blade.

Suddenly the hole was clogged with writhing Vix, trying to push past each other to climb out.

Fulton felt his stomach churn, the bile rising in his throat as Ota hacked and slashed into them, creating a growing mound of brains and bone.

In the basement, Tate heaved Monkhouse up, who gasped as his ankle racked him with pain.

Rosse laid down on his stomach and reached down.

"Gotcha," he said, grabbing onto Monkhouse's outstretched hand, and pulled him up with little effort.

Wesson took over, pulling him onto the floor as Rosse reached down for Tate.

"Come on, Top," urged Rosse.

"I'm trying," Tate growled between fear and frustration. The rice sacks were shifting and unstable, threatening to throw him at the feet of the Vix.

Knowing it was a gamble, he jumped, reaching up and trusting in Rosse's reflexes.

Relief flushed through Tate as Rosse's meaty hands grabbed hold. Tate's feet lifted off the sacks, knocking one over.

Hearing the noise, a Vix turned away from the stairs and Tate suspended in the air.

Growling, it charged across the room and vaulted. The Vix rammed into Tate, ripping him out of Rosse's grip.

With a yell, Tate fell back in a tangle of thrashing arms and clashing teeth. The Vix was a force of insanity, blindly snapping the air, inches from Tate's face. In the haze of dust, its hands found him and fingers dug painfully into his shoulder and waist.

Flashlights from above backlit the monster as it lunged, jaws gaping. Instinctively, Tate grabbed for his tomahawk and jammed the handle in its mouth.

The Vix violently thrashed its head and Tate pulled his knees to his chest and kicked.

Snarling and spitting, the Vix cartwheeled into the air, slamming against the wall. A living thing would have been knocked out, but the Vix scampered to its feet and flung itself at Tate.

"Eat this," he barked and swung his tomahawk, putting all his anger and fear behind it.

The sharpened steel axe crashed onto the Vix's head, cleaving down, through its jaw, into its chest.

The Vix went limp and slumped to the floor, bloody bubbles wheezing from its cleft throat.

With trembling hands, Tate climbed back up the sacks, fearing a hell where he'd never make it out of this hole.

Pain shot through his shoulders as Rosse pulled him up with sudden force. He wasn't going to lose Tate a second time.

"He's safe," shouted Wesson.

"Close it," gasped Ota, hardly able to hold onto his swords.

Fulton kicked the trapdoor, crashing it down on the Vix, still trying to claw through the horrific gore of Ota's work.

"Clear?" asked Wesson.

Fulton watched the trapdoor faintly bumping up and down, but no Vix would be coming up anytime soon.

"Clear," he said.

Wesson grabbed Tate under the arms as he sat on the floor, breathing hard.

"I need a minute," he said, waving her off.

Her angry face appeared in front of his as she knelt in front of him.

"Don't you ever do that again," she said, her voice cracking.

Tate began to protest when Rosse cut him off.

"Top, shut your fricken mouth," he said. "If she don't kick your butt, I will."

Tate was too happy to be alive to be insulted. He laid back on the floor, filling his lungs with stale air, feeling exhaustion and euphoria at the same time.

"I think," he said, climbing to his feet, "I'm about Japan'd out."

Monkhouse chuckled and it spread to the rest of the team until all of them were laughing.

．　．　．

The frigid night air sobered them up as they walked out of the building and closed the door.

The old monk must have been waiting for them, because he opened the temple door as soon as they knocked.

"I'm sorry," said Tate. "There's nobody alive in there."

He monk's chin sank to his chest for a moment, his lips moving in a silent prayer, before looking up at the team.

"We will miss our brothers," he said gravely. "But perhaps we will meet them again after they are reborn. You honor them with your courage."

He bowed deeply, then produced several strings of wooden beads.

"Please take these," he said, handing them to each of the team. "May they help you find peace in this life."

They bowed, thanking him, and he disappeared behind the door and closed it.

With Rosse supporting the hobbling Monkhouse, they walked back to the SUV, finding Mullen asleep in the back seat.

"I'd forgotten about him," said Monkhouse.

Several cars and armored trucks had collected nearby, their flashing lights strobing the building walls.

As Tate and the team emerged from the shadows of the temple, they heard shouts of alarm and a group of police started to charge.

"We're alive," called Tate, waving them off.

He never got over how strange it felt to say that. The police stopped and returned to their group.

One face looked over at him from the knot of police and headed towards him with two officers in tow.

"We can keep going," said Wesson, "but I don't know how much we have left."

Tate was watching the police heading towards them and glanced at his watch. They'd been at this for hours.

"I think they're about to pull the plug on tonight's adventure," he said. "Get inside and tell Mullen not to say anything to the cops."

"Copy that," sighed Wesson, and climbed into the car.

"Good evening," said Tate as the police approached him.

"There's a curfew in place," snapped one of the cops. "What are you doing here?"

"Yes," said another, "What *are* you doing here?"

He took off his helmet and removed his bite mask. To Tate's surprise, it was the same detective he'd met when he bailed out Monkhouse.

"Tate-san, right?" said detective Makado.

"Yes," said Tate. "We were going for coffee when the Vix appeared." He hoped to head off Makado's suspicions but wasn't going to bet money on succeeding.

"Your hotel doesn't have coffee?"

"It's not very good," shrugged Tate.

"Officer Satomura," said Makado. "Inspect the people in that car. Make sure no one's been bitten."

Tate knew it would be pointless to interfere and only arouse Makado's suspicions more.

Makado glanced down and noticed the beads hanging out of Tate's pocket.

"Souvenir shopping?" he asked.

"They were a gift from the monk in that temple."

Makado frowned, glancing back at the temple entrance.

"He asked us to rescue his missing brothers," said Tate. "I'm sorry to say, we were too late."

Makado saw Tate's ripped and blood-smeared clothes, connecting the pieces.

"You are foreigners," said Makado, making it sound like a question. "You didn't have to do that."

"Yes," said Tate. "We did."

The two men shared a quiet moment, broken when the officer returned from the car.

"Nobody's been bitten, Detective Makado," he said. "Should I bring them in for questioning?"

"No," said Makado. "They didn't have anything to do with this attack."

"Attack?" asked Tate, his ears perking up.

"We have seen this happen in cities around Japan," said Makado. "We believe these are targeted suicides."

"Targeted?" Tate couldn't believe it.

"Detective Makado," yelled a man, marching angrily towards them.

"Chief Shota-san," said Makado, snapping to attention.

"What's so important that you are neglecting your duties with your men?" Shota demanded.

"This man was informing us of recent sightings of Vix, sir."

"Of course he saw Vix," barked Shota. "They're everywhere. Stop wasting time with this tourist and get back to your men."

"Sir," saluted Makado.

He turned and left under the glare of his boss.

Shota frowned at Tate and his ragged condition, disliking everything about him.

"Return to your hotel," he said. "Don't stop anywhere or I'll have you arrested."

"I was told the area's been walled off," said Tate.

Shota glared down his nose at him for a moment.

"Satomura," he barked.

"Yes, chief," saluted the officer.

"Write up a pass for this man," said Shota.

"Yes, sir."

Satomura hurriedly scribbled out something on his notepad and handed it to Shota, who signed it without looking away from Tate.

Satomura tore off the page and handed it to Tate.

"Thank you," bowed Tate simply. He wasn't going to give the chief any excuse to change his mind.

He got back in the car, sighing with the sheer luxury of sitting down.

"We're dropping off Mullen, then heading to the hotel," he said, exhaustion weighing him down.

"With all due respect," groaned Wesson, "if you had said anything else I'd have kicked you out and left you here."

Tate laughed with her as she put the car in gear and settled back into the seat.

"Car," she said, clearing her throat. "Are you still working?"

"The power steering is operating at seventy-three percent," said the car. "The left headlight is not functioning. The right headlight..."

"Can you drive without hitting anything?" asked Wesson, not feeling like arguing with a car.

"Yes."

Tate craned his head to look at Mullen in the back seat expectantly.

"My meeting's a complete bust, if that's what you're asking," said Mullen.

"Thanks," said Tate. "I was a little iffy on that. I mean, where do we drop you off, unless you'd rather walk."

Mullen hesitated a moment, reluctant to give the location of his safehouse, but he wasn't about to be left on the side of the road.

He gave them the address and the car pulled into the street, its crumpled bodywork rattling as they went.

It had been two days without a word from Mullen, and if Tate was being honest with himself, he didn't care.

The team had just begun shaking off the effects of the Vix outbreak and a couple of the team weren't sleeping or were woken up with nightmares.

Fulton couldn't look at anything with ground beef without feeling sick.

On the positive side, Rosse reported that Monkhouse's ankle was only a bad sprain, but he'd have to stay off it for a few days.

Tate had gone down to the hotel's onsen, passing the door to the gym without a tinge of guilt.

He bathed before getting in the onsen and sat on the small stool to lather up. His body was a crisscross of bruises, cuts, and scrapes, and the ones he couldn't see, the sting of the soap helped him find.

After finishing up, he found himself standing at the edge of the onsen, having second thoughts about getting in.

This is going to really hurt.

A wrinkled old Japanese man sat in the steaming water, his eyes crinkling as he chuckled at Tate's dilemma.

Taking a deep breath, Tate lowered his foot into the hot water. The heat made him suck in air, but he was committed now. That's what he told himself until his scraped-up shin touched the water.

He hissed in pain to the entertainment of the old man. He couldn't stop now; it was a matter of pride. He wasn't going to turn tail in front of this guy.

Beads of sweat covered his face as he continued to sink into the water. His body screamed bloody murder and Tate used every ounce of his will to hold onto his poker face.

He asked himself why he was torturing himself and was about to get out when the pain miraculously faded away, leaving only soothing but intense heat sinking into his body.

He nodded and smiled at the old man who said something in approval.

When he finally got out of the onsen, Tate felt drowsy but refreshed.

The sensation didn't last long after he returned to the hotel.

Wesson was talking to Monkhouse when she saw Tate walk in and came over to him with the latest news.

"Mullen called," she said.

"Not good?" Tate guessed, judging from her expression.

"Not even close," she said. "Tanaka and his entire security team are dead."

Tate swore under his breath.

"They were at the meet when the Vix hit," said Wesson. "Hang on. It gets worse. Mullen's gone into hiding, saying he's not stepping foot outside until someone can guarantee the Vix have been wiped out."

"He's not calling off the meeting? You said Tanaka's dead, right?"

"Very," said Wesson. "Mullen said Tanaka was just a spokesman for the decision-maker."

"Mullen gets talkative when he's under pressure," said Tate, considering the larger implications. He didn't like the delay. The longer this went on, the greater chance The Ring might get nervous and call Mullen home.

Mullen had a lot of information about The Ring, but The Ring also knew a lot too. Inside information about what's going on in the government and names of people willing to use their influence to undermine the government to their advantage.

"I think he's feeling isolated and nervous," said Wesson.

"What else did he say?" asked Tate, getting the sense they must have had a long conversation.

"Tanaka was the face-man for someone else. Mullen doesn't know who it is, but they're considering if they want to call off the meeting. They hinted they might move the meeting to another country."

Tate shook his head, wondering what else could go wrong.

"Besides getting someone else to handle whatever deal Mullen's involved with, they have to put together another security team," said Wesson.

"I feel like you're leading up to something," he said.

"So," she said with a long sigh, "we could be here two more weeks before we know what's happening."

"You say that like it's a bad thing."

"Which part?" asked Wesson. "All of us living on top of each other in this hotel with no privacy? Or spending all night fighting off armies of Vix?"

"Don't forget almost everything has seafood in it," offered Monkhouse, listening in.

Wesson gave him a humorless look. "Yes, that too. If we're stuck in this hotel for two more weeks, the team's going to be bouncing off the walls."

"I've been thinking about that. Tell the others we're having a meeting over lunch."

"Okay," said Wesson.

It sounded like the conversation was over, but she stood there, looking at Tate in a way that made him want to squirm.

"What?"

"Can I be honest with you?" she asked.

"Of course," he said, feeling less confident than he sounded.

"What's wrong with you?"

He knew exactly what she was talking about but didn't have an answer. Instead, he only shrugged.

"Going after Monkhouse like that..."

"Truthfully, I was already down the hole before I thought about what I was doing," he said.

"It was reckless," said Wesson. "That's not how you trained us."

"I agree," said Tate. "If any of you had done that, I'd be chewing them out for days."

"Then how do you explain that?"

Tate couldn't. He knew Wesson was angry with him and he deserved it, but he had to hold back a smile. He had chosen Wesson as his second in charge and she had taken the role seriously, but until recently, that hadn't included him. It was clear that she was holding him accountable to the same standards as the rest of the team.

"I couldn't stand back and let Monkhouse die."

"None of us would," she said. "That's what I'm saying. We, including you, are a team. You don't get to be an individual when it suits you."

The last puzzle piece fell into place. She wasn't just talking about what happened at the temple.

Tate remembered the look of disappointment on her face when he was running out to intercept the Ring's security team.

"I understand," he said. "And you're right."

"I know you feel like we're not at your level," said Wesson, "but you have to give us a chance to prove you're wrong."

"And if proving me wrong gets one of you killed?"

"None of us get out of this life alive," she said.

Tate looked at her, arching his eyebrows.

"Are you getting Zen lessons from Ota?"

He'd gotten chewed out by everyone in the team, in their own way, and Wesson was making sure he got the message loud and clear.

He did, but in the back of his mind that little voice told him if he had to do it all over again, there was a fifty-fifty chance he would do the same thing.

He'd seen friends die. He'd nearly died trying to save them, but in his heart he blamed himself for not trying harder. Survivor's guilt is what the base psychologist called it.

It's normal. Very common, they say.

Like somehow that was supposed to make the guilt go away.

He realized that Wesson was watching him, reading his expression. She recognized he was dealing with a deeper struggle and gave him the needed space to deal with his demons.

He pushed the thoughts away and took advantage of the lag in conversation to change the subject.

"Did you notice what detective Makado said the other night?"

"Yes," she said. "The Vix didn't happen by chance, or something like that?"

"Right before his boss interrupted," said Tate, "he said the suicides were targeted."

"Like the suicide bombers years ago?" she asked.

"That's what I was thinking," he said. "There hasn't been much news about what's going on in the world since the big outbreak. Is it possible there's still active factions chasing their holy war?"

"Don't ask me?" said Wesson. "You're the one that made a living hunting them down. Why would a little thing like an apocalypse slow them down?"

"It wouldn't."

"I would have guessed they'd keep their heads down until the outbreak was over," she said.

"Isn't it?" asked Tate.

Wesson looked at him a long time, not sure if putting words to her fear would make it real.

"I don't think so," she said. "I think it's still going on, but on a smaller scale. The way aftershocks follow a big earthquake."

Tate couldn't think of anything more horrific. He wanted to

believe the same thing everyone did. The Vix were contained. More accurately, the human race was contained; protected inside walled cities. But if Wesson was right... In a way, it made sense. Every baby born was a point in favor of the human race. Every death was a new Vix.

Was anyone in the government keeping score which way the numbers were going? Was the human race running out of people faster than they could be replaced?

"What happened at the train station," he said, "I think the police are hiding something and Makado knows what it is."

Wesson gave him a knowing frown.

"What?" said Tate, feeling self-conscious.

"You're thinking about digging into the Vix attack. Top, we're supposed to keep a low profile."

"How's that been working for us?" he asked.

"Not great," she said. "That doesn't mean we should go all in. If you're asking my advice..."

"I ..."

"Let the police handle it. Seriously. We have enough on our plate."

"You're right," said Tate, clearing his throat and looking at his battered team. "Thanks for the reality check."

"Sure."

"I think I have a solution to us sitting on our thumbs for the next couple of weeks," he said.

"Am I pleased or frightened?" asked Wesson.

"You won't know until we do it."

"Then I'm frightened," she said.

17

NOMADS

The team sat around the coffee table covered in plates of food and ate in awkward silence, waiting for Tate to reveal why he'd called this meeting.

He felt their eyes on him and decided he couldn't finish his lunch with them watching his every move.

Everyone stopped eating as he wiped his mouth and cleared his throat.

"You already know our mission has been extended for another two weeks," he began. "There's pros and cons to that. I want to focus on a big con."

He put his sword on the table.

"I was going to say we're lucky none of us got killed the other day, but there was no luck about it. Ota saved our collective hides."

Everyone murmured in agreement, giving him approving nods.

Ota took the attention of his teammates with an easy smile.

"We're between a rock and a hard place," said Tate. "The agents have an asset who can supply us with guns. That's the good news. If Kiku catches us with those guns, it's a good bet she'll take off an arm. That's the bad news."

"I thought she was on our side," said Fulton.

"She is," said Wesson. "As long as we follow her rules."

"That brings me back to our first day in Japan," said Tate. "Ota, you said you could help us train us."

"Almost," said Ota. "I said I could help you with training. I'm not qualified to teach you."

"Are you joking?" said Monkhouse. "You're a human woodchipper. How is that not qualified?"

"All right," said Tate. "If not you, then who?"

"I was here before," said Ota. "And I met master Masuhiro Oinshi. He taught me swordsmanship. I could take you to him. There's a chance he might teach you some basics, if I ask him."

"A chance?" asked Wesson.

"He can be... strongly particular," said Ota.

Tate caught himself before loudly sighing. He recognized code for taskmaster.

"That's great," he said. "Give him a call and let's see what he says."

"He doesn't use phones," said Ota.

"Or computers?" asked Wesson.

"They're a distraction," he said.

"Then we meet him in person," said Tate.

"This sounds cool," said Fulton. "Does he live in one of those really old castles with the yard where everyone's doing martial arts?"

"Calm down, kid," said Rosse. "That stuff's just in the movies."

"Yes," said Ota. "But it's called a temple. Top, it's not a sure thing. He might say no."

"We won't know until he does," said Tate.

"In that case," smiled Ota, "when do we go?"

"We can be ready tomorrow," said Tate.

"It would be a good idea to pack ahead of time," said Ota. "If he accepts you, you must stay until he says you can go."

"So like what?" said Rosse. "We can't leave if we want to?"

"You could," said Ota. "But it would be a show of grievous disrespect."

"What's grievous mean?" asked Rosse.

"It's what happens when you piss off a sword guru," said Tate. "We'll respect his rules," he said to Ota. "All of us."

Breaks in the grey winter sky revealed hints of blue through the large living room windows as the team gathered early the next morning.

Outside, the city was busy with people and traffic, but there was tangible anxiety in the air. People were constantly glancing around, watching, anticipating a wave of Vix to erupt out of nowhere.

The latest news reported that the area of Tokyo was still walled off, but the elimination of Vix was progressing, and police were confident the "inconvenience" would be over soon.

Before leaving the hotel, everyone had agreed it would be a good idea to wear their bite masks. People were jumpy enough. They didn't need to add to it.

Ota explained the dojo was 'out of the way' and would take several hours to get there.

The first leg of their journey started with a bullet train. As it pulled along the platform, Tate saw the front of it had been modified to deal with Vix, but the need for this addition wasn't realized until after a disastrous collision.

The invention of the bullet train was an engineering masterstroke of the mid-twentieth century, with the goal of reducing travel time between long distances. Developing a power plant capable of achieving 180+ mph was the easy part. Keeping the train from flying off the rails was the real challenge.

Slower trains could manage a bump or wobble in the track, but the bullet train's inertia and momentum were unforgiving. The tracks had to be engineered to exacting standards. This was especially important because the north and south-bound trains passed within inches of each other.

After the outbreak, with the needs of an entire country demanding instant attention, it was foreseeable that mistakes would be made.

When the bullet train had been designed, the engineers had anticipated the likelihood of the train hitting an animal. When the bullet trains were put back into service after the outbreak, nobody had considered the new dynamic of not one animal but groups of Vix on the tracks.

Disaster struck when Japan restarted use of the bullet train, nine months after the outbreak.

Twenty minutes outside of Osaka, the north and south-bound trains were approaching each other. The southbound train hit a small knot of Vix. One of them was wearing a motorcycle helmet, which was sucked under and hit the train's forward wheel. The ripple effect caused the train to come off the track in front of the north-bound train.

Moving at a combined speed of three hundred and sixty-four miles an hour, the two trains hit head on.

The sound of the impact was heard eighty miles away and debris from the collision was found as far away as a mile.

Learning from that tragedy, the track system was torn down and replaced with an elevated track. The nose of the train had been fitted with a plow. There hadn't been another Vix related accident since.

The team sat in comfort, shielded from the roar of rushing wind by the trains sound-deadening shell.

They pressed Ota for more details about their destination, but he was his typically cryptic self.

"The temple is very old," he said. "It's passed through several hands. Each with their own... unique vision of its purpose."

"We don't have to shave our heads or wear robes, right?" asked Rosse. "Cause even if I was Irish, I ain't wearing a dress."

"You mean Scottish," said Monkhouse.

"It's a kilt," said Wesson.

"I. Ain't. Wearing. A. Dress," said Rosse.

"You won't have to," said Ota, leaving it at that.

"Are they like those warrior monks?" asked Fulton. "Can I learn to use all kinds of weapons?"

"That depends on which teacher is there," said Ota. "They come and go."

"We only have a week to learn sword basics," said Tate. "Unless you want to give up your worldly ways, Fulton. You could take your vows and stay there."

Fulton's eyes went wide at the possibilities.

"You'd have to give up sex," grinned Tate. "But it's a small price to pay for learning how to catch flies with chopsticks."

"Pass," said Fulton, making everyone chuckle.

By the time they reached the small village of Mimata, they had switched four trains, a taxi and two busses. The team was bone weary.

"That's where we're going," said Ota, pointing to a range of mountains shrouded in clouds.

"That's a heck of a hike," said Wesson.

Tate glanced around at the small town, considering how far away they were from any large cities, then looked up into the mountains. Their true shapes were hidden under a blanket of dense forests. Combined with the grey shreds of clouds, the place had a primordial feel to it.

"How did you find this place?" asked Tate.

Ota looked up to the mountains, peering at them as if he could see the temple through the clouds and trees.

"By chance," he said. "I met someone who knew someone."

Tate tried to imagine what would happen in his life to drive him into the isolation of these mountains. The answer came with unforgiving clarity.

The death of his daughter.

Losing her had hollowed him out, leaving behind an empty shell of a man that wanted to stop existing. If he had known of this place back then, this is exactly where he would have ended up.

The conclusion made him wonder if he and Ota shared a common tragedy.

They needed a ride into the mountains. The local villagers were friendly and uniquely accepting of the foreign strangers roaming their streets.

"I get the feeling we're not the first pilgrims that have passed through here," said Wesson.

"Oshima will take you," said a woman, smoking a pipe as the team walked by.

"Oshima?" asked Tate.

"He's got an old truck," said the woman. "About as old as he is. You'll find him down there." She gave a short nod, pointing with her chin.

"Thank you," said Ota.

The village was small and it wasn't hard to find the truck and Oshima sitting next to it.

He studied them as they explained they needed a ride.

"I don't remember you," he said. "This must be your first time."

"We're ready now," said Ota, as the others frowned in confusion.

"First time?" said Tate.

Ota only shrugged, reverting to his customary silence.

The driver let out a breath edged with disapproval.

"You don't seem the type, but I'll take you," he said. "I can wait for you, if you change your minds."

"Thank you," said Tate. "We won't."

"I only go as far as the end of the road," said the driver. "You have to walk the rest of the way."

"Yes," said Ota.

"Okay," said Oshima. "Let's go."

They climbed into the back of the truck and the old man threw them a couple of large, padded blankets.

"It gets cold up there," he said.

"I thought it was cold already," said Wesson, pulling her coat tighter around her.

Oshima was right. It got much colder.

The road out of the village was more like a dirt track and soon it angled steeply up as they began their climb into the mountains.

It didn't take long before they felt the bite of real cold on their faces.

They hunkered under the blankets for warmth as the truck

bumped and squeaked over the uneven road through the old, dense forest.

"I'm feeling a little exposed out in the open like this," said Monkhouse.

"What Vix would be stupid enough to want to climb a mountain for a bunch of monks?" groused Rosse.

"Nobody in town was worried about them," said Tate. "Maybe it's too cold for them."

"Do you think they freeze?" asked Monkhouse.

"Huh," said Tate. "Yeah, maybe they do."

After several miles, the truck finally swayed to a stop and Oshima shouted out his window.

"This is it."

Nobody wanted to move at first. The padded blankets didn't feel like they'd kept out the cold until they got out from under them. They climbed out of the truck bed and their breath fogged in the chill.

"The hike will warm us up," said Tate, tucking his gloved hands into his armpits. "Thanks for the ride."

"You sure you don't want me to wait?" asked Oshima.

"Yes," said Tate, turning to Ota. "Do you know why he keeps asking that?"

"Being polite?" said Ota.

"That's not what I... never mind," said Tate.

It was pointless to chase Ota for an answer. Whatever the reason, they were about to find out soon enough.

At the edge of the dirt road was a small path that wound upwards.

Tate was right. They warmed up quickly as the path turned into a long stairway made of dirt and logs.

"I'm start'n to wish we took that old guy up on his offer to wait for us," said Rosse, feeling the ache in his legs.

Tate was thinking the same thing. His legs were aching and each stair felt like his last. He wanted to call a rest break, but that would be admitting he was old, or out of shape... or both.

Instead, it was Monkhouse who spoke up.

"I can't do this much more. The cold and these stairs are killing my ankle."

Tate smiled inwardly. Relief was in sight.

"We're almost there," said Ota. "I can help you."

"Yeah, me too," said Rosse.

Tate clenched his jaw, silently cursing the inventor of stairs, remote temples and winter.

Ota hadn't exaggerated. They'd only gone a short distance when they rounded a turn and were met by the high walls and sturdy doors of the temple.

"Wow," said Fulton, taking in the ancient structure.

Ota left Monkhouse with Rosse and went up to a thick rope that hung from a hole beside the door.

Flakes of snow began to fall as he pulled twice and they heard the muted sound of a bell somewhere inside.

Everyone looked at the door in anticipation, but nobody came. The snow was really coming down and the group was stamping their feet and shivering.

Tate glanced at Ota who seemed unconcerned, but after several more minutes, his patience gave out.

"This is a bust," he said, suddenly wishing he had let Oshima wait for them. "No one's here, or if they are, they're not interested in visitors."

The sun was getting low and the gentle flurries had turned into heavy snowfall.

Returning down those snow-covered stairs would be brutal, but the real threat was hypothermia.

He scanned the surrounding woods, going into survival mode and looking for kindling for a fire when they heard a thud against the temple door.

The door opened, hardly making a sound and a man walked out, his lined face lit by his lantern.

"What kind of monk is that?" whispered Fulton to Rosse.

The man was dressed in brown chinos and hiking boots. He peered at them from under the brim of his weathered bush hat until he saw Ota.

"It is good to see you again," he said, smiling.

Ota stepped forward and the two men hugged.

"You look good, Walt," smiled Ota.

"Let us find someplace warm," said Walt. "Then you can tell me who these people are."

Walt turned and disappeared through the door, followed by Ota and the rest of the team.

Through the door was a large courtyard, ringed by several buildings on every side.

They heard a snap and saw a lone figure at the other edge of the courtyard. The figure held a tall bow and stood so motionless they almost mistook it for a statue. Then they heard the thwack of the bowstring. The arrow hit the distant dummy, the arrowhead so razor-sharp it didn't disturb the snow covering it.

The team's eyes were drawn by the warm, inviting glow of the light coming from the windows of the buildings and the promise of something hot to drink.

Walt turned left and led them to a small building with a low roof. As they entered, a row of automatic lights faded on from the ceiling above.

"They have power," whispered Fulton to Rosse.

"Stop doing that," said Rosse, fanning his ear like he was waving off an annoying insect. "I can see it."

A table and chairs were arranged near a crackling fireplace, and Walt gestured for them to sit down while he took off his parka and hat.

In the light they could see a scar creasing his black skin that ran down the side of his head and across where his ear used to be.

He took an empty chair and sat down. He looked at them from over his folded hands, quietly studying each of them.

Tate had seen many people pull this act, trying to give off an air of someone with deep insight and judgment of character. Walt was one of only a few that didn't feel like an act. The fire glittered off the man's dark eyes, lingering on them, coaxing out their secrets.

It made Tate feel uncomfortable.

Finally, Walt turned to Ota and spoke, breaking the heavy silence.

"They don't know this place," he said.

Ota merely shrugged, making Walt laugh.

"You haven't changed," he chuckled.

It didn't look like Ota was in a hurry to explain the situation and Tate was too tired, cold and hungry to wait.

"My name is Jack Tate. We were in the middle of a Vix outbreak a couple of days back..."

"Yes," said Walt gravely. "A terrible thing. Did you lose anyone?"

"It was a close thing, but luckily we had him," said Tate, pointing to Ota. "His ability with swords is stunning."

"Thank you," said Walt.

"Then you're his teacher," said Tate. "Great. We're here because we are in serious need of training."

Walt looked at Ota, who nodded in agreement with Tate.

Walt put his hands on the table, lacing his fingers together.

"Mister Tate," he said. "I believe you have the wrong idea about this place."

"I was picking up on that," said Tate, glancing at the electric lights.

"A very long time ago, this was a temple for Buddhist monks. That has not been the case for many generations, although in some ways we share similar traits."

Everyone at the table was forming their own ideas of where this was going and hoped it didn't end with them walking back down the mountain.

"This place was left abandoned a long... long time ago. I've never known anyone who knows why. I think that story is lost to time. Now it belongs to our unique society of nomads."

"Nomads?" said Wesson.

"I suppose that's the best way to describe the travelers that come here," said Walt. "Men and women who need a rest from their wanderings. An escape."

"We're not here to join," said Tate. "We're hoping someone can train us to use a sword without cutting off our own heads."

"Mastering the sword is a challenging commitment," said Walt.

"We only have a week," said Tate, inwardly cringing. He expected Walt would laugh them out the door.

Walt looked at him with speechless surprise.

"A week," he said, turning to Ota. "What do you think they can learn in a week?"

"A fighting chance," said Ota.

Walt sighed and ran his finger along the table, seemingly lost in the texture of the wood.

Ota's gaze drifted to the window, looking out to the courtyard and Walt followed his stare.

"You should go outside," said Walt. "I'll call you when I'm done."

Ota nodded, smiling, and got up.

"You might be surprised to know she hasn't changed," said Walt.

"I thought..." started Ota, then noticed the team were listening to him with interest.

They didn't know what this was about, but they sensed they had seen a small glimpse into his history.

"I'll be outside if you need me, Top," said Ota. He paused for a beat at the door, as if preparing for something, then left the room.

All of the team had watched his every move, seeing more emotion from him in the last few minutes than they had since meeting him.

"Mister Tate," said Walt. "I will let you stay, but you and your people are not welcome here. This is a unique place, as are its people and most definitely its rules."

"I vouch for my people," said Tate. "We will follow the rules."

"You are very committed, or very foolish to agree without knowing the consequences."

"I imagine they're serious," said Tate, glancing meaningfully at his team.

"Severe," said Walt, "and permanent."

"Before we go laying our necks on the chopping block," said Rosse, "what rules are we agreeing to?"

"The people who come here are... nomadic. They are here to be left alone. No matter the reason, you must not speak to anyone that is not wearing a blue scarf."

Walt pointed to the simple blue bandana around his neck.

"Outside our walls, our people may be nobody of consequence, or they may be monstrous. Violating this rule, you will suffer whatever punishment they choose." Walt leaned forward and fixed them with cold intensity. "Refusal is fatal."

Rosse leaned back, looking pleased with himself while others gawked in shock.

"No problem," he said. "I can go for days without say'n a word."

Wesson leaned over to Tate. "He's going to die," she whispered.

Tate nodded gravely, knowing she wasn't joking.

"What else ya got?" asked Rosse.

"Nothing," said Walt. "Except for your training. It will be demanding."

Rosse looked up, frowning at the last thing Walt said and started to say something.

"Thank you," said Tate, cutting off Rosse. "Everyone will work hard."

"Very well," said Walt, a smile softening his face; he stood up. "This will be your quarters. I'll take you to where you can get your bedding. But first, follow me, and I'll take you to the dining area."

They all perked up at that and everyone got to their feet.

Walt led them outside towards the main building.

Fulton stopped in his tracks with a gasp, making everyone else stop and follow his stare.

Torches ringed the borders of the courtyard, casting flickering light on two figures. One was the girl they'd seen with the bow. The other was Ota, and they were embraced in a kiss.

Monkhouse's mouth dropped open and Wesson jabbed him with her elbow before he said something.

"Nobody says a word," hissed Tate.

"Like I said," said Walt. "It is a unique place."

He led them into the main building, leaving the distant couple to themse

18

OL' JACK

Tate had been in the 1st Special Forces Operation Detachment - Delta Force. He would never forget what it took to pass the intensely grueling selection process and training to make it into Delta.

He anticipated the coming week was going to be hard; not Delta hard. He chuckled, proud of himself for making it through, yet knowing if he had to repeat that process, it would kill him.

He was up for whatever challenge Walt had for them. He looked forward to being tested. Wesson had said the team wanted to prove themselves. Tate suspected they were about to get their opportunity.

He wasn't wrong.

It was oh dark thirty when Walt stuck his head into their room.

"It is time," he said simply and left.

Wesson rose to the moment; shivering and bleary-eyed, she made sure everyone was up, dressed and hustling out into the courtyard in a few short minutes. The change from the warmth of their beds to the ankle-deep snow blasted away the remaining cobwebs of sleep or fatigue.

By the time Walt handed them their practice swords and belts, they were eager for any exercise to warm up.

"Between the instant your mind thinks of drawing your sword and the moment it returns to the scabbard a million things can go wrong," said Walt. "Balance, the way you grip your sword, breathing, how you place your feet... these things take years to learn."

Fulton was thinking if their teacher was going to discourage them, he wished Walt would hurry up because he was losing the feeling in his feet.

"Instead of knowledge," said Walt, "I will train your instinct."

"What does that even mean?" said Rosse under his breath.

"Each of you stand in front of the practice targets," said Walt, pointing to the five, snow-covered shapes at the other end of the courtyard. "Put your sword in your belt and stand arm's length from them."

He waited until each of them were standing in front of their targets.

Tate's hands were already red with cold and he wondered if he would be able to grip the sword without dropping it.

"On my command," said Walt, "draw your sword and strike once. Don't try to impress me. Don't show me what you think I want to see. Your movement must be an honest result of what your mind tells you to do. Ready? Strike!"

All of them grabbed their swords and swung, hitting their targets on the head, shoulders and sides.

The instant their swords landed, the targets sprang to life, snarling and swiping their arms, trying to grab them.

All of the team jumped back, yelling in shock; Fulton and Monkhouse tangled their feet and fell.

Clumps of snow flew off the thrashing Vix, but heavy ropes held them firmly against stout pylons.

"Get up," said Walt, as several of the team swore, angrily glaring at him. "Return your swords to your belts."

Shaken, the team snugged their wooden swords in the waistband of their belts.

"Stand, arms-length from your targets," said Walt, unconcerned about the writhing Vix.

One by one they moved within arm's reach of the Vix, the sharp bones of the Vix's fingers slashing the air inches away.

All of them had forgotten the cold. All of their thoughts were on the squirming nightmares in front of them.

"This is sick, Top," said Wesson under her breath.

"Now your enemy has a face," said Walt. "It sees you. It has a purpose. Strength. Its only focus is to kill you. Strike!"

Some of the team immediately drew their swords; Monkhouse and Wesson hesitated, but all of them hit the Vix.

"Did you see how you changed your strike from the first time?" asked Walt. "Why? Was it anger? Fear? Was it pity?"

He let the question hang in the air for a long time.

"When you strike, your mind must be empty," he said. "Not only of what scares you, but of what you want. When your mind is empty, there's no obstacle to action. Strike!"

They drew and hit.

"Strike."

As they trained, over and over, a strange transition began to take place. The Vix changed from a monster to an object. Feelings of revulsion, hate and fear faded away. The aura that the Vix possessed the power of death was gone.

Drawing and striking wasn't driven by the conflicts of emotions, but by muscle memory.

———

"That's it for today," said Walt, jolting Tate into the present.

The sky was tinged with purple and orange and the sun was touching the horizon. Tate had lost all sense of time, which was a troubling realization. He glanced at the others, who seemed to be coming out of their own haze.

The Vix, in front of him, was a wrecked mess of pulp and bone, and Tate's stomach churned, not from the sight as much as the dawning awareness that he was the one who had done it, repeatedly striking long after the gory thing was no threat.

"We'll begin again in the morning," said Walt.

Wesson yelped, feeling the sharp pain of her tortured limbs.

"I can't lift my arms," said Monkhouse.

Everyone, including Tate, were wincing at the pain in their arms.

"Brooklyn will take you to the baths where you can clean up and soak," said Walt.

The girl they had seen with Ota walked into the courtyard and greeted them with a smile.

"Evening guys," she said. "Come on. I'll show ya the way."

"Was that you I saw last night?" asked Tate.

"Kissing Ota?" she said, chuckling.

"Uh, I was going to say with the bow," he said. "But yes, that too."

"Ota and I go way back," said Brooklyn. "He never mentioned me?"

"He never mentions anyone," said Tate. "Oh!"

He suddenly realized she wasn't wearing a blue bandana around her neck. She laughed, guessing his surprise.

"The scarf?" she said. "I love Walt to pieces, but I don't take much to that rule. At least, not for myself. But you don't want to make that mistake with anyone else, all right?"

They stopped at a low door that opened to stone fashioned stairs. Warm air flowed over them and they wasted no time following Brooklyn inside.

She led them into a well-lit underground chamber. The walls and ceiling were smooth, cream-colored plaster and the floor was covered in fresh, grass woven mats.

"You can bathe over there," she said, pointing to several barrels of water with brushes and buckets hanging from their sides. "There's been a lot of changes to this place since the monks left it behind, but the new owners had the good sense to keep the hot tubs."

She led them around a massive beam, hewed from a single tree, supporting the arched ceiling. On the other side were three steaming pools of water.

The team stood there, caked with frozen gore and dirt, their bodies aching from cold and endless training.

"I think I'm going to cry," said Monkhouse.

"I'll leave ya to it," said Brooklyn, but hesitated when she saw Wesson frowning. "Come on. I'll show ya where you can get a little privacy."

She led Wesson to another area, screened off from the others.

"Thanks. I'm Wess... Lori. I can't place your accent."

"New Zealand," said Brooklyn. "American, right?"

"Yes," said Wesson. "I'm sorry if I'm staring, but I'm still trying to get my head around seeing Ota... with you."

Brooklyn's smile faded and she paused, looking solemn.

"Oh. Are you guys having sex?"

"What?" blurted Wesson, flushing red. "No!"

Everyone in the team was comfortable with each other, but they didn't share their private lives. She had female friends at the base, but their conversations had avoided intimate details of their relationships. Wesson loved Ota as much as she loved everyone on her team, but it was a family bond of trust.

"No," she said honestly. "He's not my type."

"I'm glad to hear it," said Brooklyn, her green eyes brightening up. "I'd feel awful putting you on the spot like that."

"No," said Wesson. "No spot. We're okay."

"Fair enough," said Brooklyn. "Ya look like hell, if ya don't mind me saying. That's a good thing. It shows you're putting everything into your training. Walt'll appreciate that."

"I'm happy to hear it," said Wesson, wincing as she tested her shoulder.

"See ya around, Lori," said Brooklyn.

"Yeah," said Wesson, eager to sink into the neck-deep water of the hot tub.

———

The morning sun was still beneath the horizon but the sky was lightening as the team entered the courtyard. Walt watched them as they wordlessly lined up for the days instructions.

Like the day before, their training was a grueling repeat of drills until the sun had arched across the sky, disappearing behind the mountains.

Before his aching body surrendered to fatigue, Tate had laid on his bed, feeling a wave of pride for everyone in the team.

During their sessions, nobody complained or made excuses. It was clear to anyone watching that all of them struggled, but they kept it to themselves.

The groans and complaints only surfaced after their day was done.

By the fourth day, all of them had broken past natural physical and mental resistance to learning something new.

Movements were becoming more natural. Their reflexes improved in speed as their muscle memory took over.

At the end of the fourth day, Walt told them he was giving them the next day to rest and recover.

Tate's shoulders could have cried with joy. Having a day off was such a simple thing, yet it had the effect of lifting everyone's spirits.

Rosse said he was going to spend the entire day sitting in a hot bath with a plate of food within arm's reach. Fulton wanted to explore the rest of the temple, which prompted Tate to remind everyone of the rules. It was a sobering moment as they all remembered to watch their step.

The following morning, Wesson had finished piling her plate with breakfast and saw Brooklyn wave her over.

"Walt tells me you're doing all right," she said.

Wesson took a bite of a freshly baked roll and mumbled thanks.

"Our supplies are a tad low and since the snow's melted, Ota and I are going out for a bit of hunting," said Brooklyn. "He tells me you're very good at tracking. Feel like stretching your legs?

"That would be great."

"Right then. Meet us at the main door when you're done eating."

Excited to get out of the temple and more than a little curious to see Ota and Brooklyn together, Wesson hurried through her breakfast. She got to the temple door first but didn't have to wait long before they showed up.

Brooklyn carried a quiver of arrows on her back and a longbow in her hand. Ota only carried his sword.

Once they were outside of the temple, Brooklyn led the way onto a worn path that climbed up into the mountain.

Wesson had been away from her usual exercise routine and her thighs were burning by the time the path eventually ended where the ground leveled off.

"Where do we go from here?" she asked, noticing an inviting game trail where the forest thinned out.

"Let your instincts lead the way," said Ota.

"Happy to," she said.

Gold light filtered through the trees and they moved deeper into the woods. Brooklyn and Ota both moved with the same easy quiet and always near each other's side.

After half a mile, Wesson slowed, choosing her path with more care as she scanned for game.

"Are you looking for boar?" she asked.

"Any game will do, but sure," said Brooklyn. "Boar will do nicely."

"There's tracks," Wesson said, pointing to a break in the carpet of fallen leaves.

"Nice work, eagle eye," Brooklyn said. "I would have skipped right past that." She glanced at Ota who was grinning at her. "I'll never hear the end of this."

"Ota knows how to track?" asked Wesson.

Brooklyn looked at her with open surprise. "You didn't know?"

She frowned at Ota, who only shrugged. "I thought you said these were your friends."

"He's a blank page," said Wesson. "We don't even know if Ota's his real name."

"It's the only name I've known and we go way back," said Brooklyn. "What do you know about him?"

"He's into Zen and he's an amazing sniper. The rest of the team have a secret pool about how he learned how to shoot."

"I'm glad he's got some friends, but it sounds a bit one way," she said, frowning at Ota. "You never did tell me how you got interested in Zen," she said. "He told me his shooting story years ago. Your friends fight alongside you, Ota. It seems only right Lori knew something about her friend."

Wesson felt strangely embarrassed being a spectator to his scolding.

"It's not important," she said. "All of us respect each other's privacy."

"There's private and then there's stubborn private," said Brooklyn. "I'll start the story about his shooting while you lead us to the boar. Ota will jump in, I'm sure."

Wesson turned her attention to the tracks, studying their surroundings until she discovered further signs, and then the hunt was on.

"When he was a kid, Ota's dad made a living as a wilderness guide," said Brooklyn quietly. "He'd lead folks into the Canadian backcountry to hunt and when they were done, he'd go back in and lead them out."

Wesson pointed to a tuft of stiff hair snagged on a bush and gestured the direction they would move.

"Did you go with him?" asked Wesson.

"All the time," said Ota.

"The hunters were supposed to check in every couple of days," said Brooklyn. "It's remote country out there. There's nobody around for a fair bit of miles. His dad was annoyed when a party of hunters missed their first check in. That sort of thing happened a lot. But when they missed their second check in, he got worried. So, he takes Ota and together they hike back into those woods."

A gentle breeze puffed against their faces as Wesson spotted another sign of the boar. The animal's signs were leading them to the edge of the woods and they crouched as their cover thinned out.

"Did they find the hunters?" she asked.

"What was left of them," said Brooklyn.

"Bear?"

"Wolves," said Brooklyn.

"A wolf," said Ota. His deep blue eyes grew dark...

Tobias Ota frowned at the mangled bodies of the hunters. All of them had been killed the same way; their throats ripped out. Each of the hunter's faces were stiff with horror, their eyes wide in shock.

"You see here? No claw marks on any of them."

"I see," said Kasey.

He wanted to look away from the bloody sight, but his eyes refused to let go.

"Do you, now?" said his father. "What else do you see, boy?"

Kasey's gaze moved over the hunters, taking in more details.

"They haven't been eaten."

"That's right," said Tobias. "The animals who did this weren't after food. They wanted to kill, not feed."

"But other animals," said Kasey. "There should be nothing left but bone and bits of cloth by now."

"I don't know, son."

Tobias stood up with a sigh and glanced at the woods around them. He backed away from the dead several paces and started walking in a wide circle around them.

"One of them is missing," said Kasey, counting the bodies.

"Yes."

"He got away."

Tobias stopped, looking at the ground at his feet.

"I'm afraid not," he said.

Kasey joined his father and saw a trail of disturbed dirt and pine needles leading off. The drag marks were from something heavy.

Tobias nudged the marks with his boot and shouldered his rifle before following them.

He'd only taken a step when Kasey wrapped his arms around his father's leg, making him stumble.

He could see the fear in his son's face and the shine in the boy's eyes threatened to fill with tears.

"It's all right, boy. I'm always with you."

He stroked Kasey's head then patted his shoulder, signaling it was time to let go.

Kasey clutched his rifle as they stepped into the woods. The natural sounds of the forest he'd heard hundreds of times before felt different today; more menacing and deliberate.

His father was calm but watchful. The drag marks were easy to see and they followed them to where they led into the middle of a clearing.

From the edge of the woods, they could see the rumpled pile of the dead hunter lying alone.

Kasey jumped when his father rested a hand on his shoulder, his strong fingers giving him a squeeze of reassurance, but that sensation disappeared when Kasey looked up and saw his father's troubled expression.

Tobias shifted his rifle in his hands and walked slowly into the clearing. Kasey didn't want to go but staying meant being alone with the dark woods at his back.

When they reached the body, Tobias continued to scan the edge of the clearing.

Kasey felt drawn to look at the hunter but forced himself to start at the man's boots instead of the grisly sight of his face and neck.

The hunter wore dark green wool pants, his knees scuffed and dirty. Bits of grass and pine needles clung to his waxed cotton hunting jacket.

Kasey knew he was getting closer to the terrible wound; what was left of the throat.

He saw a mark on the jacket and looked closer in curiosity. It looked like a wolf's print, but strange.

"Father?" he said.

His father followed his son's pointed finger and the color drained from his face.

"It's Ol' Jack," Tobias said, hardly above a whisper.

Kasey had heard the stories for as long as he could remember. Men would sit around the fire, drinking and telling tales about their travels, lost loves, or the war. Before the fire guttered into glowing embers, the name 'Ol' Jack' would be spoken and the men would go quiet for a moment before the stories would begin.

Ol' Jack was a timber wolf, though some people thought was less animal and more vengeful spirit. He didn't hunt to eat. He hunted to kill and his prey were the women of the village. They could always tell it was him because of his three-toed paw print.

After the fifth victim, they realized he was being selective; choosing only women, like Jack the Ripper. Someone called him Ol' Jack and the name stuck.

Several times the men went into the woods, determined to hunt the wolf down, but they never found him.

Some said his tracks would disappear as if the animal vanished into thin air. Others said the paw prints would end and the bare foots prints of a man would begin.

The stories spooked folks who were given to such nonsense, but they were the stuff of nightmares for the young Kasey.

Even though the men from the village never hunted him down, the attacks on the women stopped. As weeks turned into months, people relaxed. Life went back to normal until the morning was shattered by the screams of a little boy.

He had been playing with his twin sister and their mother was starting on the garden. They were playing chase when there was a blur of shadow and fur. The girl was gone. In the soil of the garden they found a paw print with three toes.

Outraged, a rescue party of five men waded into the forest,

swearing they wouldn't leave until they brought back the girl and Ol' Jack's head on a pike.

They found the wolf's prints next to the small girl's drag marks. The men didn't know what to make of it because the wolf could have easily carried her in its jaws.

As the light began to fade and the woods darkened, the men discovered the wolf wasn't only evil; he was cunning.

They found the girl, her leg badly mangled, laying in the middle of an open clearing. In the waning light, the edge of the woods came alive with the sound of barks and snarls.

Ol' Jack had set a trap and used the little girl as bait.

Of the five men, only one returned.

After that, nobody ventured into the woods. Armed villagers walked the streets during the day and people barred their doors and windows at night.

Nobody felt safe, not even in their own homes. Something more had to be done.

In a heated town meeting, the folks shared their anger and fear until it was decided that if Ol' Jack was the devil, then they'd make the forest his personal Hell.

In the crisp cold of the next morning, everyone man and woman carried cask after cask of oil into the woods and set the thing to blaze. The fire burned for days until there was nothing but the blackened skeletal remains of the trees and scrub.

One, then two, then three years went by. The forest came back, but nobody ever saw another three-toe print again.

Not until Kasey and his father had walked right into the middle of Ol' Jack's trap.

Yaps and howls started at one end of the clearing's edge and were picked up by others from other directions.

Tobias quickly glanced around, spotting a rock ledge in the distance. It was as good a guess as any that Ol' Jack had been watching them from up there.

It was empty now, which meant that the wolf was on his way.

"Listen to me, boy," he said. "We're going to turn Ol' Jack's trick back on him." He pointed to the ledge. "You run to that as fast as you can. Climb to the top and when that wolf steps into the clear, you put a bullet right behind his eye."

"He's going to chase us," said Kasey.

"I'm staying here," said Tobias, glancing at the growing sounds of howls coming from the woods. "I'm going to draw his mangy hide into the open. He won't give you a second thought. Imagine the look on his face when you shoot him."

He smiled at Kasey like they were playing a great game. The young boy didn't understand the trade his father was making to save his life, but he knew something terrible was happening. He just didn't know what.

Kasey glanced at the distant ledge, then at his father, feeling the strength melting from his legs.

"I can't," he said. "I'll miss or hit you."

"Shhhh, son. You'll do fine."

"No, come with me. Please," begged Kasey. "It's too far. I need you to show me how to shoot him."

Tobias squeezed his arm so hard it made the boy gasp.

"I'll be there," he said, looking into his son's eyes. "When you look through the rifle scope, listen carefully. You'll hear me whispering to you. As long as you keep your eye to the glass, I'll be right next to you. You know I wouldn't lie to you."

"No. You never would."

"Then trust me now," said Tobias. "Run, boy. Get up that ledge."

He pushed Kasey away, who turned and ran like the wind.

The howls were fading in the distance as he reached the outcropping of rock. Without stopping, he started to climb. With the rifle slung over his back, he hugged the rock face, clawing for purchase, chewing up his fingertips as he scrabbled up to the top.

Kasey threw his leg over the edge and froze. A scream echoed flatly from the clearing.

Snapping out of it, he clambered to the ledge. A flash of terror ran through him as he imagined dropping his rifle over the edge and he looped his arm through the sling.

He shouldered the rifle, squeezing it hard, like his father had squeezed his arm, and peered through the scope.

He saw a cluster of wolves, jerking and pulling at something. One of them looked up and he saw blood on its muzzle.

He knew under all those gnashing jaws was his father.

Kasey's finger went to the trigger.

I can stop them all.

As if they could read his thoughts, the pack of wolves backed away.

His heart twisted and a whimper of anguish escaped his lips as he saw the mangled wreck of his father. He must have known Kasey was looking at him because he looked right back at him. The white of his eyes stood out starkly from his blood-splashed face.

Kasey blinked the tears from his eyes and saw his father was pointing.

He panned the scope and saw a large, ragged timber wolf approaching his father.

He instantly knew this was Ol' Jack. His eyes weren't like other wolves. They were dark and cunning. When he looked at Tobias, Kasey could see an intelligence in them.

Kasey could feel his heart thudding against the rock and his hands were sweating. He pressed his eye to the scope, mumbling over and over, "Please talk to me. Please."

He could see what was coming. Ol' Jack was relishing the moment before he killed as he paused over Tobias.

"Father, where are you?"

The scope's crosshairs wavered, briefly sliding to the point above the wolf's eye then gone.

Kasey began to tremble, his hands flexing for a better hold of the rifle.

"Fathe..."

I'm here, son. You're not alone.

Kasey nearly leapt off the ground and whipped his head around, but there was nobody else on the rock but him.

He put his eye back to the scope.

Slow your breath. Rest your finger on the trigger.

"I'm doing it," said Kasey. "Can you see me? I'm doing it."

Yes, boy. Now, wait for the shot. Don't rush it. You'll know when it's time.

Kasey steadied the crosshairs on the wolf's head, but it disappeared as Ol' Jack dropped his head, clamping his jaws around Tobias' throat.

A tremble of ache rippled through Kasey as he lowered the crosshairs to the patch of fur above the wolf's eyes, but the wolf was thrashing his head as he tore into Tobias.

With the last of his strength, Tobias wrapped his arms around the wolf's head and held him still.

Here you go, boy. Now.

At the moment he pulled the trigger, the wolf must have sensed danger. Kasey saw understanding and fear in the wolf's eye.

The rifle kicked Kasey hard in the shoulder and Ol' Jack's head snapped back, his body tumbling in the air before landing in the grass, unmoving.

Kasey kept his eye to the scope, looking at the still form of his father. His breath coming in pain-filled gasps.

"Did it hurt?"

No, son. I never felt a thing. I was with you the whole time. You can put the rifle down now.

"No," said Kasey. "I'm never leaving. I don't want you to go."

It's all right, boy. Every time you look through a scope, I'll be right next to you.

"Promise?"

I love you, son.

Wesson stood, speechless. If there was any way to express what she was feeling, it was a mystery to her. She felt an urge to hug Ota, but just as quickly the impulse vanished.

He smiled at her. Maybe he understood what she was thinking.

"My father's been with me ever since," he said.

Wesson waited until he had walked down the trail before turning to Brooklyn.

226

"I never thought he could be so sentimental."

"That's not sentiment," said Brooklyn. "He really believes his father talks to him when he looks through a scope."

Wesson looked at Ota's retreating form as she reshuffled everything she thought she knew about him, but each time the same word rose to the top.

"But, that's..."

"Crazy?" finished Brooklyn. "It wasn't that long ago I would have thought the same thing if someone had told me the dead would come back to life and eat me."

19

OUR WAYS ARE NOT YOUR WAYS

Four days later, the team walked into their hotel room and cheered. Crossing the threshold was a symbolic finish line to their sword training.

In spite of the long journey, they were energized and Tate could see a new level of confidence in them and the bond between the team had strengthened.

Tate was happy to dump his bag on his bed and not think about unpacking for the foreseeable future.

All he wanted was the simple luxuries of padded furniture, carpet underfoot and time to mentally unwind.

That wasn't going to happen.

Among the casual activity, he couldn't help but have his attention drawn to Kiku as she kept herself busy, but always on the periphery of his view.

Her sidelong glances at him were a signal that she needed to talk but felt it would be rude to throw something at him the moment he walked in the door.

Now that he was aware of Kiku, Tate couldn't ignore her.

"Why?" he groaned to himself. "All right, Kiku-san. Is there something you want to talk to me about?"

They both knew it was a rhetorical question, but Kiku reacted as if she hadn't known Tate was in the same room as her.

"Tate-san. Welcome back," she bowed. "When you have settled in, I have..."

"I'm here right now," he smiled.

"This note came for you while you were away."

She handed him a folded note with a business card attached from Detective Makado. Tate briefly mused over discovering his first name, Takeshi, then turned his attention to the handwritten note.

'Tate-san, I'm investigating the Vix attack in Tokyo and require you and your people for further questioning.

Detective Makado.'

Tate looked at his watch, already knowing it was early enough in the day that he couldn't put off the visit until tomorrow.

This won't earn me any friends.

"Listen up, everyone. Detective Makado wants us at the police station A-sap."

"We just got here," groaned Fulton.

"Can I at least take a shower?" asked Monkhouse.

"Believe me," said Tate, "I wish you would, but we need to get Makado out of our hair. The sooner the better."

He saw Wesson giving him a knowing look.

"This wasn't my idea," he said, showing her the note.

She nodded with a wry smile and left to get her jacket.

Tate wasn't sure about this emerging dynamic. In some ways he saw the value of Wesson as a source of a second opinion, even if he wasn't asking for it, but he was used to acting on his own without passing his decision through committee.

He caught himself in mid-thought, recognizing the door-kicker in him liked his current independence and was painting a worst-case scenario of being mother-henned to death. That wasn't Wesson's style.

We'll work it out along the way.

He shrugged as his grumbling team pulled on their coats and gathered at the door.

The novelty of the police station had worn off long ago as the Grave Diggers, especially Monkhouse, weren't happy about being back there.

Tate showed the cop at the front desk Detective Makado's business card, who glanced at it before picking up the phone.

They didn't have to wait long before Makado came in and ushered Tate inside and led him to his desk.

Tate looked at his watch, thinking that this was going to be a long day if Makado was planning on questioning all of them one at a time.

He waited as Makado leafed through a stack of files before taking one out and putting in on his desk.

Tate didn't hide a long sigh as Makado took out a sheet with numbered questions. He'd just sat down and the hardwood chair was already uncomfortable.

"Tate-san," began Makado, "where were you when the Vix attack began?"

It suddenly occurred to Tate that this meeting with Makado had the same feeling as what Kiku was doing this morning. Instead of approaching him directly, she had hovered on the edge of his attention until he brought it up.

If Makado was going to dance around the real topic, Tate would help him get to the point.

"What direction..." began the detective.

Tate leaned forward and whispered, "What's really going on here?"

Makado was momentarily taken aback by the question. He glanced anxiously over his shoulder at his chief, at the back of the room, and just as quickly, his expression returned as if nothing had happened.

He dropped his head and returned to his question.

"What direction were you..."

"The night of the attack, you said these were targeted suicides."

"My English is not very good," said Makado. "I uh, misspoke."

"Misspoke?" smiled Tate. "Pretty good word for someone who's

not good at English. Stop playing games. We both know you're ly..."
He caught himself before insulting the detective. "... Hiding the facts.
Me and my team put our lives on the line to save people from that
attack. Maybe we can help save more."

Makado noticed the paper was trembling in his hands and he put
it down.

"The details of these events are restricted from the public. It
would be a serious breach of duties to reveal details in an ongoing
investigation."

"Makado-san," said Tate, "you didn't bring us down here for this."
He tapped the questionnaire. "You wanted another look at us to
decide if you can trust us. You must have watched the video of us
from all the street security cameras. You know we're capable."

The detective folded his hands on his desk and looked at Tate for
a long time, his thoughts completely hidden behind his deadpan
mask.

Makado wasn't speaking and Tate felt like he had reached a
dead end.

The detective leaned forward, but only enough to keep his voice
from carrying.

"My chief has said these are nothing but random suicides," he
said. "I believe there's more to them and wanted to broaden my investigation. Chief Shota accused me of seeking to further my career at
the cost of needless panic to the public. He took me off the case and
assigned it to other detectives who are more disciplined and will
follow his orders."

"I get it," said Tate. "I've had officers in a hurry to sweep a problem
under the carpet. We both know that's going to backfire. You want to
stop this from happening again. So let's stop it. Look at their case
files, see what's going on."

"Spy on another detective?" flushed Makado.

"I don't mean that."

"I am Japanese," said Makado, his voice rising alarmingly. "We
don't break the rules simply because we don't like them. I am a sworn
officer of the law."

"You're right," said Tate, hoping to salvage the situation, but it was too late. Makado's boss was coming and the man was not happy.

"What's going on here?" barked Chief Shota. "Who is this man? What's he doing here?"

Makado couldn't have looked more guilty as he stood ramrod straight.

"I'm interviewing a witness regarding the event, sir."

"What event?"

"The suicide at the Tokyo metro station," said Makado.

The chief balked and a vein appeared on his forehead.

"There's no evidence it was a suicide," he said. "That's a reckless rumor. You should be ashamed of yourself for entertaining this gossip."

"I was the one who said suicide," said Tate. "Detective Makado was only quoting me."

The chief shifted on his feet and glared at Tate as he struggled to decide how to vent his anger.

"I won't have shouting in my office," he said. "It's unprofessional."

"Hai, Chief Shota," bowed Makado.

"You," snapped the chief, leveling a finger at Tate. "If you don't stop spreading these wild accusations, I'll have you arrested. Got it?"

"Yes," said Tate, glancing at Makado. "I apologize for provoking your detective."

Fuming, the chief fixed on Tate a beat longer before turning back to Makado.

"I want this visitor out of my station."

"Hai," said Makado, bowing sharply. He came around the desk and stood next to Tate. "You and your friends are not needed here," he said officially. "I will escort you out."

Tate stood up, saying nothing. He suspected the chief was hoping the foreigner would give him a reason to have him arrested.

The other detectives watched as Makado ushered Tate back into the front desk area.

If Makado was going to confide anything else about the investigation, now was the time.

"Thank you for your time," said the detective and disappeared behind the door.

"Let's go," said Tate disappointedly, and headed outside.

"I heard shouting," said Wesson.

"We all heard shouting," said Rosse.

"What happened?" asked Monkhouse.

"Looks like you get that shower after all," said Tate.

Kiku must have summoned the SUV because it pulled up next to the curb and the doors opened. There was nobody in the driver's seat. He didn't know why that still unsettled him, but it did.

"Just a moment," called a voice behind them.

They turned around as Detective Makado came out of the station with a scarf in his hand.

"You forgot this," he said.

He pushed the wadded-up scarf into Tate's hand and went back inside with Tate looking on in astonishment.

"He's an odd one," said Rosse.

"It's not mine," said Tate.

He felt something inside the soft folds of the material and unbundled it. Inside was Makado's business card. He turned it over and found a handwritten note with the detective's home address.

"You can stand here if you want," said Rosse. "I'm getting in the car."

Tate nodded and climbed in. The warmth of the heater was a welcome relief.

"What's that?" asked Wesson, seeing the card.

"We've been invited to the detective's home tonight," said Tate, handing it to her.

"His place?" said Monkhouse. "Are we friends now?"

"Maybe," said Tate.

Wesson looked up from the card, frowning at Tate.

"I hardly said anything about the Vix," he said. "Blame Makado."

He sat back, closing his eyes as the SUV pulled into traffic.

A blanket of grey clouds masked the night sky as the SUV turned into the narrow street. Light spilled out of a small restaurant tightly wedged between the rows of apartment buildings and Tate suddenly felt a longing to be like the people sitting at the counter; casually passing an evening with friends with no other demands on him.

He saw the address on the building that matched Makado's note and put the card in his pocket.

"This is the..." he began.

"We have arrived," said the SUV.

Tate frowned at the dashboard, not knowing which of the multiple interior cameras was looking at him.

He considered telling the car to stop interrupting him but changed his mind. He didn't want to be that guy who argues with a car.

Everyone got out except Kiku.

"I will leave you to visit the detective," she said. "Call when you are ready to leave, or you need my services."

"I will," said Tate, imagining the surrealistic scene of him calling her to decapitate someone.

He turned and led the way through a front gate of the building. Their path opened to the narrow stairway leading to Makado's apartment on the second floor.

Tate knocked on the door and Detective Makado quickly answered.

"Please, come in," he said, bowing and motioning with his hand.

Just inside the door was a small landing where they were expected to take off their shoes. By the time they were all inside, the landing was crowded with shoes.

The small apartment opened directly into the kitchen where the lingering smell of cooked noodles mingled with ginger.

Makado guided them into the living room, most of which was taken up by a small, fold-away couch meant for two people. The group shuffled to fit, standing shoulder to shoulder. Makado attempted to make more space by folding up the couch and storing it out of the way.

"Thank you for inviting us," said Tate. "Sorry if I got you in trouble with your boss."

"It could not be avoided," said Makado, taking a seat on the floor. "He is angry all the time."

"Is that you?" asked Tate, seeing a photograph on the wall of a small figure clinging to the face of a sheer cliff.

"Yes," said Makado. "I like, uh, outdoors."

The other photographs were equally impressive and Tate realized his earlier opinion of the detective had been short sighted. He was not an empty suit, too timid to think for himself.

A pot began to whistle from the kitchen and Makado stood up, frowning.

"I was making tea, but... I'm sorry. I don't have enough cups for all of you."

The team started talking at once, thanking him and politely declining the offer.

Tate looked at his team, amused. They were tough and combat tested, none of them would shy away from a fight, but were just as quick to show their softer side.

Makado wove his way through the group and into the kitchen to turn off the stove.

When he returned, Tate saw it as a good time to get to business.

"I'd like to hear more about the Tokyo attack," he said. "It was an attack, wasn't it?"

"Hai," said Makado grimly. "One of many. Yet it was decided by members of the National Police Agency that disclosing the truth to the public would only result in unnecessary panic."

"It's also kept the public unprepared," said Tate. "What's really going on?"

Makado pursed his lips and started to speak and stopped several times.

"Tate-san," he finally began. "This is very difficult for me. I have sworn an oath to uphold the law, but I must also follow orders. These things are now in conflict."

"We're not Japanese or cops," said Tate. "If you wanted to get technical, that means we're not restricted by the same rules."

Makado's eyebrows raised as he understood the loophole of Tate's logic.

"You are clever, Tate-san, but it is a very thin line I am walking."

"You can trust everyone here that whatever you say will never be repeated to anyone else," said Tate.

The sincerity of his words were reflected in the solemn faces of the rest of the team.

Makado studied each of them, weighing his decision. His shoulders sagged as he sighed heavily and glanced at his teacup.

"There have been four of these suicide attacks," said Makado. "Each one in a different city. And each one more lethal. The first was a woman who jumped from an office building. The outbreak was minimal because everyone had their masks on. The man who killed himself, in this most recent attack, used gas to induce others to remove their mask."

"That made it easier to create more Vix," said Wesson.

"Hai. I had spoken to detectives in the other cities and was convinced these weren't random suicides. My chief wouldn't listen, but the use of gas forced my higher-ups to recognize that someone was coordinating these events. They're also changing their tactics to kill more people with each attack."

"Do you have any leads?" asked Wesson.

"Unfortunately, the bodies of the earlier suicides were burned, leaving no evidence. Except... this last one. The man who used the gas. I saw that the coroner has finished his examination of the body."

Makado took a folder from the bookshelf and withdrew a printed sheet.

"I took the coroner's request to destroy the body before the chief saw it."

Tate was about to compliment him on the good move, but Makado looked ashamed of himself.

"What does it say?" he asked instead.

"Among the personal effects is a suicide note," said Makado. "It does not elaborate on what it says. It may not be significant."

"Or it could tell you everything you need to stop whoever's behind this," said Tate.

"It don't take a rocket scientist to figure out we need to see what's on that note," said Rosse.

"I've never been to a morgue," said Monkhouse.

"I'm afraid that's impossible," said Makado. "I have been forbidden from working on this case. The clerk at the morgue would surely report me."

Tate nodded in understanding then looked at each of his team. Each of them met his gaze with a knowing nod and confident smile.

"Who said anything about going in the front door?" said Tate.

The plan to break into the morgue was simple, but that was mostly because there wasn't time to study, detail and organize what to do.

Tate and Wesson did a quick assessment of the simple, one-story building and boiled down their actions to the most basic.

They would enter through the rear of the building while the rest of the team waited out of sight.

The small parking lot was empty except for one car. The receiving desk was clearly visible in the bright office lights, but there was no sign of the clerk. Except for the front of the building, the rest of the exterior was poorly lit, if at all. Since the Vix outbreak, security hadn't been given a second thought. After all, what sane person would want to break into a morgue?

Tate's bet was the kid was sleeping on a couch in the boss's office.

Wesson gave him a questioning look.

"Sometimes you just operate on your best guess until you learn otherwise," he said.

Tate and Wesson carefully peered through the windows on the sides of the building but saw nothing but darkened rooms.

They moved around to the back of the building, where they found a bicycle leaning against the wall, and a dumpster.

One by one they checked the most likely window to force open.

"What about the door?" said Wesson, standing next to it.

All they had was her sword and his tomahawk. Both would lose the battle of trying to pry open the metal door.

"We don't have the right tools," said Tate. "I'll try the window over..."

Wesson turned the knob and opened the door.

Neither of them expected that and gawked in surprise.

Together they slipped inside and found themselves in a small room that opened into a dark hallway. The only light came from the front desk at the other end.

Following Makado's description of the building, they quietly moved down the hall until they reached the fourth door on the left. Unlike the others, this one was all metal with a wire mesh window. Cracking it open, their nostrils were instantly assaulted by the reek of embalming fluid and decayed flesh.

In the weak light, they could just make out eight square refrigerator doors on the opposite wall.

"Which one?" asked Wesson with no enthusiasm.

"You start at one end. I'll start at the other," said Tate. "One of us are bound to find Mr. Right," he shrugged.

"Or," she said, "I could watch the door and you can demonstrate your leadership qualities by checking the meat lockers alone."

Tate couldn't see her face clearly but was sure she was grinning at him.

"Fine," he said.

Wesson stayed by the door, occasionally peeking out of the window as Tate checked the first locker.

Cold air spilled out when he opened the door. It was impossible to see into the dark and he started to reach inside but stopped. A voice in his head yelled that he was about to stick his hand into a dark hole that might contain a Vix.

His rational mind told him it was stupid to think they'd transport a live Vix and keep it a locker.

Better safe than sorry.

Tate rapped his knuckles on the side of the locker and listened for any movement. The quiet remained unbroken, and he felt inside until his hand bumped against an empty tray.

He went to the next locker and knocked again. No response.

"What are you doing?" whispered Wesson.

"You do it your way," said Tate. "I'll do it mine."

Each of the lockers were empty, but as he opened the last door a horrible but familiar stench trickled out, mingled with the frosty air.

All of his instincts told him not to reach inside. With his free hand, he grabbed his tomahawk, then reached inside.

His hand touched the bottom of a shoe and he felt around until he found the tray's handle and pulled.

The metal casters gently rattled as the tray rolled out and stopped with a loud click.

"I just figured out why the back door was unlocked," said Wesson, ducking down from the window.

Nothing in her voice sounded good.

"That's how the clerk snuck his girlfriend inside and they're coming this way."

20

SEA OF TREES

Tate tugged on the tray, trying to push it back in, but it had locked into place and he couldn't find the release catch in the dark.

Worse, there was nothing in the room to hide behind.

Wesson saw him glance at the locker doors and went pale.

"I am not getting in there," she hissed.

"Monkhouse," whispered Tate over his radio, "knock on the front door!"

"Did you say..."

"Now," said Tate. "Right now."

"Too late," said Wesson.

Tate could hear muted voices and giggling from the hallway.

"Hold the door closed," he said.

Wesson stuck her shoe in front of the door a hair's breadth before the clerk pushed. They heard the surprise in his voice and Wesson hunched out of sight behind the door.

He pushed harder, cracking the door open before she shoved it back closed.

So much for stealth.

They were out of time and Tate knew they had to find the corpse's personal effects and blow out of there.

He grimaced as he blindly patted the naked Vix, searching for the bag of items.

"Monkhouse, where are you?" he asked.

"Almost there," panted Monkhouse. "We parked down the street."

"Are you running?"

Something meaty fell off the tray and landed on Tate's boot. He reached down and picked up an arm. They'd dissected the Vix.

Light from the hallway came through a gap in the door as the clerk pushed with more determination.

"I can't hold it," said Wesson.

Tate's hand landed on a face and flinched. Everything in him screamed against putting his hand near a Vix's mouth. The head rolled on the tray and he realized it had been severed from the body for examination. Plastic crinkled when his hand landed on something he was sure was the bag of personal effects.

With nothing to brace herself, Wesson was losing the battle of the door.

"We're screwed," she said.

"Bring the car around back," said Tate. "This instant."

Biting back the rising bile in his gut, he grabbed the Vix's head by the hair and ran across the room. He shoved the face against the mesh window. Outside the door, the hallway filled with screams of holy terror.

Pounding footsteps echoed down the hall and the glass front door shattered as the clerk threw it open as he charged for his car.

Tate tossed the head and helped Wesson up. They ran into the hallway and bolted for the back door. Thankfully, the SUV was waiting for them and they dove in.

"What the heck's going on?" yelled Monkhouse over the radio. "A kid jumped in his car and almost ran me over."

"Stay put," said Tate. "We're coming to you."

Rosse gunned the SUV and they swung around the corner to the front of the building.

Standing under the lights of the parking lot was a very confused Monkhouse holding a young girl, sobbing uncontrollably.

"I bet that's the last time she ever dates that guy," said Wesson.

After dropping the girl at her home, they drove back to Makado's apartment to examine the contents of the bag.

This time, Tate, Wesson and Monkhouse gratefully accepted the offered tea and watched as the detective studied each of the suicide victims' possessions.

Makado picked up a wadded-up piece of paper and carefully unfolded it. Tate could see it was written in Kanji and quietly waited for him to translate it.

Makado went rigid, cursing under his breath.

"Excuse me," he said, standing up and threading through the group. He opened a draw and rifled through it, talking to himself with a troubled tone.

He came back with another folder and sat down. He opened the folder and flipped through several pages before stopping.

Tate watched Makado's face crease with worry as he placed the crumpled paper next to the page in the folder.

Everyone watched him closely, searching for meaning. The detective sighed deeply, dropping his head and muttering something in Japanese.

"You know this ain't gonna be good," said Rosse.

"No Rosse-san," said Makado. "This is very, very bad."

Tate could see Makado struggling with his thoughts but couldn't wait any longer.

"What's going on, Makado-san?" he asked. "What does the suicide note say?"

"It is not a suicide note. It's a verse from the book of a death cult."

Makado could hardly bring himself to touch the paper as he turned it towards Tate.

"It says, 'An enlightened death saves all'."

"I don't understand," said Wesson.

"Nobody does," said Makado. "Twelve years ago, a lunatic, Yoshikaw Ichizo began a religion called The Society of Light. They believed the world was besieged by evil spirits, uh, bad karma. Ichizo had written a book called Warriors of the Sacred Gate. Into it, he poured all of his madness and paranoia.

He proclaimed himself as The Keeper, the holder of all truths and tasked his followers with selling his book. I don't understand how anyone made sense of his gibberish, but his cult grew."

"I knew this wasn't gonna be good," said Rosse.

"The swelling of followers convinced him that he was operating under divine instructions. The few details we know from there are from the handful of followers that deserted the cult. They said Ichizo had become convinced the bad karma would soon sweep across the earth and curse everyone that fell under its power. He believed people could be saved if they were killed by someone possessing true enlightenment."

"An enlightened death saves all," said Tate.

"Hai," said Makado. "Ichizo would select a follower and give them instructions to go to a populated area, then kill as many people as possible."

"That's nuts," gasped Fulton.

"The police cornered him, but before they could reach him, he burned himself alive. They couldn't identify the body, but they assumed Ichizo was dead."

"Until now," said Wesson.

"And now he's using his followers to commit suicide," said Monkhouse. "That's sick."

Makado picked through the other items from the bag.

"What could make someone want to die for this guy?" asked Tate.

"More like where does he find someone who wants to die?" said Rosse.

"The sea of trees," said Makado, holding up a train ticket.

The group looked at him, not understanding.

"The Aokigahara forest," explained Makado. "It is a place at the base of Mount Fuji, believed to be full of spirits. Sadly, people who have given up on life often go there to die. If the person behind these attacks really is Ichizo, it makes sense that he would go there to take advantage of those who are completely lost."

"Do you have a picture of this man?" asked Tate.

"Yes," said Makado.

"Then we go to this forest and stop this from happening again."

"No Tate-san," said Makado, alarmed. "This is a matter for the police. If they learn you are involved, you will be arrested for interfering with an investigation."

"Makado-san," said Tate. "How are you going to explain to your chief how you learned that Ichizo is behind these attacks? Are you going to tell him you broke into the morgue, stole evidence and disobeyed his direct order to stay off the case?"

Makado glanced from the evidence to Tate as despair filled his eyes.

"What have I done?"

"You solved the case," said Tate.

"I have disgraced myself, ignored the law and shamed my entire department," said Makado, his eyes stinging with tears.

"Whoa, hang on," said Tate. "Your chief and his bosses are the guilty ones. Instead of enforcing the law and protecting the public, they've done everything they can to block you from doing your job. They're more concerned with protecting their careers than finding the truth. They're the ones who have disgraced the force. What honor is there in being obedient to dishonorable people?"

Makado stared at the floor for a long time. Tate could his him wrestling with his words and trying to see through the complex layers of duty and truth.

The detective looked up and Tate and saw the change in his eyes. Makado had the same rugged confidence as the man in the photographs.

"We will go and finally stop this evil," he said. "I will accept the consequence of my actions, but I will always know my actions were honorable."

The sky was a brilliant blue and the air crisp and cool. Stepping off the train, Tate closed his eyes and enjoyed the warmth of the sun on his face. Something good was cooking nearby and he inhaled the scent, making his mouth water. The food from the train's snack cart had been enough to take the edge off his hunger, but now that he smelled real food, his appetite had come to life and he was eager.

Small mom and pop restaurants had set up to take advantage of the people coming off the train, and it didn't help that everything smelled good.

Wesson steered clear of the shops displaying bowls of 'sea creatures' and unidentifiable things sticking out of the broth.

Kiku didn't like everyone splitting up as they scattered to see what to eat. She found a spot in the broad walkway where she could see everyone and watched them with a diligent but relaxed eye.

The cook handed Tate a couple of bamboo skewers with breaded chicken and he walked over to Kiku, handing one to her.

"Domo," she said, happily taking the food.

"Wow," said Fulton, gazing at the distant giant of Mount Fuji. "We don't have anything like that back home."

"If you are interested," said Kiku, "you can hike up the mountain."

"No kidding?" he grinned.

"No way," said Rosse. "Gemme flat ground any day."

"What are we talking about?" asked Wesson, holding a half-eaten steamed bun.

"We're going to hike Mount Fuji," said Fulton.

"Hang on, kid," said Rosse with growing alarm. "Nobody said 'we'. You can knock yourself out climbing that thing. Just find me one of them hot tubs an' I'll be happy as a clam."

Tate imagined how rewarding it would feel to meet the challenge of hiking the mountain.

Out of reflex he glanced at his stomach and the self-defeating voice in his head told him he'd be lucky to make it halfway up before he was gasping for breath and giving up.

Before leaving Delta Force, he'd been toned, fit and muscled. When his daughter died, everything fell apart, including his body and spirit.

He shook his head, clearing that dark time from his mind. He had found life again and slowly but surely he had picked himself up and put himself back together. Yet, in spite of hard exercise and mostly sticking to a reasonable diet, he couldn't get rid of the persistent fat around his waist.

He was beginning to wonder if gaining weight came with the wrinkles and grey hair of getting older.

Someone laughed and he snapped out of his doldrums.

It's the miles, not the years.

That much was true. His time in special forces had added a lot of miles to his life. Somedays he felt them more than others...

Knock it off! Focus on the here and now.

Annoyed, he yanked on his focus like the leash of an unruly dog and tried to catch up on what everyone was talking about.

"Tate-san," said Makado. "We will need a car to get there while the light is good."

They couldn't find a rental big enough to hold everyone and ended up with two cars.

With Makado in the lead car, he guided them out of the town and towards the Sea of Trees.

As they neared the forest, the change in the landscape was unmistakable. Tall, full pines thinned out, replaced by dense, stunted trees and thick foliage.

They pulled into a small parking lot bordered by the forest on every side. Iron grey clouds had crept in, cutting them off from the sun. The air smelled damp with earth and mold. Everything about the place seemed foreign and ancient.

"This is one of the most common paths into the forest," said Makado.

They looked at the gloomy, wide, dirt trail with instinctive reluctance.

Tate noticed Wesson's hand was resting on the hilt of her sword. Looking at the others, he saw she wasn't the only one.

"All right kids, let's go," he said. "Everyone remember where we parked."

It wasn't long before the entrance to the forest was gone from sight and the trees had closed in around them.

Tate had been all over the world, in all kinds of places, but there was nothing he could compare to this.

Roots came out of the ground like gnarled fingers, twisting and bent. The trees were crooked and bent, their limbs heavy with moss. The ground was a jumble of uneven mounds of rock and earth with ferns and shrubs twisted around each other in a fight for what beams of light could find their way through the dense canopy of trees.

"This is gotta be the most depressing place I've ever been," said Rosse.

"How far does this trail go?" asked Wesson.

"Several kilometers," said Makado.

"We'll be here for days," said Fulton.

"Everyone dial it back a little," said Tate. "This guy isn't hiding under a rock. He's looking for new members to his cult. It's a good guess he's in the woods watching who's on the trails."

"He's watching us?" asked Fulton. "Like right now?"

"Maybe," said Tate.

"If that's true," said Wesson, "he's not going to show himself to a crowd."

"Yes," said Makado. "He will not approach us."

"But we don't look like a bunch of people out for a hike," said Tate. "If he's seen us, I'm betting he's curious why we're here and hasn't run off."

"So what then?" said Rosse. "We just bumble around this haunted forest like a bunch of morons while he hides in the bush, laughing at us?"

"Isn't that what we've been doing for the past half hour?" asked Monkhouse.

"Yeah," said Tate. "We're not getting anywhere doing this. Let's change tactics."

He cupped his hands around his mouth and took a deep breath.

"Yoshikaw Ichizo. Why does the Keeper of the Sacred Gate hide?"

"Tate-san," hissed Makado. "You'll drive him awa..."

"Am I hiding? Or is it that your unbelief keeps you from seeing me?" cried a voice.

Everyone looked in different directions, hearing his voice coming from everywhere.

"We believe enough to come looking for you," said Tate. This time he brought down the volume of his voice, using it to range how close Ichizo was able to hear him.

"Knowing of me and believing in me is not the same thing," said Ichizo.

"But we serve the same purpose," said Tate, lowering his voice even more. "To stop evil from destroying the world."

"What do you know about evil?" snapped Ichizo. "I have seen it. Made it wither under my divine light."

"He's close," said Tate. "When I give the signal, everyone head in the direction you hear his voice."

"You think you can stop me?" screamed Ichizo. "I will send an army of my followers into every corner of Japan and wipe you from..."

"Go now," barked Tate. "Run him down."

Ichizo's words cut short as the group charged into the woods, fanning out in every direction.

Tate had no idea where everyone was and couldn't risk a single glance as he ducked and vaulted limbs, roots, rocks, and vines. The forest was alive with the sounds of people crashing through branches and brush.

In spite of the cold, sweat was already trickling down Tate's face and the frigid air raked painfully into his lungs.

He was hoping the group's mad dash would panic Ichizo and flush him out, but Tate was running out of steam and his legs were starting to lose their strength.

Movement!

Something white flashed between the trees. It took a second for his brain to register the form of a running man.

"Got you," said Tate.

His body protested with mounting fatigue, but he had his prey in sight and pushed himself harder than ever.

He'd lost sight of the running figure for only a few seconds, but in these woods, that was all it took to disappear.

SNAP!

It came from Tate's right. He had to keep the pressure on. He bolted deeper into the woods towards the sound and was rewarded by the fleeting sight of someone in a white shirt before they disappeared again.

Breathing hard, Tate took off, trying to close the distance. He raced through the obstacle course of rocks, trees, and branches, ducking and jumping, refusing to slow down.

A large fallen tree blocked his path and he vaulted over, but the other side was a tangle of roots that snagged his foot.

Tate heard his ankle pop and pain shot through him as his foot folded under. He stumbled with his next step, his foot refusing to hold his weight and he fell to his knees.

Snarling against the pain, refusing to let it win, he got up and drove himself harder. He caught sight of the shirt to his left. He was close. Really close. Just behind the thick tree.

Tate raced around the tree, coiled, ready to fight.

There was no one.

He looked in every direction, convinced Ichizo was right here, but he'd disappeared. His mind raced back to a memory when he and his team of Night Devils were chasing down a group of hostiles. They were in a dry riverbed and the bad guys had just turned a corner. The Night Devils were a second behind, but when they came around the corner, the bad guys had vanished. Gone, into thin air... all except their footprints.

They led around what looked like a solid wall of the ravine, but it was an optical illusion, a fold in the wall of the wadi that blended against the background, hiding a cave.

That's where he went.

Tate only had to take a few steps and the mouth of a cave, neatly camouflaged by a trick of light and foliage, revealed itself.

The mouth of the rocky cave was ancient, dark and foreboding. Tate didn't give a damn.

His jaw clenched, grinding dirt and grit between his teeth as he stalked into the dark.

With his hand on the cave wall as a guide, he went deeper inside and came to a sharp.

Stepping around the corner, he entered into a pool of weak light.

Waiting for him was Ichizo.

He stared at Tate between strands of sweat-soaked hair. There was no mistaking the glint of insanity that shined in his eyes.

Around him was strewed his camp. A makeshift desk held papers, books and a laptop.

"Your time's up," growled Tate, panting hard.

"I have nothing but time," hissed Ichizo. "An eternal gift from my followers."

"Do all you nut jobs read from the 'how to run a sick cult' book?" said Tate.

"Cult?" scoffed Ichizo. He nodded to the laptop. "I have hundreds of followers. I speak to them every day."

"Once you're in prison," said Tate, "you won't be talking to anyone."

"I won't need to," chuckled Ichizo. The confidence in his voice sent a tremor of worry through Tate.

He was missing something; something big.

"I'll be in front of news cameras for days before my trial," said Ichizo. "A moment is all I need to send a message to my followers. Did you hear about Tokyo?"

"I was there," said Tate.

"I did that with one message," said Ichizo. "One! Just imagine when I'm on television in front of all of my followers at once and give them the same message. On that day, they'll spread out into every city in Japan. All over the country, my followers will commit themselves to an enlightened death. Millions will be saved."

Tate took a step and Ichizo recoiled with a shout.

"Yruku!"

A young girl appeared from the shadows behind him. He grabbed her, putting her between him and Tate.

Her bite mask, like the rest of her was dirty and smudged with grime. Her vacant eyes wandered over Tate's face with a distant smile.

"How long have you been keeping this kid?" asked Tate, as fresh waves of anger surged through his limbs.

Ichizo bent to the girl's ear and whispered something, who nodded and cocked her head towards Tate.

Her hand appeared from behind the folds of her filthy dress and light winked off polished steel as she drew the sword from the scabbard.

Tate's tomahawk was in his hand before he thought of drawing it.

"I'm not fighting a kid, you sick bastard," he said.

"You're not supposed to."

Ichizo's hand unhooked the girl's mask, letting it fall to the ground. Tate's mind refused to accept the meaning.

"This child will save you," said Ichizo, squeezing her shoulder.

The girl raised her sword, spinning it around to point at herself and pulled the sword down.

Tate's tomahawk whistled through the air. Her head rocked back and the axe's blunt handle walloped her above the eye.

With a groan, she staggered and crumpled to the ground. The sword clattered to the cave floor, unstained by her blood.

Ichizo stared at the girl, unable to accept what he was seeing.

"You want to save me so bad," growled Tate. "Pick that up and drive it through your own gut."

Ichizo's eyes fixed on the sword as though it was about to bite him.

"I am the keeper of the sacred gate," he muttered. "I can't die."

"I've heard that before, too."

"I will speak to my followers," said Ichizo, dashing for the laptop.

Tate rushed forward and hammered on the lid with his fist, smashing it closed on Ichizo's fingers. Gasping in pain, he jumped away from Tate and picked up the fallen sword.

"You can't keep me from my followers forever. They'll find a way to see me. And then... and then they'll spread my word to save everyone. EVERYONE."

21

AMBUSH

One by one, the scattered team returned to the trail where they had charged off after Ichizo.

They looked at each other with scratched and dirt smudged faces, hoping for a sign of success that one of them had found him.

With each return, the more defeated Makado looked and the more worried Kiku became.

Monkhouse wandered into the group, battered and bleeding from his cheek.

"What happened to you?" said Rosse, reaching for his med kit.

"I thought I saw him hiding under a log," said Monkhouse, wincing as Rosse cleaned the wound. "Easy!"

"He bit you?" asked Fulton.

"No. A gopher bit me."

"You mistook a gopher for a full-sized man?" smirked Wesson.

"Hey, it was a big gopher," said Monkhouse.

"We must look for Tate-san," said Kiku.

"She's right," said Makado. "It's getting dark. Finding him after nightfall will be impossible."

Behind them was a rustle of brush and Tate and a young girl came into the clearing of the trail.

Everyone looked from the girl to Tate in confusion.

"Who's that?" asked Wesson.

"Long story," he said. "Someone take the kid. Oh, and keep her away from your swords."

"I got her," said Fulton.

"Ichizo," said Makado, looking anxious. "He's escaped again?"

"I found him," said Tate.

Everyone waited, anticipating the rest of the story, but he only sat down on a rock and brushed the dirt off his pants.

"Where is he?" asked Makado.

"Dead."

Makado looked into the darkening forest as Tate stood up to leave.

"Tate-san," said Makado gravely. "What happened to him?"

"I guess he didn't like the sound of prison life," said Tate.

"He killed himself?"

"Like the man said," sighed Tate. "An enlightened death saves all." He started hobbling back towards the car with Makado frowning at his back. "Let's get out of here. I'm hungry."

Tate had little to say and generally ignored the side-long glances from Makado.

It was late in the evening by the time the train pulled into Tokyo station, and everyone was heavy with the fatigue of a long day.

"It will be difficult to explain the girl to my chief," said Makado.

"Give him credit for finding a lost kid and he'll get over it pretty quick," said Tate.

"Tate-san," said Makado, fixing him with a stare. "Back at the forest..."

Tate straightened and looked Makado in the eyes.

"Come on, Makado," he said. "Say what's on your mind. Put it out there."

"I think you killed Ichizo."

"See?" he said. "That wasn't so hard."

He turned to leave and Makado put his hand on Tate's shoulder.

"Did you?"

"After what he's done," said Tate, "would you have killed him?"

The detective paused, letting go of Tate, but said nothing.

"That's not an answer," said Makado.

"Would you believe me if I told you no?" Tate paused a beat, seeing the indecision in Makado's face.

Tate turned and walked away. "Hope you find the girl's family."

Tate woke up the next morning with a headache and throbbing ankle. He blinked the grit from his eyes and wiped muddy drool off his chin.

Last night he fell into bed, unwilling to wait for his turn to take a shower. He looked at the dirt-smeared disaster of his bed and remembered he was still wearing yesterday's clothes.

Yeah, house keeping's going to really love you.

Standing up, he nearly fell over as his ankle refused to take any weight. The shock of pain blew away the remaining cobwebs of sleep and he gingerly made his way to the shower.

Before long, billows of steam were pouring over the top of the shower door and Tate gratefully stepped into the hot stream of water.

Every cut and scrape had its moment to sting before it succumbed to the soothing heat.

By the time he got out of the shower, he felt lighter and refreshed. He rolled up his pile of filthy clothes in a large bath towel before heading back to his room.

Ota's bed was empty, which didn't surprise him. Ota routinely woke early.

Tate felt like a new man as he got dressed in fresh clothes. He rubbed the stubble on his jaw, checking himself in the mirror. The scratches on his face discouraged him from shaving and he shrugged, content to live with the whiskers for a while longer.

He went into the living room, seeing room service had come and gone, along with most of the breakfast buffet. If he was expecting probing looks from the team about Ichizo, he didn't get any.

He was their friend, teammate and leader. If he said the man killed himself, that was all they needed.

"Hey, Top," said Rosse, pushing himself away from the table. "Why don't ya plant yourself on the couch, an' I'll tape up your ankle."

"I thought you'd never ask," said Tate.

"I didn't," scoffed Rosse.

Tate suspected one of the things Rosse enjoyed about being the team's medic was telling people what to do. Tate couldn't object because the man was good at what he did and usually didn't get too pushy about it.

He was thinking about asking if he had anything for the pain when the sat phone started chiming.

I bet he doesn't have anything in his bag for the pain on the other end of this call.

"I'm here," said Tate, picking up the call.

"The other side just called," said Mullen. "They want to meet today."

Tate sat up, feeling the morning's relaxation drain away.

"No chance," he said, squeezing his eyes closed, instantly regretting his response.

"I say what's chance and no chance," snapped Mullen. "I'm the guy running the show, remember? You're the hired guns, or do I have to explain what hired means?"

"We don't have guns," said Tate.

"Whatever," said Mullen.

"Sir, this doesn't give us any time to prepare..."

"There's nothing to prepare for," said Mullen. "It's the same location as the first meeting."

"We haven't coordinated with the other team."

"You're not the one sticking his neck out," said Mullen. "I'm doing the meeting today and then I'm out of here. You tell your FBI guys to be ready to take off the minute I get to the airport. The longer I'm exposed, the easier it is for The Ring to get me."

"No one's going to get you," sighed Tate. "What time's the meeting?"

"One thirty. Don't be late," said Mullen and disconnect the call.

Levi took off the headset and turned to the other members of the team.

"We're on. Check your gear and get ready to head out."

The room broke into activity as everyone pulled out their equipment and prepared.

Cowboy put down his book and took his gun case off the wall. He put the heavy case on the table and unzipped it. He nodded with satisfaction at the six magazines of armor-piercing ammo.

Oh yes, he was ready. Screw what the boss said. This job was going down his way.

Tate looked up at the SUV's vanity mirror to check on Mullen, still fidgeting in the back seat.

Rosse was sitting back in the driver's seat with his big arms crossed over his chest, smiling as he watched the steering wheel move under the control of the car's onboard computer. The novelty hadn't worn off.

Fulton, sitting next to Mullen, looked every inch the professional and Tate smiled to himself, thinking how far the young man had come.

He checked the map display and keyed his radio.

"Four miles out," he said over the radio. "Status?"

As part of the advance team, Ota was already perched high up in the building across the street from the meeting. He swept the street below with his binoculars, seeing nothing out of the ordinary.

"Ota checking in," he said. "The other group arrived two minutes ago. Everything's clear."

Wesson was on the ground floor below Ota, and did a quick glance up and down the street.

"Wesson checking in. Everything's normal."

"Monkhouse checking in. Not that anyone cares, but the parking lot is free of bad guys."

"Keep the channel clear," said Tate, smiling in spite of himself. Monkhouse had drawn the short straw and was half a block away, babysitting the car.

The SUV turned onto their primary street and Tate straightened up in his seat, feeling the concealed Colt .45 dig into his back.

He was unconcerned about the meeting and saw it as more of a training exercise, but his 1911 was a part of him as much as his tomahawk. It was a point of professionalism that he'd left that at the hotel room, but the Colt? He just felt naked without it.

"I have eyes on you," said Ota over the radio.

The SUV turned into the mouth of the underground garage and disappeared from view.

As they came off the ramp, they saw the other team's car with two of their security team standing next to it.

"Looks like they brought more guys than the last time," said Rosse, taking hold of the wheel. "I got this, car."

"You have control," said the car.

"Park us a few spaces closer to the exit," said Tate.

Rosse glanced at him but did as directed.

"Nothing's wrong," said Tate. "I just want first shot at getting out of here if we're in a hurry."

Rosse stopped the car and he, Fulton and Tate got out. Tate stood overwatch while Fulton came around and opened the door for Mullen.

The other men watched them with mild interest.

Fulton stayed with the car while Tate and Rosse escorted Mullen to the elevator.

"We're inside," said Tate.

His radio clicked twice as Ota and Wesson acknowledged the message.

The elevator came to a smooth stop and opened into a large, glass-walled room. Four security people stood in each corner of the room.

Tate didn't like the situation. No matter where he stood, there would be someone at his back.

He took a breath, reminding himself that this was not a meeting between two hostile enemies. He scanned for the tell-tale bulge of a gun under their jackets but saw nothing to indicate they were armed.

Mullen crossed the room and shook hands with his counterpart and the two men sat down to begin their meeting.

Twenty minutes later, Monkhouse was getting bored and the sushi shop across the street was putting a keen edge on his hunger.

He put his hand on the radio, thought better of it and let go; changed his mind again and keyed the radio.

"How long's this supposed to go?"

Wesson hotly squeezed the radio.

"Get off the channel," she growled. "That's an order."

Monkhouse let go of the radio like it had bit him.

"I have a degree in engineering and what did that get me?" he fumed. "I have to watch this stupid car."

"While my designers have strived to make my artificial intelligence the most advanced of its kind," said the car, "unfortunately, I am limited by current technology. I apologize if I have disappointed you."

"No," said Monkhouse. "You're fine. I'm just hungry."

"I noticed your eyes dilate every time you looked at the restaurant across the street."

Monkhouse's' stomach growled.

"That's it," he said, getting out of the car. "I'll be right back."

He put on his bite mask and jogged towards the sushi shop.

Yamutsu watched him from the van parked behind the SUV and picked up his radio.

"He's left the car," he said. "I'm planting the override now."

He slipped out of the driver's door and, keeping low, moved to the SUV and opened the door.

He took out the device and switched it on. He watched the two small displays showing different digital waveforms and typed a series of numbers on the keyboard.

The second waveform changed, matching the one above it.

"I've accessed the target car's AI," said the man.

Hearing the report, Levi smiled.

"Good job," he said.

"The pre-program route is set and manual driving option is locked out," said Yamutsu.

"Perfect," said Levi. "Assemble back here."

"Copy," said Yamutsu, as he fastened the override under the dashboard.

A half-eaten tray of sushi in hand, Monkhouse was about to cross the street when a black van pulled out of the parking lot. The driver stopped and let Monkhouse pass in front.

"Thanks," he waved.

The driver waived back and headed down the street.

Careful not to spill the soy sauce, Monkhouse climbed back into the SUV and set the tray on the dashboard.

"How are you, car?"

"Running at operational levels," said the car. "How's your sushi?"

Rosse had done a good job of taping up Tate's ankle, but the meeting had gone on for an hour and a half and the pain killers were losing the battle.

He could see light at the end of the tunnel when Mullen and his counterpart stood up and shook hands.

"The meeting's wrapping up," he radioed.

He heard confirmation clicks as the others acknowledged.

Mullen was all smiles until the elevator door closed and he didn't have to pretend anymore.

"I want you to take me directly to the airport."

"That's the plan," said Tate.

"Your FBI guys better already be there," groused Mullen. "I don't want to be sitting on the tarmac like a... a sitting duck."

Tate wanted to say they weren't 'his' FBI guys, but knew Mullen wouldn't understand, or care.

The elevator doors opened to the garage and everyone and everything were right where Tate expected them to be. Fulton was standing by their SUV and the other team's men by theirs.

Mullen quickened his pace, threatening to leave Tate and Rosse behind, but Tate took him by the arm, cautioning restraint.

"Calm down," he said. "You're going to make those men wonder why we're running from the meeting."

Fulton opened the passenger door and Mullen ducked inside.

"We're getting in the car," reported Tate. "Be ready to meet us on the street."

"Monkhouse..." began Wesson.

"I'm coming," he said, starting the car.

Wesson and Ota came out of the building as Monkhouse pulled up. As they got in, they saw Tate's car appear from the parking garage.

"We see you," said Wesson.

Tate's car pulled out and Monkhouse pulled away from the curb to follow.

Instead of straightening out, Monkhouse's car continued to turn.

He looked at the steering wheel in confusion as he tried to pull it.

"What are you doing?" asked Wesson.

"It's not me," he said.

The car made a full U-turn and began accelerating away from Tate's car.

"Car," said Wesson, "release control."

"You have control," said the car.

Monkhouse tugged on the wheel but couldn't move it.

The gap between them and Tate was growing quickly.

"Return to your position behind us," said Tate as he watched the other car in the side view mirror.

"Top, the car's driving," said Wesson. "We can't control it."

It could have been a random malfunction, but the chances of it happening right now? Tate didn't think so.

"Speed up, Rosse," he said. "We need to get out of here."

Rosse pressed the gas and the SUV sped up the street.

"What's going on?" asked Mullen, looking nervously around.

"Maybe nothing," said Tate. "We're..."

"Crap," shouted Rosse, as two vans charged in front of them and stopped.

The SUV's anti-collision took over, throwing everyone against their seatbelts.

"Reverse," barked Tate, as men in balaclavas piled out of the vans.

Rosse threw the car into reverse and nailed the gas pedal.

It took a split second for Tate to register all of the men were snapping assault rifles to their shoulders.

"Down!"

Everyone ducked as bullets ripped into the front of the car. Keeping his foot glued to the gas, Rosse was doing his best to steer using the rear camera, but he oversteered and swerved into a row of parked cars.

Tate risked a glance, seeing the SUV had stopped with the passenger side facing the assault team.

He ducked back down as the front tires exploded, the gunmen shredding them before walking their fire up the front of the car.

The air crackled with gunfire. The car vibrated with the stream of bullets drilling into the grill and destroying the engine.

Mullen started wailing uncontrollably and Fulton looked at Tate with wide, fear-filled eyes.

"Rosse!" said Tate. "Get out. Use the car for cover." He risked another fast look around. "There's a store behind us. You and Fulton take Mullen inside. Find a rear exit and get out of here."

"What about you?" asked Rosse, his face covered in sweat.

"Don't worry about me," said Tate. "I'm not dying for that idiot."

Levi watched as chunks of metal and plastic flew off the wrecked SUV.

"Keep the pressure on," he said over the radio. "Force them out of the car. As soon as they're out, they'll split up. And watch your fire. We can't risk shooting the target."

His smile widened when he saw the SUV's driver side door open. "Perfect. Team two get ready to pursue."

The air was a deafening wall of gunfire as Rosse opened the rear door and waved Mullen out. But the man had shut down, swallowed by fear; he was curled into a ball and crying to himself.

Rosse grabbed him by the jacket and yanked him out of the car like a toy.

"C'mon kid," he said, and Fulton eagerly scrambled out of the car.

Tate climbed past the driver's seat and got out behind Rosse, holding him by the shoulder.

"Get ready to run into that store," he said.

Crouched behind the car, he listened for a break in the noise.

There it is.

The constant cracking of assault guns dipped, and he knew they were reloading.

"Go! Go! Go!" said Tate, with a sharp squeeze on Rosse's shoulder.

Staying low, Fulton, Mullen and Rosse dashed into the open and disappeared into the store.

"Team two," said Levi, "Go now!"

Three men broke away from the van and quick walked towards the store, while the remaining three men kept Tate pinned down.

Tate grabbed his mic, flinching from shards of glass bouncing off his head.

"Wesson! I need you."

"We don't have any control over the car," she crackled over the radio. "Doors and windows are locked. We're trapped."

"Copy," said Tate. "Keep me... "

He dived to the ground as three ragged holes punched through the car next to him.

. . .

Everything was going perfectly when Levi saw Cowboy break from cover. Red tracers jetted from his gun and Levi realized he was shooting armor-piercing rounds.

"Cowboy! Get back here."

Cowboy yanked out his earpiece and pumped another burst into the car.

"Judas, mother of...!" spat Tate, as bullets ripped through the metal over his head. Whoever was shooting wasn't taking prisoners. He rolled behind the rear tire, hoping the gunman didn't see his shadow.

"Team two," said Levi. "Hurry up. Get the target and get back to the van now!"

Rosse lead Mullen and Fulton through the small grocery store, staying low and threading past terrified shoppers.

"Come on, come on," he said, looking for a back door.

"They're going to kill me," cried Mullen. "We're all dead."

They reached the back of the shop and found the back door.

"Aw crap," groaned Rosse.

The entire wall was blocked with racks of food. In the narrow aisle, there was nowhere for the racks to go.

"Kid," said Rosse. "Go past me and hide behind the end of the aisle."

"I can flank them," said Fulton, squeezing past Rosse. "While they're looking at you can..."

"No you can't," snapped Rosse. "Yer follow'n orders, an' I'm telling ya that you keep your head down an' stay outta sight."

They heard the screams of shoppers and knew the gunmen were closing in.

"Cowboy," screamed Levi.

He put his sights on Cowboy's head, feeling the trigger against his finger.

Swearing, he let go. He couldn't risk leaving a body behind and even if he chewed up valuable time to drag his useless corpse into the van, what was he going to do with a dead body?

"I told you I'd be back," shouted Cowboy. "Did I kill you yet?"

Fire blazed from his gun as armor-piercing rounds cut into the side of the car.

Tate paused, recognizing the voice.

"What the...?"

Cowboy should be locked up somewhere. He'd trusted those two morons and now they were about to get him killed.

Reaching back, Tate grabbed his Colt, turned, and came up to shoot. The car disintegrated around his face, stabbing him with splinters of hot metal.

For a fleeting second, he saw Cowboy. He held the Colt over his head and blind fired.

CRACK CRACK CRACK, until he emptied the pistol.

He wedged himself between the open rear door and side of the car, hoping at least one of his bullets found his target.

"Nice try," yelled Cowboy as he came round the front of the car.

22

TAKE THE DEAL

Inside the grocery store, Rosse watched, helpless to do anything, as three gunmen came around the corner and trained their guns on him.

"Kill them," screamed Mullen, pounding his fists on Rosse's back.

"Easy guys," said Rosse, reaching back to Mullen. "He's all yours. Just don't hurt the kid."

One of the gunmen motioned with the barrel of his gun towards Mullen. Rosse dragged Mullen out from behind him and shoved him towards the gunmen.

"Traitor! Coward," screeched Mullen.

Two of the gunmen latched onto him and dragged him towards the front of the store, while the third kept his gun leveled at Rosse's face.

"Please, kid," muttered Rosse under his breath. "Don't try to be a hero. Please."

The gunmen's face was hidden behind dark sunglasses and a balaclava, making it impossible to read his expression.

"We're done here, right?" said Rosse.

Any second now, he expected a blinding flash and the instant blackness of death.

The gun barrel dipped, just a hair, and the gunman backed away until he was satisfied Rosse wouldn't charge him. He turned and quickly left the store.

Life-giving air rushed into Rosse's lungs as he slumped back and sat on the floor.

"You okay?" said Fulton, rushing to his side.

"Not even close," said Rosse.

The Colt's slide was locked open, the gun empty. Tate heard the crunch of Cowboy's boots on the broken glass as he came around the front of the car.

Adrenaline careened through Tate's body and he tried to steady his hand as he fumbled for another magazine.

Cowboy saw Tate hunched on the other side of the open door and kicked it.

The door slammed into him, knocking his hand, sending the magazine clattering to the ground.

"Told you I'd find you again," said Cowboy.

Crouching, Tate came around the door, drawing his sword. Cowboy saw the flash of metal and lashed with a high kick, catching Tate in the chest and sending him sprawling to the ground.

He hit the ground hard, grunting as the wind got knocked out of him, but he kept his grip on the sword.

He started to lift the sword, but Cowboy charged at him, stomping down on the flat of the blade. Tate heard a metallic PING and knew the sword had been snapped in two.

Cowboy leveled his assault rifle at his chest. Tate kicked out with all he had, driving his boot into Cowboy's knee just as he pulled the trigger.

Bullets splattered the pavement next to Tate as Cowboy screamed, his leg bent in a direction it was never meant to go.

Fighting for balance, Cowboy staggered back, but didn't fall. Spit frothed at the corner of his mouth as he raged at Tate.

Staggering, he yanked on the trigger, but nothing happened. The gun was empty. Cowboy hit the mag release.

At the same instant, Tate spotted his Colt's magazine laying in the street and lunged for it. He felt like he was moving through molasses and any second bullets and blood would spout out of his chest.

Cowboy felt the snap as his own fresh magazine locked into place and raised his gun.

All rage and pain was forgotten as he looked down into the gaping barrel of Tate's Colt. Fury exploded from the big .45, and Cowboy's face disappeared in a storm of blood, gore and splintered bone.

Levi jolted as he saw the back of Cowboy's head blow off. Tate rose from behind the cover of his smoking SUV and fixed Levi in his sights.

The air ripped around his ears and he ducked down.

The situation had just changed for the worse.

"Team two," said Levi.

"We have the target," crackled his radio.

"Put him in my van..." he began.

A stream of bullets ripped through the side of his van and Levi dove to the ground.

He's got Cowboy's gun!

"Disregard that," he shouted. "Put him in your van and get out of here."

He saw Team two disappear inside the other van. Its tires screeched in a cloud of smoking rubber and the van fishtailed as it pulled away.

Levi popped up and sprayed the side of the SUV. Tate's head disappeared, and Levi jumped into the van.

"Move!"

The driver didn't need to be told twice and stomped down on the gas.

Tate came up in time to see the back of the van swing around the corner before it was gone.

"Rosse," he said, gazing at the mouth of the grocery store, dreading that he may never hear the man's voice again.

"Yeah. We're okay."

Limping, Tate jogged into the store, breathing deep with relief seeing his friends unharmed.

"I kinda lost Mullen," said Rosse.

"Don't sweat it," said Tate, unable to keep the smile off his face, patting Rosse and Fulton on the shoulder.

"Turn it off," yelled Wesson as Monkhouse franticly pressed buttons on the dashboard.

"I've tried everything but kicking it," he said.

"Then kick it!"

Both of them pulled their knees to their chest and stomped into the dashboard. Bits of plastic and glass snapped and flew off as smoke and sparks shot out from the cracks.

They kicked again, breaking the dashboard mounts and rocking it up. Monkhouse saw something fall on the floor and picked it up.

"What's that?" asked Wesson.

"Manual steering engaged," said the car. "You have the wheel."

The car violently veered to the left and Monkhouse gripped the steering wheel, narrowly missing another car.

"It's working," he said.

"Toss that thing and take us back," said Wesson.

Monkhouse opened the window and threw out the device, watching it shatter as it hit the asphalt.

"Top," called Wesson over the radio. "We got it back. The car's working again."

"How far are you?"

"Not far," she said. "It's been driving in circles around the same block. We're on the way back to you."

"Negative," said Tate. "The hostiles just left. Heading west of our location in a dark green van. Intercept."

"On it," said Monkhouse.

"You are exceeding the lawful..."

"Shut up," he said, punching the dashboard.

They raced down the street and Wesson pointed to the upcoming intersection.

"Turn here."

The SUV leaned hard as Monkhouse pulled into a sharp left. They flew past a couple of side streets and Wesson told him to slow at the next street. As it went by, she scanned the traffic but didn't see a dark van.

Monkhouse grunted in frustration. "I think we lost..."

"There," she said. "Right! Right!"

People dodged out of the way as the SUV swung wide around the corner.

"See it?" pointed Wesson. "It's a dark green van."

"I see it," said Monkhouse, speeding up.

"Sergeant?" said Ota from the back seat. "What exactly are we supposed to do when we catch up to the van full of heavily armed men?"

"I'm working on it," said Wesson, her jaw clenching.

They quickly closed the distance and it was only a matter of seconds before the gunmen realized they were being chased.

"Okay," said Wesson. "Monkhouse, speed up and get next to..."

The dark van leapt forward.

"They saw us," he said, accelerating.

They caught up to the van, which tried to swerve between cars, hoping to lose the SUV.

"If you have a plan," said Ota, gripping the front seat as the SUV suddenly changed lanes, "now would be the time."

"I have one," said Monkhouse.

Before Wesson could ask, Monkhouse whipped alongside the van and yanked the wheel, smashing the SUV into it.

The van slewed wildly, the driver fighting for control. The van pitched left as the driver oversteered. It snapped into a hard turn and the van tilted over and slammed onto its side.

"Uh oh," said Monkhouse.

Inertia bounced the van off the ground, flinging it up into a side roll. Broken glass and sparks flew into the air as the van crunched over and over until its wrecked carcass lay smoldering in the middle of the street.

"Ota with me," said Wesson, as she got out of the car and bolted for the van.

Both drew their swords as they reached the van and looked inside. Among the scattered bodies of groaning men, they spotted Mullen's rumpled form.

Wesson passed her sword to Ota and crouched through the glassless front of the van.

Without checking for a pulse, she grabbed Mullen by the jacket and pulled him free of the gunmen. Once outside, Ota took him by the feet and they hustled him back to the SUV as Monkhouse opened the rear hatch.

"Is he dead?" he asked, his voice cracking.

"Do you mean did you kill him?" said Wesson, as they laid the limp body in the back of the car. "I'll ride back here. Let's go."

Ota ran around to the passenger's side and got in.

She felt for a pulse as Monkhouse pulled away.

Mullen's eyes fluttered but didn't open and she felt a reassuring pulse on his neck.

"Top, we got him," reported Wesson.

"Great work," said Tate. "Come and get us. Things are heating up here."

———

Hands on hips, Kiku scowled as she watched the team climb out of the SUV.

Rosse rolled the high gate closed behind them, closing the courtyard of the small house off from the street.

"Thank you for setting this up at the last minute," said Tate, his bow stilted by the protests of his aching body.

"It's one of many safe houses I have used," she said. "You told me nothing would happen."

"Nothing was supposed to happen," he said.

"You could have been killed," said Kiku.

"Thank you for your concern."

"Who would have executed you? All of you are my responsibility."

"I promise," said Tate, "I won't allow anyone to die if you're not there."

Kiku huffed, but grudgingly accepted Tate's pledge, not understanding the joke.

Wesson and Fulton helped Mullen out of the back of the car. He was conscious, but from what Wesson described of the crash, he probably had a concussion.

"Rosse," said Tate. "Check him out, will you? We might have to move him soon."

"I'll let ya know," said Rosse.

"I assumed you would not be returning to the hotel," said Kiku. "Your bags are in the living room."

"Thank you," said Tate.

He hadn't noticed or had time to notice his throbbing ankle, but it was quick to remind him he had abused it in no uncertain terms.

Biting his lip, he limped into the house, pausing at the entrance and looking at his foot.

He considered not taking off his shoes. He was sure that he'd never get a shoe back on his swollen foot.

He was at the top of Kiku's list already. Breaching this basic display of respect could be the last straw and frankly, Tate didn't want to see what she was like angry.

Gasping, he gingerly slid off the shoe and hobbled into the living room.

Opening his bag, he took out the sat phone, unsurpassed by the double digits of missed calls.

He had missed the scheduled drop-off and knew the FBI agents must be sweating bullets over the status of their prized defector.

After what they'd just been through, Tate couldn't have cared less.

He hit the return button and listen to the static while the phone connected.

He didn't have long to wait.

"Where are you?" growled Jones. "Do you have any idea how badly you've screwed up?"

Tate barked out a laugh, painful with irony.

"Before your mouth digs you into a hole you can't get out of, shut up and listen," he said. "We got ambushed right after we left the business meeting."

"Impossible," said Jones. "Nobody knew the time and place but the defector and you."

"Don't forget the guy I took the sat phone from."

"The Ring's security team? My people are sitting on them."

"You might want to check on that because they just shot the crap out of my car, nearly killed me and almost took Mullen."

"But... our people."

"Have your people been checking in?"

"How should I know? I'm the operational lead on this mission," said Jones. "I don't do admin."

Intel operations were so full of their own hype they were totally blind to their own incompetence. It was that way when he was in Delta Force and still that way today.

"Back up," said Jones. "What about the sat phone?"

"He's been listening to everything we've said from the beginning."

"He's..."

"Listening right now? I would be. This is the last shot he's got at getting the defector and the gate drive. I killed one of his team. He's got to be looking for some payback. Maybe I should say where we're supposed to drop off Mullen. I can imagine the look on your stupid faces when he comes rolling up with a full assault team. Well, minus one."

"Are you threatening me?" asked Jones darkly.

Tate heard the sound of rustling and Smith came on the line.

"Let's take a step back," he said. "Yes, everyone made mistakes..."

Tate gripped the sat phone, flushing red and fighting to keep his anger in check. Normally, he could roll with the punches. What was it about these guys that pushed his buttons?

"... Tate, you there?"

"I didn't catch that. The signal dropped."

"Bring in Mullen and the gate drive."

"We'll be there in three hours," said Tate.

"Three hours," said Smith. "We'll be ready.

Tate ended the call. Behind him were the sounds of his team, settling in and trading their versions of what had happened during the ambush.

He saw forward, still holding the sat phone and looked at it knowingly.

A smile curled the corner of his mouth when the phone chimed. He answered the incoming call.

"Sorry about your man," said Tate.

"No, you're not," said Levi.

"Yeah. No, I'm not."

"He was a problem from the beginning, but you work with what you have."

"You heard we're handing Mullen over in a few hours," said Tate.

"I don't suppose you want to tell me where?"

Tate laughed, appreciating Levi wasn't the type that gave up.

"As much as I'd like to see the look on their faces when you rolled up with guns blazing," he said, "I'm sorry to say I can't help you."

"Or we can help each other."

There it was. The line that separated what you believed in today and what you might believe in tomorrow. Tate had been there before. Sometimes that line was sharp, clearly defined and you would never cross it. But... if the circumstances were just right... that line could get very blurry; maybe even disappear. Then one day, you wake up and realize you're standing on the other side, thinking that there wasn't much of a difference between the two sides after all.

Levi had just brought Tate to that line. He wondered how blurry Levi would make it.

"Mullen's causing a lot of concern in The Ring," said Levi. "Enough that the head man himself has come here to personally oversee the operation."

"That's a heck of a monkey you have on your back," said Tate.

"Brother, you aren't kidding," chuckled Levi.

"I wish I could help you," said Tate, "but I have my own monkeys."

"Not like mine, and he's serious about getting Mullen and the gate drive back. Listen, just between you and me, this man is powerful and dangerous. You do not want him on your back."

"I appreciate the warning," said Tate. "I've got broad shoulders."

"There's a way we can make everyone happy and no one will point the finger at you. Let's split the difference. Your guys get Mullen. My guy gets the gate drive. Everyone loses a little and wins a little. You would end up with enough money to retire early..."

"How much is enough?"

"That's between you and the big guy," said Levi. "He doesn't blush when it comes to spending money. Which is why you don't want him making it his mission in life to kill you. He will get the job done."

"Why would he settle for the drive?"

"Between Mullen and the drive, the combined information could be fatal to The Ring. Individually, they can wound, but not kill. My boss can live with that."

"Hmmm," said Tate.

He was aware that Levi knew a lot about the inner workings of The Ring and the man who ran it. Much more than a rent-a-merc could possibly know. He knew the damage Mullen and the gate drive could do to The Ring, the temperament of the organization's leader and how he'd react based on the circumstances. These were details and nuances only a close adviser would know.

A ripple of electricity ran through Tate as the last piece fell into place. Levi must be The Ring's head of security. The head of the organization would want his best man running the operation in person. But that wouldn't be good enough. Not with The Ring's neck on the chopping block. The 'big guy' is nervous and wants the ability to instantly react to the situation. He couldn't risk a delay in status reports.

He was here! Tate stood up, his ankle forgotten. The head of the snake was in Tokyo.

"You know as soon as your side gets what they want," said Levi, "they disappear. We're the ones on our backs in a hospital with bullet wounds and broken bones. We pay the real price."

"I don't move the way I used to," chuckled Tate.

"The knees, right?"

"You too?"

"We can't do this forever," said Levi. "Sooner or later we're out of the game. Either we decide or someone with a gun will."

"What's your bosses' offer?"

"I don't know the number," said Levi, "but like I said, the man's not shy about spending money if it's for the right reason, and brother, you are the right reason."

"I'll call you later," said Tate.

Levi paused a beat.

"Is that a yes?" he said cautiously.

"I'll call," said Tate and hit end.

23

HEAD OF THE SNAKE

Two SUVs appeared around the hanger and slowed as they neared the waiting jet.

Several men with compact assault rifles stood guard around the aircraft.

"That's them, right?" asked Mullen, looking at the two FBI agents standing by the jet.

"Yes," sighed Tate.

The air was tinged with the smell of jet fuel as a squat tanker truck refilled the jet's tanks for the return flight. A man in coveralls came out of the jet and stuffed his hands into his coat.

"Thanks for letting me use the toilet," he said, passing one of the guards.

The guard nodded but kept his gaze on scanning the area.

Tate took a breath, not looking forward to this face to face with the agents.

Everything about them irritated him. What annoyed him more was that he had to work with them. The alternative was sitting on his butt in Fort Hickok, watching months go by without a mission.

"I thought you'd never get me here," said Mullen.

"You're welcome," said Tate.

The cars rolled to a stop and everyone got out.

Even though the sun was nearing the horizon, the agents wore their dark sunglasses.

Tate grinned, seeing the agents shiver, pretending to ignore the cold wind biting through their thin suitcoats.

"Mr. Mullen," said Jones, "I'm agent..."

"Yeah, great," said Mullen brushing past him and climbing the jet's short stairs. "I hope you have something warm to drink in this thing."

"What about...?" stammered Smith, following Mullen into the jet.

"Here," said Tate, holding out the gate drive.

"Why do you have it?" asked Jones.

"Safe keeping," said Tate.

"Did you look at it?" Jones looked meaningfully at him.

"Didn't you say it was encrypted?"

"Yes, but..."

"Thanks for the compliment," said Tate, "but I don't have super hacker skills. Besides, I've had enough of this operation. Whatever's on that drive would only suck me in deeper. No thanks."

He put the drive in Jones's outstretched hand. The agent nodded and stuffed the drive in his pocket.

"Between Mullen and that drive, you'll have enough actionable intel to destroy The Ring and lock up the big players."

"That's for us to determine," said Jones.

Tate leaned in, staring through Jones's sunglasses. "I suggest you make that determination soon," he said. "Something like that has a limited shelf life before it loses its usefulness."

"You stick to kicking in doors," said Jones. "We'll do the rest."

"I don't believe this," scoffed Tate. "You're going to slow-walk this. This isn't about taking down The Ring. It's about you two numb-nuts making yourselves look good so you land a fat job in the Pentagon."

"Your part in this is over, Tate."

"Don't say it," he growled.

"We'll take it from here."

"I should drag him off the jet and give him to someone who's serious about protecting our country."

Jones shifted uncomfortably and his hand drifted towards his coat, where Tate assumed was a holstered gun.

A grim smile curled the corner of Tate's mouth.

"I'm keenly interested in how you see the next few seconds of your life playing out," he said.

The agent's hand stopped and he saw the rest of the team watching him with cold menace. None of them were touching their swords, but their coats were open and the handles exposed. The tension disappeared on the wind as the agent brought his hand up and looked at his watch.

"Our window's closing. Get on board."

Everyone picked up their bags, each saying their goodbyes and bowing with appreciation to Kiku before filing onto the jet.

Wesson paused at the foot of the stairs.

"That's everyone, Top," she said. "It sounds crazy, but it'll be nice to be back home, even if it is an ugly hole."

"Keep the light on for me," said Tate.

Wesson's eyebrows furrowed.

"You're not coming?"

"It's been all work," he said. "I'm going to take a couple of days. Decompress."

"Uh... okay," she said, not certain it really was. She glanced at the agent then back at Tate. "Everything all right?"

"Yes," he said, smiling.

"Very touching, you two," said Jones. "On or off the jet. We're leaving."

Wesson's eyes threw daggers at the agent before she disappeared inside.

"You have a way with women," grinned Tate.

The agent brushed past him and started up the stairs.

"I shouldn't have to remind you," said Jones, "from this moment on, you're no longer operating under our protection. If you get in trouble, it's all on you."

"If feels like nothing's changed," said Tate.

Jones disappeared inside. A moment later the stairs folded up into the side of the jet and the engines powered up.

"I'm afraid this ends my service as well, Tate-san," bowed Kiku.

"Thank you, Kiku-san," said Tate, bowing deeply. "I am honored to know you. Please let me drop you at the hotel before we finally part ways."

Behind them, the sleek jet taxied towards the airstrip for its take-off and long flight back.

Kiku nodded and they climbed into the SUV. They turned to leave with the empty SUV trailing behind.

The lights were off in the living room of the hotel suite. The lights of Tokyo spread out like a blanket of multicolored stars, but they couldn't distract Tate from the emptiness of the room.

He turned the gate drive over and over in his hand, not taking his eyes from the scenery outside.

The sat-phone vibrated in his other hand and he picked up the call.

"You didn't strike me as a man who gloats," said Levi. His voice was edged in restrained anger.

"What are you talking about?" asked Tate.

"We saw you hand over the gate drive."

"You were there?"

"You had me thinking we could work something out," said Levi.

"We can," said Tate. "I'm holding the gate drive in my hand."

"The second your agents try to read the one you gave them," said Levi, "they'll know it's a fake. The encryption on the drive can't be duplicated."

"It doesn't have to be if the drive is damaged," said Tate.

"You're good," said Levi. "I have to know. What made you take the deal? You're not fickle with your loyalties. You and I don't see things in dollar signs."

"It wasn't the money," said Tate. "The way I see it, The Ring won't last forever. It'll be wiped out sooner or later, but not by me. I mean, yes, we can hurt them, but how many of my people would die trying to deliver the killing blow? This way, your boss gets the gate drive and me and my team are left alone."

"I thought you'd say that," said Levi.

"And forty million," said Tate. "I'll provide the account. Tell your boss to wire the entire balance using the one-time cipher I give you."

"That's going to make him nervous," said Levi. "I'm familiar with the technic. As soon as the forty mil hits that account, it'll trigger an automatic transfer to a blind account. The original account deletes itself and any records of activity."

"So, you have heard of that," said Tate.

"I've used it," chuckled Levi.

"Don't worry. I'm not interested in screwing your boss. I'm after peace of mind. I'm not going to shoot myself in the foot by making an enemy of him."

"Give me the place and time," said Levi. "I'll be there."

"Just you," said Tate. "If you're not alone, I disappear."

"Come on. We've done this kind of thing before. It'll be just me. Trust me. You're not the only one who doesn't want to make an enemy out of my boss." When he spoke again, his voice was deadly cold. "And Tate, don't play games with us."

Levi hung up.

Tate rolled the gate drive in his hand.

I'm not playing.

Tate drove the SUV onto the long bridge, leaving the mainland behind. It didn't matter that he was sure he wasn't being followed, his eyes drifted to the rearview mirror out of habit. Satisfied, he turned his attention to the distant island ahead.

It was a holding yard for freight containers, but after the outbreak, imports were nearly non-existent and nobody went there.

He left the mainland behind as he started across the long bridge that connected to his destination.

The sparse streetlights created the strange sensation that there was nothing beyond their reach but emptiness and icy, black sea.

He thought of his friends flying home. Probably asleep, but like him, suspended over the same cold, dark waters.

His tires bumped over the gap where the bridge returned to solid ground and Tate turned onto the neglected road that led into the storage yard.

Hulks of stacked freight containers towered over the SUV like a rusted ghost town. Clumps of weeds snaked up through the cracked asphalt, dragging against the sides of the SUV like feeble fingers trying to grasp it.

A single car sat alone at the other end of the open yard as the SUV slowed to a stop.

Tate felt tense, but looking around, didn't see signs of anyone else.

So far, so good. Now it was Levi's turn to get out of his...

Bursts of gunfire exploded from the shadows around Tate's car. The windows blew out and bullets ripped through the steel with a dull thwack.

The SUV slumped like a drunken animal as a tire exploded, chunks of shredded rubber flying off.

All of the guns suddenly stopped at the same time. Darkness greedily filled the yard with only the faint hiss from the destroyed SUV.

The door of Levi's car swung open and he got out, zipping up his coat. As he walked over to the smoking wreck, he took out a pair of latex gloves and put them on before getting a flashlight from his other pocket.

He stopped at the driver's door and turned it on, filling the SUV with harsh, white light.

From his vantage point, high up on top of a stack of containers, Tate watched as Levi tensed, sweeping his flashlight inside the SUV, looking for a body that wasn't there.

Tate smiled.

I guess those smart cars are good for something after all.

Levi saw a note under the broken glass in the driver's seat and picked it up.

'Like you said, we've done this before. I'm calling in twenty minutes. If your boss doesn't answer, I hand the gate drive over to the FBI.'

Watching Levi, Tate could almost see him shaking with rage as he stormed back to his car.

"Op's over," yelled Levi. "Debrief tomorrow."

He leaned in and took out his sat phone.

"Oh crap," said Tate, fumbling for his sat phone. He mashed the button, silencing the ringer a split second before the phone lit up. He didn't answer the call and Levi threw the phone back into the car.

Levi fumed as two cars rolled out of the shadows and his assault team drove away. He took the sat phone out and stopped, tapping it in his hand while staring at the ground.

Which is the safest way to tell your boss you screwed up? Over the phone, or in person?

Levi tossed the phone into the car and got in.

"In person," said Tate, scrambling off the containers.

He jumped down, cursing himself before he landed on his bad ankle. The pain stopped him and he took a moment to push past the pain. He hobbled to his car and waited until Levi wouldn't see him following.

Tate had hoped his note about the limited time would force Levi to cut corners, and it paid off.

Following behind, Tate could tell that Levi wasn't concerned about a tail. Instead of the traditional techniques of changing lanes, speed and multiple turns down streets, he was driving directly to his destination.

He had to. Tate had given him a deadline and the clock was ticking.

Driving into the heart of Tokyo, Tate could see the towering glass monolith of the Imperial Yagura hotel and his instincts told him that was where Levi was heading.

Tate nodded to himself, thinking how it never changed; when the mighty were winning, you'd find them in mansions, expensive cars, and five-star hotels. When they were running for their lives, you'd find them in holes in the ground, dressed in rags.

A few minutes later, his guess was confirmed when Levi drove into the Imperial's underground parking.

Tate pulled up to the front and got out, leaving the door open for the parking attendant. He gave the questioning doorman a curt nod, leaving him to assume Tate must belong there.

There wasn't time to appreciate the opulence of the lobby as he quickly crossed to the elevators. He spotted a doorman standing next to a lone elevator door and knew it must be exclusive to the penthouse.

"May I help you, sir?"

"Going up," said Tate. "Meeting a friend and I'm in a hurry."

"Yes sir," said the doorman, pressing the elevator button. With the doorman's back to him, Tate took his Colt from behind his back and concealed it under his coat.

He glanced up at the display above the door. Garage level four.

He's still down in the garage.

Intercepting Levi was his only way into the penthouse and reaching the leader of The Ring.

"May I have your keycard?" asked the doorman.

He could call the elevator, but without a card the doors wouldn't open.

The elevator display changed to G3.

He's coming up!

G2...

There wasn't time to spin a lie and talk his way into the elevator.

G1...

Tate saw an ornate card clipped to the doorman's pocket, betting it was a master key for the elevator.

"Excuse me," he said, snatching the card off the doorman's coat and held it in front of the scanner.

Lobby...

"Sir," said the doorman as the elevator chimed.

Inside, Levi was glaring at the floor and looked up in confusion as the doors unexpectedly opened.

"There he is," said Tate, dashing into the elevator.

Blocking the doorman's view with his body, Tate shoved the Colt into Levi's ribs.

"I was just thinking about you," said Levi, and nodded to the alarmed doorman. "We know each other."

Tate kept his back to the doors as they closed and felt Levi tense, ready to make a move.

"Don't," he warned, putting the barrel of the Colt under Levi's jaw. "You're brains are one trigger pull away from decorating the walls."

Levi relaxed, knowing the slightest flinch and he'd be dead.

"He is here, right?" asked Tate. "I'd feel pretty stupid going to all this trouble and walking into an empty room."

"He's here," said Levi. "But you really want to rethink your next move. The guy's more powerful than you can imagine. Waving a gun in his face will be the biggest mistake of your life."

"I have an ex-wife who would disagree with that," said Tate.

He looked up at the display over the elevator door and saw they were nearing the penthouse.

"I'm going to need your belt," he said.

The elevator doors opened to a spectacular view of Tokyo. Tate stepped out into a dimly lit room, dragging a tied-up Levi behind him over the polished wood floor.

He swept his gun to the left, pointing it at the man sitting behind a handsome wood desk.

Tate let go of Levi and cautiously walked towards the man. The bookcase behind the desk covered the entire wall and was an interesting mix of books, photographs, and mementos. The items were too specific to be hotel decor.

"You're correct," said the man. "This is one of my homes."

Tate scanned for hidden threats, but the man was surprisingly alone.

"Just one?" asked Tate, reaching the desk. His gun never wavered from the man's chest.

"My interests involve extensive travel."

From the man's expression, Tate couldn't tell if he was pretending to ignore the big .45 pointed at him, or genuinely didn't care.

"I'm disappointed you decided not to work with us," said the man, as he tilted his head to look at Levi.

"No," said Tate. "I don't think there's an us. You're the top of The Ring's food chain."

"Guilty as charged," smiled the man.

The answer sent a shiver of thrill up Tate's spine. He was really standing in the same room as the leader and mastermind behind the covert takeover of the United States.

"Since you're guilty," he said, coming around the desk, "let's get to the sentencing."

He shoved the Colt to the man's temple and pulled back the hammer. The sound of that distinctive click had shattered the resolve of many people and Tate wanted to rip this man down from his lofty pillar and see the fear in his eyes.

Instead, the man smiled.

"How much is my life worth?" he asked. Careful of the gun at his head, he turned his computer monitor so Tate could see it.

On the screen was a video feed of his team, Mullen and the two agents sleeping in the cabin of a jet.

"How?" asked Tate, feeling his gut twist into a knot.

"It wasn't easy, but where there's a will... You see the clock?" the man asked, tapping the corner of the screen.

The meaning was instantly clear to Tate.

"If I don't enter the password, let's say because I've been shot, the bomb on the plane goes off."

"That's your life insurance policy?" hissed Tate, digging the gun barrel into the man's head. He crushed the grip of the gun until his knuckles were white.

"Come on, Mr. Tate," said the man, nervousness creeping into his voice. "We both know there's a line you won't cross."

BOOM!

The Colt bellowed in Tate's hand, leaving a smoking hole in the fine leather chair next to the man's head.

"You're looking at the wrong line," he snarled.

The man swore in pain, cupping his ringing ear. His smooth veneer had vanished, leaving doubt and fear.

"Don't you get it?" he said, between a question and a plea. "If I don't put in the code before seven hours is up, they all die."

"That's not my decision," said Tate, crouching down to eye level with the man. "I was in Delta Force a long time, but you already know that from your file on me. I bet it doesn't tell you about all the horrific things I've seen. You can't imagine the kinds of things I've witnessed sick, evil psychos do to people."

With his free hand, Tate took out his tomahawk and buried it into the desk.

"I picked up a few of their tricks along the way. Now, seven hours isn't enough time to show you everything I've learned, but if I rush, I might have time to squeeze in a couple extra."

The color had drained from the man's face and he folded his hands to keep them from trembling. It didn't help.

Tate yanked the man's hands apart and flattened one on the desk.

"Let's get started," he said, pushing the Colt's barrel onto the joint of the man's finger.

"Or," yelped the man. "We can skip to the end and I stop the bomb now."

Tate let the gun barrel linger for a long time.

The man let out a long breath as the gun lifted off his finger. Careful not to make a sudden move, he took a gate drive from his shirt pocket and plugged it into the computer. He placed his hands on the computer's keyboard but stopped.

"You could kill me as soon as I put in the code," he said, eyeing Tate with fearful suspicion.

"You have my word I won't kill you," said Tate.

"What kind of guarantee is that?"

"An important one. You'll learn that if I say I won't kill you, I won't. And if I say I will kill you, you'll know it's a stone-cold fact that it won't matter what you do, or how far you run... I will take your life."

The man sat, locked in Tate's pitiless stare.

"I believe you," he croaked.

"That's the smartest thing you've said," smiled Tate.

The man turned back to the computer and typed in a string of characters.

The timer on the screen turned to zeros and stopped.

Tate held out his hand and the man unplugged the drive, putting it in Tate's palm. The man nervously watched Tate, but relaxed when he holstered his gun.

"That's it," said Tate with a long sigh. "I'm done knocking heads with you guys."

"What do you mean?"

Tate sat on the corner of the desk and pulled his tomahawk free, making the man flinch.

"Personally, I think you, The Ring," he said, making a circle in the air with his finger, "are running on borrowed time. One by one, your closest allies will start disappearing. Snapped up by the DOD or CIA. They'll stick them in a black site. Your power brokers are what, CEO's, politicians? Soft. My bet is after they get their first taste of enhanced interrogation, they won't be able to throw you under the bus fast enough."

The man straightened his shirt and smoothed his hair, trying to reclaim his previous air of self-control.

"Then we're done here," he said dismissively.

"Just about, yes," said Tate. "Two things."

"The money," said the man. "Give me the account details and I'll have it done."

"Forty million," scoffed Tate. "Don't insult me. Sixty."

The man didn't even blink. Levi was right; the man didn't worry about money.

"What's the second thing?" said the man.

"Leave us alone," said Tate. "Forever."

"You have my word."

"No," said Tate. "You have my word. If you threaten us again, I will come for you. Don't test me on this."

"Are you finished?" asked the man, sounding annoyed.

"Yup," said Tate, pushing himself off the desk.

He walked out of the study, passing Levi without a glance and got into the elevator.

The doors closed and the elevator started its smooth ride down.

Reaching the lobby, the doors opened with a chime and Tate half expected a firing squad of Ring gunmen waiting for him.

Instead, it was exactly how he'd left it; a milling crowd of guests and employees.

Back in his car, Tate let the computer do the driving. He stared, unblinking, out the windshield until his body started shivering. He gripped his hands together, trying to stop the shaking.

"Holy crap," he said, his voice quivering. "That was a seriously stupid risk."

"Can I help you with something?" asked the car.

"Yeah," he said. "Take me someplace where I can get drunk."

"All right."

"I mean really, really drunk."

"I know just the place," said the car and turned around.

24

SEVEN DEADLY SINS

A bead of sweat rolled down Tate's jaw as the heat of the jungle got an early start that morning.

Heading over to their ready room, he glanced around the familiar scenes of Fort Hickok and smiled. The smell of damp earth and cooking; a sergeant chewing out a new recruit and soldiers trading stories about their last patrol. It was as if the camp had been frozen in time the moment they'd left for Japan and only reanimated when they returned.

But the bustle of activity and the heat of the fat sun pushing down on him couldn't dispel the melancholy weighing heavily on his shoulders.

His encounter with the leader of The Ring...

Why didn't I ask his name? Would it matter?

He knew he'd left a lasting impression on the man.

The door creaked as he walked into the ready room and the welcomed coolness out of the sun.

Tate was early and the sight of the empty chairs made the room feel hollow.

He had meant everything he said to the leader, including the torture; if provoked, Tate would return and kill him.

But how long would that threat hold that man in check? He was powerful, driven, and used to getting what he wanted.

Tate shook his head slowly, conceding to the truth. Sooner or later, the man would come after Tate and his team.

Mullen and his gate drive were likely the poison arrow that would bring down The Ring, but when those FBI fools would finally strike was anyone's guess.

Tate replayed that night for the hundredth time, except instead of shooting the chair, he blew a hole in the leader's head. That victory would only last until the timer on the computer screen ran down. He imagined the camera indifferently staring at his friends. There'd be a sudden flare of light and then static. Thousands of miles away, the jet would do its death spiral into the sea.

He squeezed his eyes closed, cursing himself for being weak. He couldn't trade the lives of his friends for the death of The Ring. Tate knew if he had to do it all over again...

Damn it!

He still wouldn't make that trade.

He had fought and sacrificed much for his country. Keeping it safe had taken even more. But this one time, he chose to be selfish.

He could live with that.

He looked up and grinned as Kaiden came in. He knew she'd see the wear and tear from the mission on him.

"I know," he said, preempting her commentary.

"It's a big day," she said. "I wondered how long before the nostalgia of the old days caught up to you."

"I couldn't do it without your connections."

"Does the team know?" she asked.

"They will in a few minutes," said Tate, glancing at his watch.

"Are they ready?"

Light poured in as the door banged open.

"You knew I had my eye on that bacon," growled Rosse.

"I said I'd share it with you," said Monkhouse.

"Who wants half a bacon?"

Tate smiled as the team walked in and took a seat around the room. As close as they were, it never failed to amuse him how they took up the whole room, never sitting next to each other.

"Morning," said Wesson.

Her glance lingered a beat longer than usual and he knew she was trying to gauge if he was back to his old self. She'd noticed something had been weighing on his shoulders since he'd come back from Japan.

He put a little extra into his smile, letting her know he was fine.

"What's up, Top?" asked Fulton.

"Kinda last minute," said Rosse. "We got another op already?"

"There's a couple of things I want to cover with you," said Tate. "But first, Sergeant Wesson?"

Tate's sudden change of tone and formality took everyone by surprise. They watched, baffled, as Wesson quickly got to her feet and stood at rigid attention.

"Yes, Sergeant Major," she barked.

"Call the team to attention."

"Grave Diggers," she snapped. "Attention!"

Chairs squeaked across the floor as everyone got to their feet like they'd been bit by a cattle prod.

"Specialist Jeff Fulton," said Tate. "Step forward."

Fulton bumped into a desk, nearly tripping, as he rushed to stand in front of Tate.

"Here, Top... Sergeant Major," he blurted.

Tate picked up a folder from the desk behind him and opened it.

"The Secretary of the Army," he announced, "has reposed special trust and confidence in the patriotism, valor, fidelity, and professional excellence of Jeffery Fulton. In view of these qualities and his demonstrated leadership potential and dedicated service to the United States Army, he is, therefore, promoted to the rank of Corporal."

Grinning, Wesson replaced Fulton's old insignia with his new rank as everyone applauded.

"Congratulations Corporal Fulton," smiled Tate.

He saw Fulton didn't know whether to shake his hand or hug him, and put out his hand before the corporal wrapped his arms around him.

Fulton was enveloped with smiling friends all congratulating him.

Eventually, the room quieted down enough for Tate to speak up, signaling he had more to say.

"I'm very proud of everyone here," he said. "Japan wasn't the easy op we had planned for, and all of you showed a great degree of adaptability, courage and grit."

Everyone's back straightened and chest filled with pride at the rare praise.

"Delivering Mullen into the right hands might be a fatal blow to The Ring, and you were the ones that did it."

He paused, considering what he was about to say.

"What are you working up to, Top?" asked Rosse.

"I think it's time we become an independent unit," said Tate.

"What does that mean?" asked Wesson, perplexed.

"Mercenaries?" said Monkhouse.

"Huh?" said Rosse. "I thought you didn't like mercs."

"Hang on," said Tate. "No, not mercenaries, but close. We'd be more like free-agents."

"What would we be doing?" asked Fulton.

"A lot," said Kaiden, joining in. "The world changed forever when the outbreak hit, and news of what's happened since is hard to find, but believe me, things are still changing out there. Not all for the better. In fact, some of it's very bad."

"And nobody's doing anything about it," said Tate. "But we can."

"We can't just pick up and go wherever we want," said Monkhouse. "We have to report to..." He

ran out of words as he realized he'd never actually seen a commanding officer in charge of their unit.

"The Grave Diggers designation allows us to operate as its own entity," said Tate. "Our CO used some loose interpretations to get us authorized, but that's the long and short of it."

"You mean we could do this from the beginning?" asked Rosse.

"Yes," said Tate, "but it wasn't until Japan that I felt we were ready to take that step."

"Go where we want, when we want?" said Rosse, leaning back in his chair. "I'm game."

"It's not exactly that simple," said Tate. "But I can answer your questions as they come up."

"Hey, Top?" said Fulton, raising his hand. "We're living in the boonies. Our uniforms, heck, even our weapons are hand-me-downs. All of a sudden, the army's going to pay for us to go freelance?"

"No," said Tate. "We pay our own way. But we recently received a generous donation that will set up our team for the foreseeable future."

He left the vague explanation hanging there, and the team realized he wasn't going to elaborate.

"It's a lot to think about," he said. "We'll meet again on Thursday. Then we'll decide if we stay here, keep things the way they are, or we make the move and up our game. Dismissed."

Kaiden leaned quietly against the wall until the last of the team had left.

"What do you think?" she asked.

Tate stared at the door as if able to see his friends outside.

"I don't know," he said. "Some already decided, they're in. A couple... I hope they go for it."

"If they don't?"

"It's all or nothing," he said. "I won't break up the team."

"I wasn't exaggerating before about what's going on out there," frowned Kaiden. "Details are always sketchy, but it's getting scary."

"We've handled everything thrown at us so far," he said. "I think they can handle it."

"I never get tired of that can-do spirit," she said. She pushed off the wall and started for the door. "Let me know how they vote. I have a job for you already picked out."

Tate watched the door close behind her. Alone, in the empty room, doubt crept back in. He wondered what 'things' Kaiden was hinting at.

What am I getting us into?

The question taking center stage in his mind was which was better; going into the unknown or rolling the dice on if, or when, The Ring came gunning for them.

The constant hum of insects filled the night air as thickly as the humidity.

Two MPs walked their assigned patrol through blocks F and G, living quarters of Fort Hickok. Neither of them were aware they were being watched.

Once the MPs turned the corner and were lost from view, the shadows came alive.

A figure, clothed in black, crept along the side of building F. Keeping his assault rifle at low ready, he swept the area with his night vision optics.

"This is Limbo," he whispered into his radio. "I'm clear and ready to move."

Five more identically geared people broke from concealment and lined up behind Limbo.

"You have five minutes to reach your positions," said Limbo. "Verify your target, acknowledge when ready to execute."

Each of the team tapped a data pad on their forearm. A holo-image of their target appeared in the corner of their goggles.

Satisfied, the team separated, slipping into the darkness like smoke.

Limbo watched until they were gone from sight before moving. He studied the features of Jack Tate in his goggle's display before turning it off.

Gravel bordered the concrete sidewalks, but Limbo's boots were specially made to cancel the sound of his movements. He could walk behind on walnut shells and they'd never hear him.

The technology didn't come cheap, but the boss had pulled out all the stops for this mission.

Limbo froze as a voice whispered in his ear.

"This is Heresy. My target's door is in sight. Standing by."

Limbo took a long breath, slowing his thumping heart. The clarity of their communication gear was unnerving. Without the static hiss he was accustomed to, it sounded like someone was right next to him.

The superimposed mini map on his goggles showed him the route to Tate's quarters. Part of the route meant he'd have to travel several yards without any concealment. It was the riskiest of all of the targets, which is why he chose it for himself.

"Treachery checking in," said a voice in his ear. This time Limbo kept his heart from jumping out of his chest. "In position. Standing by."

Limbo paused at the corner of Tate's building. He would wait here until everyone was ready. On his order to move, he'd dash into the open, breach Tate's door and eliminate the target.

The sub-sonic rounds in his assault rifle made as much sound as crinkling up a piece of paper. Very impressive, but pointless. The crash of him breaking through the door negated all of his expensive stealth gear.

The advantage would come when it was time to exfil. The light-absorbing material that covered him, head to foot, would make escape effortless. Even at twenty feet he'd be invisible in the beam of a flashlight.

"This is Greed. I'm good to go."

"Anger reporting. I'm set."

Seconds passed and there was no word from the remaining team member.

"Violence," said Limbo. "What's your status?"

There was no response. Limbo was quick to blame it on the cutting-edge comms. He always considered the new stuff too finicky.

But, in the back of his mind, his instincts felt the subtle tremor of worry.

"Everyone stand by for my..."

It was only a split second of muffled sound that came over his radio, but it was sound that shouldn't have been there.

"Everyone check in," hissed Limbo.

"Anger, here."

"Greed, here."

... Nothing else.

"Heresy?" said Limbo. "Treachery?"

There was no reply.

There wasn't time to wonder what was happening. They had a mission to complete.

He broke from the corner, flipping the safety off his gun and dashed for Tate's door.

"This is Limbo. Execute, execute, execute!"

Without slowing, he lowered his weight and drove into the door with his shoulder. The door swung open in a cloud of debris and splinters.

The layout of the room was exactly the same as the mock setup he'd practiced in. Muscle memory guided his aim where it needed to go.

Limbo squeezed the trigger, sending a stream of bullets lancing through the dark. The strobe of gunfire overwhelmed his goggles, blinding him. He gripped the gun to keep it steady, but it was already over, the gun empty.

Limbo hit the mag release, dumping the empty magazine. A fully loaded magazine was instantly locked into his gun, and he was ready to fire.

He put his hand down, feeling for the body but the bed was empty.

Limbo wheeled around, knowing the bathroom was behind him.

Before he moved, a voice broke over his radio.

"This here's Sergeant Crenshaw of the military police. When ya'll done making a mess of that room, how about you come outside and let's have a little talk about what you're doing in my base."

Limbo risked a glance through a crack in the curtain and felt his stomach drop.

His team were kneeling on the ground, flex-cuffed and stripped of their gear.

A row of soldiers crouched behind ballistic shields with their automatic weapons trained on the front door.

Forty-two thousand feet over New Mexico, the Gulfstream T80 banked a few degrees east, avoiding the storm front. Jack Tate and his team were sound asleep, enjoying the comfort of the executive leather, convertible chairs.

Under the half-eaten sandwich on the table next to Tate was a red striped folder with Classified stamped on it.

The label read simply, 'Montana - Cyborgs'.

The End.

Thank you for reading Lethal Passage.
Your reviews help keep this series growing.

25

SUICIDE IS NOT THE WAY

If you are questioning your reasons for living you are not alone. Whatever you are experiencing is personal to you, but believe me, it is not unique. You may feel isolated, trapped and that there's no way to a better future, but I can tell you from personal experience that is an illusion. Being in distress can blind us to the answers we need.

Right now, at the very moment you are reading this, there are people who understand what you're feeling. More importantly, they can help.

Take a deep breath. Now call them.

United States - National Suicide Prevention 1-800-273-8255

Canada - Suicide Prevention Service 1-833-456-4566 or text 45645

New Zealand - Suicide Prevention 0508 828 865 (0508 TAUTOKo) or text 1737

Australia - Suicide Lifeline 13 11 14 or text 0477 13 11 14

ENJOY THIS FREE BOOK

Add this free prequel to your library!

A simple mission turns into terrifying fight for survival.

This special forces team is about to walk into something more horrifying
and relentless than they could ever imagine.

BOOKS IN THE SERIES

Is your Grave Diggers library complete?

———————

ABOUT THE AUTHOR

Chris Fritschi grew up on George Romero, Rambo, Star Wars and Tom Clancy, a formula for a creating a seriously good range of fantasy, science fiction, action, paranormal, and adventure novels.

———

Chris has been a script writer, Kung Fu instructor, competition shooter and mall Santa. He lives in a haunted house with his wife in Southern California.

———

website: chrisfritschi.com